Soul's Emancipation

Soul Series Book 1

Felicia D Gibbons

BBF (BooksbyFee) Publishing

Soul's Emancipation (Soul Series Book 1)

This is a work of fiction. Any similarity to real people or events is coincidental and unintentional.

BBF (BooksbyFee) Publishing https://everydaylovewithfee.com/

Printed in the United States of America.

Ingram Spark-Distribution Services

Acknowledgements

Finally! I wrote this book for my friends when I was in college because we had run out of black romance novels in our local library. Then I put it on a shelf and let it sit for over 20 years! Now, after many revisions, motivational speeches, and finally finding a safe space in writer's mind, I get to share it with you. Thank you to Vickie, Crystal, and my Gaston crew who read the story of Soul and Anthony so many years ago and encouraged me to share their story with others. Thank you to the one who read all my articles and poems in the meantime and in between time and encouraged me to "just keep writing". KIRC, thanks ladies, for encouraging me when I had to be reminded God's timing is never late. J. Monique girl, you are the entire bomb! I appreciate you walking me through the process, and giving me writing opportunities. And to (insert your name just in case you thought I forgot about you lol), thank you for the motivating conversations when they were most needed. You may never know how much they meant to me, but I genuinely appreciate you. For my new readers, I hope you all enjoy this story and look forward to learning more about the characters in future stories, and I can't wait to hear your thoughts. Fee

Dedicated to love. May we find it, experience it, and thrive from it.

Contents

Chapter 1

Message received from (972) 555-1152

"Hey Danny. It's your baby Shawntay. That was me that just called you, but your phone went to straight to voicemail. Metro tripping so I had to get a new phone and just in case you want to come back for a lunch quickie, you the first person I called to give my new number to. I know you just left this morning, and you probably tired from all the work you put in this morning and then having to be at the gym so early for your first session, but I couldn't get you off my mind after the way you put it down last night and this morning. Lock me in boo.

Message received from (972) 555-2371

It's Sandy. You do remember me right. I mean I'm not sure since I haven't heard from you since last week. Let me refresh your memory, we met at the gym a few days ago, and we woke up the next morning together if my memory serves me right! Give me a call so we can see about recreating that magic. I think I might need a bit of personal training.

Soul slammed her glass so hard on the counter, the bottom cracked. During his lunch break, Danny, her soon to be ex, stopped by in what was quickly becoming a rare appearance for someone who she was supposed to be in a relationship with for the last few months. It just happened that during his pop-up visit, in what Soul suspected was a piss poor effort to calm her complaints down about the lack of time they had been spending together, Danny claimed he didn't have time to charge his phone the night before and since Soul's place was closer to the gym, he stopped to get his spare charger. While he was charging his phone, he had used her Mac to log into his iMessage account to check his messages. During the visit they argued about their relationship, or lack of, and Danny got so mad he had snatched his phone and charger and stormed out without logging out of his IMessage account. As soon as he left, Soul grabbed her computer to finish working on the school project he interrupted her completing and it was like hitting the jackpot, when right there on her computer screen was access to Danny's messages.

"I'm about to fuck this nigga up," Soul yelled as she grabbed her phone to text Danny. As soon as she opened their text message thread, a meme she sent to Danny yesterday popped up, "If the conversation is getting short with you, it's getting longer with someone else."

"LOL," he had replied.

"I got his LOL," Soul grabbed another glass from the cabinet, tossing the cracked one in the trash, and refilled her mimosa with way more champagne than orange juice for an extra kick. "Sorry muthafucka!" Before now she couldn't put her hand on it, but she knew something had changed between she and Danny and based on history, she knew it was only a matter of time before Danny's dirt would be revealed. One of Soul's grandmother's favorite sayings was that every dog would have his day in court, and Danny was about to appear before the judge, jury, and executioner.

The phone's ringing jarred Soul out of her thoughts. She looked at the caller ID and couldn't believe whose picture was flashing across the screen.

"Yeah" Soul said in the driest tone she could produce as she felt her breathing become more labored and her blood pressure rise but she was determined to remain calm to see how the conversation would play out to determine how she should best handle Danny.

"Hey baby!"

"Danny."

"I'm sorry baby. I just didn't want to stay and argue with you, plus I need to run back to the gym to finish some business?"

"Umph your business must be named Shawntay", Soul mumbled under her breath.

"What?"

"Nothing Danny, "I'm here. What's going on? I mean you come here for whole minute even though I haven't seen you in days. If I didn't know better, I would think you had another woman"

"Nah baby girl, never that. Work just been keeping me busy, you know I'm trying to be a better man for you baby, and I just didn't like how we left things earlier. Plus, I got some great news. The company finally got me a personal receptionist. They couldn't have their number one personal trainer trying to balance clients, answer calls, and schedule sessions," he laughed.

"Not when you have so many other things you could be doing with your time right"

"Exactly, hey what are you doing when you finish working on your project?"

"Oh, you know me, same old same old."

"Well, I was wondering if you wanted to come over for some home cooking and then you could be my meal a little later."

Apparently, dogs didn't ever get tired of searching for a bone, or just *someone* to bone. Even though, Soul wanted to give Danny the cursing out he deserved, only the thought of seeing the look on his face when she busted him for cheating helped her to control her anger. "Sounds good to me baby. I'll need a couple of hours. What time should I be there?"

"Well, let's see you know Saturday is my busiest day. I've got to handle some more gym business, you know meet with a few clients, then shit, shower, and shave, so let's say around 8:00."

Soul glanced at the time on her phone. 12:45. That would give her plenty of time to figure out a way to bust Danny's trifling ass. "O.K. baby, see you then," she ended the call and screamed at the top of her lungs. "Old moth ball head ass fucker!"

Soul paced the floor for a few minutes until a plan begin to form in her head. She was sure that as soon as Danny left her earlier, he had returned his missed messages and knowing how much he liked to brag he probably couldn't wait to brag about his new receptionist. As one of the top personal trainers in the entire Dallas area, Danny had a long list of A-list clients, some upscale, some ghetto fabulous. He had been threatening to quit the upscale gym he worked for if the company didn't give him a secretary to handle, as he called it, trivial details. Of course, not wanting to lose their number one moneymaker, Danny and Soul both knew it was a matter of time before the company would give him exactly what he wanted.

Soul waited 30 minutes then called Danny's direct work line. The pleasant voice of a seemingly young woman answered the phone. "Celebrity Bodies for Ordinary People, this is Mary, would you like to schedule an appointment today with the number one trainer in Dallas," she said with so much enthusiasm Soul nearly gagged.

"Hi, this is Soul, Danny's girlfriend, is he available?"

"Oh," Mary said wistfully. Danny had probably flirted with the poor girl so much her head was spinning. Don't worry sweetie, you can have his sorry ass as soon as I am finished with him, Soul thought to herself. "No ma'am, he's in the back getting ready for his 1:00 client and then he has four more appointments immediately after that. Then, he's leaving for the day." Soul was sure Danny wouldn't be pleased with the fact that Mary gave his itinerary to a complete stranger over the phone, simply because she said she was his girlfriend. "Would you like to have his voicemail?"

"No Mary, that's fine. Thanks anyway, I can tell you are going to be a great asset to Danny. Don't worry about telling him I called. I'll just catch up with him later."

"Are you sure?"

"Mary, I insist."

Ok, you have a great day."

Soul looked at the clock. It was nearing one o' clock, which meant Danny would be with clients until at least four or five. She threw on some workout clothes and pulled a baseball cap on her head. Grabbing some oversized sunglasses, she put the mimosa in the fridge and grabbed her keys.

Twenty minutes later she was pulling into an empty space at Danny's job. Soul pulled the baseball cap over her eyes and put on the sunglasses. She knew Danny's office was near the back, and when he worked with clients, he always worked them in the back gym the first half of their session. Soul walked to the front where a tall blonde gentleman was answering the phone. "Excuse me sir," she said with a smile. "I'm supposed to meet my friend to workout," she said flashing her member's pass Danny had given her when they first started dating. "Do you mind if I use your phone, to see where she is? My cell died," Soul explained."

"Sure, use that one on the end," he said with a smile.

"Thanks," Soul said before walking to the phone. She looked around nervously hoping that no one who knew her would recognize her. She and Danny had worked out several times together and he even used to have a picture of the two of them on his desk when the relationship was still fresh and new, but since he had decided to become the freak of the week, he had probably put it out of site in case his new booty showed up. Soul quickly pulled out the numbers she had jotted down from Danny's messages and began to dial the first number. She glanced at the guy who let her use the phone, but he was too busy flirting with one of the customers to pay her any attention. Soul pulled her hat even further down over her face before quickly dialing the number of freak number one.

"Hey Daddy Long Stroke!" she said probably looking at the caller ID, which was one reason Soul came all the way to the gym to make her calls.

"No ma'am, this isn't Mr. Alexander. This is his secretary Mary. He asked me to give you a call, and let you know he is planning a surprise for you, and you are to be at his home promptly at 8:15.

"Yessss bitch," she said sounding excited.

Soul giggled. He will be with clients for the rest of the day, so he will be unavailable if you need to speak to him prior to that time. Do you need the address?"

"Hell nah, not after the things we did in that joint! I got that address memorized sis! Okayyyy!!!"

Rolling her eyes, Soul swallowed hard. "Yes ma'am. I'll let Mr. Alexander know he can expect you tonight." Soul hung up the phone wondering how long Danny's little escapades had been going on while she thought they were moving to something serious.

Soul breathe quickly, glancing around before dialing the next number.

"I thought you had forgotten about me." Boo number two Sandy said purring into the phone.

"Good afternoon. This is Mary, I am calling on behalf of Danny Alexander. I'm his new receptionist."

"Oh, that's right, he did mention he was trying to get some help. You know he has been so busy we couldn't even catch up so it's good to see the company did what was right. I'm sorry I'm rambling, I just thought you were Danny calling."

"No worries ma'am. Danny wanted me to call to schedule a meeting with you tonight at 8:25. Can I let Mr. Alexander know you are available, or would you like me to request a different time?"

"No, no, no," she said quickly. "8:25 is perfect."

"Ok I will let Mr. Alexander know."

"Wait. I need the address. Our first *meeting* was at my place. I uh don't know where he lives."

"Sure, no problem." Soul quickly replayed Danny's address to Sandy. "He has a very nice surprise planned for you. I think you will enjoy it. He will however be unavailable for the remainder of the day due to his schedule."

"No problem. Anything I need to tell him I will do tonight. Tell Mr. Alexander I will see him promptly at 8:25, and he can expect his own little surprise," she said with a giggle before hanging up.

"Where you able to reach your friend?" blonde guy asked finally breaking his attention from the girl he had his eyes glued to.

"I sure did. You will never know what a great help you have been," Soul said before exiting the building.

***

"So, I like what I see when I'm looking at me When I'm walking past the mirror," Soul sang at the top her lungs as her Mary J playlist piped through her bedroom sound system. Soul gyrated in a circle as she examined the form fitting black dress that she knew would get a rise out of Danny as soon as he saw her. Stepping into her red "fuck-me" heels, she turned around to see how the heels would make her legs and butt look. Perfect.

Soul pinned her braids into a neat bun at the top and let the rest hang down stopping just short of her butt in what Soul affectionally called her thot length braids. Applying her make-up, she sang loudly to next MJB song on the playlist *Glow Up*. Soul worshiped Mary J. Blige. Mary had been her girl since back in the day with her *What's the 411* CD. She played that CD so much it scratched to the point it would barely play anymore and of course instead of throwing it out, she went and bought two more copies just in case one of them scratched. With each of her albums, Mary's music had gotten Soul through some tough moments, especially in the relationship world.

With *What's the 411*, there was Alex, Soul's broke, ex-boyfriend with the Jeri curl, who still lived at home with his mother, didn't have a job, and had no ambitions of getting one.

Then there was *My Life*. Soul laughed as she remembered swearing to her friends that Mary had a spy watching her. How else could she have written lyrics so real that had Soul crying and breaking up with her boyfriend Jamal because of their religious differences. In other words, he thought he was God, and she didn't."

When *Share My World* was released Soul was right in the middle of her relationship with Fidel. Fidel was tall, well built, and had a body like a star NBA player. He lived in a condo in downtown Dallas, drove a Lincoln Navigator, and had a six-figure salary. With all of that going on for himself, Soul could have probably overlooked one simple affair with another woman, if the "other woman" was a woman! The problem was that she walked in and caught him lounging in her lingerie feeding grapes to another man!

Then there was *The Tour* and the *Mary* album. When *Mary* came out, Soul was dating this fine stripper named "I got 10 N U." Things were laid back and cool between the two of them until she met Cedric. Cedric wasn't easy on the eyes, to say the least but he was funny, made her smile and seemed to worship the ground she walked on. Even though he looked like a cross between K-C Hailey, and Lou Rawls, Soul really began to like him. Besides with the luck she had with good-looking brothers, maybe an ugly brother was just what she needed. So, she stopped seeing "10," and started kicking it exclusively with Cedric. Big mistake! That was like moving from a mansion to a crack house. But hey, Cedric was good to her as far as she could tell. Things were great in the beginning until he got the big head and started thinking he was running the show. He even had the nerve to start putting her down and trying to act like she wasn't good enough for him! Then he had the nerve to hint that he didn't want to be with her anymore. And there she was, instead of having "10" in her, she had about three, and then this fool had the nerve to trip.

"Maybe it's me, I need to do a better job of picking the company I keep," Soul thought to herself as she put the finishing touches on her makeup. Soul sprayed perfume on her neck and wrist and blew herself a kiss in the mirror before heading out to what was sure to be an enjoyable night.

Soul arrived at Danny's door, looking and smelling like she stepped off the cover of a magazine. She could tell Danny liked what he saw by the immediate bulge in his pants. The thought of Danny and his "Mandingo warrior" skills almost made her weak, but then Mary J's song "No Playa Shit" popped in her head. That's why Mary was her girl. Her songs always provided strength in moments like this.

"Hey baby," Soul gave Danny a long, sensuous kiss. "I know I'm a little early. Uhm, something smells good," she added, walking into the apartment. Before the door could close, Danny had his hands all over her.

"So, what you want first, good loving or good cooking?"

"As good as that loving sounds, I'm starving," Soul said taking a quick look at the clock. Shit, it was already 7:45. She would have to do some quick thinking if this plan was going to go off right. Danny was still rubbing his hands all over her trying to make her lose her focus.

"Baby, I think I've changed my mind. Why don't you run to the store, and get some whip cream and chocolate syrup? I'm feeling a little freaky tonight."

"Hell Yeah! You ain't said nothing but a word!"

It never took much to get Danny's hormones rising. Sex was the one problem they never took ownership of.

"Be right back babe and hey take the garlic bread out of the oven. I made spaghetti and there's salad as well on the counter," Danny gave Soul a quick kiss before hurrying out the door.

As soon as Danny left, Soul walked into the kitchen to take the garlic bread out of the oven before she started fixing a plate of salad, spaghetti and garlic bread. Opening the cabinet, she pulled out four wine glasses and filled each of them with wine from Danny's stock. Normally she and Danny would eat in the kitchen because Danny hated when people ate or drank in his living room because of the expensive white leather furniture and white carpet, Soul didn't hesitate to carry her plate and one of the wine glasses into the other room and plop down on his sofa. She connected his Bluetooth speaker with her phone finding the perfect song. As Boosie sang about not fighting in here, Soul smiled before digging into her plate of food and waited patiently for the "shit to hit the fan."

Just as she began to eat her food, there was a knock on the door. Soul sat her plate on the glass end table before walking to the door. Peeping through the peephole Soul clapped her hands together. "Guest number one has arrived!". Taking a deep breath, she opened the door and put on her best smile.

Now this sister was ghetto, straight up ghetto to be more exact. Although Soul loved weave as much as the next sister, the rainbow weave that hung just past her booty was a bit much even for Soul. And with long curvy fingernails that matched her hair, Soul didn't even want to think about how she wiped when she went to the bathroom. When Soul opened the door, the gold-tooth smiled from Danny's guest turned into a frown.

"Who you?"

"Hi, I'm Soul. Come on in. Danny told me he was expecting you. He just stepped out, but he should be back any minute now."

At the mention of Danny's name, she suddenly relaxed. "I'm Shawntay. It's pleasurable to meet you," Shawntay said stepping through the door.

Soul smiled. Really! Pleasurable. Shawntay was even more ghetto than Soul originally gave her credit for. "Would you like something to drink? There's wine."

"Girl, you know I keeps me a bottle of Crown in my bag, but I ain't turning down nothin' but my collar. Ayeee!"

"I know that's right girl," Soul laughed before walking back into the kitchen and grabbing two of the glasses of wine she had poured earlier. As Soul handed Shawntay one of the glasses, there was another knock at the door. "That must be our other guest!"

"What other guest? Danny shoulda told me this was a party. I didn't bring enough weed for a whole bunch of people."

"Oh, I don't think you'll need that much. Soul said as she opened the door for guest number two who was standing with a trench coat on, wide open to expose her butt-naked body! When she saw Soul standing there instead of Danny, she quickly closed her coat.

"Uhm, I'm sorry," she said obviously embarrassed. "I must have the wrong apartment."

"Are you looking for Danny?"

"Yes," she stammered obviously confused. "Is he here?"

"Come on in. You must be Sandy." Soul looked back at Shawntay, who had finished her glass of wine and was now pouring some of her crown into the wine glass.

"Yes, I'm Sandy. I was under the impression this would be a private affair. You are?'

"Not staying long. Just doing some favors for Danny. Come on in. Sandy, this is Shawntay; Shawntay, Sandy." Sandy quickly sat down and pulled her coat tightly around her body. It was a good thing Shawntay was too busy pouring her Crown and searching through her purse to catch the view Soul was given at the door, or she might not still be so calm.

"Sandy, would you like a glass of wine?"

"Please," Sandy said quickly, looking away. She must have been embarrassed out of her mind, and it took everything in Soul's power not to laugh.

Just as Soul handed Sandy the other drink she was still holding in her hand, Danny walked in.

Soul cursed herself for not being close enough to her phone to capture Danny's face as he walked in and saw all three of his "girls" in his apartment.

"Hey baby. I poured you a glass of wine. Let me grab that cause you look like you could use a drink."

"Baby! Ah hell nah! Danny what the fuck is going on here?" Shawntay jumped up from where she sat rolling a blunt.

"Shawntay baby, let me explain!"

Danny what is going on?" Sandy interrupted.

"Ladies, calm down. Let me explain," sitting back on the sofa and picking up her plate of food, Soul propped her feet on Danny's glass table. "Danny, why don't you have a seat as well."

Everyone sat down, except for Danny who seemed to still be in shock that three of his women were together in *his* living room.

Soul took her time taking a bite of the food. "Um Danny, this is delicious, not too much pepper this time. You know," she said turning to the two ladies, "Danny has a bad habit of putting too much pepper into the spaghetti. Danny," Soul laughed, "do you remember the time you opened the pepper from the big end instead of the sprinkle end and put so much pepper into the spaghetti that"

"Excuse me," Sandy interrupted, "but could you please tell us what's going on here?" she said jumping up hastily to face Soul. In her haste of standing so quickly, Sandy's jacket accidentally flew open. Sandy had tears in her eyes, but Shawntay looked as if she were ready to pull out a knife and shank somebody, and Sandy's little expose' only added fuel to the fire.

"What the," Shawntay screamed as Sandy quickly attempted to close her jacket. "I ain't down for no menagerie," Shawntay said.

"What?" everyone said turning to face Shawntay.

"You heard me the first time, a menagerie!"

"Oh, I think she means a ménage a trois" Sandy said.

"Whatever, I aint here for no English lesson just get on with the story for I start beating ass," Shawntay said rolling her neck and eyes.

Where in the hell did he meet this one? Soul wondered. "I'm so sorry," Soul continued taking another bite of spaghetti. "It's just that this spaghetti is sooo good! But you are right, back to the task at hand. Well, let me just say that it is a *pleasure* to meet both of you. As I'm sure you have already guessed, Danny here, has been playing all three of us. See, Danny and I have been seeing one another for about eight months. Now somewhere along the line, he met the two of you. Now I'm not blaming any of this on you, because we, my friends, are the victims. See the problem with most sisters, is that in situations like this, the women tend to blame one another, and not the dog ass man," Soul glanced over at Danny. "Now when I first met you ladies, I knew that would not be the problem. I could tell that both of you were very classy and intelligent women." Soul could tell she had them exactly where she wanted as they both nodded their heads in agreement. "Ladies, our anger should not be directed to one another, but instead at the man who has made us puppets in his sick little game."

"Danny," Soul sat down her plate and walked over to him, "I am extremely disappointed in you. All those nights you screamed *my* name, all the freaky things you did to me," she said taking the syrup and whip cream out of the sack Danny was still holding. "Goodbye Danny," Soul whispered, letting a single tear roll down her face. She kissed him lightly on the cheek and whispered into his ear, "You punk ass bitch." Where was the academy when true acting was going on, Soul wondered to herself.

Picking up her glass of wine, Soul walked to the back of the apartment to ensure the few belongings she still might have in Danny's place were retrieved. Soul could hear the beginning of what seemed and sounded like a war, going on in Danny's living room. Grabbing her few belongings, she made her way into the kitchen, and filled a plastic container with spaghetti, salad, and garlic bread. She tossed back the remaining wine glass she poured earlier. Fuck it, she thought, I'm taking the rest of this bottle. As Soul walked back into the living room, all hell had broken loose. Sandy was breaking things, and Shawntay had Danny hemmed up in a corner with a box cutter to his throat.

Soul paused to better arrange her things so they wouldn't fall, including Danny's bottle of wine, took another bite out of the plate of spaghetti that she had left on the table, and walked towards the door.

"Bye ladies, it was such a pleasure to meet you. I wish we could have met on better circumstances, but feel free to give me a call. Maybe we could all hang out sometime. Danny's got my number, and remember ladies, direct your anger towards the right person," Soul shouted as she walked out the door.

***

Chapter 2

"Ms. Jackson, May I see you for a minute?" her principal asked sticking her head into Soul's classroom.

"Sure. Guys turn to page 76, and go ahead and complete part A. This will be due at the end of the period, so make use of your time wisely," Soul said before stepping into the hallway. "Hey Mrs. Divers, what's going on?" Soul was blessed to have taught at Dunlap High School for the last seven years with Mrs. Divers serving as her principal the entire time. To Soul she was more like a mother figure. She could be bitchy when she wanted to, but for the most part she was fair, and for the last five years had pestered Soul into returning to school to get her Masters and Principal Certification. "Someone's got to take this job when they rest this old cow to pasture," Mrs. Divers often joked. Now that Soul was close to graduating, her principal was giving her more and more duties each day. Today standing before her was Alejandro and Shakeem, two of Dunlap's most challenging students. They were known gang members, and drug dealers. Alejandro had just gotten out of jail and unfortunately was headed down that same path again.

"Ms. Jackson, I am going to let you handle this situation because for some reason they like you, and maybe they will listen to what you have to say because they sure as hell ain't listening to me." Mrs. Divers said before walking off. That's why Soul liked her principal, she kept it real. Teaching in the inner city, her principal always stressed how important it was to know the culture and environment you worked in, and it never surprised Soul to hear the older lady walking down the hall singing the latest rap song.

"Alejandro, what have you and Shakeem done this time?"

"Ah Ms. Jackson, Mrs. Divers just tripping cause she thinks we high."

"Well, you look high, and" "Soul said grabbing Shakeem's jacket, and pulling it to her nose, "and you smell high. So, if it walks like a duck and quacks like a duck, it's probably a duck." Both boys began to laugh. "I'm not trying to be funny. You both know Mrs. Divers is getting tired of this mess. Alejandro, you know your parole officer can show up any time. Now what would happen if he came up here and you were high?" Alejandro didn't answer. "Oh, the situation ain't that funny anymore. I keep telling you both, life is about choices."

"Man, you don't know what it's like in this neighborhood."

"Shakeem, I don't want to hear that mess. You got more excuses than a hooker in church. And at least the hooker is in church, you are barely at school even though you already have a truancy case with the court. You control how things turn out in your life. If you want to be a thug, you will get treated like a thug."

"Yeah well, the ladies like the thugs," Alejandro said giving Shakeem a fist bump.

Soul had never seen so much gold in her life. Who would have known the day would come when Hispanics liked gold teeth as much as blacks. "Yeah, and men in jail like thugs too. You boys know I like both of you and I believe in you. There are plenty of teachers here who think I'm wasting my time, but I want you prove them wrong. I know in my heart you boys are going to make a difference in someone's life. If you believed in yourself half as much as I believe in you, we would be at a good starting point. There are two ways you can make a difference in someone's life, positive or negative. You both need to think long and hard and decide what kind of difference you want to make. Now come in here and sit at the back of my room until the bell rings," Soul said sighing. At twenty-nine, Soul was one of the top teachers in her district. Noted for her teaching qualities, several people were telling her it was time to get out of the classroom, and eventually that is just what she decided to do. Already in her last year of the Educational Master's program at John Timothy University, she couldn't wait to begin the second phase of her educational career.

Single again, Soul found herself even more focused on getting her degree, to forget about this last situationship that tried disguising itself as a relationship.

Usually when it came to relationships either Soul would give her all or nothing at all, but if she gave her all, it was one hundred percent. Which is why she had to set Danny up. It was her belief that no man, or woman for that matter, should be allowed to trample on a person's feelings. As a radio DJ had boasted one morning, "men are like grapes, and it is a woman's job to stomp on them and hope that they mature into something that a woman would one day like to have dinner with." After the recent fiasco with Danny, Soul had been wearing the hell out of her "stomping boots.

Chapter 3

"Soul, can you open the door?"

"Hold on girl!" Soul said running to open the door before her cousin could start banging on it. "What's up Simone? Girl, what do you have in all those bags?" Soul asked motioning to the several bags Simone had with her.

"You know me. I never know what I'm going to wear to the club, so I have to bring my whole closet!"

Simone was Soul's first cousin. They had been tight since the days of playing kick ball in her grandmother's backyard. At the young age of twenty-seven, Simone had it going on as the youngest nursing administration at Metropolitan Hospital, one of Dallas's largest and best medical facilities. She owned her own home, and always drove the latest Mercedes reminding her friends that "bad bitches drove bad Benz". In Soul's eyes Simone was a man's ultimate dream: smart, successful, gorgeous, and in her words, "rides a mean dick." The only problem was how easily intimated men were by her, especially with her attitude. Simone, of course, felt the only reason her attitude was so foul when it came to dating was because all the good brothers were either dating white women, or black men. Soul, on the other hand, suspected Simone's dating attitude came from her own fears and insecurities with falling in love, and for once, not having control of a situation. Despite her bad bitch attitude, Simone often found herself with the street hustler type who wasn't ready to settle down, especially not with a woman like Simone who demanded a lot from a man. It was true that sometimes when you're used to shopping at the Bazaar, where everyone has or has had what you're buying; you don't know how to act when you shop at Nordstroms. Simone was Nordstroms.

"Girl, has that fool Danny been harassing you lately?"

"Hell yeah. That fool keeps bugging the hell out of me, texting me, calling me, sending gifts to my job."

"Did you keep 'em?"

"Hell yeah!" Soul gave Simone a high-five. "But I tell you one thing, if he doesn't stop calling me, I'ma have to take it back and break out my old Destiny's Child CD and just call him and when he answers, let *Bugaboo* play in his ear."

"You make me wanna throw my pager out the window. Tell MCI to cut the phone off. Break my lease, so I can move, Cause you a bugaboo, a bugaboo." Simone and Soul sang loudly.

Simone started dumping clothes onto Soul's sofa, "First of all, do you even still have a CD player. Wait scratch that, I forgot you are a music head. Second. you know who should be singing that song?"

"Danielle! Is she still trying to hang on to that broke-ass, no good, no job having Jackson?"

"Girl, she's still with him. I called her house the other day, and do you know that fool had the nerve to answer her cell and tell me to call back!"

"Simone, please tell me your kidding! What bill has he started paying that negates him trying to regulate her household? She hasn't even met his family and they've been together what"

"Too damn long! But Soul, you know a man only dishes out what a woman is willing to take in."

"Facts! I tell you one thing, any man that I have to constantly make excuses for, I don't need. There isn't a damn thing out here that I need a man to give me. Hard work and determination can get you anything."

"Now you know there's one thing a man can give you that you can't get by yourself."

"What?"

"A good orgasm!"

"See that's where you are wrong, cause with these fingers," Soul said, twinkling two fingers at her, "and my rose, I can get that by myself too."

"Uh! You are so nasty! That's why you don't have a man now."

"Uh Simone, you don't have a man either in case you've forgotten," Soul reminded her. "Now where the fuck is Danielle?"

"I thought you were going to stop cursing so much." Simone began to sort through the pile of clothes she had dumped on Soul's sofa that were now spilling onto the floor.

"Hell, I'm trying."

The knock at the door interrupted Soul from further explaining this week's attempt to stop using profanity in every other sentence.

"I'll get it," Soul said, since Simone was now surrounded by clothes. She ran to the door and peeped out the peephole. Danielle.

Danielle was a tall, caramel sister, with a head full of beautiful golden locks and a heart of gold. She was the most forgiving person Soul had ever met and could find something positive in a terrorist. Simone and Soul thought she was too forgiving, but Danielle loved to remind them that there was no such thing, which often got her in many compromising positions. Like the time, she let a homeless family she met coming out of the store stay in the daycare she owned one weekend, and when she went to drop them off some food, they had stolen all the toys and electronics out of the facility and were nowhere to be found. For most people that would be a wake-up call, but Danielle still hadn't banked all the sense she bought. Like Jackson. With all the positive things going on in her life, Soul could never understand what Danielle saw in a low-life snake like him.

"Hey Danielle, I can't believe Jackson let you out of the house." Soul said opening the door.

Danielle rolled her eyes and walked inside, "Girl, Jackson doesn't run me!"

"Oh, really now, when did he stop?"

"What the hell is that supposed to mean? Soul, I'm so tired of your"

"OK you two." Simone intervened. "Damn Soul, can you at least let her in the door before you two go at it? I swear, no one would ever think the two of you have been friends for seventeen years."

"Yeah well, pity is a mutha...."

"Soul!" Simone screamed. "How can you try to stop cursing, when every word that comes out of your mouth, is bitch this, muthafucker that. I don't even know how you make it through the school day without using profanity!"

"I save it up for when I'm when I'm with the two of you, cause y'all are my bitches and hoes," Soul said sticking her tongue out at Simone.

"Simone," Danielle walked over and sat on the sofa in the only free space that wasn't covered by Simone's clothes, "you know you can't teach an old dog new tricks, especially an old, broke down –ass dog like Soul."

"Oh, hell nah. I got your broke down-ass dog."

Simone rolled her eyes towards the ceiling. "Here we go again!"

Chapter 4

C *lub Explicit* was packed. Everybody who was anybody was in the house from the city's NBA team to the city's NFL team and everyone was dressed to impress.

As Soul, Simone, and Danielle walked to their usual spot, the bar, Soul noticed an extremely fine brother looking her way. When he noticed that she was looking at him, he raised his glass of what appeared to be a dark liquor as if he were giving her a toast. Not wanting him to think she was interested, Soul ignored his toast and smile and proceeded to the bar. The brother was definitely giving sexy vibes, but a brother that fine couldn't be anything but trouble, and after that last fiasco with Danny, Soul didn't have the time nor energy needed to deal with this current generation of daters.

Simone ordered her usual Sex on the Beach, and Soul her normal Amaretto Sour, but the surprise came when Danielle, who hardly ever drank, ordered a Hurricane! As soon as the word *Hurricane* came out of Danielle's mouth, Simone and Soul gave each other "the look."

"OK Danielle, what's wrong now?"

"Simone, who said anything was wrong?"

"Well Dani," Soul interrupted, "anytime *you* order an alcoholic drink, and not just anything, but a Hurricane, something has got to be wrong, and I bet that something goes by the name of Jackson."

Danielle sighed as her eyes suddenly became glossy, "You're right, I mean, I don't know. I love Jackson, and I really hate to lie to him."

"What do you mean lie?" Simone said touching Danielle's arm.

"Well, I kind of told Jackson that I was going to visit a friend at the hospital."

"What! Girl, you don't have to lie to him! He's not paying any bills. Hell, has he even found a job?"

"Simone, please don't start with me. You know he is *between* jobs, and he really wanted to spend some time with me tonight."

As Simone and Danielle began to argue, Soul took her drink from where the bartender had placed them on the counter and handed him thirty dollars. "Keep the change," she smiled choosing to remain out of Danielle and Simone's conversation knowing it was better to keep her mouth shut, rather than go off on a hopeless tangent about an even more hopeless situation.

Jackson and Danielle had been together for several years and it seemed they had more bad times than good. Jackson was constantly "*between jobs*" and Danielle was the one who always ended up compromising to please him. He couldn't stand Soul and Simone and loved to refer to them as "those two meddling bitches". Soul knew he was just worried that one day they were going to help Danielle see him for who he really was.

Taking a sip of her drink, Soul's thoughts were interrupted by a deep voice, as she turned to find the fine brother from earlier standing directly behind her.

"Do you mind if I sit here?" he pointed to the empty barstool next to her.

"Sure. It's a free world."

It wasn't like the brother wasn't as fine up close as he was from afar, because he was. Too damn fine, in fact. Smooth, jet-black skin, a shiny baldhead, and a beard that made Soul's thoughts wonder if it would tickle the inside of her thighs, not to mention a body that was definitely to be worshipped. The navy fitted suit looked like it was made specifically for his tall frame. And that smile, God that smile, could make the projects feel like a mansion. He obviously never missed his dentist appointments. Soul immediately noticed his fraternity letters and a simple initial necklace dangling from the two simple gold chains he wore. Yeah, his middle name had to be fine, or sexy, or Greek God, and based on his confident smile, she could tell he knew it. Too bad for him that after her recent Danny escapade, Soul decided to take a break not just from fine men, but all men. The games they played and the lies they mastered were enough to make her scream.

Her eyes soaked him in from head to toe one more time as a sigh escaped Soul's lips. Before her body could betray her, she turned her back hoping he would take the hint that she wasn't interested. Soul knew she was being standoffish, but she really didn't care. She had come here tonight to enjoy spending time with her girls, and that was exactly what she was about to do.

Simone eyed the handsome stranger who sat next to Soul but was now trying to get the bartender's attention. Lifting her eyebrows and nodding her head in his direction, Simone shot Soul a questioning glance.

"Are you even listening to me?" Danielle whined as Simone shifted her focus back to her.

Soul shook her head as she heard Danielle explain to Simone how Jackson was so devastated when she told him they could not see one another due to her friend's "illness."

"Girl, you should have seen him! He almost had tears in his eyes. He really wanted to spend some time with me."

"I see," Simone took a long sip of her drink to avoid saying what she really wanted to say about Jackson.

"Simone, I would expect this negative behavior from Soul, but I can't believe that you find it so hard to believe that Jackson wants to spend time with me." The tears that were threatening to come earlier fell down Danielle's face before she stormed off in the direction of the women's restroom.

"Damn, the effects of a Hurricane are already taking over I see. I'm glad it wasn't me who made her cry this time."

"Shut up Soul. I guess I better go check on her. Watch my drink."

"Yeah, cause we're supposed to be having fun not crying in the club," Soul shouted to Simone's retreating figure.

"Excuse me, were you talking to me?"

Oh shit! Mr. Fine again. Soul took another sip from her drink hoping that if she ignored him, he would leave her alone.

"Excuse me," he leaned in to where Soul had no choice but to turn in his direction.

Rather than answering him, Soul simply turned towards him and gave him a bored look.

"Hi, I'm Anthony, and you are?"

"Not interested."

"Well, 'not interested,' it's very nice to meet you," he said looking her up and down. "Ms. Not Interested, can I buy you another drink? What are you having?"

Soul swirled the drink around with her straw, "I'm fine thank you."

"Well, it looks like there's nothing left in that drink," he replied pointing to the near empty glass.

Anthony wasn't quite sure what it was about her but there was something about the woman in front of him. Maybe it was the way she seemed to be trying so hard to ignore him, or maybe it was her stunning beauty. Her skin had a glow that reminded him of a shiny copper penny, and her long braids that stopped just above her butt made him think she had a little fire in her. The way her jeans hugged her ass made him want to pull her into his arms and run his hands up and down every inch of her body. He wasn't sure, but he knew he had to get her to at least talk to him.

Soul finally noticed his eyes and she felt like he was reading directly into her soul. If she wanted to keep her promise to stay single, she better get away from Anthony quickly. But not wanting to lose her spot at the bar nor try to walk around and find another place at the bar with three drinks Soul sighed and gave him her attention.

"Listen I'm not interested. I just came here to have a good time with my girls."

"Well since your girls aren't here, or are they, he asked looking around her, "let me at least buy you a drink."

"Fine. Amaretto Sour."

"Excuse me."

"You asked could you buy me a drink. Amaretto Sour. That's what I'm drinking"

"Bartender, can I have another glass of Crown and Coke and a Budweiser, and another Amaretto Sour for my friend 'Not Interested'."

"I see you've got jokes. Although I'm still, *not interested*, my name is Soul."

"Well Soul, that's a beautiful name for a beautiful lady, but can I ask exactly what it is you're not interested in?"

"Basically, the bullshit that you will eventually try to throw my way."

"Well, I can tell you believe in saying exactly what's on your mind, and lucky for you, I do to. So, let me be blunt. Yes, I do think you are a beautiful sister, but I think it's pretty arrogant for you to think that A. a brother wants to get with you, and B. that he would have to throw bullshit your way to get your attention. In fact, if you think that, it isn't saying a lot for your self-esteem. I would think that a real man would know better than to step to you without coming correct. This is my first time in this club, but if all the women in here have as much attitude as you do, I might as well drink the rest of my Crown and call it a night. Oh, and by the way, if this is the thanks I get for buying you a drink, you can just give me my $7.25, and I'll move on."

"Damn! I guess I asked for that. Maybe I should offer to buy you a drink!"

"Or maybe you should stop making assumptions and give a brother a chance. Anyways what makes you think I'm trying to holla at you?" Anthony said handing the bartender money for their drinks and sliding Soul's drink in her direction.

"Damn. It's like that! My bad!" Soul picked up a white napkin and waved it in the air as a sign of surrender, bringing a laugh from both of them. "Maybe we should start again. Hi, I'm Soul, and you are?"

"Anthony, nice to meet you."

"So, is this your first time at Explicit?"

"Yeah, it's a pretty nice club, but a lot of the women seem to have bad attitudes," he teased.

"Really, I never would have imagined."

"Yeah, this looks like two attitudes coming our way now," Anthony nodded his head in the direction of two women, who unfortunately were Danielle and Simone.

"Now what makes you think these two women have bad attitudes?" Soul asked hoping he was just joking and had saw the three of them walk in together or noticed them together when he sat down next to her.

"Well, just look at them. One is working her neck; the other has her lips all poked out. I don't understand why women like that come to the club, where people are obviously trying to have a good time."

"Is that right."

"Yes indeed. I used to see women like that on the yard all the time and even now in my everyday life. Mad at the world for no reason."

"Humph." Soul was doing her best to remain cool, but the fact that he was passing judgment on her friends without knowing them, was pissing Soul off which was too bad. Despite her vow to take a break from men, Soul knew that she was attracted to him as soon as he opened his mouth and put her in her place.

"Anthony, what exactly do you mean by 'women like that'."

"You know," Anthony began, "like I said mad at the world for no reason. Women who probably sit around watching soap operas all day, and waiting for that particular club night, usually Ladies Night, so they can get in free. Then when they get to the club, they come with that ghetto attitude that turns brothers like me off and makes good sisters like you look bad."

Soul sucked her teeth, but Anthony didn't seem to notice as someone he knew walked up and dapped him up.

Who did this negro think he was anyway? He didn't even know her girls, yet here he was making assumptions about them. Soul rolled her eyes. He probably did that to everyone, like he was so high and mighty. Soul silently opened her purse and pulled out a ten. She took a couple of deep breaths because she was about to go left on this fool. Anthony focused his attention back on her, but his smile turned into a puzzled expression when she handed him the ten.

"What is this?" he looked at the ten dollar bill she placed in his hand. "Are you leaving. Did you decide to change your name back from Soul to Not Interested, or did I offend you?"

Soul took a deep breath and finished off the remainder of her Amaretto. "Nah Anthony, you didn't offend me, but my cousin and best friend would probably slap the shit out of you."

Anthony laughed. "Damn, I guess it's a good thing they're not here."

"Nah, but they are over there," Soul pointed in the direction of Anthony's so called 'ghetto sisters." Putting her glass on the table, she picked up Simone's and Danielle's drink. "Oh, and by the way, keep the change."

Soul didn't stick around to see the look on Anthony's face, as she walked to join ghetto ass Simone and Danielle!

Chapter 5

"Hey girl, I saw you talking to that cutie I was eyeing before Danielle had her entire meltdown. Who is that and please tell me you got his number and that he's got a cute friend for me!"

"Trust me, he's no one worth mentioning," Soul said as she handed Simone her drink.

Simone took a sip and swirled her straw around as she continued to look in Anthony's direction, "Well, as cute as he is, he definitely looks worth mentioning. But why is he looking at us so strangely?"

"You don't want to know." Soul laughed. "Speaking of Dani, where did she go? I'm not walking around with her drink all night. Don't tell me she's in the bathroom crying again."

"Hell no. She left."

"What!"

"Yes girl, she said she felt so bad about lying to Jackson, that she was going home to tell him the truth, and I quote 'beg his forgiveness'."

"The hell you say! I need another drink on that note, and this Hurricane is not going to cut it. Come on I need another drink."

"Well here hand me her drink. I feel like I'm playing catch up to you dealing with all Dani's drama.

"You sure are playing catch up. I'm about to be on drink number three," Soul laughed as she headed back to the bar noticing Anthony's gaze following her every move. As they got closer to the bar, she stopped just short of where Anthony still sat sipping on his drink, "Simone, let's go to the bar on the other side. It's just too damn ghetto over here." Soul turned abruptly and began to walk off putting a little extra sashay in her hips just in case Anthony was still watching her.

Simone gave her a puzzled look but followed anyways. "Soul, what was that about?"

"Nothing. I just need another drink." No need to mention Anthony's comments to Simone who was not only known for her attitude but her temper as well. It would be just up his alley to have Simone go off on him and prove him right about his presumptuous judgements.

As they headed to the bar across the room, Soul turned one last time to look at Anthony. Soul wasn't sure why but the fact that he was still watching her gave her an unexplained satisfaction.

Soul made an overexaggerated effort of rolling her eyes at him before proceeding to the other side of the club.

What a waste, Soul thought to herself, now wondering why she even accepted his offer to buy her a drink? Besides who could possibly meet their soulmate in a club. Wait, why was she even thinking about soulmates. Get it together girl, you're tripping. You should have never allowed him to invade your space anyway, even if it was just for a moment. Soul shook her head to clear her head.

"Hey what's going on over there?" Simone asked, interrupting her thoughts.

"I don't know. It looks like two chicks are about to fight," Soul said glancing in the direction Simone was looking.

"Uh Soul, one of those 'chicks' is Danielle."

"Oh Shit, Come on!" Soul grabbed Simone and started dragging her through the crowd.

"Soul, hold on, you gone break my damn neck!"

"Well, it looks like Danielle is about to break somebody's neck if we don't get over there."

It was no easy task making their way through the group of people who were gathered around thinking they were about to see a fight. Soul could never understand why people would stand around and watch two fools fighting. More importantly, she would never understand why two people would embarrass themselves just for the amusement of others. Soul knew there were times were you just had to throw down. In fact, she had several fights herself growing up, and of course in college when she didn't know any better, but for two grown women to fight in the club usually meant they were fighting over one thing, a man.

After what seemed like forever, Simone and Soul finally made their way to the center of the action. As they got closer, they could see Danielle and some light, damn near white, sister in a neck rolling, finger pointing contest.

"Danielle, what's going on here? Simone was the first one to reach the action.

"This bitch is all over my man, slow dancing and shit!" Danielle screamed with tears streaming down her face.

At what seemed like the exact same time, Simone and Soul spotted Jackson standing at the edge of the crowd with a smug look on his face seeming to enjoy this spectacle.

Grabbing Danielle and turning her to face her, Simone angrily whispered, "Danielle, I can't believe you are in here acting a damn fool over that no-good dog."

"Don't start with me. That bitch," Danielle yelled loudly turning in the direction of Jackson's companion, "thinks she's all that! Well, I'm about to see if she can take 'all this' ass kicking I'm about to give her!"

"Look Danielle," Soul began, "first of all, Jackson is the one you should be directing your anger towards. If I'm not mistaken, he's the one who was supposed to be at home heartbroken. He probably came here thinking you were at the hospital, and while the cats away, the dog will play. Furthermore, what kind of man is going to sit around and let his woman make a fool out of herself by fighting over him in a club?"

At that moment Jackson walked over and grabbed Danielle. "Come on Danielle, let's go."

"Excuse me, I didn't see you trying to help at first, so get to steppin'." Simone shouted.

"Look Bitch, when I want your opinion, I'll ask. That's why you ain't got no man now!" Jackson said grabbing Danielle and beginning to walk off.

"Did he just call me a bitch. I knew those kickboxing classes would pay off."

Before Soul could grab her, Simone had karate-kicked Jackson in his back.

Jackson fell forward and stumbled on the floor.

"Now who the bitch, bitch!" Simone stood over Jackson.

"Bitch, I'm a kick yo," Before he could finish, and before anyone could stop her, Simone jumped on the ground putting Jackson in a headlock, she unleashed a barrage of wildly thrown punches on his head and neck.

"Simone stop!" Danielle screamed trying to pull Simone off Jackson which only caused all three of them to fall backwards awkwardly.

Soul stood in shock before coming to her senses to try to pull her friends apart. She thought about getting in a sucker punch on Jackson, but before she could figure out who was who so she wouldn't end up accidentally hitting one of her girls, security had reached their area, and grabbed Simone, who now had Jackson in an awkward figure four move as he tried to wrestle his way out of her hold.

"Bitch, you better not ever come over my house!" Jackson screamed.

"Well, that won't be a problem since you don't have a house, you bastard!"

"Alright you two, take it out of here!" security yelled pulling Jackson, Simone and Danielle apart.

"Stupid bitch!" Jackson said from the safety of the security hold.

"Yo mama!" Simone lunged at Jackson. One of the big security officers grabbed Simone and threw her over his shoulders as she swung wildly trying to get free. The punches she pounded on his back seemed not to faze him as he began to carry her outside.

The other security guard still had Danielle and Jackson separated in each of his arms.

"Come on Dani," Soul grabbed her hand before turning in the direction security was carrying Simone who was now kicking and screaming at the top of her lungs.

"No Soul, I think I better go with Jackson."

"What! Man, whatever," Soul sucked her teeth in disbelief. Grabbing Simone's purse, Soul headed to the exit. As she weaved her way towards the exit, she caught Anthony glancing her way. When he saw her looking, he smirked, and once again toasted her with his raised glass.

Chapter 6

It had been over three weeks since the club incident and Danielle and Simone were still not speaking. Soul, stuck in the middle of the entire situation, was pissed and over it all. The three of them had been friends since the days of kickball and dirt, and Soul never thought she would see the day when any man would have the ability to come between their friendship. In Soul's opinion, both of her girls were wrong, and the way things were looking, it was up to her to set them straight.

Danielle would be a problem. She could be *too* forgiving as evident with Jackson. Simone, on the other hand, was a different story. She could be as stubborn as a mule and hold a grudge longer than anyone this side of the grave.

Danielle and Soul had plans to go to the movies at 8:00, so Soul figured tonight would be as good as any to do some friendship repair. She picked up her cell and scrolled to her favorites to call Danielle.

"Hey Soul. What's going on chick? We still on for tonight?"

"I'm actually really tired, how about we just chill at my place, and watch a movie or something."

"I really wanted to go to the movies."

"Come on Dani," Soul begged, "you can't even imagine how tired I am. I'm so sick of these kids, I don't want to even risk seeing them at the movies."

"I guess," Danielle sighed. "You still want me to come over there at eight?"

"Yeah, that works for me. I may even stop and pick up your favorite dessert on my way home from work."

"Listen, don't play with my cheesecake emotions. Either you are, or you aren't."

"Whatever! I guess I'll go ahead and get you some."

"Then, I'll definitely be there."

"Cool, see you tonight," Soul said before hanging up and dialing Simone's number. "Hey girl, what are you doing?"

"Watching *General Hospital*. I can't believe Lucky is dead!"

"What? Oh my God! Again? How did he die this time? Wait, my class is about to start. I was just calling to see if you wanted to come over. Our movie is on Netflix!"

"I know you're not talking about *Petey Wheatstraw*!"

"The devil's son in law!" Soul and Simone sang in unison.

"I'm already there. You want me to bring wine?"

"Of course! And I'm picking up cheesecake and ordering pizza. Do you want Meat lovers?"

"That's cool, don't forget the buffalo wings."

"Uh, I'm on a budget. Black folks love to splurge on somebody else money."

"Believe it! Girl, I got to go. Laura just found out Lucky is dead. Girl, she breaking down, I said she breaking down!" Simone sniffled into the phone, "Oh Lord Jesus, she gone have me over here crying too!"

"Well, it sounds like it's too late for that. Get off my phone and focus on your show"

"Alright. What time does the movie start?"

"8:30, see you later!"

"Yeah, and you better have my hot wings."

***

It was 8:15 and Soul was getting worried that Danielle still hadn't arrived at her house. If Simone arrived before Danielle, and Danielle saw Simone's car, she probably wouldn't even stop, more less come in, especially if she wasn't ready to face Simone.

Soul dialed Danielle's number but after a few rings it went to her voicemail. Soul hoped that Danielle was in route and that's why she wasn't answering her phone.

Sitting on the couch, Soul scrolled her social media for a few minutes before dialing Danielle's number again. When voicemail picked up, Soul started to leave a message but was interrupted by a knock on the door.

"Why the hell are you so late?" Soul asked snatching the front door open.

"Excuse me?"

"Oh, hey Simone."

"Well, hey Simone to you too. And what are you ranting about? It's only a few minutes after 8:30," she said glancing at her watch. I had to run back to the store, I forgot my Black n' Milds!"

"Child, ignore me, I'm tripping."

"You sure are," Simone pushed past Soul handing her the bag with two bottles of wine. "Is the pizza here and did you order my wings?"

"Nah, it should be another ten or fifteen minutes."

"Well, they need to hurry up because a sista is hungry like a mug. I took a shower after work and came straight here. You ready to start the movie or should we wait on the pizza?"

"Let's wait on the pizza."

"I don't know why Rudy Ray Moore didn't get the Oscar nod for that role. Now that's acting."

"Shut up," Soul laughed.

"It's the truth anyhow. Let me put this wine in the freezer?"

Soul made sure Simone was in the kitchen before shooting Danielle a text. With each passing second, Soul became more irritated. If Danielle was somewhere laid up with Jackson, Soul was going to kill her, she thought glancing down at her phone to see if Danielle had texted back.

"Hey girl, who are you on the phone with?"

"Nobody, just checking my social media.

"Oh. Well anyway, let me give you a soap opera recount. I'll start with Bold and Beautiful. I could not believe this mess. You know the little Forester girl, what's her name, has split personalities like her crazy mama and..."

Simone continued to rattle on about the soap operas, but Soul was too busy wondering what would happen when Danielle arrived and saw Simone's car to really pay attention. Soul couldn't shake the feeling that something was wrong. Ten minutes had passed, and Danielle still hadn't called or texted. Somewhere in the back of her mind her irritation was turning into an unsettled feeling that something was wrong. Soul considered telling Simone that Danielle had been invited.

"Are you listening to me?"

"Huh. Sorry I was just thinking about something,"

"Well apparently it's more important that what I have to say, so what is it?"

Soul sighed heavily. May as well get this over with. Simone would be pissed but Soul was just trying to help her friends get out of their own stubborn way. It wasn't like she was doing anything wrong or trying to set her friends up like she had Danny, Soul just wanted to see them back together.

Just as she opened her mouth to tell Simone the truth there was a knock at the door. Soul took off in a mad dash. She was running so fast she didn't see Simone's boot lying near the entryway and tripped over it practically rolling the rest of the way to the door.

Soul could hear Simone laughing loudly behind her. Opening the door, Soul was disappointed to find the pizza delivery guy.

"Hey dudes, is everything OK? I thought I heard a loud noise."

"Everything's fine!" Soul snapped taking her pizza and wings from his extended arm. She closed the door without even saying thank you which only made Simone laugh even harder.

"Dang Soul, I guess you're hungrier than I am!" Simone noticed Soul wasn't laughing or smiling. "I'm sorry cousin did you hurt yourself?"

"Simone, I need to tell you," At that moment her cell phone started to ring, and Danielle's picture flashed on the screen. Soul grabbed the phone. "Hello! Yes, What! Oh my God! We'll be right there!" Hanging up the phone Soul turned to Simone, "It's Danielle, she's in the hospital."

Chapter 7

On the way to the hospital, Soul explained everything to Simone who was extremely quiet, only nodding her head once or twice to show that she was listening. The short ride to the hospital seemed to take forever.

"If Danielle is not OK, I'll never forgive myself," Simone said breaking the silence and wiping the tears that were beginning to form in the corner of her eyes. Soul placed her hand on top of Simone's hand without saying a word. They drove the remaining way in silence with Soul holding Simone's hand for the remainder of the drive to the hospital. Finding a parking spot in the hospital garage, Soul and Simone rushed through the huge metal doors, quickly approaching the tired looking woman sitting behind the desk.

"Yes, may I have Danielle Allen's room number?"

"Are you members of the family?" the attendant asked typing something into her computer.

Simone gasped. Soul squeezed her hand gently to keep her from crying. "Yes mam, we're her sisters."

"Humph," the woman looked over her glasses as if she was searching for the family resemblance, "OK. She's in room number 612. Go around this corner, take a left by the plaques, and you'll see the elevators."

"Thanks." Soul grabbed Simone hurrying in the direction the attendant had indicated. As they got on the elevators, Simone began to cry. Not those soft tears, those hard, funeral, Lord why tears. Soul struggled to hold Simone's sobbing body in an upright position. The other people in the elevator either weren't fazed by a sobbing woman or had their own worries and stresses to deal with.

"Simone, get a hold of yourself." Simone's outburst surprised Soul since Simone was not in the least bit the emotional type. Soul figured the fight between Danielle and

Simone contributed more than anything to Simone's emotional outburst more than her emotions themselves. Soul resisted the urge to remind Simone about her insistence that she call Danielle to resolve their issues on more than one occasion during the past few weeks. Even though past experiences taught Soul tomorrow is not promised to anyone, she didn't want to pour salt on Simone's obviously open wound.

"Soul, it must be bad. I don't think she was even going to let us in, until you told her we were Dani's sisters. What if she doesn't make it. Here I am mad at her over Jackson's stupid ass, and now Danielle is in the hospital."

"Calm down. Don't get ahead of yourself. We don't even know what happened to Danielle. And whatever it is, you need to get yourself together before we go in this room. I'm usually the crybaby, not you," Soul nudged Simone with her shoulder trying to make her cousin smile.

"Your right, but,"

"But nothing! Now get yourself together, and let's go."

Simone took several deep breathes as they made their way down the hall to Danielle's room. When they reached the door, Simone grabbed Soul's hand before gently pushing the door open.

"Oh my God!" Simone put her hand over her mouth. The nurse who was checking on Danielle turned around.

At the sound of Simone's voice, the nurse turned towards the door, "Oh hello, I didn't see you standing there."

Soul looked past the nurse towards Danielle who had a bandage around her head, bruising on her face, and her arm in a sling.

"Is she ok?"

"She's way better than she looks," the nurse said as she jotted down information on a chart she held in her hand.

Soul walked over to get a closer look at Danielle, "What happened?"

"Apparently, she fell down some stairs and suffered a slight concussion and a broken arm. She'll be as good as new in a couple of days."

Simone let out a sigh of relief. "How did she get here?"

"Her brother called the ambulance, once they got her admitted and checked over, he told me to call this number and left." Soul looked at the piece of paper the nurse handed her recognizing her own cell number along with another phone number that Soul didn't recognize, listed underneath.

"You said her brother? How did he look?"

"Tall, light complexion, bald head, a very good dresser, and damn good looking," the nurse smiled.

"Jackson," Simone and Soul said at the exact same time.

"Do you know where he is now?" Soul asked.

"No, I think he left. But he gave me his cell number and told me to call him sometimes! So, I'm sure I'll be seeing him real soon."

Soul glanced at Simone and could see the steam rising. She quickly thanked the nurse, hoping she would leave before Simone tried to do one of those wrestling moves on her. "Do you know when she should be awake?'

"I don't know. The doctor gave her something for the pain, so she's been out of it. She should be awake soon though.

"Thanks," Soul mumbled.

The nurse disposed of her gloves before washing her hands in the sink and exiting the room. Soul noticed she picked up the paper with Jackson's number on it. As soon as she left, Simone finally let out the breath she had sucked in, "Can you believe that!" Simone walked over to Danielle's bed and immediately began going over the basic information listed on her charts.

Soul walked over to Danielle, gently touching her cheek.

Danielle began to move around. "Ouch."

Simone put the chart back and rushed to the other side of the bed. "Hey boo, you ok?"

"My head hurts like I've been drinking those Hurricanes again, and my arm feels like someone slammed me into a wall." Danielle whispered clearing her throat and trying to sit up.

Simone gently pushed Danielle back into a resting position, "Hold on. Take it easy." Danielle, tired and in pain, did as she was told not even bothering to argue.

"Boo, what happened?" Simone asked.

Danielle sighed heavily, and tears began to form in her eyes.

Simone touched Danielle on the shoulder as Soul sat on the edge of the bed. Danielle began to cry silently. "I was on my way to Soul's, and Jackson asked me where I was going. I told him, and he didn't believe me. He started yelling and talking about me always lying about going to see a friend. I went to walk away, and he grabbed me by my hair. Then I started trying to jerk away, and I tripped over something, and the next thing I know, I was falling down the stairs."

"So, he pushed you?" Simone hissed.

"No, no! Jackson didn't mean to. It was my fault."

"Danielle, when are you going to wake up, and smell the damn coffee? He ain't even here now!"

"Simone," Soul shot a warning glance in her cousin's direction.

"No Soul, this needs to be said. Dani, I love you like a sister, and I can't keep watching you go through this bullshit with Jackson. You are too good for his ass, besides the fact that he doesn't appreciate the things you do. It's time you stop overemphasizing your role in other people's life, especially when they keep auditioning people for the role you think you have."

"Simone, if you feel this way. How do you think I feel?" Danielle cried. "You don't see us when we're happy. As my friends I tend to tell you the bad things, and you only hear my side of it. But Simone sometimes he's so good to me that the good things count way more than the bad. Don't you think I want to be happy? Don't you think I know I deserve to be happy? But how do you think I feel when I'm alone. Jackson and I have been together for so long, that being with him is like second nature. Yeah, he makes me sad, but what do I do when he also makes me happy? Do you know how many times I have prayed to God to help me stop loving him? And just when I think I can let go and be strong; things become better. We start having a good time, and laughing, and making love, and just being together. It's like when I start pulling away, he feels it, and pulls me back. And I began to think, OK, God is letting this happen for a reason, he's going to help us make this work. There must be a reason why I can't leave. So yeah Simone, I'm tired of the bullshit too, but what do I do when the bullshit feels so good?

Simone walked over and sat on the bed, and held Danielle as she cried, "Sis, when it's from God, you don't have to work this hard."

Soul lightly rubbed Danielle's leg in a soothing manner. What Danielle was feeling was no stranger to so many women, Soul included. There were times in the past when Soul knew she was in a bad situation and should cut her losses short, but like Danielle, Soul knew walking away from the very thing or person bringing you pain wasn't always easy even when they were the source of the pain. Knowing that people find it easier to judge a situation when it's not their own helped Soul to at least try to sympathize with Danielle's situation.

Danielle, Simone, and Soul all sat silently, deep in their own thoughts. Soon the effects of all the medicine Danielle had been given started to take their toll and she drifted back to sleep.

"Do you want to get some coffee?" Simone asked interrupting Soul's thoughts of a time in her past where she could have easily traded places with Danielle.

"I don't know about coffee, but a sista is hungry than a mug."

"Now that you mention it, my stomach is growling."

"I know. I heard it a few minutes ago."

"Whatever! Besides I didn't get to eat any of that pizza," Simone said, "and hospital food isn't as bad as people say it is. Let's go grab something to eat, while *sleeping beauty* is resting."

"Do you think Dani wants something back?" Soul asked as they headed back down the long hallway.

"Probably, let's sneak some cookies back, and if she's still hungry, I'll run back to the cafeteria and get her something."

"Where is the cafeteria anyway?'

"I'm not sure; wait let me ask that paramedic. Excuse me sir," Simone said to the tall white paramedic standing on the corner of the hallway looking at his cell phone."

"Yes ma'am," the paramedic glanced up from his phone. "Hey, don't I know you?"

"Oh no, never mind." Simone began to walk off but not before Soul caught the strange expression that crossed her face.

"Wait, I do know you, give me a sec, I never forget a face."

"Look, I'm sure you don't know me, I'm sorry to have bothered you," Simone said over her shoulder not bothering to look back.

"Girl why are you tripping, he's a paramedic, and you're a nurse. He probably knows you from the hospital." Simone was walking so fast, Soul almost tripped trying to catch up with her. When she finally reached her, Simone had the same nervous look on her face, and for the life of her, Soul couldn't figure out why her cousin had bugged out.

"Dang girl! What's your problem?"

"Nothing, I'm just hungry that's all. Come on I think the cafeteria is this way."

As Simone and Soul were finishing up our meals in the cafeteria, Soul looked up to see the paramedic from earlier approaching their table with a smile on his face.

"Excuse me miss,"

Not even glancing at Simone, Soul could feel Simone's body tense as soon as she heard his voice. Again, Soul didn't understand the nervousness etched onto Simone's face. Obviously, the paramedic didn't notice, because he continued to talk.

"Now I remember where we met. I'm Ray's partner, you do remember Ray," the paramedic laughed. "Boy, you and Ray were something else! The whole crew is still getting a laugh from the two of you. And poor Ray, that guy will never live that down."

Simone coughed as she choked on the lemon she was sucking trying to look anywhere but at the paramedic.

"Who is Ray, Simone, and what is this guy talking about?" Soul asked patting her on the back as Simone continued coughing.

For a paramedic he seemed oblivious to the fact that Simone was damn near choking, as he stood in front of the two women with a goofy ass look on his face, "Yeah, I can't wait to tell Ray that I saw you. He is going to flip. And we both know how Ray likes to flip," the paramedic laughed hysterically as he winked at Simone. You want me to tell him to give you a call?" Just as he was about to continue, his walkie talkie notified him of a call. "Well, duty calls, I'll see you around *"superwoman"* he winked again before walking off.

"Simone what the hell was that about?"

"What?" Simone took a drink from her water calmly with a blank expression on her face.

"Bitch, don't play with me."

"Look Soul, I don't have to tell you everything that goes on in my life."

"Oh yes the hell you do! Wait! I know you and the white dude didn't have something going on. Gurrl!"

"No dummy, you know I only like dark meat."

"Then what was all that about, and come to think of it, who is Ray? Girl you better start talking."

"You know Danielle is probably wondering where we are," Simone attempted to get up, but before she could make another move, Soul snatched her back down into the seat.

"Look, I am not letting you leave, until you tell me what that was all about."

From the serious expression on Soul's face, Simone knew her cousin was not going to stop hounding her until she gave her the details.

"You gone make me act a fool up in here, up in here," Soul gave her best interpretation of the infamous rapper DMX.

"Alright, nosy butt, but if you ever breathe a word to anyone, I will pour gasoline on your shoes strings, and light you up!"

"Yeah, Yeah, Yeah Firestarter. Now come on with the come on."

Rolling her eyes, Simone sighed, "Alright, during my first year as a nurse, I met Ray. Ray was a paramedic who did routine drops at the hospital. Anyway, he was always flirting with me, and so one day I finally took him up on a dinner date offer. We dated for about two weeks, and I broke on down and gave him some."

"Dang girl, so soon!"

"Well, it had been a while, and this brother was slap yo mama fine. Plus, the brother was a straight freak. I'm talking about toes, arm pits, everything. So, one night he comes over talking about doing some role-playing, and at first, I was like whatever, but he talked me into it, talking about he was gonna be Superman, and to let him tie me up. I mean, the brother was talking like he was going to tear something up! So, I let him tie me up."

"No! You didn't!"

"Can I finish? Anyway, he ties me up with my arms and legs spread open to each bedpost, exposing my *va jj* for all to see, then he goes in the bathroom, and comes out butt-naked with a cape on. By now I was like 'yeah superman, dive all up in this!' Okay, why did I have to say that, cause this fool decides he is truly going to *dive* in it. He decides he's going to jump from my dresser and land on top of me in the bed. I kept telling him that was too far to jump, but he was like he's superman and shit, and there's no task too great. So, he climbs on top of the dresser, and stands up, and is talking mad shit, about how he was going to tear me up, and put me back together again."

"Heyyyyy!"

"That's what I thought too, until he went to 'jump in the pussy,' and he didn't quite make it. I told him it was too far to jump, but nooo, he didn't listen. Why did this fool, bump his head on the edge of the railing of my bed, and pass out!"

"Stop it!" Soul screamed in laughter causing a few people to glance in their direction. "What did you do?"

"Hell, what could I do? The man was passed out on the floor. At first, I thought he was playing, but after ten minutes he still wasn't moving. Hell, I thought he was dead. So, I started screaming at the top of my lungs, and one of my neighbors must have heard me, and called the police. The next thing I know there was knocking on the door, and a big crash, then police, paramedics, and all sorts of damn people were busting into my apartment. Girl when those people rushed in and found Ray bucked naked on the floor, with a cape on, and me tied up, with my legs spread apart for everyone to see, they fell out. And why did the paramedic crew have to be the same crew that came to the hospital, and the same unit that Ray worked on. Girl, I thought I was going to die."

Soul fell out of her seat laughing so hard she thought she was going to pee on herself. She knew the people in the cafeteria thought she was crazy.

"Can you calm down, it ain't that funny."

"I'll be damn, I can't wait to get upstairs to tell Danielle," Soul said wiping tears from her eyes.

"Wait, hold up, sit down, you are not taking your happy-go-lucky ass anywhere. This stays between us! That's why I never told you in the beginning!" Simone said forcefully.

"Shiiiiiit, this is too good to hold onto," Soul said taking off in a mad dash, before Simone could grab her. By the time Simone made it to Danielle's room, Danielle and Soul were laughing hysterically.

Chapter 8

J ust as Soul was preparing to lock up and leave her classroom, her cell phone started ringing. Soul struggled to lock the door, hold the bag full of papers she planned to grade at home, and search the deep *jungle* that she called a purse. As soon as she got the door locked and placed her hand on something she hoped was her cell, the phone stopped ringing. It never failed.

Hoping whoever was calling would either call back or leave a message, Soul made her way into the main office to sign out. Making her way to her car, Soul prayed a silent thank you that she was able to find a close parking spot this morning and wouldn't have to carry her heavy belongings far. Just as she unlocked her door and sat her bags on the empty passenger seat, her phone rang again. Once she got settled in the car and turned the air on full blast, Soul dug in her phone for her purse to check her missed calls. One from Danielle and one from Simone. Soul scrolled through the phone and tapped on the voicemail icon.

"Hey Soul, this is Dani, I was calling to let you know you don't need to pick me up from the hospital, I already have a way home."

"Soul, this is Simone, I just received a message from Danielle saying not to come pick her up, please tell me you're going early or something. Because if she doesn't want either of us to come by to take her home, that could only mean one thing, and I'll be damn if we go down this road again."

Soul sighed heavily, "Not today, Jesus. Not my business." If Danielle wanted to continue thinking she had the ability to turn a hoe into a husband, that was on her. All Soul knew was that she was tired as hell and had tons of essays to grade before progress reports were due.

***

Soul pulled the phone away from her ear as Simone screamed into the phone, "Can you believe this? I'm so sick and tired of this! Doesn't she know the next time it might not just be a push down the stairs! It might be a push into a damn grave!"

Soul couldn't help the giggle that escaped her mouth although she knew Simone wasn't joking.

"Ain't nothing funny!"

"I know. It's just the way you said it. Listen, Simone, you need to calm down. Danielle is a grown ass woman, and it is time we let her make grown ass decisions and have to pay the grown ass consequences and just be there for her when it's all said and done. Dani made it clear at the hospital that it's always easier to see things from the outside. And that's true. Just because we see the house, does not mean we can see within her walls."

"Well, I don't need to be a fly on the wall to know their relationship is full of shit"

"Dang Simone, you starting to curse as much as me! Look, I agree with you. You are probably right. We don't need to be a fly on the wall, to know the shit stank, but it's her shit, and she's the only one who has to smell it everyday. Now please, go smoke a black and mild, and drink a beer or a glass of wine so you can chill out and leave me the hell alone!"

"Fine!"

"Ok!"

"Hey"

"What Simone?"

"Call me back when Grey's Anatomy comes on, so we can watch it together!"

"Girl, get off this phone!"

***

Soul breathe a sigh of relief as she slid the essays she had finally finished grading in her bag and placed the bag on the sofa near her purse and jacket so she could grab everything on her way out the door in the morning. Walking to the kitchen she poured a huge glass of wine and went to draw her bath. Pouring lavender bubbles into the water, Soul opened her Spotify app and scrolled to her Anita Baker playlist. After her long day, a bubble bath, wine and Anita was just what she needed. Stripping out of her clothes, Soul prepared to step into the tub full of steaming bubbles when Ms. Anita's smooth voice was interrupted by the ringing of her phone. Soul considered letting it go to voicemail, but she knew it was no one but that dog-gone Simone, and she would only call back if Soul didn't answer. Not even bothering to look at the Caller ID, Soul hit the answer icon.

"What Simone?"

"Excuse you! You must a' lost yo last mind answerin' ya phone like you don't have no home training'. This ya granny, and I know you know better than to answer that phone like some thug on the street."

"Dang, granny I'm sorry. I thought you were someone else."

"Well, it doesn't matter who it was on the phone, you don't answer nobody's phone like that. I don't care if you are paying the bills. For all you know, that could a been the good Lord on the phone."

"Granny, you know the Lord ain't calling my damn house!" Soul giggled into the phone.

"Girl, you better watch the way you talking to me. I know ya mama didn't raise you to use curse words in front of grown folks."

"But granny, I didn't mean to"

"Don't you but granny me. Lil girl I ought to come over there right now and wash ya lil' nasty mouth out with soap. I knew there was a reason that the Lord put it on my heart to call you, cause the Lord knows that you probably curse like that everyday. Help her Jesus. She turnin' into a little heathen!"

Soul's grandmother, or Granny Lewis as she was affectionally known, was one of the best dressed, sweetest, wisest, and most religious women a person could ever meet. She was like "Big Mama" from the movie Soul Food, except she loved fashion, and everybody loved her. Raised in the dirt roads of the East Texas back country woods, she could bake a peach cobbler that would make you want to slap her, but you knew better. Soul's grandmother was the reason she pledged her sorority. There was not a sorority meeting or event that her grandmother missed, and if Soul became too AWOL her grandmother would call her and remind her of the oath she took. There was never a day when you could catch her in public with even a hair out of place. She always represented the epitome of finer. Soul loved her grandmother to death. When her mother died a few years ago, Soul wanted to die, but it was her grandmother and grandfather who brought her through the storm. Each time that Soul thought she couldn't take her mother's death, her grandmother would remind her that in every death comes a blessing, and where God took from your life, he would add even more. Soul's family was the kind of family that enjoyed being around one another, and every weekend it wasn't unusual to find Soul sitting at her grandmother's house laughing at her crazy uncles and aunts. They had family talent shows, and even Soul's ex-boyfriends still begged her to let them come to her family reunion. The only thing about her grandmother was she would church you to death. She was the first one at Sunday school and the last one to leave evening service. Soul's grandparents were the funniest couple she had ever laid eyes on. After fifty-two years of marriage, they still fought like teenagers, but loved each other like newlyweds. If her grandmother was a fashion icon, her grandfather was the exact opposite. All he ever wore was a pair of blue jean overalls, and a white t-shirt. It was a wonder her grandmother even got him to put on a suit to go to church every Sunday. He was a true God-fearing man, a Mason, head of the brotherhood and deacon board; but he believed every man had to come to God in their own way. When Soul's grandmother would chastise the family about their worldly ways, her grandfather would chastise her grandmother about not letting "the kids live their own life". Oil and water was how Soul's mother used to refer to her parents, and who would have thought they would mix so well.

"Granny, I'm sorry. I really don't curse a lot," Soul closed her eyes praying a silent prayer of forgiveness. Today had been a long day and her granny's lectures could go on for hours. "It's just that I am really tired, and Simone keeps calling. I also have tons of work to finish before I send failure notices to parents."

"That's my baby, always looking out for the young folks. How is work anyways?"

"School's fine Granny. You know I love working with kids, no matter how much I complain about them, and no matter how much money we don't make, I wouldn't give this up for anything. This year's group is much better than the knuckleheads I had last year. You know one of my students I had last year just went to juvenile for bringing a gun to school. As much as I love teaching, I can't help but wonder everyday, if I will one day be involved in the next Columbine or Parkland," Soul said with a sigh.

"Baby, now don't you go to talking like that, the Lord knows what is best. You love those kids, which is why you went back to school so you can help them even more, and as long as you keep your faith in God and continue to pray, he will watch over you."

"Amen! Now Granny, what do I owe the pleasure of this phone call to?"

"Well baby, I told you the Lord put you on my heart, and I was calling to invite you to church on Sunday. Your granddaddy can't make it and I sure would like some company. Besides, it ain't gone be no evening service, so don't try to use that as an excuse."

"Well granny, I actually have a previous engagement," Soul said teasing her grandmother.

"What kind of engagement you have on a Sunday morning cept' some football or that Lifetime network you like so much."

"Uh,"

"That's what I thought. So, I'll see you Sunday morning."

"Granny, you think you know me!"

"I take it that means yes?"

"Yes ma'am."

"I'll see you at 11:00, but Sunday school starts at 9:45."

"Granny," Soul warned.

"I know. I'm pushing it. Well, I'll see you at eleven, and wear something pretty, I gots me somebody I want you to meet!" Soul's grandmother hung up the phone before she could say anything else.

Chapter 9

♥

Saint Luke Baptist church was always packed. Ever since Reverend Crawford decided to build a new sanctuary, the membership kept growing. It also didn't hurt that Reverend Crawford could preach a mean sermon! He always told the church, "Bring ya steel-toed boots, because this sermon is about to step on a lot of toes." To add to the preaching there was St. Luke's choir, The Gospel Movers, who had recently made a record that was blowing up on the gospel charts. With the amazing preaching and singing, Soul had no idea why she did not go to church with her grandmother more often besides the fact that as her grandmother mentioned on the call the previous night, Soul was lazy and wanted to watch football. Even though she had only visited on occasion as her grandmother's guest, Soul really enjoyed the church and Reverend Crawford's messages were always relatable, but Bible based and centered on scripture.

When Soul's grandmother had chosen St. Luke as her fellowship home, Soul was surprised mainly because it was three times bigger than her old church in East Texas, but Granny Lewis favorite saying was the Lord didn't limit his spirit to small churches.

This Sunday was not any different than most other times Soul had visited, the pews were already filling up and it wasn't even 11:00. Soul spotted her grandmother sitting way at the front looking around, probably searching for Soul who tried slipping quietly into a back pew, but her grandmother spotted her and started waving frantically for her to come to the front. Soul tried pretending like she didn't see her grandmother, but then her phone started ringing.

"Yes grandmother."

"Soul, baby, come on up to the front. I don't want you to miss a word the good Rev has to say!"

Soul sighed before hanging up the phone and making her way to the front, sitting down just as the choir began to sing the opening hymn.

"Baby, you sure look good in your royal blue pants suit, and I love those nude heels. I'm glad you took granny's advice and dressed up nice."

"Well, Granny you know true ladies always wear the finest royal blue," Soul said referring to the colors of their sorority. Growing up around her grandmother and seeing the true sisterhood found in their sorority, when Soul went to college there was never a question of where her loyalty would lie.

Granny Lewis continued looking around as if she was looking for someone else, "What's the matter, Granny?"

"I was just looking for Sister Jenkins baby, don't worry about me."

Soon Soul's grandmother was all into the service, and the choir was jamming so hard that even Soul was on her feet clapping along with the melody. One thing about St. Luke that Soul loved was no matter how long you were away, it always felt like coming home. Soul wasn't sure what it was, but there was something special about this church. Even though she was raised in the church, what started out as missing one service became two, then three. Now she was at the point where she qualified as a CME, Christmas, Mother's Day, and Easter church goer. And for some reason *Lifetime* always put the best movies on at 11:00, not to mention that online services had made it too easy to stay home and catch the word. The problem was, as soon as the word started, Soul often found herself falling back asleep with the phone beside her and the word preaching to the lights and walls. Along with the fact that school could get so hectic during the week, and the many meetings on Saturdays, Soul wanted at least one day of rest. The problem was Soul's upbringing in the church as a child only served to convict her as she knew deep down, she had to give God his time too.

Born and raised in the church, Soul used to sing in the choir, taught Sunday school, lead youth meetings, and much more. Her grandmother was constantly on her back about her lack of church going, and no matter how much Soul kept trying to explain that a person could serve and believe in God, and not be in church, in her heart Soul knew that growth came through fellowship. Drifting in thought, Soul wondered if she went to church more often, would she have already met her a good man, who could tame her and help her become more submissive but soon found herself giggling at the thought of anyone taming her.

"The Lord is always protecting me," Rev. Crawford said interrupting Soul's thoughts. "See sometimes my money is running low, and my phone might get cut off. I can't call on my friends no more. But I tell you who I can call. Jesus! T-Mobile nor Verizon can't stop this conversation. See I don't need a phone line to talk to him, I just fall on my knees and pray. I don't worry about call waiting interrupting, don't have to worry about him not being home, don't have to send him a text or a message in Facebook messenger, cause he's right there!" the pastor said almost singing his words. "Can I get an amen!" See some of us only call him when we need something, moneys running short, spouse ain't acting right, people plain and simple getting on your nerves! I ain't on ya toes yet."

By the time Reverend Crawford finished, the church was on fire. Women were shouting in the aisles, and men were standing on their feet. It never ceased to amaze Soul how every time she did come to church the message was right on time. This man could truly bring the message.

"Well, baby, how did you enjoy the service?" Soul's grandmother asked turning to her after the benediction.

"Ah Granny, you know I love to hear the good Rev. speak. He is one of the most motivating speakers I have ever heard. In fact, I think I'm going to go speak and let him know how much I enjoyed his sermon."

"That's right baby."

"Granny, did you hear what I said?"

"Oh baby, I'm sorry, I was just looking for Sister Jenkins. Oh, there she is! Come on baby, I want you to meet Sister Jenkin's grandson."

Bruh!!!!! Soul knew she was just wondering about meeting a good man in church, but she did not feel like suffering through another of her grandmother's blind date moments. Before she could even respond, her grandmother dragged her over to Sister Jenkins.

"Hey Sister Jenkins," Granny said hugging the older lady tight.

"Hey Sister Lewis, you looking good as ever. I know this ain't that granddaughter you were telling me about. Such a beautiful young lady."

"And a beautiful, single young lady," Soul's grandmother quickly added.

"Ya grandmother tells me you are a teacher."

"Yes ma'am, it's a challenging job, but someone has to do it," Soul smiled politely even though she wanted to run right out of the church before Sister Jenkin's grandson came over. He was probably some jerry curl, gold tooth having, ugly brother who wore some of those old MC Hammer glasses.

"Ain't that the truth. You know your grandmother was telling me you didn't have a boyfriend. That's a shame, seeing how pretty you are and everything. How long has it been since you had a boyfriend?"

"I know she didn't," Soul thought to herself. Sister Jenkins better have been glad that Soul was raised to respect her elders, because this lady was getting a little too nosy. "Well, Sister Jenkins, it hasn't been too long, but I'm not looking. You know I'm trying to work on my career, and I'm also going to graduate from graduate school soon, so I just don't have time for a relationship right now." Soul finished with a tight smile hoping that would satisfy the old nosy heifer.

"You ain't hom e sexual are you," Sister Jenkins asked loudly.

What! No, I am not homosexual," Soul added correcting the older woman. Soul could tell the question even caught her granny off guard, because she looked like she was about to go upside Sister Jenkins head.

"Look here Luella, I didn't bring Soul here for you to get all in her business, I thought you was going to introduce her to your grandson."

"Well, I was just trying to see who I was going to fix my grandbaby up with," Sister Jenkins said with an equal attitude. It was as if they had forgotten Soul was standing there and that was fine with Soul if she could just figure out a way to slip out during the old lady stare down.

"Ladies, really, thank you both for being so concerned with *my* love life," Soul said stressing my, "but really I don't need to be fixed up with anyone."

Her grandmother pulled her to the side, "Baby, listen you know I only have your best interest at heart. I am only asking that you meet the nice young man, and besides, I already promised Sister Jenkins that you and I would go out to dinner with she and her grandson. And if we cancel now, you know she would run her mouth telling everybody that I ain't a woman of my word, and Lord knows I don't want that," Granny Lewis said sniffling.

Soul's grandmother obviously missed her calling as an actress because she was sure laying it on thick. Yes, she was religious and all, but she could manipulate her way through any situation, especially a situation that was regarding Soul's love life.

"Fine Granny." Soul said with a sigh," Just this one time, but you have to promise me that you will never fix me up again after this."

"Thank you baby, you know your granny just wants to see you happy, and besides after today, you might not need to be fixed up with anyone!"

It amazed Soul how quickly her grandmother's solemn demeanor changed, as she happily walked back over to Sister Jenkins. "Come on honey," her grandmother said over her shoulder as she linked arms with Sister Jenkins, "we riding to the restaurant with Sister Jenkins and her grandson. He's outside getting the car."

"Whatever Grandmother. I'm right behind you. Just remember this is the last time you will try to set me up on a blind date, right?"

"Of course, now come on. We don't want to keep the young man waiting."

The walk to the back of the church seemed to take forever since Sister Jenkins and Soul's grandmother had to stop and talk to everyone they knew. Soul wished they could just get this mess over with. Her grandmother must have noticed the agitated look on her face, because she quickly finished what seemed like her fourth conversation and grabbed Sister Jenkins arm. "Come on Luella, we don't want to keep your grandson waiting."

They walked outside, and the day was beautiful. All Soul really wanted was to go home to enjoy this beautiful day. One thing was for sure Soul's grandmother owed her big time, especially since she could think of a million and one things she could be doing besides going on a blind date with two old ladies. Tomorrow there had better be a Sock-It-To Me cake waiting on her doorstep when she got home from work.

"There he is," Sister Jenkins said waving to a fine brother in a late model SUV. "Anthony," Sister Jenkins screamed waiving her arms frantically, "over here!"

Chapter 10

"This cannot be happening." Soul thought as the SUV pulled up to the curb and the driver rolled down his window.

"Hey nana, what took you so long? Let me guess, you ladies had to fight all the men off to get out of the church," Sister Jenkins's grandson stepped out of the SUV and wrapped his arm around the older woman.

"Boy stop," she laughed obviously enjoying her grandson's comments. "Let me introduce you to Sister Lewis and her beautiful granddaughter."

Taking Soul's grandmother by the hand, Sister Jenkins' grandson turned on the charm, "The pleasure is all mine Mrs. Lewis, but surely my nana is mistaken. You are much too young to be someone's grandmother".

"Isn't he respectful," Soul's grandmother smiled, elbowing Soul in her side at the same time. "Let me introduce you to my granddaughter Soul."

As Anthony turned his attention towards her, Soul noticed a look of familiarity cross his face, as a smile threatened the corners of his lips, "Soul, so nice to see you again," he said extending his hand. "I've been thinking about you."

"Again? Do you two know each other?"

Leave it to Sister Jenkins nosy ass to start asking questions, Soul thought as she rolled her eyes.

"Soul, don't be rude," Soul's grandmother whispered noticing that she had not shook Anthony's outstretched palm.

"We've met," Soul extended her hand.

"Yes, we have." Anthony said looking deeply into Soul's eyes. Taking her outstretched hand, Anthony caressed Soul's hand rubbing his thumb slowly in her outstretched palm. "Haven't we Soul?"

"Even better," Sister Jenkins remarked. "So, where do you kids know one another from?"

"We met at a previous social engagement," Anthony said still holding her hand and looking into her eyes.

"Yes, a previous engagement," Soul said snatching her hand from Anthony.

"Well, isn't that nice that you kids already know each other?" Soul's grandmother added looking more at Sister Jenkins than at Soul and Anthony. "Well kids, let's get this show on the road. I'm hungry! Anthony, me and your grandmother can sit in the back, that way you and Soul can get reacquainted."

Soul shot her grandmother the evil eye. Thank goodness for love or she would have pushed her old butt down right on the spot.

As Anthony helped Sister Jenkins and Soul's grandmother into his SUV, Soul couldn't help but notice how his navy slim fit suit seemed to be tailor made for his body before she began to walk to the passenger side of the Range Rover and get in. "Hold on Soul, let me help you." Anthony said closing the back door and jogging around to the passenger side of the truck.

"Thanks, but I can get it," Soul said as started to open her door.

"Soul, a lady always allows a gentleman to open her door," her grandmother remarked sternly from the backseat.

"Fine!" Soul said taking Anthony's hand and stepping into the truck.

"That wasn't so hard," Anthony whispered in her ear, before closing the door and walking back to the driver's side. In spite of herself, the deep sound of Anthony's voice in her ear sent chills through Soul's body.

"Well, I can't believe I have the luck of enjoying the company of three beautiful women. I am really going to enjoy this lunch!" Anthony said turning to Soul with a smile.

***

Although the restaurant was only a short distance from the church, it was as if Anthony drove as slow as the speed limit would allow simply to torture Soul.

"Anthony, let me and Sister Lewis off at the front door baby while you and Soul find a parking spot. You know us old women can't walk as far as you young people."

"Sure Nana, anything you say."

Anthony pulled in front of the restaurant and jumped out to open the door for their grandmothers. As Anthony helped his grandmother out of the truck, Soul's grandmother leaned to the front seat "That Anthony sure is a gentleman, and a nice dresser."

"Whatever Granny, just know that you owe me big time."

"You the one that ought to be thanking me, that boy got it going on as you young folks say, and it doesn't hurt that he's easy on the eyes. Look at this car. He seems to be doing well for himself. Did I tell you he was in real estate? Girl, If I was a little younger and didn't love your granddaddy like I do! Heyyy," Soul's grandmother said snapping her fingers.

Soul couldn't help but laugh at her grandmother's antics. She was right about two things. Anthony was definitely a good dresser, Soul thought as she snuck a few glances his way. Just like that night at the club, his outfit of choice was a flawless-navy slim fit suit, white button top dress shirt, dark brown dress shoes, and a navy and brown multi print tie. The starched white dress shirt did little to hide his ripped muscles. Soul's thoughts were interrupted when Anthony jumped back in the SUV to find a parking spot.

"So, Soul, you were quite quiet on the way over," he said shooting a sideway glance in her direction.

"Yeah well, I try not to hold conversations too much with people I don't like."

"My my, we really do have to work on that attitude," Anthony said expertly backing his SUV into an empty space. "By the way, how are your two friends," he asked with a smirk. Before Soul could respond, Anthony had turned off the SUV and gotten out.

By the time Soul got her thoughts together to formulate a smart aleck comeback, Anthony was opening her door and grabbing her hand to help her out. Anthony led her into the direction of the restaurant. It didn't immediately register with Soul that her hand was still inside of Anthony's but once she did, Soul quickly snatched her hand away from Anthony which only seemed to amuse him even more. Placing his hand into the small of Soul's back, Anthony's whispered into her ear, "methinks the lady doth protest too much! Come on, I promise it won't be as bad as you think."

Before Soul could give Anthony a piece of her mind, she was interrupted by her grandmother waving them to the back of the restaurant as they entered the door, "Over here dear!"

"Excuse me," Soul huffed pushing past Anthony. She walked to the back of the restaurant where her grandmother and Sister Jenkins were sitting in what appeared to be a two-person booth. "Granny, I thought you guys were going to come in to get seats for *all* of us," Soul asked folding her arms.

"Well baby, there were only these two small booths left when we came in, so we figured we had better grab what we could get. You and Anthony can sit in that booth together. Besides Luella and I really need to discuss some things that the Willing Workers auxiliary needs to do at the church."

"Granny," Soul warned through clenched teeth.

"Well," Anthony interrupted, "personally I think that is a great idea. It would allow Soul and I a chance to get reacquainted even more."

"See baby, Anthony doesn't mind," Soul's grandmother said smiling knowingly at Sister Jenkins. Soul swore to herself that if it wasn't a crime, she'd fight both of those old biddies.

Soul didn't say a word but instead stomped over to the empty booth that had been selected for she and Anthony.

"You know Soul," Anthony laughed sliding into the booth across from her, "we could make this a horrible lunch, or we can start over."

"Whatever," Soul sighed. "Let's just get through this so we don't ever have to see each other again."

"Do you really dislike me that much?"

"Does it matter?"

"Yeah, it actually does."

Before Soul could determine if the look on his face was one of seriousness or tease, they were interrupted by the waitress. "Hello, what can I start the two of you off with today?"

"I'll have a coke," Anthony answered, "and the lady will have"

"A tea please."

"Will this be together or separate?"

"Separate. Together" Anthony and Soul both said at the same time.

"Uh, which one, separate or together?"

"Together," Anthony said, "and could you add the tickets of those two gorgeous girls over there as well," Anthony said pointing to their grandmothers.

"Sure will darling." The waitress winked at Anthony before leaving to go get he and Soul's drinks and allow them time to decide on their orders.

"Look," Soul began, "I can pay for my meal and my grandmothers. You really didn't have to do that."

"Well, I figured since you insisted on paying for that drink, I owed you!"

"Yeah, you actually do," Soul smirked as she tried to appear engrossed in her menu.

Anthony shook his head with a smile and started to peruse the menu as well.

The truth was, something about Anthony was getting under her skin. Maybe it was that deep voice, or that pearly white smile that she was sure had broken a heart or two or three. And let's not even get started on that body. Despite his apparant arrogance, Soul had to admit he was no less attractive than when she first laid eyes on him that night at the club. Soul took a sip of water hoping it would cool her thoughts of Anthony before thanking the man above that the waitress had returned with their drinks. The sooner she could get out of Anthony's presence the more likely she was to keep her panties on.

Are you two ready to order?" the waitress asked looking at Anthony.

"Well since what I want is not on the menu,' Anthony said staring at Soul and licking his lips, 'I'll start with a salad, and for the main course can I have the pork chops, with collard greens and an order of candied yams. And can you also bring me two pieces of hot water corn bread."

This guy was a piece of work, Soul though to herself even though she once again felt herself warming under Anthony's magnetic stare as he continued staring at her with that silly ass grin on his face.

"Ma'am'," the waitress said waving her hand across Soul's face, "I can see how you could get lost in those pretty brown eyes over there sugar, but are you ready to order?"

"Actually," Soul said glaring at the waitress, "I am. Could I have the fish and fry dinner basket with corn instead of coleslaw.

"Sure honey." The waitress seemed oblivious to the daggers that Soul was throwing her way. "Let me get those menus out of your way."

"Hmm do you always order seafood at a soul food restaurant?

"I guess some of us aren't as big on soul food as others," Soul took a sip of her tea and looked around. When she found Anthony once again staring at her with a smile, she pretended to look through her purse to avoid any conversation with him.

"So, Soul, are you a member at Saint Luke?"

"Yes." Soul answered pretending to still look through her purse.

"That's funny, I've been going there faithfully for the past few months since I moved back to Dallas, and I don't remember seeing you, and I go to bible study and everything." he said smiling knowing he had caught Soul in a lie.

"Actually, I mean, I haven't been in a while so that's probably why you haven't seen me there lately." Soul quickly took another sip of her tea. She could almost feel the laughter threatening to erupt from the corner of Anthony's mouth.

"Probably," Anthony said with a smile before taking a sip of his coke.

"What do you do for a living, Soul?"

Soul sighed in exasperation, "Since you are so insistent on having a conversation with me, I'm a teacher, but I'm attending school to obtain my masters degree with an administrative certification."

"Really?" Anthony said clasping his hands together. "I really admire teachers. It takes a special person to deal with kids. What grade do you teach?'

"Ninth." Soul said dryly.

"Oh, you really are a brave person! You know I don't remember the teachers being as cute as you when I was in ninth grade."

"Really," Soul replied nonchalantly wondering why her stomach did a little flip.

"Really." Anthony paused looking at her again.

"I guess polite conversation would call for me to ask what you do for a living?"

"Actually, it would, but since you seem to know nothing about being polite, it's OK. But for the record, I'm in real estate. Actually, I'm now a loan officer, but on occasion, I still do some real estate every now and then. I work with a couple of my fraternity brothers at a growing real estate office in North Dallas."

"Hmm, Soul said thoughtfully as she leaned back into the booth. "I guess being your own boss explains the reason for your arrogance."

Anthony ignored her comment, "Tell me something Soul, are you always this much of a bitch, or is it just me that brings out the bitch in you?'

"If you must know, you bring out the queen bitch in me." Soul smirked not missing a beat nor reacting to Anthony's shade which caused Anthony to laugh loudly just as the waitress brought their meals to the table.

"Here you go sugar. You know, you two sure make a cute couple," she said smiling and looking back and forth between Soul and Anthony.

"Thank you. I think so too." Anthony replied looking directly at Soul.

"Well eat up sugar, let me know if there is anything else you need," the waitress said before walking off.

As she walked past their grandmother's table Soul rolled her eyes as she saw the waitress give them the thumbs up sign.

Anthony and Soul ate the meal in silence with the exception of Anthony's occasionally smacking of his lips or remarking how good the food was. From the way he acted, you would think the man had never had good cooking.

"Must not have a woman at home to cook for you the way you acting." Soul gasped as she realized she had actually verbalized her thoughts.

"Why, you trying the fill the spot?" Anthony asked licking his spoon and staring at her with a mischievous look in his eyes.

"No! Not at all!" Soul stammered.

"Sugar that food sure must have been good to you the way you cleaned that plate. Do you want anything else?" the waitress said walking up to their table.

"Yes ma'am my compliments to the cook. Anthony said wiping his mouth. "What you got sweet in that kitchen?"

"Well, besides me Sugar," the older lady giggled, "what you want?"

"You got any sweet potato pie?" Anthony said laughing.

"Sho nough. You want that for here or to go?"

"Can I get it to go and can I also get our tickets.

"Sure, baby," the waitress turned to retrieve the tickets.

"Do you have to flirt with everyone you come in contact with?'

"Why, are you jealous?"

"Jealous! Why would I be jealous?" Soul exclaimed loudly. "Excuse me I have to go to the ladies room." Before Anthony could get up to help her out of her chair, Soul grabbed her purse and hurriedly brushed past him.

The nerve of that son of a bitch. Who in the hell does he think he is? Just because he's cute, he might be used to other women's panties dropping at the sight of that sexy bald head, but he would not have the same effect on Soul. "Boy as soon as he drops Granny and I back at the church I'm really going to let her have it," Soul was glad the bathroom was empty. She couldn't understand why Anthony's comment, hell Anthony himself, had her so flustered. "Ugghhhh," she moaned rolling her eyes at her reflection in the mirror. Soul reapplied her lipstick and grabbed a makeup blotter from her purse to take the shine off her face.

By the time she came out of the rest room, Anthony had paid for the meals and he, Sister Jenkins and her grandmother were standing at the front of the restaurant waiting on her.

"So, did you kids have a good lunch?" Soul's grandmother asked.

"It was more entertaining than you will ever know. In fact, I was just about to ask Soul to go out with me Friday."

"What!" Soul said turning to Anthony with a shocked expression on her face.

"That would be a lovely idea," Sister Jenkins said.

"Actually, I'm busy," Soul said quickly.

"Oh, I understand, what about Saturday, or Sunday, I'm pretty much available for the entire weekend," Anthony said smiling deviously.

"Well," Soul began.

"She'd love to," her grandmother interrupted.

"Great," Anthony said. "How about Saturday, let's say 7:00. Why don't you give me your address and I'll pick you up then."

"Uh why don't we discuss this later, Anthony."

"Actually, I'd like to go ahead and get it so I don't forget," he said grabbing a napkin off the counter.

Before she knew what was happening, Soul's grandmother grabbed the napkin and wrote Soul's address and phone number on it. Anthony took the paper back from her grandmother and placed it in his chest pocket. "I need to keep this as close to my heart as possible! Ladies," he said holding the door open.

Soul wondered what the hell just happened, but she knew one thing for sure, she was going to wring her grandmother's little old wrinkled neck. She stomped over to where Anthony had parked his SUV. Anthony jogged ahead of her and opened the door.

"What the hell was that?' Soul whispered fiercely.

"What?" Anthony asked innocently. "It was us planning a date. And you thought we'd never see each other again. You should really quit selling yourself so short. I find your company quite entertaining," he added before jogging around to the other side of the truck to open the door for Sister Jenkins and her grandmother.

Her grandmother must have felt the evil looks Soul was giving her through the rearview mirror, because as soon they were settled into the SUV and Anthony was pulling out of the lot, her grandmother tapped Anthony on his shoulder, "Anthony baby, could you please drop Soul off at her car first, your grandmother and I need to run in the church to get some things, and I don't want my baby to have to walk by herself."

"No problem Mrs. Lewis," Anthony said looking across the seat at her with a smile, as he began to hum an old Prince tune.

Chapter 11

The one part of the workday that Soul enjoyed the most was meeting with her lunch brunch. The group of ladies always had a lively discussion whether it dealt with sex, religion, or politics. Like songs on an R Kelly CD, they were so different, there was no telling what could be said at any given moment.

Soul knew today's conversation would be no different as she began to tell the lunch brunch of her time at church, and her impromptu upcoming date.

"Well hell, you ain't got no man, and Anthony seems like he has it going on. What the hell are you complaining about?" Mrs. Alice asked, as she sucked on a piece of neck bone she had brought for lunch. As the oldest member of the lunch brunch, Mrs. Alice was like the crazy mother figure everyone wanted. With twenty-seven years of marriage under her belt, she was the person the entire crew sought out when there was a relationship problem. Her oldest daughter was Soul's age, but Ms. Alice was so cool, that everyone considered her to be like a sister *and* a mother. With Mrs. Alice there was always a joke to tell, a story to share, and an opinion to give, desired or not. She and her husband lived in a huge five-bedroom house in an elite Dallas suburb area with their youngest two children. Her favorite piece of advice to the lunch brunch was not to rush into things for appearance sake, with her constant reminder that she ate beans five different days and ways, drove an old beat up station wagon that you had to start from under the hood, and struggled from job to job until she and her husband were able to live as she says "hood rich."

"Mrs. Alice, but he is so conceited." Soul continued to complain.

"Ain't that the prostitute calling the stripper a hoe. Damnit, I got a stain on my shirt," Mrs. Alice said trying to wipe out today's stain. There were two things in life Soul could bet money on when it came to Mrs. Alice, she was going to give you her opinion and she was going to get something on her clothes every time she ate!

"Mrs. Alice you're crazy girl," Kayla laughed as she ate her second dessert. For someone so skinny Kayla, another member of the lunch brunch ate like a football player.

"No really, what is the problem?" Marie asked bringing them back to the topic at hand. "You said the brother was foine, and had a job. Hey that's ten points if you ask me." Marie and Kayla were complete opposites. Marie, a city girl, was married with kids, with a little, no, make that a lot of ghetto in her. One of those women who knew she had it going on, Marie didn't take anything from anybody. Kayla on the other hand, could best be described as cute and country. Her smile and outgoing personality had men falling at her feet, but Kayla was still one of the most down to earth people a person could ever meet. Kayla could be a bit naïve' when it came to common sense things, but as far as being a man's fantasy, she was currently working on her doctorate degree, single, no kids, cute, nice shape, and pushing a new Mercedes.

"Marie, you know, I just hate blind dates. Haven't you guys ever had a blind date that was horrible?" Soul asked.

"Hell yeah! Did I ever tell you about when I was in high school and went on this blind date with this college dude?" Mrs. Alice asked while still attempting to wipe the collard green juice off her white blouse.

"What happened Mrs. Alice?" Janice asked in an exited tone. Janice, a newlywed, was so in love with her husband, it sometimes disgusted Soul to no end. Janice always came up with the most random questions. Sometimes Soul wondered if Janice asked stupid stuff just for attention, or if she really wanted to know about the random stuff she asked. Like a few months ago she called Soul to simply say "Girl, why didn't you tell me that if you plucked your eyelashes it hurt!" Soul had cursed her for calling her at 6:00 AM on a Saturday morning, and then hung up the phone on her. After that phone call, Soul put Janice on phone restrictions with no calls before 7:00 AM, and 12:00 PM on the weekend.

"I didn't tell ya'll about that?" Mrs. Alice asked knowing she probably had, but also knowing the girls wanted to hear one of her famous stories anyway.

"Well, Mrs. Alice, you probably told us, but tell us again, because I know it's probably some mess," Soul said with a smile.

"Girl," she began, "I was in high school, and I went to this party with this college guy. You know I thought I was the shit, right? Anyway, when we got to the party, his ass left me by myself. Well, I didn't know anyone at the party, so I just sat in the corner most of the night. After about an hour, I noticed some brownies sitting near the punch. So, when I went to get some punch, I also got a brownie. Girl that was the best brownie I had ever had in my life. So, I got another and another. By now I was feeling pretty good. I noticed a few people were staring at me, but I didn't give a damn. My big ass had pulled me a chair up at the table and was eating the hell out of those brownies. Girl when my date finally found me, he was like 'Alice what the hell are you doing?' shit I was giggling and stuff, and for some reason the look on his face was sooo funny. He tried to pull me away from the table, but I wouldn't move, girl I was too busy trying to get my grub on. I sat there and ate that whole damn plate of brownies."

"Mrs. Alice, don't tell me they had weed in them?" Soul asked laughing.

"Hell yeah! My date was so mad and embarrassed; he left me at the party, and never called me again. I mean it wasn't my fault, his ass shouldn't have left me by myself."

"Mrs. Alice you are too crazy," Janice added as she began to collect all the trash from their table. "I guess I am blessed when Jude and I met it was love at first sight."

"For real?" Kayla asked, "And you guys never had problems?"

"You know what, actually we did, now that I think about it. Soul remember when I called you from over his house, asking you to come help me fight!"

"Hell yeah," Soul laughed, "A mess and a half!"

"What happened?" Kayla asked turning to Janice.

"Well," Janice began, "Jude and I were sitting at his house watching movies, when his phone starting ringing. Every time he answered the phone, the person would hang up. Then we heard some noise outside, and the next thing I know, we heard glass breaking and his car alarm going off. So, Jude jumped up and ran to the door, and as soon as he opened the door, a brick came flying through! Girl you should have seen me getting off that sofa, and diving on the floor. Why was his crazy ass stalker ex girlfriend standing outside screaming, talking about I know you got a bitch in that house. You'll always belong to me; I don't care what that damn restraining order says!"

'What!" Marie screamed. "Don't tell me he had a restraining order put on her!"

"Girl yes!" Janice laughed. "So, Jude was running through the house talking about call the police, that bitch is crazy, and the next thing I know we hear glass breaking in the kitchen. Girl how about I dove on the floor and crawled on my elbows like I'm in the damn army, trying to get to the back room where the phone was. When I made it to the back I could here some tussling going on in the front, cause by now this crazy ass girl has started trying to crawl through the kitchen window. So, I'm still laying on the floor whispering to the police about what's going on. As soon as I hung up the phone with the police, I call Soul. I'm on the phone giving Soul directions when I hear a female voice yelling 'help me get the fuck out of this window.' So, I tell Soul to hold on and I run to the front. Tell me why this crazy trick had gotten stuck in the window! I tried to punch the hell out of whatever part of her that wasn't trapped in that window! Scaring me like that! You should have seen Jude trying to hold me and her twisting and turning to get out that window!"

Mrs. Alice, Marie, and Kayla were holding their sides from laughing so hard.

"Girl, something similar to that happened to my husband and I before we got married, but when that bitch stepped to me, I straight got out of the car," Marie said demonstrating as she stood up from the table and proceeded to get into a boxing pose, "and straight whooped her ass. Then I told my husband to get in the damn car and drive off before I whip his ass too." Maria smacked her lips and rolled her eyes dramatically.

"Maria, you think you are so tough," Soul laughed.

"And you know this," Marie said giving Soul a high five.

"Girl you all are something else, I guess since we are talking about bad dates, I might as well tell my story of what happened to me a while back," Kayla said. "I had vowed not to tell anyone, but you guys are my lunch brunch."

"What has your crazy ass done?" Mrs. Alice asked with a smile.

"I ain't right, am I?" Kayla joked. "Okay, listen, listen. Remember me telling you all about Mr. Football?"

"Right, Right," Soul commented.

"Ok, so we went on a date to that Italian restaurant, in the art district," Kayla continued. "It was Mr. Football, his homeboy, one of my good girlfriends, and myself. Anyway, I was looking cute, I had on my jazzy pink slacks, with a little cute top. And I had decided to wear my good new wig."

"Hey!" Soul said. "The big curly wig we bought at Wigs to Fit?"

"Yeah, girl that one!" Kayla said twinkling her fingers at Soul. "Anyway, we were having a good time, everyone was eating and drinking. Now ya'll know I cannot drink, but I had me two good Cadillacs."

"Cadillacs!" everyone said in unison.

"Yeah!" Kayla started to giggle. "So, we left the restaurant and decided to walk through the arts district. Everyone was hitting it off and feeling good. My girlfriend and Mr. Football's friend were walking ahead of us, and Mr. Football and I were walking behind them holding hands and laughing and talking." Kayla said as she began to laugh hysterically.

Soul, Mrs. Alice, Maria and Janice begin to laugh in anticipation of what Kayla was going to say.

"Kayla, finish the damn story," Mrs. Alice said laughing.

"Anyway," Kayla said trying to stop laughing, "we were walking, and we went under some trees, and" Kayla laughed even harder now, "I felt a snag, but I thought that was the liquor, and so I kept walking," Kayla paused trying to regain her composure. "I started feeling a little cool air begin to hit my head. And all the sudden, Mr. Football's friend turned around to say something to us, and he just burst out laughing, which of course caused my home girl to look, and she let out a slight scream!" Kayla could hardly finish the story she was laughing so hard. "Friends, why had I walked out of my wig, and it was dangling from a branch a few feet back!" Kayla screamed with laughter.

By now Soul, Mrs. Alice, Maria and Janice were all laughing hysterically, and rolling on the floor with laughter, as the bell rang indicating that lunch was over, and students begin to trill into the room wondering what was so funny that their teachers could not stop laughing.

Chapter 12

"**I**'m not going," Soul said for what had to be the twenty-fifth time that night.

Simone rolled her eyes and continued scrolling on her phone. "Soul, quit with the dramatic bullshit.

"Seriously Simone, I don't have anything to wear."

"Trick, I don't care if you have to go on this date butt booty ass naked, you are going on this date," Simone said stressing the word *are*. "You came into this world naked, no need to change now!"

"Forget you Simone," Soul laughed, throwing a shirt in Simone's direction.

"Besides," she continued, "you said you don't even like Anthony, so why are you stressing over what to wear!"

"Matters all that," Soul walked into her closet to once again look through her wardrobe, "I represent whenever I go out."

"I guess it has nothing to do with the fact that you are going with a long, tall fine drink of water like Anthony!"

"Please! You haven't even met him! Well technically you have, but you know what I mean."

"Whatever! I was tipsy at the club, but I do have a slight recollection of his fineness. Besides, the way you described the brother, he just *sounds* like he looks good.

"He is fine," Soul admitted, "and arrogant, let's not forget that part."

"Now that wasn't as hard as you thought huh. I hope Anthony gives you some tonight, because it would do you some good to remove the stick from up your butt and replace it with some di"

"Simone! Ugh! Ain't nobody putting nothing in my butt!"

"Not even if it gives you a nut," Simone giggled at her lame attempt to rhyme. "I mean seriously when was the last time you had a good shot of Dr. D? And I'm not talking about Danny with his lying ass."

"It hasn't been that long," Soul peeked her head from out of the closet. Well, ok it's been a minute. But not like Sahara Desert dry, but yeah dry."

"Looks like someone is looking to get their thirst quenched! Heyyy!" Simone sang, throwing one leg up, and dancing in a gyrating circle.

"I can't stand you! Girl, I already told you Anthony is not my type. I'm only going out with him, so Granny and Sister Jenkins can get off my back."

"And Anthony can lay you down on it," Simone teased as she did an old school version of MC Hammer's typewriter across the room.

"Look here old broke down version of Oaktown 357. Sit your crazy butt down somewhere or come and help me find something to wear."

"Alright," Simone said flopping down on the bed, "but you know I'm right."

"Whatever, besides you know I love me some thug love, and Anthony definitely doesn't strike me as the thug type." Soul shouted from the closet.

"Well, I wouldn't be so quick to judge Anthony, because some brothers know how to carry themselves appropriately in all situations, but there is one thing I can't argue with you about."

"What's that?" Soul asked coming out the closet, with several outfits in her hand.

"Ain't nothing like some thug love!" Simone said giving Soul a high five. "Yes Lawd! Baby, a thug can rock your body all night long."

"Hard as hell by day and eat the best coochie by night!"

"Facts! A thug don't bar none. They lick it all. Toes. Fingers"

"Bootyholes"

"Bootyholes! That's just nasty!" Simone pretended to throw up with a look of disgust on her face.

"Simone, you are telling me you never let anybody eat the groceries?"

Nope, aint' no grocery shopping over here," Simone said shaking her head with the same look of disgust on her face from earlier.

Yeah, well, don't knock it until you've tried it. If I ever find a businessman, that has some thug in him, I'll marry him on the spot. You know the kind I'm talking about, the kind of brotha where if the lights are about to get cut off, he's not gonna wait for me to do something, he'll find his own way to hustle up on the light money. I don't care if it means going to cut other people's lawn after he gets off his nine to five."

"Okay! And if you find a thug like that, make sure he has a brother for me. Cause all the thugs I find, I have to pick them up because they don't have a car."

"Hold on Simone, you ain't said nothing! What about the kind of thug that you have to wait until around 1 or 1:30 in the morning to pick them up because they have to wait for their parole officer to call to make sure they are in the house, before they sneak out!"

"Hmmmm! It doesn't make no damn sense that those are the ones that put it down in the bedroom the best." Simone added. "I'm a tell you somebody else that put it down. Those broke ass thugs that always want to borrow money. You know the type. The one that always want to borrow fifteen dollars for a dime bag and a beer."

"What! But you know to qualify as a true thug, he must have at least three tattoos, one of which must be a RIP for one of his homies, and he has to have at least two gold teeth."

"And don't forget," Simone added, "when you ask him his occupation, he is either a rapper, who is in the studio and about to drop his album; or he is a semi- pro football player."

"Boy, it ain't nothing like a what"

"Thug!" they both laughed in unison.

***

"Girl, you look good if I do say so myself," Simone eyed Soul with a look of approval. "That outfit says jazzy, yet sophisticated. You sure you aren't trying to impress Anthony?"

Soul looked in the mirror. She did look good. Finally settling on a tan dress that hugged her curves in all the right places, and stopped mid-thigh paired with an earth tone multi print duster and nude heels. The blonde wavy bob she was currently sporting brought the entire outfit together and seemed to set off her gold accessories and golden skin.

"Well, you know I have to represent," Soul said putting her necessities into a small tan clutch bag. "And what are your plans for tonight, cutie pie?"

"Well, as you can see, I'm wearing an elegant evening gown," Simone said waving her hand across her faded-out jean shorts and a 'Kiss a Nurse' T-shirt. "So, darling, I have an exclusive date with Rhahab, the 7-eleven clerk, being that I am down to my last black and mild," she said in a mock English accent.

"You, my friend, are crazy," Soul laughed. "What time is it?"

"6:58, what time is Anthony supposed to be here?"

"He said he would be here around 7:00, but pretty boy is probably"

"Right on time," Simone smirked as the doorbell began to ring. "Score one for Anthony," Simone skipped down the stairs to get the door.

Soul took another quick look in the mirror; then proceeded down the stairs to where Simone was already opening the door for Anthony.

At the sight of Anthony, Soul felt those same butterflies she fought so hard to ignore the other day in the restaurant. Damn, this man was absolutely breath taking, even if Soul would never admit it to him. Anthony was looking good in dark jeans, a cream sweater with a dress shirt underneath, and brown polo boots. Different from the dress looks Soul had saw him in prior but definitely no less sexy. The sweater hugged his chest so perfect she could count the ripples in his well-defined chest.

"Anthony," Soul said coming down the stairs. "It's good to see you again."

"No, the pleasure is all mine. You look fabulous," Anthony licked his lips as his sexy bedroom eyes swept over Soul before he grabbed her hand and pulled her into him, giving her a light kiss on the cheek.

Soul savored the smell of his cologne as Anthony's soft lips brushed against her cheek. Checking herself, Soul quickly reminded herself that she was only going on the date to please her grandmother.

"Uh um," Simone cleared her throat "Do y'all need a room?"

"Simone!"

"What! I mean you sniffing him. He licking his lips like he LL Cool A," Simone said giggling at her own joke, "I'm just saying. Maybe ya'll should skip the date part and go right to the mate part," Simone pumped her body.

"Oh God! Simone, stop it! Anthony I'm sorry."

"Why! I find her quite delightful, and her advice is worth listening to," Anthony winked at Simone and once again licked his lips as he glanced in Soul's direction.

"Anthony, this is my cousin Simone. Otherwise known as doesn't know when to stop talking."

"Hello Simone, it's nice to meet you," Anthony said, kissing her hand.

"It's so good to meet a man with manners."

"Thank you, but I felt obligated to kiss your hand."

"Why," Soul asked hoping he wouldn't bring up the club incident, especially since she had failed to tell Simone about his stupid comments. For some reason, she didn't want Simone to think bad about him.

"Well, her shirt says kiss a nurse, and I'm assuming she's a nurse."

"Yep, I'm a nurse. I save lives every day."

"Is that right. Well thank you for your service. It's good to see a sista doing her thing," Anthony remarked.

Soul almost believed he was genuine in his compliment. "Yeah, she's not half as ghetto as she looks," Soul smirked in Anthony's direction.

"Okay," Simone said drawing the 'kay' out, and giving Soul a strange look. "You kids have a good time, and Anthony it was very nice to finally meet you, especially since you are all that Soul has talked about for the past week," Simone gave Soul a sly grin. "I hope to see you soon. Soul, call me later," Simone said as she began to walk to her car.

"Oh, I will definitely call you later," Soul rolled her eyes at her cousin before she and Anthony stepped out of the door so Soul could lock up.

"So, you've been talking about me?"

"Whatever, you just better be glad that I never told Simone about your little club comment, because if I had, she probably wouldn't have cared about your polite manners or your little flirting kiss since you might have been next on her Taebo ass-kicking list!

"My, my, my, you have got to get that jealousy in check. You have my full attention all night long. And no one, not even Taebo himself could take my attention from you tonight the way you look in that dress." Anthony said biting his lips and staring Soul up and down before taking her elbow and steering her towards his truck.

Chapter 13

“You know,” Anthony said as he opened the door to his SUV for Soul, “I never did apologize for my stupid comments, so if you’ll let me start over, I truly do need to apologize. What I said that night was stupid of me. I really don’t even know what made me say those things. I was pissed off about something that happened earlier that day, and believe it or not, before our grandparents even decided to do their little hook-up thing, I’d thought about you several times, wishing I had gotten your number so that I could call you and apologize. What a way to impress a beautiful woman! So, I would love it if we could start over,” Anthony said flashing a dazzling smile.

Soul found herself once again memorized by Anthony’s smile and although she had vowed to stay mad at him, if she was honest with herself, she just wanted to relax and enjoy a night on the town. She studied his face hoping she could find something that would help her remain committed to being the bitch she had planned to be for their date, but the only thing she found was a look of someone who seemed truly apologetic. It was possible that Soul was wrong about Anthony. Lord only knows there were plenty of times Soul said things aloud before thinking them completely through in her head.

“Soul,” Anthony spoke interrupting her thoughts, “so, do you accept my apology? Oh yeah, before you answer that,” he said reaching into his back pocket and pulling out his wallet, “here is that ten for your drink. A wise man told me never to ask to buy a lady a drink, then piss her off, and make her pay for her own,” Anthony said smiling and biting his lips in that sexy way that he had a habit of doing Soul was discovering.

“In that case,” Soul laughed, relaxing a bit, “apology accepted, and Anthony, just so you know, I plan on keeping these ten dollars! We’ll just call it an investment in our date.”

“Well, in that case, Anthony said reaching back in his wallet, “here’s another twenty!”

“You’re crazy! We might make it through the night after all.”

"Shall we?" Anthony said taking her hand to help her into the truck.

***

True Visions was one the hottest spots in Dallas. A few nights a week, the club hosted a "for the culture" night with jazz, neo soul, open mic, and some of the best food in town. Unlike some of the clubs other nights when the hip hop crowd came to jam to Megan Thee Stallion and UGK, tonight the crowd was an older, after work crowd mixed with a little cultural eclectic ness.

"Have you ever been here before?" Anthony asked leading her to a table up front.

"Actually, I've been here a few times with Danielle and Simone, and I have a couple of friends that perform here."

"I've only been once or twice, but I didn't have the pleasure of seeing you here," Anthony whispered in her ear sending chills through Soul as he pulled out her chair.

"Maybe you weren't meant to see me. I mean look at how our last club meeting went," Soul jokingly jabbed at Anthony.

"Hello," the waitress said interrupting, "how are you guys doing tonight? Will you be eating from the buffet, or would you like to have something from the menu?"

"Whatever is fine with the lady is fine with me."

"If it's cool with you, I think I would prefer to just order from the menu. Can we start with the famous platter as an appetizer, then as my main course, can I have the smothered chicken with garlic mashed potatoes and a Caesar salad and a glass of Sangria. Soul said not bothering to take the menu the waitress had laid on the table.

"Ok, I like a woman that takes charge."

"Hey never put the ball in my court if you don't want me to bounce it. Besides, I order that every time I come in if that makes you feel any better."

"Sir, would you like to actually look at the menu, or do you know what you want as well," the waitress said with a smile.

"Uh, the lady seems to be on to something, so could you bring me the same thing she's having, except I'll have a class of crown and coke"

"Sure, I'll get those appetizers and drinks out to you as quick as I can. Is there anything else you guys need at this time?"

"No that seems to be it for now. Soul?

"Nope, that's it."

"So, Soul, how has your beautiful grandmother been? She's quite a character!"

"You don't have to tell me. Remember I have known her my entire life. She's definitely a character. She and my grandfather are completely opposites. It's amazing their marriage has lasted so long."

"What do you mean?"

Well, my grandmother is really outgoing, she loves to be in the center of everything and is always in everybody's business. My grandfather, on the other hand, is quiet, wise, and stays out of trouble. He's still working at the age of 72, and we don't think he will ever retire. They have 8 children, 3 of which have passed."

"Did your grandparents raise you?"

"Nah, my mama raised me, but being a single parent, my grandparents played a huge role in me and my upbringing, especially since my mom worked a lot.

"Well, if your mom is half as entertaining as your grandmother. I can't wait to meet her. Does she go to Saint Luke?

"She passed away a few years ago," Soul said feeling that old familiar pain in her heart.

"I'm sorry," Anthony said reaching over to take her hand.

"That's okay. You didn't know." Soul wanted to change the subject before she became depressed, which happened a lot whenever she thought of her mother's death.

"How many siblings do you have?" Anthony asked sensing she needed to change the topic.

"I'm an only child. And you? Tell me about yourself?"

"Do you want the short or long version?"

"Here you guys go," the waitress said sitting their drinks and a large platter of steaming hot wings, fried pickles, and mozzarella sticks on the table."

Anthony and Soul both looked at the food, "Short!" they laughed simultaneously.

"Okay, my parents were born here in Dallas, but moved when I was three to Charlotte, North Carolina. My mom worked at the city library most of her life and my dad was an electrical engineer before retiring a few years ago. When I graduated from high school, I moved to Atlanta, where I attended Morehouse, and I graduated with a master's degree in business and finance. After graduation I moved back home where I worked for five years as a buyer for a large corporation, until I decided to return to the Dallas area to pursue a career in the real estate business. I've been in real estate for four years. About two years ago, my parents moved back to the Dallas area to take care of my grandmother, my mom's mom, not that she needs taking care of as you have probably noticed, but I think my mom was a little homesick, and I am sure she missed her baby. Now you have the short version, so let's eat!" Anthony said digging into the wings.

"Remind me to get the long version later, Soul laughed as she grabbed a wing and dipped it into ranch dressing."

Anthony and Soul ate the rest of the food in silence only stopping when the waitress placed their entrees on the table, which they promptly dug into as well."

***

"I am officially stuffed," Soul said sliding her chair back. "If I eat another bite, I think I will burst."

"You did put away some food."

"Hey, you didn't just pick over yours. I can almost see my reflection in that plate as good as you cleaned it," Soul teased.

"Well at least I don't have food all over my face," Anthony laughed reaching over and wiping some sauce off her cheek.

The touch of Anthony's hand once again sent electric chills through Soul's body. She had never imagined that a man's hands could be so soft. Soul couldn't help but wonder if his lips were as soft as his hands.

"Soul," Anthony interrupted breaking her train of thoughts.

"Huh," Damn Soul hoped he didn't catch her starring at his lips. Noting the smile forming in the corners of his mouth, she figured she had once again been busted. She was going to have to watch herself around him. He seemed to catch her slipping on several occasions.

"I asked you did you want anything for dessert or a refill on your drink?"

"Oh no, I definitely can't do dessert, but I would definitely like another glass of wine."

"Cool," Anthony said flagging down their waitress, and giving her their drink orders.

"Soul I must say that I have truly enjoyed this evening with you so far. You have been great company."

"Thanks, you haven't been half as bad as I thought you would be," Soul admitted smiling at Anthony. "You picked a great place to come. I can't wait to they start open mic."

"Looks like your wait is over," Anthony remarked gesturing to the MC who had walked over to the mic on stage.

"Hey! How is everybody feeling tonight?" the short bald man asked the crowd. If you're living and here tonight, you can at least say you're blessed! So let me try that again. How is everybody feeling tonight?"

"Blessed," the crowd including Soul and Anthony shouted towards the MC. "That's what I'm talking about! Hey, we want to thank you guys for spending your night with us here at True Visions. You know what time it is. Tonight, we've got some new musical talent, and of course our jazz band is always in the house but first we're going to start with one of my favorite segments. Coming to stage we've got a special guest. She's an old favorite, and many of you know her because you've supported her by buying her first poetry book, and she is about to release her second poetry book. Please give it up for J. Monique Gambles."

"Hey that's my girl. We used to work together, and we took some college classes together."

"Really! She has some talent! I've heard her read some of her stuff the last time I was here."

The lights dimmed on the stage as Soul's friend gave the MC a hug and walked over to the mic.

"Hey! What's up people? It is good to be back home among my peoples. You guys know True Visions is my home away from home, and I just want to thank you guys for all the love and support you gave me with my first book.

I'm excited to share something from my new book. I'm a little nervous since this is my first time sharing them publicly, and as Erykah Badu would say 'keep in mind that I'm an artist and I'm sensitive about my shit! Nah seriously," J smiled as the crowd laughed, "I hope you like it and I'm willing to bet that many of you in here can relate to this struggle that I am about to talk to you about, and if you can't, maybe you need to reevaluate your life. This poem is called *Lover's Quarrel (Fighting with GOD)*"

"I know ya right!" Someone shouted from the back.

"Thank you brother. This one is going to be for you."

Love so sweet, like golden paved streets

Through rain, snow or sleet we often meet.

An invocation, exaltation, my tribulation, &contemplation

Your love unconditional, awesome, merciful, and filled with dedication.

O' but I, torn & scorned, ignored the horn

As I listened to the beat, which ultimately became my defeat.

My actions became my words, and I got what I deserved
Confused & ambivalent, I did not the will of my Master but another I served.
Adamant and block headed I ignored my path
Until you stopped me & rocked me with your wrath.
Then I realize my wrong and the pain that I caused
As you wiped away my tears and reminded me, I'm still yours.
My path for you has now truly begun
We are no longer quarrelsome but are one.

"Thank you again for inviting me into your minds," J remarked before making her way off the stage.

"Dang, your girl sure has some skills."

"Most definitely! Hey, hold on, she's coming this way. Gambles! Over here! What's up girl?" Soul asked hugging her long-time friend.

"What's up Soul, you trying to sneak up on a sista? Oh hey," she remarked noticing Anthony.

"Nice to meet you. I'm Anthony." Anthony said, standing up to shake her hand. "I really enjoyed your poetry tonight. I must say I've heard you read before, but I didn't know you had a poetry book out, I'm going to have to pick it up."

"Hey, handsome and smart! I like that. Soul, you did good girl!"

"Shut up ol' crazy girl."

"What? I know I didn't embarrass you," she teased. "Soul, when are you going to bless the stage?"

"One day."

"And you've been telling me that how long?"

"No seriously, I just need some motivation."

"Well, I'm sure this fine brother here will provide all the motivation you need."

"She doesn't need me for motivation. She could just look at herself in the mirror, that would be enough motivation for me."

"Okay, I feel you brother," J Monique said as she dapped up Anthony.

"Ms. Gambles, would you like to join us?" Anthony asked

"Nah, I'm cool, but thanks for the invite. And call me J. I've got my people waiting for me," she said pointing to the back of the dark room. "But it was nice to meet you. If Soul's no fool, I'll be seeing you around!" she winked before walking off. "Call me girl!" she shouted over her shoulder.

"She seems cool!" Anthony remarked.

"Cool and crazy!" Soul laughed.

"So," Anthony began in a playful tone, "are you a fool?"

"The jury's still out on that one!"

Anthony and Soul listened to two more poets and a singer, who might one day give Anthony Hamilton a run for his money, before the jazz band took the stage. After their second set, they decided to call it a night. As they left the club a light drizzle had begun to fall. Anthony ran to get the truck while Soul waited at the door. Tonight, really had been cool, Soul thought as she watched Anthony jog to the truck. It had been a while since she had been on a date as nice as tonight had been, and Anthony had proved to be great company and Soul really enjoyed being around him.

Anthony pulled his SUV to the front of the club where Soul stood waiting. He jumped and walked over to Soul taking her hand, "Hey beautiful, you ready to call it a night?" he asked helping her into the SUV.

"Sure."

"Did you have a good time tonight?"

"Believe it or not, I really did," Soul said smiling down at Anthony. "And I guess I owe you an apology as well, for blowing things out of proportion, and being such a bitch last Sunday."

"Shh!" he said placing his hand on her arm. "Today we start fresh, okay?"

"Okay," she whispered before Anthony closed the door.

Anthony jumped in the truck and sped off.

"Do you mind a little music?"

"I'm a music head, so I never mind a little music."

"Is that right?"

"Yes, music is my soul medicine. I love all genres and fair warning I do consider myself something of a music connoisseur, so if you put on some trash, I will let you have it!"

"Ok music connoisseur what you know about this?"

Bilal's smooth voice quickly filled the truck as he sang sexily about his Soul Sista. Anthony sang the lyrics of the song sliding his hand over to hold Soul's hand interlocking his fingers with hers, as the rain now fell steadily on the windows. Soul leaned back into the seat and closed her eyes. Hand holding. Anthony was an old school guy, but Soul liked that. This truly had been a nice night.

***

She must have drifted off into a light sleep, because the next thing Soul knew Anthony pulled to a stop in front of her apartment.

"Wake up sleepy head," he said as he lightly stroked her face with the back of his hand. "You're home."

"I'm sorry, I guess those glasses of wine relaxed me more than I realized. I didn't mean to fall asleep on you," Soul said noticing the rain had stopped.

"No problem. Let me get you into bed. I mean let me get you in your house." Anthony smiled sexily before sauntering out of the truck to open her door.

"Look Bitch! Don't you even try it," Soul whispered looking down at her vagina feeling the heat growing between her legs.

Anthony and Soul held hands and walked slowly to her front door. "So, Soul," Anthony said stopping as Soul opened her front door, "now that we've fulfilled our promises to our grandmothers, can we go out again but this time as a promise to each other," he said facing Soul.

"You know what Anthony, I'd really like that. Why don't you call me when you have some free time."

"So, I'll call you tomorrow," he said with a short laugh.

"You are too much! You have a good night," Soul said before reaching up to give Anthony what was supposed to be a light kiss on the lips, but once their lips touched Soul knew this kiss was going to be anything but light as Anthony slipped his tongue inside her mouth and pulled her closer in his embrace. Just as Soul felt herself melting into Anthony's touch, he pulled away.

Looking at her with a smile in his eyes, Anthony gave Soul a kiss on the forehead, "I'll call you in the morning. Go in. I need to hear you lock the door."

"Huh?" Soul could still feel Anthony's lips on hers.

"I need to be sure you are safely in the house ma'am."

"Oh ok. Well, I guess this is good night." Soul walked into her apartment. "Close the door Soul," Anthony said smiling. "Good night Ms. Soul, sleep well."

"You too Anthony," Soul said before closing the door. Soul locked the door knowing tonight she would have to find the satisfaction Anthony had awakened from her nightside friend she kept in the top drawer.

Chapter 14

S oul leaned against the door and sighed. Kicking off her heels, she tossed her clutch bag onto the sofa and began stripping her clothes off. Not a minute after she had finished undressing, her phone started ringing.

"Who in the hell is calling me at this hour?" Soul wondered walking over to dig her phone out of the purse.

Looking at the caller ID on the screen, Soul shook her head. Simone. "What nosy!"

"Soul, good, you made it in from your date." Simone spoke into the phone.

"Simone what the hell are you doing up at 1:00 in the morning," Soul asked glancing at the clock above the fireplace. "You are one nosy little heifer; you couldn't wait til' tomorrow morning to see how my date was?" Soul joked as she sat on the ottoman.

"Girl, I wish that was all, and I'm assuming your date must have gone well by the tone in your voice. I can't wait to hear about it, but right now I need your help."

"What's the matter girl," Soul stopped as she noticed the slur in Simone's voice. "Are you drunk?"

"Yep," Simone slurred, "but that's the least of it, Danielle is tore up from the floor up, and we all know she can't drink. She found out Jackson is cheating, and he's over some hoe's and I came over to calm her ass down, and now we both fucked up. Now I know, you and I both know, Jackson is a Biatchhh, but Danielle is our girl," Simone said as she slurred Danielle's name.

"Damnit Simone, I literally just walked in the house and undressed, and I have had a few glasses of wine myself."

A few glasses of wine ain't nothing to a slush like you. Is you drunk or are you tipsy." Simone burped into the phone.

"I'm relaxed, but I'm assuming that's over. Give me a second to put on some clothes, and I'll be over there as soon as I can. Your place or Dani's?"

"We're over Dani's," Simone slurred, "and Soul,"

"Yeah Simone," Soul said as she started to walk upstairs to throw on something comfortable. "I love you bitch."

"Bye Simone!" Soul laughed before ending the call. Soul could never understand why every time a person got drunk, they want to tell you how much they love you or start telling truths that they only have the courage or foolishness to tell you when they are drunk. Soul giggled recalling one time in particular when she and Simone were at her place playing dominoes with their then current boyfriends and drinking Tequila shots. Simone and her boyfriend were constantly on and off in their bipolar relationship. During the middle of the domino game, Simone's in her drunken glory decided to blurt out, "OK Bobby, I'm fucking somebody else!" Bobby could hold his liquor better than Simone, and he reminded her of her outburst once she sobered up! Needless to say, the on and off of their relationship moved completely to off after that night.

Soul's phone had dinged the entire time she and Anthony were on their date, but a quick glance at her phone let her know it was Simone, Danielle and her grandmother, all of which Soul assumed were simply being nosy so she didn't bother answering or texting them back at the time. Changing into a pair of black leggings and an old black Mary J *Share my World Tour* concert t-shirt, Soul checked her messages. There were nine messages, three from Danielle talking about the Jackson situation, four from Simone regarding the Jackson/Danielle situation, and two from her grandmother wanting to know how her date went. Soul shook her head as she threw on some old black Nikes, and walked downstairs, grabbing her keys from the rack near the door. Walking out the door, Soul's phone beeped indicated a new text message.

Hey beautiful, I hope I didn't wake you, but I wanted to let you know I had a really good time I tonight, and I'm looking forward to seeing you soon. Sleep tight sweet lady.

Hey! I had a really good time tonight too. Can't wait to talk to you again too. Sweet dreams Anthony.

Soul smiled and pressed send.

Oh, they will definitely be sweet, I'll be thinking of this sexy lady I know and planning my next date with her.

Soul smiled before setting the alarm to go put out whatever fire Danielle and Simone had surely planned to set.

Chapter 15

By the time Soul arrived at Danielle's, it had started to rain again. She jumped out of her truck, hit the alarm, and jogged to Danielle's front door. The sounds of Bettye Wright's "No Pain, No Gain," flowed from inside. She knocked on the door for at least ten minutes before Simone snatched open the door.

"Welcome to our pity party," she slurred. "Come on in."

"Where's Dani, Oh Great Drunk One?"

"She's in the enter, the enter," Simone paused thinking.

"The entertainment room fool!" Soul said laughing. She took her shoes off and left them by the door before following Simone.

Danielle had recently purchased a modern four-bedroom brick home in a suburb that sat on the outskirts of Dallas, when her daycare reached its peak attendance. Her home reflected her personality, colorful and cheerful, and the entertainment room was no exception. There was a tan leather sectional sofa placed in the center of the room with a colorful array of beanbags placed strategically around the room. An oak wall unit took up most of the space as it held a 65-inch TV with surround sound Bluetooth speakers giving the room an extra theatre effect. Framed 17x21 pictures of Tupac, Michael Jordan, Venus and Serena Williams, Counte' Baisse, and Simone Biles hung around the room, and sprawled out in the middle of the floor with a damn near empty bottle of vodka was Danielle.

"Hey Sugar," Soul said flopping on a beanbag near Danielle. "What has the great Jackson been up to now?"

"Soul?" Danielle said squinting her eyes and trying to focus.

"Yes."

"I hate men," she slurred as she attempted to get up.

Danielle looked a complete mess. Her locks were wildly strewn around her head. Eyeliner ran down her face, and by the look of her eyes, she had been crying all day.

Danielle again attempted to get up, but the effort was too great as she eventually gave up and plopped her face back into the expensive hand-woven oriental style rug.

"What happened Dani?" Soul asked kneeling down beside her to help her sit up.

"Jackson needs me to whoop his ass again," Simone announced as she walked back into the room sucking on a chicken bone.

"Simone, shut up and how are you supposed to be over here helping, and you done got drunk ya' damn self?" Soul asked.

Simone stood up from the couch, "My name is Simone and I'm an alcoholic," she slurred placing the chicken bone across her heart.

"Simone, if you don't sit your old greasy lips down somewhere," Soul laughed. "Go on baby," Soul said turning back to Danielle.

"Well, things were good about the first two weeks after I got out of the hospital, then Jackson started tripping, coming home late or not at all. He stopped wanting sex, and I know Jackson likes sex too much to just stop cold turkey. Then whenever I would walk into the room, if he was on the phone, he would get off, and," she added raising her voice, "he would always turn his phone off whenever we were together, or if he did answer he would go into another room to talk. Now I know Jackson has cheated on me a few times, but he promised he would never do it again."

Simone and Soul gave each other knowing looks, but didn't say anything.

Danielle continued, "So tonight he said he was going to spend the night over his uncles', and that was the last straw. What grown man do you know has a slumber party over his uncle's house. So, I followed him over to some apartments off Jonesburg, and I watched him go into an apartment, and I didn't know what to do. I must have sat in my car crying for about two hours, and the more I cried, the madder I got. I thought about everything I had done for Jackson. All those designer suits and clothes that I bought, that nice ass Cadillac Escalade that I put in my name, sitting on rims that I bought, and I couldn't take it anymore."

"Well, I told you that no matter what kind of clothes you put a dog in, his bark will still sound the same," Simone interrupted.

Soul shot her a piercing look across the room, "Go ahead Dani."

"Anyway, I jumped out of my car and walked up to the apartment that I saw Jackson enter and knocked on the door. I could hear laughing and music in the background.

Then I heard a voice ask who it was. I screamed Jackson's girlfriend. Well, the laughing stopped then. Child you will never guess who opened that door. The nurse from the hospital. I could have slapped the taste out of her mouth. As soon as the door opened, I pushed my way inside her apartment and Jackson comes running to the door with his boxers on talking about 'what the fuck are you doing here?' Can you believe that shit? And the trick is in the background screaming how she thought I was Jackson's sister. Do you know Jackson had the nerve to say and I quote, 'Baby, she ain't shit, you, my girl. She just some crazy hoe who won't leave me alone."

"No the hell he didn't!" Soul shouted angrily.

Danielle began to cry again. Despite their cynical remarks to one another, and their fights, Soul, Simone, nor Danielle could stand to see the other hurting, and Danielle was really hurting. If there were ever a group of friends who loved each other, it was them. They had been through it all, boyfriends, deaths, fights; it didn't matter. Even when they disagreed, they still had each other's back.

"How could I let this happen?" Danielle sobbed.

"Danielle, listen to me," Soul said grabbing Danielle's face in her hands, "Jackson is a fool, he does not deserve you. You are a successful and gorgeous woman, and if Jackson can't treat you like the queen you are, fuck him. His loss. And if I catch that nigga on the street, I'ma' kick his ass!" she said meaning every word of it.

"Danielle," Simone said calmly sipping yet another drink of something or other. "Soul is right. It's not your fault that you can't predict doom and gloom. Hell, I wish I could, and then maybe we would all be happily married. Now I know you don't want to hear it, but you have to face up to your fuck ups as well. You took on all the roles and responsibilities of girlfriend duty, but you never required Jackson to step up to the plate. You became ok with comfortable toxicity. See you had Jackson on a leash, but when he would stray too far instead of snatching his ass back with enough force to snap his damn neck, you simply went out and added another leash to the one you already had, which only made a longer leash," Simone said as she swallowed the last of her drink.

"Simone," Soul warned as Danielle began to cry even harder.

"Don't Simone me. The truth hurts, but my point is it hurts us all. We have all, at some point, built our castles and dreams on quicksand and then later wondered why they sank. But in turn you to either build your castles somewhere else or cover that quicksand with cement to create some foundation. So, Danielle, wipe your tears, Soul get your keys, we are about to roll over to Jackson's and put some cement over his quicksand.

***

By the time they arrived at the Jonesburg apartments, it had stopped raining, Danielle had stopped crying, and Simone was lying across the backseat. As Soul pulled into the apartments, she noticed that sure enough, backed in like he lived there, was Jackson's maroon Cadillac Escalade, all shined up, rims glistening from the rain. She glanced at Danielle and Soul could see the steam shoot from her head. She turned the radio down and slowed to a crawl. They rode past Jackson's car two times before backing Soul's truck in several cars down from Jacksons'. Soul turned off the headlights and turned the ignition off.

"Okay ladies, what now?"

"What do you mean what now? What now is we go into that bitch's apartment and kick Jackson's ass!" Danielle screamed.

"Calm down boo," Simone said sitting up suddenly. "No need to take such drastic measures. Here," she said reaching into her coat and pulling out two bottles of fluorescent yellow spray paint.

"Simone where in the hell did you get those?" Soul asked.

"Just a little something I pulled out of my hat, or should I say my coat," Simone said reaching back into the bag. "Here," she said handing Danielle a black t-shirt and black baseball cap. "Put these on." Simone glanced at Soul. "Your clothes seem inconspicuous enough. Hand me that navy headscarf," she said pointing towards an old navy headscarf lying between the console of Soul's truck. "Danielle," Simone said sweetly, as she began to tie the scarf around her head, "you have to learn that with men like Jackson, they will hit you were it hurts, so when it comes to payback, you have to hit them where it hurts! Now I usually don't agree with women who mess with a brother's car, but Jackson is an extreme, yet special case," Simone said opening her door. "Let's go!"

Danielle, Simone and Soul all filed out of the truck and headed towards Jackson's Cadillac. They walked along the shadows of the apartment just in case someone drove by.

"What are we going to do?" Danielle asked.

"Well, you and I are going to write Jackson a little note," Simone said handing Danielle one of the cans of spray paint. "Soul here, is going to be the lookout."

"Dani, doesn't Jackson have an alarm," Soul interjected.

"Yeah, I have a set of keys on my key chain, so all I have to do is disarm the alarm before it gets too loud and starts to wake up the whole damn complex." Danielle jogged back to Soul's truck to get her keys while Simone and Soul waited in the shadows.

"Simone this is not a good idea. What if"

"What if you quit worrying so damn much?" Simone slurred.

"Let's go," Danielle said jogging back to where they waited.

"OK Bonnie and Clyde, I can't have a criminal record and still teach kids, not to mention these apartments are near the school."

"Soul you worry too much. Besides," Simone added, "you're just the watch out and if any thing goes down, you can say you weren't in on this." Simone stopped just short of Jackson's SUV and started to shake the can of spray paint. "Let's see Dani, what do you think we should write?"

"I don't know what you're going to write," Danielle said as she began to walk to the driver's side of Jackson's SUV, "but I know exactly what I need to say." Danielle shook her can up furiously, and began to spray paint something that Soul couldn't see from where she stood. Her hands moved in very large circles as she sprayed so fast Soul thought her arm was going to fall off. Now Simone, on the other hand, was standing like her name was Simone-angelo, as she struck an artistic pose with one hand on her hip, and her chin rested on the top of her spray paint can. She had this thoughtful look on her face like what she chose to write was going to be a million-dollar masterpiece.

"That's it," she said, snapping her fingers. Simone began to spray paint the passenger side of Jackson's SUV stopping every so often to think about what she was writing.

"Dang, would you guys hurry up!" Soul whispered loudly.

"Calm down girly. Payback takes time. You just do your job and watch," Simone said.

"Oh shit! Oh shit!" Soul whispered pointing in the direction of a pair of oncoming headlights. "Let's go, she said as she turned towards her truck.

"Shit, here comes a car that way too," Simone said pointing towards headlights that were approaching the direction of Soul's truck.

"What do we do?" Danielle screamed, running to the front of Jackson's truck where Soul stood.

"Shut up and quit screaming!" Simone said coming around to the front and pulling Danielle and Soul to the passenger side. "Get down!"

"I told ya'll this was a stupid idea." Soul whispered.

"Shut up Soul." Both cars were now approaching each corner.

"What are we going to do?" Danielle whispered in an urgent tone.

"Come on!" Simone said getting on the ground.

"Simone, what are you doing?" Soul asked.

"This!" Simone said getting on the ground and rolling underneath Jackson's SUV. "Come on! Hurry the hell up!"

Danielle and Soul looked at one another, then quickly dropped to the ground and rolled underneath Jackson's Escalade as well.

"Ow!" Simone yelped.

"Sorry, I was rolling too quick." Danielle apologized.

"Scoot over Simone!" Soul whispered fiercely. "Half of my body is still sticking out!"

"Damn! You made me roll in a big puddle of oil." Simone said.

"Shh you two!" Danielle pleaded.

By now both cars were near Jackson's Escalade. One car kept rolling but it seemed like one car had slowed down. They could hear the voices of teenagers talking loudly.

The car came to a stop near Jackson's truck. The teenagers were laughing loudly.

"Damn dog, that's fucked up!" They heard a loud male voice say.

"Yeah," a female agreed. "I guess some nigga got caught slipping," she laughed.

"Hey, don't you get any ideas," the male voice said warning the girl.

"Hey, let me out so I can see what's on the other side, Alejandro," another male voice spoke up.

"Hell nah Shakeem. Somebody might come out here and think we did that shit and my parole officer said I couldn't get in no mo' trouble," the teenager girl said with attitude in her voice.

Soul's heart quickened. She thought the first male voice sounded familiar, but now she knew for sure. If two of her students, especially Alejandro and Shakeem, both of whom she was forever preaching to about what is wrong and right, found her underneath a spray painted truck, she would never be able to live it down.

"Bitch!"

"Bitch! Who you calling a bitch? Take me the fuck home! Neither one of y'all getting no ass tonight," the teenage girl replied.

"See man," Alejandro said sounding frustrated.

Danielle, Simone and Soul all clutched each other tightly barely breathing.

"Damn dawg, you play too much," he continued. "Girl he was just playing," Alejandro said before the car began to slowly roll away.

Danielle, Simone and Soul didn't breathe until they were sure the car was completely gone. Simone began to laugh.

"Trick, I don't see a damn thing funny," Soul said.

Danielle began to laugh with Simone.

"Do you know those were some of my students?"

This only made Simone and Danielle laugh even harder.

"Damn alcoholics! That could have been the police," Soul said in an irritated tone.

Danielle and Simone were laughing so hard by now that Simone couldn't even roll from under Jackson's SUV.

"You two have issues. I am not going to take another chance like that. I'm going to go get my truck so we can get the hell out of here," Soul announced as she began to roll from under the truck.

Danielle and Simone were still clutching each other, laughing hysterically.

As she got up, Soul noticed that Simone had been writing selective verses from the Ten Commandments, 'Do unto others as you would have them to unto you, thou shalt not commit adultery, and honor thy husband and wife.'

Danielle, on the other hand, had chosen a more ghetto approach. She had started writing 'Here drives a punk ass, dog' and the beginnings of 'he likes it in the booty' but right now it just read 'he likes it in the boo.' As she started back to her truck, Soul could hear Danielle and Simone rolling from under Jackson's truck still laughing.

"Ouch!" Simone yelled. "I rolled into another car!" This only made Danielle laugh even harder.

"Don't make me laugh, I got to pee!" Soul heard Danielle say.

"Hey help me! My hair is stuck on a wire on this car's door!"

Soul ran back to help Simone who had somehow got her hair caught on a wire that was stuck to an old beat-up car parked right next to Jackson. When she got closer Soul began to laugh. Simone was attached to a short wire. Her face looked like she was one of Jerry's kids. She had apparently rolled over a candy wrapper that was now stuck to the side of her face, and her clothes were covered with oil stains.

"Danielle," Soul laughed holding her side, "come look at Simone!"

Danielle came around to the driver's side where Simone was struggling to free herself from the wire. The sight of Simone struggling so hard only made the situation even funnier. Danielle fell on the ground laughing.

"Oh please, I told ya'll not to make me laugh," she said holding herself. "Damn ya'll are going to make me pee on my, Oh shit!" Danielle laughed. A little wet circle began to form in Danielle's pants. "Oh! I can't make it stop," Danielle laughed as she tried unsuccessfully to stop herself from peeing.

By now even Soul couldn't control her laughter. Simone had somehow managed to untangle herself. She stood up and saw Danielle and began to laugh. By now all three of them were laughing so loud they should have woken up the entire complex.

"Hey quiet down, down there!" someone screamed from an apartment above as a light popped on in the window.

"Oh crap!" Soul said as they all began to take off running towards her truck in a breathless pant as she jumped in followed by Danielle and Simone.

"Let's go!" Simone shouted.

Soul turned on the ignition and began to drive off still laughing.

"Wait!" Danielle screamed as they neared Jackson's truck. She jumped out and ran and picked up one of the spray cans. She shook one of them and began to spray something else on Jackson's truck.

"What are you doing?" Soul yelled.

"Adding a 'dy' to this, so it says booty"

"Well, hurry up!"

Danielle finished her wording, and then ran to the other side to pick up the other can of spray paint. As she approached Soul's truck the apartment security car came around the far end of the complex.

"Let's go!" Danielle screamed opening the door of the truck. Soul punched on the gas so quick, Danielle had to dive into the truck to keep from getting left. They fishtailed it out of the apartment with Danielle holding on and the door hanging open.

Chapter 16

♥

The ringing phone jarred Soul out of the deep sleep dream she was having. Wondering who could be calling her so early in the morning, Soul opened one eye and fumbled with one hand in search of her cell phone. Damn, why couldn't she find the phone? Soul leaned a little further off her bed to reach for the phone on the nightstand. It was only until she felt herself falling out of her bed that she suddenly remembered she wasn't in her bed at all, but instead on Danielle's sofa. She tried to stop herself before she hit the floor, but it was too late.

"Ouch!" A screaming Simone yelped in pain as Soul landed on top of her. "Get the hell off of me!"

"Sorry!" Soul said rolling off Simone and continuing her search for the ringing cell phone.

"Could someone please turn the alarm off?" Danielle mumbled from the other end of the couch.

"That's not an alarm, that's my phone sweetie," Soul spotted her phone lying on top of her purse in a beanbag in the corner and made a mad dash for the phone before the ringing stopped.

"Hello."

"Hello beautiful," at the sound of Anthony's deep voice a smile immediately filled Soul's face.

"Good morning yourself," Soul shook her head at the empty liquor bottles around the room before flopping on one of the colorful beanbags.

"I wouldn't quite call it morning. It's almost 1:30 in the afternoon!"

"What! Dang! I can't believe we slept that long!"

"We?"

"Yeah, I had an emergency meeting of the minds. Relationship problems always call for a sista girl party you know, so I ended up staying over my girl's place rather than driving back across town.

"Oh well, I hope everything is cool."

"Oh yeah, nothing to worry about. So, what do I owe the pleasure of this call?"

"What! You consider this call to be a pleasure. Attention America, I'm wearing her down! I was hoping that you and I could get together later for a picnic. It's a nice day outside, but I guess you wouldn't know that yet," Anthony joked.

"I guess I wouldn't!" Soul laughed.

"So, what do you think? Are you up for it or have you filled your quota for spending time with me?"

"Believe it or not, I would love to join you for a picnic." Soul said smiling

"Cool. What time is good for you, sleepy head?"

"How about 3:00?"

"That's fine. I'll pick you up then. Should I pick you up at your place?"

"Oh yeah definitely, I'm actually on my way home in the next fifteen minutes."

"Okay, see you then," Anthony remarked before hanging up.

Soul ended her call and began putting on her tennis shoes and pullover. She gathered all her belongings before walking over to where Danielle had fallen back asleep on the sofa.

"Dani," Soul gently shook her sleeping friend.

"Huh"

"I'm getting ready to go. Come lock the door."

"Okay," Danielle said before turning over to go back to sleep.

"Dani!" Soul said shaking her a little harder.

"What! Damn, can I get some sleep?"

"Hey, I'm just trying to tell you I'm getting ready to leave, so you probably want to get up and lock the door. I mean I'm sure you don't want Jackson barging in here after last night."

At the mention of Jackson's name, Danielle immediately sat up, but the effects of the last night's alcohol caused her to lie right back down as she quickly fell back on the pillow.

"Damn! I'm never drinking again."

"Yeah, Yeah, Yeah, you and every other drunk."

"Whatever," Danielle said sitting up slower this time. "I've got to get up and get these locks and alarm code changed and pack all Jackson's shit before I go on my vacation."

"What vacation?"

"Last night as we were driving back, I decided it was time for a vacation and no time is better than the present," Danielle said standing up stretching.

"I guess you're right. You have any particular place in mind?" Soul asked as she attempted to pat Danielle's wild hair into some form of shape.

"Chicago, I think."

"Chicago. Like as in Devon Chicago?"

"As in Chicago Soul. Quit trying to read more into it."

Really, so you're telling me you would go all the way to Chicago and wouldn't reach out to Devon? Like not even a phone call? Or a hey stranger! I'm in your neck of the woods lets meet for lunch, or a come blow my back out for old time's sake dinner? Nothing?" Soul asked referring to Danielle's ex-boyfriend and one true love and soul mate in Soul's opinion.

"Maybe," Danielle said smiling.

"Good for you boo. You deserve"

"Both of ya'll deserve to shut the hell up while I'm trying to sleep," Simone shouted from where she lay on the floor.

"Whatever! Anyway Dani, when are you leaving?"

"If I get everything taken care of, I'm leaving today."

"Today!'

"Yep, no time like the present. Anyway, I'll call you later and let you know since you're on the way out."

Danielle and Soul walked to the front door. "Don't forget to call," Soul said reaching for the door.

"Wait!" Danielle grabbed the door, "Make sure Jackson is not outside."

"Man! Jackson might be a fool but he ain't stupid. He don't want me to open a can of whoop ass on him!"

"Yeah, you're probably right."

"Hell yeah, I'm right. Now you go take care of business boo," Soul said kissing Danielle on her forehead before walking out the door. As soon as the door shut behind her, Soul glanced up and down the street before running as fast as she could to her truck!

***

At exactly three, Anthony knocked on her door. Opening the door, Soul was struck again by the sheer fineness of this man. Anthony had dropped the business look sporting grey joggers, sleeveless t-shirt and baseball cap with his fraternity letters, and Nike kicks. In other words, the ultimate thirst trap, Soul licked her lips taking in the bulging muscles in his arms and the one in his pants.

"Hey beautiful, you look great as always," Anthony said bending down to give Soul a kiss on the cheek.

"Yeah, I figured since you said picnic, it would be cool to probably go for the casual and comfortable look." Soul had chosen a pair of shorts that barely covered her ass, a Kobe Bryant jersey and purple and gold Nikes. She had chosen to forgo the wig and instead donned her own hair in a ponytail for today's look with huge loop earrings. It was what Soul called her LL Cool J round the way girl look. Had Soul known Anthony was going to be on some thirst trap grey sweatpants ish, she would have put on her thirst trap attire as well, a sundress with no panties.

"Casual and comfortable huh? Yeah ok." Anthony stroked his beard looking Soul up and down.

"Why you say it like that? Yeah, ok?" Soul said locking the door behind her.

"Girl, you know what all that ass in them little bitty shorts was gone do to me."

"Boy shut up," Soul playfully tapped Anthony's arm.

"I'm just saying damn ma!" Anthony licked his lips. "Yeah, let's go get in this truck before I get myself in trouble."

"Ok smooth operator! Lead the way."

"I'll lead you wherever you want to go. Unless you want to lead me, by the hand, or by a leash" Anthony said barking like a dog causing Soul to laugh.

Anthony grabbed Soul's hand and headed towards his truck. He walked around to the passenger side to help Soul in before proceeding to the driver's side.

Starting the ignition, the smooth sound of Elhae filled the truck.

"So which park are we going to?

"Actually, it's just around the corner."

"McNeese Park?"

"Yeah, that's it."

"I go there all the time when I want to get away to meditate, write, or just clear my head. Sometimes I just go to feed the ducks or walk along the trail. I love the man-made waterfall, it's one of the most beautiful things I have ever seen."

"You must not have looked in the mirror this morning." Anthony said reaching over to take her hand, while expertly maneuvering the wheel of the truck with his other hand. Anthony glanced at her from the side and begin singing the lyrics of Elhae's Needs.

I just need somebody like me

As freaky as she can be

Take it all night long. "

Anthony sang along with the lyrics giving Soul a long sexy stare.

Soul wasn't sure if it was the base bumping through the speakers or her heart pounding from Anthony's stare that was causing her body to become hot, she thought as she reached down to ensure her air conditioning vent was set to open and not closed.

But not being one to back down, Soul matched Anthony's stare until a smile crept into the corner of his lips. Glancing at the defined bulge in Anthony's thirst trap sweats, Soul silently prayed "please Lord, don't let me end up doing some bald head hoe shit today."

"Here we go," Anthony said pulling into the park and interrupting Soul's much needed prayer. He opened the door and walked around to open Soul's door.

"Do you need my help?" Soul asked as he walked around to open her door.

"I think I have everything," Anthony said reaching into the back seat to retrieve an extremely large picnic basket and blanket, and a mini-Bluetooth speaker.

"Here, let me help you," Soul took the blanket and the speaker from Anthony. "Ready?"

"Yep!" Anthony hit the alarm before leading her to a secluded area near the waterfall. He sat the picnic basket on the ground before reaching for the blanket Soul held in her arms and spreading it on the ground. "I can't believe the park is so empty. It's really a nice day."

"Yeah, it is," Soul glanced around noticing the normally bustling park was pretty quiet. "So, what do we have," Soul peered at the basket taking a seat on the blanket.

"Let's see," Anthony said sitting down close to her. He dug into the basket and began to pull out an array of foods. Fried chicken, cold cuts, cheese cubes, crackers, potato salad, grapes, watermelon slices, macaroni, rolls, strawberries, two large canteens that held two different kinds of juice, and several bottles of water.

"Dang Anthony, how much food did you pack?"

"Do you think this is enough?"

Soul couldn't tell if he was serious or joking, "Don't worry I think we have enough to feed an army."

Anthony pulled two paper plates and plastic ware out of the basket. "Here dig in."

Soul began to pile her plate with food.

"I love a woman who has an appetite."

"Oh well, you'll love me for sure," Soul said biting into a piece of chicken.

"I agree, but it won't be because of food," Anthony said looking at her before digging into his own plate of food. Anthony couldn't figure out what it was about Soul, and he had never believed in love at first sight, but the woman sitting in front of him was causing him to think differently, and he knew it from the first time he saw her walk into the club that night. In fact, his boys had given him the blues earlier this morning when Anthony kept talking about last night's date.

"Did you hit it," his friend Jonathan, who was better known as Ajax, had asked.

"Nah dog, I told you. It's just something about her."

"You ain't hit it, and she cursed you out the first time you met her. Oh yeah there's definitely something about her, she another bitch."

"Shut the fuck up Ajax, I can't wait to you find a sister that handles your ass."

"The only place a woman can handle my ass without me putting her ass in check, is in the bedroom."

"Whatever dog, you just wait."

"I don't have to wait for the future, cause I know the now. Anyway, this bitch Soul must have a banging body."

"First, she ain't no bitch. Dog I told you that you won't ever find a real woman if you keep referring to them as bitches and hoes. Second, she is fine as hell. Her nickname had to be brick house when she was growing up," he said giving Ajax a pound. "But that ain't it. I can't really explain it."

"Whatever dog, don't call me talking about you and this chick are getting married or some shit like that. And just so you know, you owe me for blowing me and the game off to go on a picnic with some bit, I mean chick."

Yeah, it was something about Soul because it was out of Anthony's element to miss a game to take a woman out for a picnic.

"So, what would the lady like to hear?" Anthony said taking a bite of the food piled on his plate and breaking his own thoughts of the earlier conversation with his boy.

Whatever you play. All your selections have been good ones so far, don't mess up now."

Damn, it's like that? Ok. Bet. Anthony opened an app on his phone as it connected to the Bluetooth speaker and Kindred the Family Soul begin playing as Anthony and Soul continued to eat in a comfortable silence, like two old friends.

"I can't eat another bite," Soul announced flopping back onto the blanket, closing her eyes and sighing contently as only a full woman could. The mellow sounds of Kindred began to pull Soul into a light sleep as she wondered why black folks always ate and then went to sleep. Soul opened one eye to find Anthony starring at her. "What?"

"That's just like black people to eat and go to sleep!"

"I was just thinking the same thing," Soul replied laughing.

"And you were still about to go to sleep on me!"

"Hey, you can't blame a sista when you stuff me with so much good food."

"I guess your right," Anthony said lying beside her. "If you can't beat em'"

"Lay with em apparently."

Anthony and Soul lay in silence for several moments before Anthony began laughing.

"What's so funny?" Soul asked glancing sideways at Anthony.

"I was just thinking about the first time we met."

"Oh no!" Soul said joining in his laughter. "I thought you were one of the most arrogant, self-centered, self-righteous sons of a bitches I had ever met; and that's my nice tasteful description."

"I bet it is! And then when our grandparents tried to hook us up at church, I could feel the daggers you were shooting at me across the table at the restaurant!"

"Who would have thought we would end up like this, relaxing and laughing." Soul closed her eyes again enjoying the sunshine on her face.

After a long pause, Anthony added, "I did."

"Is that right?"

"Very much so, and my mama always told me the truth would set you free."

"What if we had never crossed paths again?" Soul asked opening one eye to look at Anthony only to find him sitting up starring at her again.

"I knew destiny would intercede on my behalf."

Soul propped herself on her elbows and looked at Anthony. "Destiny huh?"

"Destiny or our grandmothers, cause even destiny can't touch the intercessory prayer of a church grandmother."

Soul laughed, "Amen to that! Tell me some more about yourself.

"Well, I told you just about everything last night, but I did promise you the long version later huh? So, you must be ready for the long version?

"I'm ready for anything you're ready to give to me," Soul said sitting up. Anthony wasn't the only one with smooth lines.

"Well, since everything about me is long," Anthony paused, "I don't have a choice but to give it to you any other way."

Soul took a knife and began making a slicing gesture through the air.

"Woman what are you doing?"

"Trying to cut some of this sexual tension! Whew chile."

Anthony began laughing, "Come here," he said pulling her towards him.

Soul scooted in between his legs resting her back against his chiseled chest making sure she pressed her ass into his massive junk just to be sure it wasn't an allusion brought forth by the sweats. Much to her satisfaction, it wasn't.

Anthony told Soul about his days at college where he played basketball for two years before an injury to his hamstring put his promising career on the backburner. They talked about their pledging days and love for Greek life. Anthony told Soul about life as the only child and his love for real estate and she shared her love for kids. They talked about sports, religion, politics, music, relationships, and success. Anthony shared his dream of one day moving from the business with his frat, to one day opening his own mortgage company that would target low-income families and help put them in their own homes, while Soul shared her dreams of one day becoming a principal and writing her own book. Soul told Anthony about her college days and laughed at his college stories. Soul smiled to herself when she realized talking to Anthony was like a breath of fresh air after being in a smoke-filled building with no windows. There was never an awkward moment, and when there was silence, it just felt right. Soul guessed Anthony wasn't the only one who made a mistake with first impressions. The more she talked to Anthony, the more she felt their connection.

"Dang," Soul said, noticing that it was starting to get dark, "We've been talking for hours."

"Three hours to be more exact," Anthony replied looking at his phone.

"I guess time really does fly when you're having fun,"

"So, you had a good time?"

"Very much so," Soul said gathering the picnic items together.

Anthony began to help her pack up the food items, "So," he paused, "would you say you had a good enough time that you wouldn't mind seeing me again?"

"Why? Are you asking to see me again?"

"If you will allow me the pleasure, then I'd like nothing more."

"I would love to see again. You have proven yourself to be worthy company."

"Worthy!"

"Yes worthy!" Soul joked handing Anthony the picnic basket and speaker so she could fold the blanket.

"Looks like we have everything. You about ready to get out of here?"

"Yep," Soul replied looking around to make sure they had not forgotten anything. Anthony began to hum as they walked back to his truck.

"What are you humming?" Soul asked as she tried to pick up on the tune.

"Girl, you don't recognize this jam! I thought you were a musical connoisseur?"

"I am!" Soul said pretending to be offended. "I just couldn't pick up on the tune."

Anthony hit the alarm on his truck as they got closer. "When I'm alone in my room, sometimes I stare at the wall,"

"Hey!" Soul said throwing her hands in the air, "and in the back of my mind I hear my conscious call"

"Telling me I need a girl who's as sweet as dove, for the first time in my life, I see I need love." Anthony and Soul sang.

Anthony sat the picnic basket and speaker in the backseat before breaking into the old school dance, the cabbage patch as he opened the door for Soul who was laughing so hard at his dance moves tears begin forming in her eyes.

"Oh! Oh! Oh! Oh! Go Anthony! Go Anthony!" Soul said breaking into the prep.

"Hey!" Anthony said joining in with the prep.

Anthony joined Soul in laughter pulling her into an embrace. He looked into her eyes and at that moment Soul wished time would stop. The smell of Anthony was so intoxicating, that she felt dangerously drunk with passion. Anthony's sexy eyes roamed over her body and instead of giving her the kiss that her body once again longed for, he simply pulled away, opened her door, and helped her into the truck. He closed the door slowly, before walking slowly around to the driver's side of the truck, as she watched him in the mirror. Soul couldn't stop her heart from racing like a pack of wild horses. She was afraid of what Anthony was stirring inside of her, but even more afraid of the feeling going away. Never in her life had someone invaded her soul in such a short time, but the chemistry between she and Anthony was undeniable.

Anthony pulled away from the park, as they drove several moments in silence. After a few minutes, she finally turned sideways in her seat to look at Anthony, "Is everything OK?"

"More than OK," Anthony said after a short silence taking her hand in his and driving the short distance to Soul's in remaining silence.

Pulling into a parking spot in front of Soul's apartment, Anthony turned the ignition off. Anthony stroked Soul's hand, turning to look her in the eyes, while they sat in silence. After a few moments, Anthony opened the door and jogged around to help Soul out stepping behind her and sliding his arms around Soul's waist as they walked to her apartment door. "I really enjoyed being with you today, Soul," Anthony whispered as he nibbled on her ear and neck. "In fact, I can't think of anyone I would rather have spent my time with today besides you."

"Would you like to come in?" Soul heard herself ask. So much for not doing bald head hoe shit.

"Actually, I think I better get going, but I hope this isn't the last invitation I get."

"Humph, I definitely don't think it will be your last," Soul said turning to face Anthony as he pulled her into another embrace. At this point all sense had left Soul, and there was a fire burning inside that only Anthony could put out. Soul knew it was too soon, as she kept trying to tell herself to take it slow, but her words and vagina were at odds, and old hot twat was about to win.

Anthony held Soul a moment longer before pulling away, "I'll call you later," he said kissing her on the forehead before walking away.

Soul stood there watching him walk away before turning to go inside her apartment. Closing the door behind her, Soul leaned against the hard wood with a sigh as a sudden thought occurred to her. Sprinting upstairs to her bedroom, Soul ran to the nightstand. Pulling her journal out, Soul flipped the pages that contained her most intimate thoughts, dreams, and inspirations frantically in search of the entry that she had written only a month ago,

What I am looking for in a man

    1. God fearing-willing to teach and learn about God's word and respects God's word (If I find number one, all others fall under that ***)

    2. Safe

3. Committed to me

4. Loyal

5. Trustworthy

6. Hardworking

7. Listener and a Conversationalist

8. Shares my interest

9. Good Role model

10. Well-rounded (businesslike with a little hustle)

11. Has goals of his own –supports and encourages my goals

12. Romantic but realistic

13. Open-minded

14. Makes me laugh, loves my smile, and doesn't mind when I cry

15. Doesn't have to keep me on a pedestal but doesn't want to see me on a footstool.

Soul reread the list three times, before running downstairs to grab her cell phone.
"What up trick," Simone answered obviously looking at her caller ID.
"Guess what happened to me today?" Soul said smiling.
"What?"
"I may have just met the man of my dreams!

Chapter 17

It had been two months since Soul and Anthony's picnic, and since that time they had started spending every free moment they had together, talking on the phone until the early hours of the morning, and texting each other as soon as they woke up the next day. Soul loved how romantic Anthony was, and she often joked that God must have broken the mold when he created him. He had captured her attention, and though she kept denying it verbally to everyone else, Soul knew he had also captured her heart. Even Simone and Danielle had noticed the change in Soul badgering her until Soul finally admitted how she felt.

"You are in love," Simone said drawing out her words.

Simone and Danielle had made Soul promise to have dinner with them, even threatening to call Anthony if Soul didn't show up for their scheduled dinner date. Anthony too had decided to hang with his friends, agreeing that they had been giving him a hard time since he and Soul started spending so much time together.

"I'm sorry, are you talking to me? Danielle, she must be talking to you. I didn't know you had a new love in your life."

"Whatever Soul. Simone is right. You are bonified, superfied, and all the other fieds I can't think of, in love."

"Noooooo, I'm not."

"Okay, so what? Are you telling me ya'll are just friends?" Danielle asked.

"Yeah," Soul replied calmly sipping on her drink.

"Okay, so as friends, how often do you see each other?"

"Everyday, or at least every other day. We like hanging out."

"And as friends, how often do you talk on the phone?" Simone added with an amused expression on her face.

"A lot."

"What's a lot? Please give specific answers."

"Okay Simone, every night. Are you satisfied now?"

"You met his family?"

"Simone, you know I did."

"He's met your family?" Danielle questioned although she already knew the answer.

"Okay Ms. Know it all one and two. Since you know everything about how Anthony and I feel, please explain it to me," Soul stated sitting back and folding her arms across her chest.

"Danielle, do you want to take this, or shall I?"

"Simone, you have such a way with words, please bless us with your wisdom."

"Thank you my dear. Okay here's how I see it," Simone said switching to a much more ghetto approach. "You and Anthony are both sprung, but you don't want to admit it. Anthony, well, he's probably just feeling out the situation to see where ya head at, but he's feeling you too. Trust me I know. If he stared any harder at you at the card game a few weeks ago, I thought you would melt. The two of you were about to make me throw up all googley-eyed and shit, little kisses here, and pats there. It was damn right disgusting. I'm sure just like you drive us crazy with Anthony this, and Anthony that, his boys probably feel the same way."

"How do you know? You were too busy talking trash and arguing at the last game night to know anything about Anthony or his boys," Soul interrupted.

"Whatever. Call it women's intuition."

"Or call it Simone's bullshit."

"You better listen. This bullshit may get your ass a man, because I know you like a pair of old panties. Now where was I before I was so rudely interrupted? Oh yeah, the two of you being sprung. Now what I figure, is that you don't want to admit the way you feel because you're afraid that once you do that, you'll find out he's frontin, but I want you to quit holding Anthony accountable for every other brother's past mistakes. More importantly, I want you stop doubting your love based on the past love choices that didn't work out. Trust your judgement, even it deserves a second chance. Besides, Anthony is cool, and he genuinely cares about you. Like I said he's just waiting on you. Now the cousin I know is a go-getter. And either you get it now, or somebody else gets it later. Don't be a fool. Anthony is a good catch, and you know hoes can sniff out when a man is off limit, or at least I know you could, and we all know you a hoe!"

"Shut up Simone," Soul laughed. "I guess you would know, since hoes of a feather flock together."

"Hey! You and Simone speak for yourself. I am a reformed hoe, thank you very much!"

"So, it's okay to admit that you're in love and stuff, cause once Anthony finally gives you some, it won't be any denying it."

Soul sighed, "I guess you're right," she whispered.

"I'm sorry, what was that?" Simone said with a smug expression on her face.

"Fine! I got it bad."

"You got it bad, or you're in love," Danielle smiled knowingly.

"Okay I'm in love. There I said it. Now if you don't mind, we can switch the subject." Soul's cell phone started vibrating, as Anthony's picture flashed on the screen. "Hey you," Soul answered smiling and rolling her eyes at Simone and Danielle who had burst into huge fits of laughter.

"To love," Simone laughed raising her class.

"To love," Danielle agreed as she clanked her glass against Simone's.

***

Once Soul had finally admitted how she felt, she felt like a burden had been lifted from her shoulders, but it was the remaining feelings of uncertainty and fear that still frightened her. From the moment she leaned into his arms during that picnic, Soul knew Anthony was dangerous. One conversation after another slowly peeled away Soul's guarded layers that had been spun from one failed relationship after another. And even though she was still afraid of how strong her feelings had become for Anthony in such a short time, he had almost succeeded in turning her skepticism of relationships into a belief that love was still available and waiting. Soul loved his friends and family, and everyone who was important in Soul's life adored Anthony. Sometimes she couldn't even make it through the day without sneaking off to the teacher's lounge to call him to just hear his voice, not to mention the numerous text messages they sent daily.

Anthony fit every description Soul had of the perfect man, if there was even such a thing. He was one of the most romantic, intelligent, and real men she had ever known. One minute he was having a professional conversation with his clients and the next minute, he was talking cash money noise with his boys on the basketball court. Anthony made Soul feel safe, and that should have scared her, but it didn't. Soul recalled how just the other day, it was the getting close to the one- year anniversary of the death of one of her favorite students Alisa Morgan who died in her class as Soul held her in her arms. Alisa suffered from heart failure, and by the time the paramedics arrived, she was pronounced dead on the scene.

As they lay on the floor listening to music and sipping wine, Soul told Anthony about the incident and how devastated and depressed she became afterwards. She even opened up and told him how she almost suffered from a nervous breakdown, and seriously considered quitting the teaching profession. Anthony held her the entire night and let her cry getting all the anger, frustration, and feelings of guilt that had for so long caused her so many sleepless nights. And when the day came that marked that awful time, Anthony sent her two dozen roses to work, one in the morning and the other at the end of the day. The first roses came with a card that read, "So you can mark this day with better memories," and the second card read, "You brighten so many lives; today it's your turn."

The only complaint Soul had about her relationship with Anthony was that they hadn't had sex. Soul knew she was being ridiculous, but sometimes it took every ounce of will power she owned not to jump on top of him and let nature take its course. There had been some heavy petting and heavy kissing, but they never took it all the way. Soul could tell Anthony wanted her as much as she wanted him, but right when Soul thought Anthony would make a move, he pulled back. She had even tried to get him to spend the night with her but no matter how late it was, he would always drive back to his place. When she confided in Mrs. Alice from her lunch crew, she told Soul that when she met her husband, she thought he was gay because he wasn't trying to have sex with her, but later he told her he didn't try to have sex with her, because he respected her. Ms. Alice told Soul that her husband said he knew that she was going to be his wife, and he needed to make sure it was about more than sex. She also bluntly told Soul to stop being such a hot ass.

Soul had increased her inventory in her nightstand, but there was not a toy in there that could scratch the Anthony itch.

Soul and Anthony had even talked about their relationship fears, and he assured her that there was nothing another woman could do for him that she couldn't. The funny thing was that when he said it, she truly believed him even without the sex. Soul felt in her heart that with Anthony it wasn't just words. Anthony could walk the walk without even trying. One thing she had come to learn about him was that if he said it, he showed it. Anthony was definitely a man of action and had done more for Soul in the short time they had known each other, than any man outside of her family and God ever did for her in all her days on this earth. And sometimes when he looked at her like she was the sexiest woman on earth, she felt like she was! Beyonce who? Not with her Anthony around.

Soul Denise Jackson was in love. She couldn't, nor did she want to imagine her life without Anthony. There were days that Soul still wondered when someone was going to come along with a needle to burst her bubble of happiness. She even found herself wondering if the day would ever come that she got one of those famous calls from some woman saying those famous words "you don't know me, but." For Soul, past wounds healed slowly, and despite her mind telling her to move slowly, she knew that no matter how hard she tried, trying to slow down the love she felt growing so quickly for Anthony would be no small task.

Chapter 18

"Simone, could you please hurry up, Anthony will be here in a minute," Soul yelled as she examined her freshly done French manicure and pedicure.

"Don't get mad at me because beauty takes time," Simone said yelling from the bathroom."

"And don't get mad at me because some beauty comes naturally," Soul got up to examine herself in the mirror.

"Bitch, you are so conceited," Simone said coming out of the bathroom to find Soul smiling at herself in the mirror. "Anthony is going to be so mad the day he goes and gets those cataracts removed from his eyes, not to mention getting that glaucoma cleared up."

"Yeah, Yeah, I guess you would know since that's how you lost all your men!"

"Oh, that was a good one," Simone said hi-fiving Soul. "How do I look?"

Simone had on a pair of tight-fitting blue jeans that hugged every curve that her mama and God had blessed her with. Her cropped T- shirt with the word "*Hottie*" imprinted across the front stopped right at her mid section, exposing her silver belly chain, and drawing attention to her tattoo of an ice cream cone that read "lickable." Her long black cornrows dangled down her back, and her make-up was flawless. She had chosen a wine lip gloss that made her lips full and pouty. Her full brown eyes always captured the attention of many men. Simone was a force to be reckoned with, and she knew it.

"You look good, and besides if I told you any different, you wouldn't believe me anyway."

"True. True. Now which shoes do you think I should wear?" she asked holding up a pair of sandals and a pair of tennis shoes.

"Definitely go with the tennis shoes, they go with you whole b-girl look." Soul replied turning back to the mirror to put on some more lip-gloss.

"I don't know why you are putting on more lip gloss. Anthony is just going to kiss it off, and to think you still haven't gotten any from that sexy ass man. Girl you must be slipping, cause if that was me,"

"Simone just because you have hoe tendencies, does not mean the rest of us have them too," Soul answered in an overly sweet tone.

"Forget you!" Simone laughed throwing a shirt in Soul's direction. "I was about to tell your stanking ass that you look cute, but now you're just going to have to walk around all day wondering if you look hot or not."

"Baby, there is no need to wonder about this," Soul replied throwing her hands in the air and gyrating her body like she was a video vixen.

"You need to be trying to do Anthony like that!" Simone shouted walking back in the bathroom.

"Yeah! Yeah! Up or down?" Soul asked referring to her freshly braided micros. Soul loved how the golden highlights made her skin seem to glow.

Simone came out of the bathroom to examine Soul as she pulled her braids up, then let them fall back down. "Up. They go with your quote, unquote look,"

The yellow romper Soul had chosen showed enough cleavage for Anthony to appreciate but not too much that his mom, whom she got along with wonderfully, would talk about her. The nude gladiator sandals would not only expose Soul's freshly done pedicure but draw attention to her gold toe-ring as well.

Soul and Simone were going to a barbecue at Anthony's parents and his entire family and several of his friends and fraternity brothers were sure to be in attendance, so of course she had to represent.

"Hey, did you ever get in contact with Danielle to see if she wanted to go," Soul asked pinning her braids up in a bun.

"Actually, I called her when you were in the shower, and she said she wasn't feeling well. In fact, I only talked to her for a few minutes before she rushed me off the phone."

"Oh yeah, she said she was feeling bad the other day when I called her too. Maybe we should stop by there later to check on her. Come to think of it, I really haven't had a full conversation with her in about two weeks. She's always rushing out, or sleep, or doing God knows what and has to get back with me."

"Now that you mention it, she's like that when I call too. In fact, the only time I talked to her this week was Monday, and she was at work, so I didn't get to really talk to her then, and here it is Saturday. Yeah, we definitely have to check on her later."

"Maybe she's throwing herself into work to forget about Jackson and Devon."

"I thought he was going to fly down here to see her,"

"The last I heard he was. I knew she and Devon would end up connecting on that trip. She even told me the time spent with Devon gave her time to really clear her head and seeing him put a lot of things in perspective regarding Jackson."

"Yeah, she told me that too. Hopefully her thing with Devon will work out, and she can put Jackson's sorry ass behind her. Even though I never met him, he seems like he's a good guy, and that he really cares about Danielle."

"Trust me. Devon is a great guy. In college, they were the perfect couple. Even the guys thought so. I didn't think she would ever get over him, when he had to transfer to another school because of his scholarship, but they have kept in contact all these years, and there must be a reason for that. Hurry up, I hear Anthony downstairs ringing the doorbell," Soul said as she grabbed her wristlet and phone before heading downstairs.

"Hey, Hey Cutie!" Anthony looked great in khaki shorts with a Carolina Panthers football jersey, and plain white Nikes.

"Hey yourself," Anthony replied bending down to give her a kiss. "Where are the girls?"

"Danielle is sick, and Simone, of course, is still upstairs primping in the mirror!"

"Simone! Come on girl! Primping is not about to help you now!" Anthony shouted up the stairs.

"Forget you, Anthony. Don't be mad because Soul can't look this good!" Simone announced as she came down the stairs.

"Yeah, you're right!" Anthony joked.

"Hey!" Soul said slapping Anthony playfully on the arm.

"I'm just kidding baby, come here and give me another kiss."

"No! Put yourself in time-out."

"OK, well I'll just give Simone a kiss," Anthony said walking over to kiss Simone on the cheek. "You look good as always."

"Thank you, thank you, thank you," Simone said blowing kisses at Anthony.

"Simone, don't get you and Anthony's ass whooped."

"You jealous baby?"

"Yes!" Soul said pretending to pout.

"I'm sorry, here let me give you a kiss,"

"I want a good kiss too, not no kiss on the cheek," Soul replied sticking her tongue out at Simone.

Anthony wrapped his arms around Soul and kissed her, slipping his tongue into her mouth as she melted into his arms. There was something about the feel of his arms that made Soul feel safer than she ever did in her life. His presence brought her a sense of peace and stability.

"Hey you two," Simone said breaking them apart, "get a room. Nobody wants to see that mess!"

"Don't hate," Soul said giving Anthony another quick kiss, while looking at Simone out of the corner of her eye.

"Yeah, Yeah, Yeah, Let's go before the thought of spending the day with the two of you causes me to change my mind," Simone said as she threw her hand in the air and walked out the door.

***

Soul loved Anthony's parents, but especially his mom. She and Marvela Robinson got along like two old friends. She reminded Soul of her own mama in so many ways which was part of the reason Soul adored her. She was a little bitty woman with the personality, voice, and heart of the wrestler Andre the Giant. The first time Soul met her and heard that huge voice come from such a small lady, she was amazed. The only problem with Anthony's mom was that every time Soul saw her, she was trying to make her eat, and the way Anthony's mom cooked, Soul always had to spend extra time at the gym for every plate Marvela put in front of her. Today of course, would be no exception.

"Hey baby," Ms. Robinson said walking up and giving Soul a hug. I see you're still taking pity on my son, and hanging out with him," she joked giving Anthony a kiss on the cheek.

"Actually, truth be told, I only hang around with him so I can see you," Soul said placing her arm around Marvela.

"Oh, is that how you gonna do a brother?" Anthony asked with a grin on his face. "Cool, let's go Simone."

"Uh Uh, I'm staying right here with the lady who holds the strings to the food," Simone began rubbing her stomach.

"Boy you women sure do stick together! What is this a conspiracy or something? No wonder men have been trying to warn each other for generations about you evil beings," Anthony said connecting his fingers in the shape of a cross. "Always trying to tell a brother what to do, and then when we have served our purpose, Boom! You want to get rid of us. And if you aren't telling us what to do, you're complaining. Did you get a degree in that? 'Yes, I have my PhD in Complaining,'" Anthony said in his best female voice. "It probably started way back in the days of Mary and Joseph. Oh, there was some room in the inn, but it booked up, because Mary was too busy complaining about not wanting to stay in an inn, and why they couldn't get a room at the Doubletree!"

"Boy!" Anthony's mom laughed, before popping him upside the head. "Get on out of here before the Lord strikes you down right here and now for playing with him!"

"Shoot. I hope he don't strike me down before I get something to eat, cause Uncle Fred's ribs are smelling good and a brother is hungry in a mug," Anthony said rubbing his stomach. "Have you ever noticed black people always got to be something in a mug: hungry in a mug, ugly in a mug, tired in a mug, broke in a mug,"

"Crazy in a mug," Soul added pointing at Anthony.

"Fine in a mug," Anthony said swatting Soul on the butt before bending down to plant a kiss on the cheek.

"Simone, have they been like this all day?"

"Pretty much Ms. R." Simone said pretending to vomit and causing them all to begin laughing.

"Well, I guess I can't complain since Soul keep my baby smiling but that's enough of that for now."

"Where's dad?" Anthony asked.

"Now where else would he be?" Marvela Robinson said putting her hands on her hips.

Anthony laughed, "Let me guess, in his lounge chair under the tree sleep."

"You guessed it!"

"Well, I'm about to go wake him up."

"Anthony, before you go harass your dad and fix you a plate, because I know that's where you are really going," Mrs. Robinson said with a knowing look, "go check on Teddy Jr. He's supposed to be in the house lying down, but as bad as that boy is, who knows?"

Teddy Jr. was Anthony's five-year-old little cousin, he was a true terror and had to be watched 24/7 he was so bad.

"Where's Lisa?" Soul asked referring to Teddy's mama.

"Probably trying to jump off a bridge if she's smart," Anthony joked.

"Boy, now you know that's just ugly. I think she had to run to the store and get a can of milk for Samantha," Ms. Robinson commented referring to Teddy Jr.'s one year old sister and the object of most of his terrors.

Lisa was Anthony's cousin. She was cool but a little dingy when it came to her choice of men. She had a heart of gold, which allowed men to run over her all too often. Her six-year relationship with Teddy and Samantha's dad was the best example of this, as he came in and out of their life when he pleased, never helped her financially, and was in and out of jail too many times to keep count. Soul figured that was probably why Teddy was so damn bad. Anthony loved Lisa like a sister, but he was always pissed off with the state of her life. "If she paid as much attention to her kids as she did that damn nigga, Teddy Jr. wouldn't be so damn bad!" He'd told Soul during one of his Lisa tirades.

"Hurry up and go on and check on him before he tears something up in my house, and I have to whoop his butt myself. In fact, bring him out so we can all see him. He's been on punishment long enough."

"What did he do this time?" Soul asked.

"Chile, do you know his bad tail went and put scotch tape over his baby sister's eyes while she was sleeping!"

"What!" Simone and Soul screamed at the same time.

"Yeah, you heard me right! Tape! Girl the baby woke up and was in there screaming and Lisa went in to get her and what do you think she found? The poor little girl's eyes taped down!"

"Boy get up." Marvela Robinson said to her son who was bent over in laughter. "Anthony, that ain't funny. That child has issues, and do you know what he said when Lisa asked him why he did it?" Ms. Robinson was trying to hold in her own laughter but couldn't contain it anymore. It took her several seconds before she could speak again, she was laughing so hard. "His little bad tail said he was tricking the baby, so she would think she was still sleep when she woke up!" By now they were all falling out with laughter.

"Hey what's so funny?" Lisa asked emerging around the corner. The sight of her only made them laugh harder!

***

"I sure hope ya'll saved some food for us," Ajax, said as he and Anthony's frat brother Thaddeus came around the corner.

"What up ya'll?" Anthony said rising from the bench where he sat with Soul, Simone and Lisa eating food. "I see ya'll fools late as usual," Anthony said embracing first Ajax then Thaddeus.

"Man, I was trying to get this hoe's number, but she was tripping, wanting a brother to stay and conversate and shit." Ajax said with a grin.

Ajax and Anthony had been friends since childhood. In fact, they were more like brothers. He and Anthony did everything together until Anthony went away to college. Then they drifted apart until recently. Ajax was a ladies' man. Standing 6'5, his bald head and light complexion, not to mention his hazel green eyes only contributed to his womanizing skills. He always had a smile on his face showing off his dazzling white teeth. Ajax used to be the biggest street hustler around until his second arrest. When the judge broke down the three strikes law to him, he realized he better do something different. He went to barber school and now owned a successful barber shop. It was always packed, and don't even think about going without an appointment. His successful business and good looks kept him supplied with a continual hoe-asis as Bernie Mac would say. When Soul first met him, she thought she would slap the taste out of his mouth with all the bitches and hoes that came out it, but eventually she realized that most of what he said was a front, and he was truly a good guy and a true friend to Anthony.

Thaddeus, on the other hand, was the opposite of Ajax. He was Anthony's best friend and frat brother. They met in college and had been close since then. Thaddeus wasn't an Ajax in the swag department, but he could hold his own. He was the type of dude you could find on TikTok if you went down the Big Tok rabbit hole. Standing about 6'1, his large, muscular football frame made him very easy on the eyes, and his smooth chocolate complexion was a definite plus. His short locks fit him well, and he always smelled so good! He worked as one of Dallas' top sports agents after a knee injury ended his short stint with the Green Bay Packers. Soul considered him cool as hell and very mild mannered until he got around Anthony or any of their other frat brothers. She didn't know what it was about their fraternity, but it was like something came over them when there was two or more of them in the same room.

"Say fool, watch your language around the ladies," Thaddeus said punching Ajax in the shoulder.

"Damn, it ain't like I called them some hoes! What up Soul?" Ajax said reaching over to give her some dap. "Lisa, what's up, where Teddy bad ass at?" he said walking around to snatch a hot link off her plate. It was at this moment that he seemed to notice Simone. "How you doing Ms. Lady?" Ajax eyed Simone licking his lips.

Simone looked around as if she didn't know who Ajax was talking to, "Oh I'm sorry. Are you talking to me or one of your hoes?"

"You, one of my hoes, it's all the same to me," Ajax smiled sweetly.

"Ah'ight you two, don't start," Thaddeus said before Simone could get her next comment in. "What's up Soul, Lisa, Simone." Thaddeus said coming around to give each of them hugs. "You guys are missing one, aren't you?

Soul, Dani, Simone, Anthony, Thaddeus, and Ajax had hung out together a few times, especially since they made a point of saying that would be the only way to get Soul and Anthony to hang out.

"Yeah, Dani is sick," Soul said licking barbecue sauce off her fingers."

"You want me to lick them for you?" Anthony whispered in Soul's ear causing her to giggle.

"Oh damn, here they go, it's definitely time for me to go get a plate now," Ajax said walking off.

"Hold up yo! I'm going to get me one too," Thaddeus said catching up to Ajax. Ajax and Thaddeus both returned shortly with their plates piled high with food.

"Damn man, ya'll leave some food for anybody else," Lisa asked getting up from the bench. "Here ya'll can have my seat. I'm going to take a nap."

"That's why ya ass spreading now, all that eating and sleeping," Ajax said before sitting down.

"Or it could be because she's had two kids," Simone said rolling her eyes at Ajax as she sucked on a piece of rib.

"Damn Simone, you sure sucking on that rib good. I like the way you all thorough and the way you suck it straight to the bone," Ajax eyed Simone.

"You know what, go to hell Ajax, you nasty bastard!"

"Man, can you two get along for a second?" Anthony asked shaking his head.

"What can I say bro, she wants me," Ajax said in a nonchalant tone as he bit into a piece of barbecue chicken.

"Ajax, I'll become a lesbian before I give you some."

"You sure about that," Ajax asked looking Simone directly in the eye.

"You know what? Fuck you Ajax! Simone said getting up to throw her plate in the trash.

"That's ya problem now," Ajax mumbled to himself.

Anthony, Thaddeus, and Ajax became engrossed in talk about the latest Maverick's game. Soul gave Anthony a peck on the cheek and excused herself. Soul knew she could hang with any man when it came to sports talk, but sometimes men needed to be by themselves.

She went looking for Simone and found her in the house plopped in a chair talking to Lisa and Marvela.

"Hey baby, I thought you would still be outside playing referee between the three amigos from the hood," Mrs. Robinson said looking up.

"Now that's a game, I'd never want to call," Soul said plopping down on the sofa beside her. "What are you guys watching?"

"Some movie with that sexy young Michael Jordan in it."

"Michael Jordan got a movie?" Soul asked with a puzzled expression on her face.

"Yeah! And he sexier than he was in that Black Panther movie." Mrs. Robinson said turning the volume up on the TV.

"You mean Michael B. Jordan Aunt Marvela," Lisa said closing her eyes.

"Whatever, A, B, C Jordan, I don't care, all I know is the boy is sexy."

"I heard that Mrs. R!" Soul said reaching over to give her high five.

***

"Hey baby, wake up," Anthony said gently shaking Soul.

"Huh, oh dang, I didn't realize I had fallen asleep.""You not by yourself," Anthony said with a sweep of his hand.

Mrs. Robinson had moved to the recliner where she slept peacefully. Simone was knocked out in her chair. Even Teddy had crawled into his mother's lap and fallen asleep while baby Samantha breathe heavily on her chest.

"I don't know how ya'll sleep with all the all the noise the domino game is creating outside from us men folk! You about ready to go?" he asked bending down in front of her.

"Sure baby, let me go straighten up the kitchen"

"Don't worry about that kitchen," Mrs. Robinson said with her eyes still closed. "I'll get to that later. You just go in there and fix Danielle a plate and Anthony, go lay Samantha and Teddy in the bed. Nah better yet, lay the baby down, but leave Teddy right here where I can see him."

"How can watch him and you sleep?" Anthony asked pinching his mother's thigh.

"Gone boy, I ain't sleep, I'm just resting my eyes." Soul heard Anthony's mom say as she walked to the kitchen.

Soul began to fix Dani a plate, straightening up the kitchen as best as she could without making up too much noise. If she took too long, Mrs. Robinson was sure to come in there and fuss about her not listening. She returned with four foil-covered plates knowing that Anthony and his mom would fuss if she didn't fix plates for everyone.

When she returned to the living room, Simone and Ajax were arguing while Thaddeus and Anthony were standing at the door shaking their heads. Mrs. Robinson still lay reclined with her eyes closed. When Soul walked into the room, she opened one eye.

"Good, you know my baby has to eat later too."

"Yes honey, plus I don't think he would let me ride home if I hadn't fixed him a plate," Soul said bending down to give her a kiss on the cheek.

"He might have, but I sure wasn't," Simone said walking over to kiss the other cheek before walking over to the door.

"Bye Mama! Tell Dad bye since and Unc outside arguing about who makes the best ribs. I'm not even trying to go outside and be pulled into that nonsense. I'll see you later this week," Anthony called from the door.

"Yeah see ya later Mrs. Robinson," Thaddeus added.

"Bye beautiful," Ajax said taking her hand and kissing the back.

"Uhm," Mrs. Robinson remarked never opening her eyes. They all headed for the door. "See ya'll kids later. Make sure you take Danielle her plate on your way home," Marvela Robinson reminded them never opening her eyes. "Oh, and Soul"

"Yes Ma'am?"

"Thank you for straightening up the kitchen."

Chapter 19

"Hey, do you think Dani is even home? Her car isn't in the driveway."

"She probably parked in the garage so Jackson wouldn't stalk her," Simone said jokingly. "I hope she's feeling better, because you know Dani can be a baby when she is sick," Simone began banging on the door and ringing the doorbell simultaneously.

"Dang, what's taking her so long?"

"Maybe she's getting some," Anthony said pinching Soul on her butt.

"Here comes her hard walking ass," Simone said referring to Danielle's loud footsteps. She covered the peephole with her finger knowing Danielle would automatically peep out the hole to see who it was.

"Baby why didn't you use the key," Danielle said snatching open the door. A look of shock came across her face when she saw Soul, Simone, and Anthony standing in the door.

"Well, *baby*, you know I don't have a key and why do I get the feeling that we weren't the *baby* you were expecting," Simone said pushing her way into Danielle's house.

Soul had a gut feeling there was about to be trouble. She guessed Anthony did too, because he was still standing in the same spot with a peculiar look across his face that equally matched her own.

"Uhm, what are you guys doing here?" Danielle asked anxiously.

"My mama sent you a plate from the barbecue," Anthony said when he noticed that Soul hadn't said a word. "It seems like we caught you at a bad time, so we're gonna go ahead and get out of here, right baby," he said turning to Soul. "Come on Simone."

"Now what kind of friends would we be, if we didn't visit with our sick friend," Simone said from the hallway.

"Simone is right baby. Besides, Dani looks so much better. I'm sure she's up for a little company. Right Danielle?" Soul breezed past Anthony and Danielle and stood by Simone.

"Well, I uh, was actually uh, getting ready to lie back down," Danielle quickly added throwing in a fake cough for added measure.

"We're not gonna stay long. Come on in Anthony," Soul said giving him a hard look.

Danielle looked at Anthony helplessly, but he knew better than to get in the middle of a battle with three women who had been friends for as long as the three standing in front of him.

"So, what's up girl, who did you think was at the door?" Soul asked following Simone into the living room. Danielle followed reluctantly, and Anthony lingered even further behind.

"Look guys, I'm about to have company, so..."

"Who ya company?" Simone glared at Danielle.

"Simone, I really don't think that's any of your," Danielle began.

"Yeah Dani, who is your company? He wouldn't happen to go by the name of Jackson?" Soul stressed Jackson's name as she stepped in Danielle's face.

"You know what, I am so tired of ya'll acting like I can't take care of my business! What if it is Jackson, what the hell does it have to two with the two of you?" Danielle challenged stepping up to Simone and Soul pointing her finger in their face.

"What does it have to do with us? You mean the same two who have to keep picking you up when that nigga put you through some more drama? The same two who damn near went to jail trying to spray paint a muthafuckin car behind some bullshit, the same two who was at the hospital after this nigga than pushed yo ass down some stairs!" Soul spat pushing the side of Danielle's head with her finger."

"Hold on ladies, ya'll talking out of anger now, and I know your friendship means too much."

"Wait a minute Anthony," Simone threw a hand in Anthony's direction to stop him, "this is between the three of us, and if they want to fight, let them fight." Simone said. "This is about friendship."

Danielle sighed, "Look guys I know you love me, and you always have my best interest at heart, and I know if this was one of you guys, the situation and attitudes wouldn't be any different, but what ya'll keep forgetting, is that I'm a big girl, and no matter how much you try to protect me, I'm the only one who has to deal with the consequences and repercussions," Danielle said taking a step back.

"But Danielle, why do you have to set yourself up for hurt?" Soul asked.

"And with Jackson!" Simone added. "That nigga don't amount to shit in a cow pasture!"

They all turned at the sound of keys jingling in the door.

"Babe! Where ya at! They didn't have the wine you wanted, so I had to pick another one! And whose truck in the driveway?"

"I'm in here baby." Danielle shouted.

Simone, Anthony, and Soul all exchanged glances. Anthony had never met Jackson, but Soul had told him enough stories about him, enough to know that this could end up bad.

Devon, sexy, black, and bald emerged around the corner smiling as always.

"Devon," Soul stammered.

'What's up baby girl!" Devon said coming to give Soul a huge bear hug. "Girl, I haven't seen you since college. Look at you!"

"Wha What are doing here?" Soul asked pulling from the embrace.

"Well, when my sweetie here came to visit me, I realized how much I missed her, so I took an extended vacation from my job, and decided to take a vacation to come spend some time with her."

"Danielle Katrina Allen, why didn't you tell me Devon was here?"

"Because I pay the bills in this household, so the only people I have to answer to are TXU, AT & T, and Bank of America mortgage company," Danielle said with a huge smile on her face, as she walked up to Soul playfully pushing Soul's head with her finger.

"That may change," Devon said walking over and putting his arms around her waist.

"I can't believe you Dani, you were about to take an ass whoopin, because you didn't want to tell us *Devon* was here?" Soul said shaking her head in disbelieve.

"You mean I was about to have to *give* an ass whoopin to prove that I am grown enough to make my own decisions and my girls, even though their intentions are in my best interest, have to learn that I can handle my own self."

"Yeah a'ight trick, we understand," Simone said reaching over and giving Dani some dap. "Devon, my man, you don't know what a pleasure it is to finally meet you! Soul and Danielle have told me plenty of stories about you from those famous college days. I see why you the man that ruined it for every other man in Dani's life!" Simone said looking at Devon appreciatively. "You have got to be Simone," Devon said extending his hand. "Danielle has told me all about you. It's a pleasure to finally get to meet you in person. And you must be Anthony!" Devon said turning to Anthony and dapping him up. "So, Ms. Soul, I was wondering why my lil' sis hadn't stopped by to see me. I kept trying to make Dani call you, but she said she didn't want nosy ass people in her house!" Devon said laughing.

"Um!" Soul said smacking her lips. "I bet this trick did."

Danielle giggled and walked over to put her arms around Simone and Soul. "So are guys staying for a while?"

"Oh! So now you want us to stay for a while," Simone said mimicking Danielle.

"Well not really! I was just being courteous!"

"See what I mean about black folks, bring em' some barbecue, and they don't want to introduce you to their company, try to fight you, and put you out the house," Soul said pretending to be offended.

"Did somebody say barbecue?" Devon asked interrupting.

"Yeah, we had a barbecue today, and my mama insisted that we bring the third musketeer a plate." Anthony replied.

"Shoot! Well point me to the plate!"

"It's over there baby," Danielle said pointing to the table where Simone had sat the plate.

"Well guys, us nosy people are gonna get out of here," Soul said walking over to give Devon another hug, as he inspected the plate of food. "Call me, and if Danielle doesn't give you my number, just throw it to her real good, and ask her during sex! I'm sure she'll give you all her contacts!"

"Alright baby girl," Devon said kissing Soul on the cheek. "Simone, I'm sure I'll see you before I leave."

"For sure, for sure," Simone said walking to the door.

"Anthony, it was nice meeting you man. Next time you guys come over, we gone have to pull out the table, and whoop these women folks in some bones or cards, or something, cause Danielle been bragging since I got here."

"She ain't no different from her friend," Anthony said reaching over to give Devon some dap.

"Well, enough chit chat, let me walk you guys to the door," Danielle playfully pulled Soul from Devon's embrace, and pushed Simone towards the door.

"Damn you ain't got to rush us, but on second thought, the way Devon is over there looking at you like you the barbecue! Yeah, it's time for us to go."

Danielle put her arms around Simone and Soul as she walked them to the passenger side of Anthony's truck. Anthony and Devon stood by the driver's side discussing the possibility of going to shoot some hoops before Devon left town.

"Dani, why did you let us think Jackson was your company?" Soul whispered.

"No! I did not let you two think anything! You *assumed* Jackson was my company. That's what I was talking about earlier. We have to trust each other to make good decisions, as hard as it may be. And no, every decision is not going to be a good one, but as friends we deal with it, and stand beside each other. Plus, I didn't want the two of you making Devon's visit into more than it is."

"Which is?" Simone asked as she opened her door.

"That's what I'm talking about nosy butts! But for the record," Danielle paused dramatically, "it's just a simple visit between two old friends who are getting reacquainted."

"Reacquainted huh? That's what you call spending over a month in Chicago and now Devon is her in Texas. Now it makes sense why we've only gotten together once for dinner since you've been back," Soul said giving Simone a high five."

"Look who's talking, we can barely pry you away from Anthony so there's that! Freak number one, you need to worry about trying to put it on Anthony tonight instead of worrying about who I'm putting it on, and freak number two, let's just hope you won't require medical help to knock down your door tonight! Bye bitches," Danielle said twinkling her fingers. "Come on baby, carry me in the house," Danielle said walking around to the driver's side where Anthony and Devon were still talking.

"Aright little lady, hop on," Devon said squatting down.

"Little! Ain't nothing little about Danielle but her little peanut head!" Simone shouted as she climbed in the back seat."

Alright number two," Danielle giggled as she climbed on Devon's back.

"Anthony, I'll holla at you before I leave." Devon said as he straightened up with Danielle hugging onto his neck tightly.

"No doubt, just give my girl a call, and she can get in contact with me," Anthony said as he pulled away from the curb. "You know, I like that kid, he seems like good people."

"He is baby, real good people," Soul said settling under Anthony.

Chapter 20

"Baby, do you want anything out of the store," Anthony asked pulling into the station to get gas.

"I do baby," Simone said from the backseat. "The black and milds are calling me."

"Simone, are you ever going to stop smoking?"

"Don't worry, I'm not going to smoke in the car, Simone said sitting up from where she had sprawled out across the backseat. Sliding her shoes on, Simone stepped out the truck just as two guys pulled up in a convertible. Simone, noticing the two guys watching her, put a little extra sashay in her walk. Anthony and Soul looked at each other and shook their heads. Soul sat in the truck and watched Anthony slide his credit card in the slot on the machine and begin to pump the gas. He blew Soul a kiss when he saw her watching him in the rearview mirror. She got out of the truck and walked over to Anthony. To Soul, there was something so sensual about pumping gas. Sliding the hose slowly in and out of the tank always reminded her of making love. Soul knew it was crazy, but she couldn't help thinking about sex every time she pumped gas. For as long as she could remember she would get completely turned on pumping gas, and watching Anthony right now didn't do a thing to put out her fire. She put her arms around him and gave him a long kiss.

"What was that for?"

"Do I have to have a reason to kiss the man I love?" Soul regretted saying the words as soon as they left her mouth.

Anthony looked at her for a long time not saying anything. It was the first time she had ever told him what she'd known since their picnic. Why did she have to open her big mouth? She really didn't mean to say it out loud. It just seemed like her mouth moved quicker than her brain could think. Now Anthony was going to feel pressured, and Soul was sure that this was the beginning of the end.

"Soul."

Soul held her breath knowing Anthony was going to say they were rushing into things. Why oh why did she have to say anything. She closed her eyes and tried to pull away from his embrace and eyes that stared into her face as her stomach began bubbling with nervousness. "Anthony, I"

Anthony pulled Soul back into his arms and hugged her so tight she could hear his heart beating. For seconds it seemed as if the world had stopped until Anthony pulled away from her and gave her a peck on the lips, "I love you too baby."

"Hey!! I got myself two phone numbers," Simone said c-walking her way to the truck. "Damn, do ya'll ever stop kissing? You need to just go somewhere and do it and get it over with."

"Whatever Simone," Soul said never looking away from Anthony. She gave him another kiss before finally turning her attention towards Simone. "Simone how did you get two numbers in that short amount of time? What? Did you get the number of the clerk too?"

"For your information, both men in convertible were trying to holla at ya girl, and I told them they were both cute, and that I couldn't decide which one I wanted. Hell, I was just playing, I didn't think they were both going to give me their numbers."

"Are you going to call them?" Soul asked breaking away from Anthony's embrace.

"Probably not, besides two friends who give the same girl their number, just doesn't seem to say much about their characters," Simone said balling the paper up in her hand and getting in the backseat.

"Your right about that. Hey, I need to run in the store and get some things. I'll be right back."

"You want me to go get them for you baby?" Anthony asked.

"Nah I got it; it'll just take a second. Be right back." Soul said winking at him.

***

They pulled in front of Soul's house and Simone said her goodbyes before getting in her car.

"Call me when you get home," Soul said closing her door.

"Yes Mother," Simone said pulling off.

"Baby, why don't you go home and get some clothes. I want you to stay over here tonight. And not stay over and leave later tonight. Stay with me Anthony." Soul said turning to face him.

"I was thinking the same thing. You need anything back?"

"Just you"

"Then I guess I better hurry up and get back," Anthony said giving Soul a quick kiss.

Soul had just enough time to pull this thing off before Anthony returned. She looked around the room and it was a mess. She knew she should have cleaned the room before she left for the BBQ. Soul started grabbing all the clothes that had been strewn around the room earlier and stuffing them into the hall closet. Ambience was the key. Everything had to be perfect, especially for the man she loved. It was funny how something like saying I love you could happen at the most unexpected moment. Soul would have never guessed in a million years that she and Anthony would confess their love for one another at a gas station of all places. Soul went to the hall closet pulling out two boxes of white tea candles and placed them strategically around the entire bedroom. Soul checked the clock. It had already been twenty minutes, and she wasn't even halfway finished, and it wouldn't be long before Anthony would be back. Starting the shower, Soul grabbed her shower cap and stepped inside to take a quick shower. Letting the water hit her face, she smiled recalling how it felt to finally tell Anthony how she felt and the relief of knowing he felt the same way. Making sure to pay extra attention to all the places Anthony may want to put his face, Soul stepped out of the shower and wrapped a towel around her before grabbing her toothbrush to brush her teeth. Walking into her room, Soul went to her lingerie drawer. Tonight, had to be perfect. She pulled out several pieces of lingerie, before finally decided on a black lace teddy. Soul rubbed her body with her favorite exotic oil-based lotion Lick me All Over and dabbed her pheromone spay lightly behind her ear and between her thighs. Surveying the room, something was missing. That's it, Soul remembered snapping her fingers. Roses! Grabbing her phone, she dialed Simone's cell number.

"I just made it home."

"Good. How much do you love me?" Soul asked.

"What do you want Soul?"

"Can you come back over here?"

"Hell nah! I just took my shoes off!"

"Please! Girl I'll tap dance at your wedding. I'll give you my new MAC lipstick that you said you liked, you name it, it's yours."

"Damn! It's like that! What's really going on?"

"I'm planning something for Anthony, and I need you to run to the store and get a dozen white roses."

"And where in the hell am I going to find white roses at this time of night?"

"Get some from the supermarket, I'm not looking for the best, I really just need the petals."

"I bet you do! So, it's going to be that kind of party. It's about damn time. What changed? I thought ya'll were taking everything sooo slow."

"Simone, tonight I told Anthony I loved him, and he said he felt the same way."

"What! When? Where was I? Details! Details!"

"Listen I promise to give you the whole story tomorrow, but I'm running out of time, can I count on you?"

"Yeah, I guess. It ain't like I'm getting some."

"Listen Simone, white roses, and Simone, I need you on white people time not CPT."

"Alright man, I'm already walking out the door. I'll be there in 15 minutes."

"Thanks girl."

"No thanks are necessary, have my lipstick in your hand when I get there," Simone said hanging up the phone.

As soon as Soul sat her phone on the nightstand to plug into the charger, it rang again. She looked at the caller ID. Anthony. "Hey you!"

"Hey yourself, what are you doing?"

"Waiting on you. You're still coming back over, aren't you?"

"Yeah, I was just calling to let you know I'm going to take a shower, and I should be back over there in about 30 minutes or so."

Thank you, Lord. "Okay baby, see you in a bit."

Soul began applying a fresh coat of makeup. Not too much, just enough to give her a natural glow. Unpinning her hair, Soul let her braids fall loose. That's how she wanted to feel tonight, free and unrestricted. Tonight, things had changed, and Soul was ready to take everything to a new level. Just as she slid into the matching black robe, the doorbell began ringing. Soul rushed downstair and peeped through the peephole, before opening the door for Simone who walked in with a bag in one hand, and the other hand extended.

"Thanks girl, I owe you big time,"

"Yes, you do. In fact, I want both of your new lipsticks because I found a bag of pre-pulled rose petals so that saves you time, and I brought my handcuffs in case you want to get freaky cause I know you! Now give me my lipsticks."

"My purse is on the counter and there should be a twenty in there, and no we don't need handcuffs! Everything will be romantic not dominatrix. I'll give you your lipstick tomorrow because the bag is upstairs. Soul said pushing Simone back out the door.

"Damn, this is the second time I have been rushed out of a house tonight. I must be losing my touch."

"Get out! Anthony will be here any minute now.

"Alright! Alright! You not getting your change, and I want my lipstick tomorrow wench. Don't make me come looking for you." Simone said turning to walk away before turning back around just as Soul was closing the door. "Are y'all planning on making a flick?"

"Go Simone!" Soul laughed as she made sure Simone made it to her car safely. As soon as she closed the door, Soul rushed back upstairs and opened the drawer where she kept her scarves. Pulling out two silk red scarves, she placed them on the nightstand near the bed. Next, she opened the roses and spread a few of them on the bed before scattering the rest on the floor, down the hall and on the stairs leading to the front door.   Soul turned on the Bluetooth speakers and glanced at the clock. Anthony would be here any minute. Just as she finished connecting her phone to the Bluetooth speaker, Soul could see headlights pulling in front of her apartment. She peered out of the window and saw Anthony pulling into a space reserved for her apartment. He stepped out in a pair of flip flops, basketball shorts, and one of his fraternity t-shirts. Taking a deep breath, Soul pressed play on the Mr. Right playlist she had created just for Anthony. Ro James voice filled the room as he asked for *Permission*. Soul glanced in the hall mirror just as Anthony knocked on the door. Soul took a deep breath to steady her pounding heart. This was it. She struck one of the sexiest poses she could think of, and opened the door

***

"Damn!"

"Hey."

"You look"

Soul prayed that Anthony couldn't tell how nervous she really was as she boldly stepped towards him interrupting whatever he was about to say and smothering him with a kiss. Soul could feel Anthony growing harder inside his thin basketball shorts as she pressed her body closer to him.

"Soul, I"

"Shh! My terms." Soul took Anthony's hand and led him up the stairs.

"Wait," he said, turning around to lock the door behind him. Anthony followed Soul up the stairs and into the dimly lit bedroom filled with candles and rose petals. "Damn baby."

Soul answered Anthony with another long passionate kiss. "I love you," she whispered as she nibbled on his earlobe.

"I love you too," he managed to get out.

Soul slowly pulled Anthony's T-shirt over his head exposing his muscular chest. Though she had seen him several times without his shirt, she was always struck breathless by how fine he was. Kissing Anthony tenderly around the slope of his neck she slipped her tongue inside his mouth as he began to massage her swollen nipples.

Anthony attempted to remove her clothes, but she swatted his hands away. "This is on my terms remember," she whispered pushing Anthony onto the bed. Standing in front of him, Soul slowly began to dance, slowly winding her hips, her eyes never leaving Anthony's gaze, his eyes following her every. Slowly climbing on top of him, Soul leaned over Anthony's body to retrieve the two scarves from the nightstand as Tank now blasted through the Bluetooth speakers explaining exactly what Anthony and Soul both knew was about to happen.

"My terms?"

"Your terms."

Soul began tying Anthony's wrists to the rails.

"What"

"Shh, my terms remember." Soul steadied herself atop Anthony, her eyes never leaving his. Leaning down she began to kiss his neck as he moaned in pleasure. "You like that baby?" Soul whispered into his ears.

"Soul," he moaned.

Soul reached inside Anthony's shorts to massage his eagerly awaiting erection. Sliding off Anthony, Soul stood up staring at the man she had so quickly fallen in love with. Soul began sliding his shorts off as he awkwardly lifted off the bed attempting to help her as best he could with his wrists still tied to the headboard. Staring at his naked body, Soul locked eyes once again with Anthony. He smiled and licked his lips slowly as Soul started slowly removing her lingerie. Anthony moaned in pleasure as Soul propped one leg on the bed and spread her legs for him to gaze at her glory. Sliding two fingers inside herself, Soul moaned in pleasure driving Anthony wild.

"Baby come sit it on my face," Anthony said almost begging.

"Uhm Anthony," Soul moaned, "My terms baby" she whimpered moving her fingers quickly over her swollen clit.

"Babyyyy," Anthony plopped his heads deep in the pillow. "Quit fucking teasing me and bring that pussy to daddy."

Anthony's words pushed Soul over the edge, her legs trembling as she came so hard, she almost lost her balance. Laughing lightly, Soul climbed back on top of Anthony her newfound moisture dragging over his chest and she slid her fingers in his eagerly awaiting mouth. Anthony licked and slurped her fingers as Soul grinded her hips on top of his naked body, his hard erection almost dipping inside of her.

Snatching her fingers from Anthony's mouth, Soul licked his chest, sucking on his nipples before landing on her prize destination. Every essence of his deliciously chocolate body took her breath away. Anthony moaned loudly as he watched himself disappear into Soul's mouth over and over while she masterfully played with his balls driving Anthony over the top his juices shooting into her mouth. Soul licked her lips greedily savoring every drop.

"Fuck! Untie me baby, my turn."

"Anthony, you are so impatient," Soul laughed sliding her fingers once again inside of herself. "We're still on my terms, and I'm just getting started. You hear what you do to me? That's that macaroni in a pot that Cardi B was trying to warn y'all about," Soul winked at Anthony as she moaned. Removing her fingers from inside of her, Soul wrapped her wet hand around Anthony's dick bringing back to life what was already almost there. Anthony moaned as Soul continued stroking him while sliding her tongue inside his mouth. Once she was satisfied, he was where he needed to be, she retrieved a condom from her nightstand. Soul tried reminding herself to go slow, but the thought of finally having Anthony inside of her became too much to bare.

"You okay baby,"

"Shh. My terms," she reminded him, but the shaking of her hands caused her to fumble clumsily with the condom wrapper. She finally got the condom out of the wrapper, and calmed herself, before expertly rolling the condom onto Anthony with her mouth as he moaned in pleasure. Slowly she slid onto his hard penis, as their bodies immediately became one.

"Damn Soul! Fuck, you feel so good. Why are you so fucking wet baby!" Anthony moaned as Soul began winding her hips in a circle. She leaned over Anthony and placed one of swollen nipples into his ready mouth as Anthony slurped at it like a starved man.

"Just call me your personal waterpark," Soul continued to move like her very life depended on it as she continued to meet Anthony's hard thrust. Their voices combined to surely awaken the world to their private affair as they could no longer take it, and their love exploded simultaneously. Tears, sweat, and love intermingled into one.

Sweat dripping from her hair, Soul collapsed onto Anthony's chest.

"You okay," Anthony whispered into her ear.

"I'm sorry," Soul couldn't contain the tears that flowed down her face.

When she rose up to untie his hands, Anthony smiled before wiping away her tears with his thumbs and pulling her back into his embrace.

"I promise you I'm not going anywhere," he said as if reading her thoughts.

Soul continued crying softly into his shoulder. She had experienced damn good sex that made her drop a tear before, but not like this. It was like the tears were a manifestation of the strings pulling at her heart.

"Hey, look at me," Anthony said pulling away from Soul to look into her eyes. "Did you hear me? I'm not going anywhere. I promise you."

"Me either," she said with a weary smile on her face.

Anthony pulled her to him and kissed her lightly on the forehead. "My baby got some skills."

"Was it worth the wait?"

"Hell yeah, plus some!"

"Shit the way you had me waiting I thought I was going to have to go find Jodie so he could do that 'beat it right dance' for me.

"What! Oh, you were going to try to give my stuff to Tyrese huh?" Anthony said tickling her sides.

"I don't know baby, you remember Baby Boy! He didn't call it the beat it right dance for nothing, the way he was hitting that, he looked like he put a patent on the pussy!"

"Oh, so you want somebody to beat it right," Anthony asked placing her hand onto his growing penis.

"Damn, it's like that. Like that quick?"

"We gotta make up for lost time baby." Anthony flipped her on her back and began kissing her breast as his fingers expertly played a song while her body hummed the perfect lyrics. Her hips rose to greet his fingers in a dance worthy of an encore. Parting her legs, Anthony made his way south and began to taste the applause that he had created. As she rubbed his baldhead, he pressed her in a deeper place of ecstasy where she soon exploded onto his expertly maneuvering tongue. Anthony greeted her screams with a kiss. Parting her legs even further, Anthony grabbed another condom and quickly put it on, before thrusting his erect penis inside of her.

"My terms," he asked.

"Yes baby," she moaned, "your terms!"

Chapter 21

"Dang, I wish Simone would hurry up and get here, I'm on a time schedule."

"You know Simone, she's always late," Danielle commented switching her purse from one shoulder to the other.

"No, you not talking about somebody being late, and you're the queen of lateness."

"Well, I'm not late today. Do you want me to call her on her cell again," Danielle asked as she reached into her purse to get her cell phone.

"Please do, it's going to take forever to find Anthony a good birthday present, and I still want to get my hair and nails done today too, that girl has"

"Has what?" Simone said walking up.

"It's about time. I thought we were going to meet at the mall at 11:00," Soul said reaching over to pinch her cheeks.

"Stop!" Simone replied as she jerked her face away, and besides it's only 11:20, and I'm hungry."

"Oh no Ms. Lady, we will not eat until we at least find something for Anthony."

"Well, do you have any ideas what you want to get him," Danielle asked as they begin to walk the mall in no general direction.

"Well, I know I want to get him something to wear, but I also want to get him something unique, so I guess we can start at Murphey's.

"Yeah, they got some banging clothes, and there's a Mexican restaurant right next door," Simone added. Come on, it's this way," she said turning back towards the way they had just come from.

"So, what do you and Anthony have planned tonight anyway?" Danielle asked.

"Well, I gave him some birthday stuff this morning, and"

"Ohh TMI," Danielle said covering her ears. "I'm just glad you two finally did it because you were getting on my last nerves."

"Mine too, but I don't know why Danielle is saying its TMI, it ain't too much information for me. Tell me, it been a hot minute since I had some, and this is the closest I'm getting to sex any time soon."

"Shut up, Simone! Something is wrong with you," Soul laughed. "Anyway, I sent him some chocolate covered strawberries to his job, and tonight I'm going to take him to True Visions, since that was where we had our first real date. What I was thinking is that I would buy several gifts and every hour I will give him a new gift. You know build up anticipation, plus he thinks he's not getting anything until next week when I get paid, but I put away money for his birthday with my last check.

"Good thinking, cause yo ass stay broke."

"True that," Simone said giving Danielle hi-five.

"Whatever tricks, I look damn good to be so broke," Soul said striking a pose as they reached the entryway of Murpheys' clothing store for men. "I think I'm going to get my baby something cream. Brown and cream colors look good on him," Soul said walking over to the shirts.

"What about this?" Danielle asked holding up a silk cream shirt.

"Uhm, that's a no! I don't want him looking like a pimp. Now this is more like it," Soul said picking up a cream sweater that would hug Anthony's biceps nicely.

"Oh yeah I like that," Simone said, "I could see Anthony rocking that with some jeans and Polo boots."

"Oh yeah me too," Danielle said walking over to examine the shirt closer.

"So is that for me," a gravely male voice said from behind Soul causing all three women to turn in the direction the voice came from.

Key.

Soul felt her stomach hit the floor, with her mouth fighting her stomach for a floor position.

"Are you going to stand there with your mouth open or are you going to give me a hug?"

"Huh?"

"Man, come here girl," Key said pulling Soul into his arms and kissing her on the cheek. "Look at you, looking all good and shit," he said pushing her back so that he could get a better look. "I been missing you girl," he said as he licked his lips.

"Uhm, I guess that's why she hasn't heard from you in over what is now, three, four years give or take?"

"What's up Simone. I see you ain't changed."

"I see you ain't either."

"What's up Danielle?" Key said letting go of Soul to give Danielle a hug. "How have you ladies been?" he said walking back and putting his arm around Soul.

Simone sighed heavily, "Soul, I'm going to walk over here and see if I can find Anthony some jeans," she said stressing Anthony's name as she looked at Soul intently.

At the mention of Anthony's name Soul quickly slid from Keys embrace. "Um' yeah that cool,"

"Well Key it's good to see you again, I think I'm going to help Simone," Danielle said, "Are you coming Soul?" she asked sensing her friend needed an escape route,

"Uh yeah I'll be there in a second." Danielle lifted her eyebrows before walking to the other end of the store where Simone was angrily going through the rack of jeans.

"I see Simone still hasn't changed," Key said with a short laugh. "I'm glad she found her a man. I was beginning to wonder if she was a dyke."

Soul wasn't sure, but for some reason she didn't bother to correct Key, to let him know that Anthony was her man, not Simone's.

"Key you know Simone is not gay. What are you doing here?" she whispered as she tried not to breathe in his intoxicating smell.

"Well, I was about to buy a shirt, but I see you have already picked one out for me," he said referring to the shirt that she still held in her hand. Again, Soul didn't bother to let him know that the shirt was for Anthony, and she feared that would come back to hunt her.

"Key," she said in an exasperated tone, "you know I don't mean here. I mean here. Back in town. Why are you back?"

"My lady," Key said as he attempted to reach for her again.

"Key don't," Soul said moving away from his grasp.

"What the fuck you mean don't, you my"

"Excuse me, is there a problem," a young very feminine salesman asked walking over.

"Boy, aint nobody"

"No sir, there's not a problem, everything is okay," Soul interrupted quickly.

"Are you sure?"

"Nigga didn't you hear the lady," Key said the tone in his voice causing several customers to turn in their direction.

"Key don't." Soul pleaded. "I'm sure sir, but thank you," she said hoping the salesman would just leave.

"If you're sure," he said before walking off with a slight switch of the hips.

"Yeah, you betta walk off old punk ass bitch," Key said in a loud voice. "Man let's get out a here so we can talk fore' I have to whup a muthafucka's ass." Key said as he began to pull her towards the door.

"Key I'm not going with you."

"What you mean you ain't going with me, oh I guess you ain't happy to see me. Baby you know I love you, and time ain't got nothing to do with me and you, we been together for twelve years."

"No Key, we've known each other for twelve years. To be with someone both people have to be in the relationship. And if I recall you were too busy out there hustling in the streets to settle down and be in a 'relationship' with me," Soul said performing air quotes as she said the word relationship.

"Soul, you know I do what I have to do to survive."

"No Key, you do what you want to do, not have to do."

"So, what the fuck you trying to say? What you got a man too, didn't I tell you this gone always be my pussy?"

"Excuse me sir," the salesman said walking back over to them, "I'm going to have to ask you to leave. You're disturbing our customers."

"Hoe, didn't I tell you to leave me the fuck alone?" Key said pushing the salesman in the chest causing him to stumble back.

"Key, you're embarrassing me, just go!" Soul pleaded.

"I ain't leaving until we talk."

"Key."

"You know I mean what I say, and I say what I mean, and what I'm saying is I'm not leaving 'til we talk."

"Key please just leave. Just call my cell and we can talk, but this is not the time."

"Oh, so it's like that? A'ight then. I'm a call you and we gone talk," Key said, "Believe that." He pushed the salesman out of the way. "Move bitch."

"I'm sorry sir," Soul said looking at Key as he made his way slowly out of the store.

"That's alright, damn negroes always got to make us look bad in front of folks," the salesman said walking back to his register.

"What did he want? I tried to mind my own business, but I almost came over here when he started getting loud," Simone said walking back over to Soul with several pairs of jeans in her hand.

"Nothing good Simone, nothing good."

Chapter 22

S oul looked at the ringing phone and sighed. Key had been calling her nonstop for the past three hours since she saw him at Murpheys.

"Why don't you just answer the phone," Danielle said as she examined the coat that Janet, her regular nail tech, had just applied.

"Why don't you just ignore his ass? You got a good man, and you don't need Key's old lost ass to come back into your life creating havoc. Should have changed your number a long time ago when it came to Key," Simone added with a pissed off look on her face.

"Look Simone, we went through this at the restaurant, and in the car! I told you I told Key to call me so he would stop creating a scene in the store. Besides I have had this number since college and I'm not changing it for no one. I love Anthony and I am not going to mess up behind Key, but he and I do have history, and I at least owe him an explanation."

"History! Okay, in those twelve years of history, how long did you and Key consecutively date? I mean during those twelve years were you ever together day to day for longer than a month. Let me answer that for you. HELL NO! Why, you ask? Cause his ass can't stay out of jail long enough to be in a relationship. Just because he was your first love, you think you owe him something. Key has never shown up for you for your important moments. He may be infatuated with the idea of a woman like you, but he has never been willing to do the work that comes with being with a woman like you. Let me tell you something, you don't owe him shit! Quit trying to be captain save a hoe. Sometimes you are the mountain that gets in your own way! To be honest, your unresolved shit between you and Key, is part of the reason you go from relationship to relationship, continually grieving for relationships that never had life from the start!"

"You know what Simone, fuck you," Soul hissed. "You always act like your shit don't stank, like you got the answer to everything. It's no wonder why you don't have a man. Who could put up with your know-it-all condescending ass? You're just mad because you'll probably be alone for the rest of your natural black life. The only time you've had a boyfriend is for the 30 minutes it took him to get the draws, and you want to give me advice about me and my man! Humph! Fuck you Simone, you can't tell me shit," Soul said blowing on her nails.

"Soul, you know what? You ain't even worth my time. Go ahead mess this up, like you do everything else," Simone said pulling money out of her purse. Simone handed the money to her nail technician as she headed for the door.

"You no dry?" the nail technician shouted to Simone.

"I no nothing," Simone said throwing a look of pure hatred at Soul. She put her shades on and strolled out of the shop.

"Soul,"

"Shut up Danielle."

"The tech who had been applying her French manicure began to speak in Chinese.

"And don't you start either," Soul said shooting her a look. The tech quickly hushed and finished doing her manicure.

***

"Hey baby."

"Hey, Soul said smiling at the sexy sound of Anthony's voice on the other end of the phone.

"What's the matter Boo?"

"Nothing."

"Come on now. You think I don't know when you're upset. I can hear it all in your voice."

"Really, it's nothing. So, how's the birthday boy?" Soul asked attempting to change the subject.

"He'll be better once his lady tells the truth."

"Baby, really let's not spoil your birthday mood."

"Soul."

"Look it's really nothing." Soul knew she should tell him about seeing Key, but instead chose not to. "Simone and I had a fight over something stupid. See that's it."

"Are you sure that's it?"

"Yes, I promise."

"Well, I'm sorry. I know how close the awesome threesome is. I'm sure you guys will work it out."

She was glad Anthony didn't press for more information. Soul hadn't lied to him, and she really didn't want to start.

"Well, I've got something to cheer you up. We're going out tonight."

"But Baby," Soul protested. "You know I have birthday plans for you."

"Oh, you do! Do they include hand cuffs?"

"If you act right."

"Umph, well in that case, I'm on my way right now."

"Anthony!"

"OK, OK, Let's compromise. We'll do mine today and yours tomorrow."

"No honey, we're not compromising. I have your birthday all planned."

"Hey! I am the birthday boy. Remember?"

Soul sighed; this day was not going anything like she planned.

"I thought we could go back to True Visions," they both said simultaneously.

"I guess great minds think alike. What made you want to go there?" Anthony asked with a laugh.

"Let's just say I found some motivation."

"Don't tell me you are going to grace the stage?"

"Quit asking so many questions. Just know I am going to let my man know how much I love him, in every imaginable way."

"That's what I'm talking about. Girl you sure you don't want me to come over there now for a quickie?"

"No Anthony. I do not," Soul said laughing. "I don't do quickies, and after last night, I know you don't either."

"Yeah, I like to take my time."

"Bye Anthony."

"Make it slow."

"Bye Anthony," Soul giggled.

"And hard,"

"I'm hanging up Anthony. Love you." Soul added before hanging up the phone. As soon as she hung her home phone up, her cell began to ring. Soul laughed to herself. That boy never quit. "I'm hanging up," she answered not bothering to look at the caller ID.

"What the hell you mean you hanging up. You just got on the phone. Why the hell haven't you been answering my calls?" Key said in the phone angrily.

God why didn't she look at the caller ID? Soul sighed and began rubbing her temple. "Key, I can't talk right now. I'm busy."

"Well, when are you going to make some time for me?" Key asked trying a gentler approach. "I got something for you."

"Key," she sighed. "I really can't talk right now." Tell him Soul. "I promise I'll call you tomorrow." Tell him Soul. "I just got a lot going on."

"Alright baby," Key finally sighed. "I'm a let you go, but you better call me tomorrow, or I'm a find out where you live and show up over there."

"Key, I'll call you," Soul said as her stomach began bubbling with nervousness.

"Hey, I love you."

"Bye Key."

"Did you hear what I said? I love you."

"I heard you Key," Soul said hanging up the phone. Soul knew she should have just told Key about Anthony and to stop calling her, and she also knew she should have told Anthony she ran into an ex. Well, not just an ex, but *the* ex. Soul convinced herself that if she explained things to Key in person, he would take it better than arguing with him over a phone call because Key wasn't just any old flame, he was the one Soul lost her virginity too, the one that in between the Dannys' and all others would run in an out of Soul's life creating havoc and mental chaos. Tonight would be all about Anthony and tomorrow she would deal with handling her past once and for all before it came back to bite her.

Chapter 23

S oul dusted her face and chest with bronzing power as she waited on Anthony's arrival. Vowing to put Key, Simone, and everything else out of her mind, her entire focus tonight would be making sure this was the best birthday Anthony had ever had. Putting the finishing touches on her make-up, Soul stepped back to examine herself in the full-length mirror. The red mini dress was the perfect choice for the night hugging her thick hips while the deep V cut dropped just above her waist barely covering her full breasts. The camel brown stiletto heels brought her long legs to life and the matching camel brown leather blazer brought the full outfit together. Soul pulled her hair into a high bun to show off her huge golden hoop earrings and added several gold chains including her small gold necklace with her name in cursive writing. The deep smokey eye and red lip she sported gave Soul the perfect sexy sultriness that she had hoped to achieve with tonight's chosen look. Soul placed Anthony's gifts into a gift bag just as the doorbell rang.

Grabbing her gold bracelets off the dresser, Soul slid them on before throwing her makeup into a small carryall which she placed into a red oversized clutch. Grabbing the gift bag off the bed, Soul headed down the stairs. "Coming," she shouted as Anthony once again rang the doorbell. Soul opened the door just as Anthony prepared to ring the doorbell again. "I said I was coming," Soul said smiling.

"Looking like that, you're about to."

"I take it you like?" Soul said spinning in a circle.

"Damn," Anthony pulled Soul into his arms and begin nibbling her neck.

"Don't even try it," Soul said, pulling away from his kiss. "We'll never leave here if you start that, and you know it."

"That's fine with me. I mean it is my birthday, and the best sex is birthday sex."

"But you look too sexy to stay in," Soul commented on Anthony's tasteful choice in clothing for the night, a pair of khaki pants, with a long sleeve navy and white pinstriped dress shirt, and a navy and red argyle vest. "Besides I can't give you my best surprise here."

"You want to bet," Anthony replied reaching for Soul, but she quickly avoided his reach and walked over to his gift bag instead.

"There will be plenty of time for that gift later," she promised. But I have another gift for you. Soul reached into the bag and pulled out two large boxes. "Here baby," I hope you like them. Happy Birthday," she said walking over and kissing Anthony on the cheek.

Anthony tore into the gifts like a child at Christmas, first opening the jeans then the shirt that Soul, Simone and Danielle had chosen earlier. "This is dope," he said with a smile as he held up the shirt to his chest.

"Do you really like it? I kept the receipt just in case."

"I love them baby, just like I love you," Anthony said giving Soul a kiss.

"Good, now you are just going to have to wait until later for the rest. Let's go," Soul said grabbing the bag and heading to the door.

"You just going to walk out of here with my gifts?"

"Yes. Now let's go."

They arrived at True Visions and Anthony pulled into the valet area. He opened the door and walked around to grab Soul's hand. It was still early so they had no problem finding a seat near the front of the stage.

"Here you go," the waitress said handing them their menus. "Can I get you something to drink to get you started?"

Soul ordered an Amaretto Sour and Anthony ordered a Crown and Coke

"I'll be right back with those drink orders," the waitress said walking off.

"I'll be right back baby," Soul said excusing herself from the table.

"Everything okay?"

"Yes, baby. I'll be right back." Soul said blowing him a kiss. She grabbed the bag that held Anthony's gifts. "Just in case you try to get a sneak peak." "Here goes nothing," Soul thought to herself, and she sought out the host of open mike and added her name to the list. Soul hoped Anthony would appreciate the poem that she had written him. She had never written a poem for a man, but Anthony wasn't just any man, and the best way she could express herself was with words. Never in a million years would Soul have imagined herself getting on a stage and sharing her most intimate thoughts, but Anthony was worth it. Soul found their waitress. "Excuse me ma'am," she said reaching into the gift bag and pulling out a small gift. "When we finish our meals, can you bring this to my date around ten or so."

"Ah how sweet. Sure, no problem," the waitress smiled.

"And can you say something like because your lady will always have your back or something like that?"

"Sure, no problem."

"Thanks." Soul would have to make sure to leave her a big tip. She walked back to the table and sat down. "For every hour up until 12 AM tonight, you will receive a gift from me, so since it is about to turn 9, here is your next gift, she said handing him a white envelope with kiss prints on it. Anthony opened the envelope, and a huge grin spread on his face. "Anthony Hamilton tickets. That's what I'm talking about baby." He said kissing her hands. You are too good to me."

"Nothing is too good for my man."

"Here you go," the waitress interrupted sitting their drinks on the table "You folks about ready to order?" she said winking at Soul.

Anthony and Soul placed their orders, then sat back to enjoy the jazz band as they made small talk about the day's events. The waitress returned shortly with their food orders as they promptly dug into the delicious food. Soul noticed the clock was approaching ten and hoped the waitress would return shortly to collect their plates.

"Did you folks enjoy the meal?" the waitress said returning to collect their plates.

"It was great as usual," Anthony said sitting back in his chair.

"You guys want a refill?"

"Sure," Anthony said.

"I'll be right back," she said. She turned around and stood behind Soul. "Now?" she silently mouthed making eye contact with Soul.

Soul nodded her head slightly so that Anthony wouldn't notice.

The waitress left to replace their drink orders and when she returned Soul could see her carrying the gift under her arm carefully. "Here you go," she said sitting the drinks on the table. "Oh, I forgot something," she said winking again at Soul. "Here you go Sir, a little something extra on the house. I hope you realize that you have a woman who will always have your back," she said placing the gift in front of Anthony.

Anthony looked at Soul with a puzzled expression on his face.

"Go ahead."

Anthony slowly opened the gift to reveal the picture that Soul had chosen. When she first saw the black and white picture entitled, *I got your Back*, she knew she had to get it for Anthony. To Soul, the picture seemed to say I've got your back through all of life's pushups as the man held the woman on his back while he did a push up, and she massaged his temples. She liked the picture so much that she even purchased one for herself but had yet to hang it up since she hadn't given Anthony his framed copy.

Anthony looked up at her with tears in the corners of his eyes. "Soul, do you know how much I love you right now at this very moment?"

"I hope as much as I do you."

"You know I'll always have your back too? No matter what."

"I know baby," she smiled faintly. Soul considered telling him about Key, but the moment was too perfect to ruin it with talk of an ex-boyfriend.

"You really didn't have to do all this."

"Yes, I did. I wanted to and it isn't over. I still have two more gifts for you."

"Baby, you didn't have too."

"I promise you are going to like this next gift."

At that moment the MC walked to stage thanking them all for coming out to True Visions. Soul began to feel the nerves bubble in her stomach, but it was too late. The MC called several poets and singers to the mic before he finally asked the crowd if they were ready for some new talent. When everyone agreed, he announced "Coming to the stage we have a virgin to the mic. I want you to be really kind to her since it's her first time. Everyone give it up for Soul Jackson."

Anthony turned to her with a surprised look on his face, "So you really getting on the stage tonight?"

Soul took a deep breath, and kissed Anthony's hand. "Thank you for being my motivation. Happy Birthday." She made her way slowly to the stage. Soul squinted adjusting her eyes to the light on the stage before her gaze found the man who inspired her to do something so completely out of her norm.

"Good evening. This poem is for a special man that I love with all my heart. Tonight, is his birthday and I want him to know that when I met him my soul was freed. So, I call this poem *Soul's Emancipation.* I love you Anthony," Soul said blowing a kiss in his direction.

"I love you more," Anthony mouthed as "Ah," could be heard from several people in the crowd. Soul took a deep breathe and closed her eyes.

Never been A robber or a thief
But from that first drink
I stole the pleasure to meet
Your essence
Your style
Your intelligence
Your smile
In my world and in my mind, there wasn't room for another friend
But months later as I reflect, I realize what a Godsend
You've been to me
And to the healing of my soul
Too many losses to count
Too much pain to unfold
It's not an exaggeration
Calling my man a Godsend
And I'm not just saying that because
You tend
To show off your bartending skills
But because you don't tend
To pretend
To be what you are not
But simply to be what you are
Never getting caught up in man's image of a superstar
If every man were created out of Anthony mold
Truth untold
It would still be hard for them to uphold
The standards
I behold
Upon you and place upon your threshold
No wonder your ex was tripping
And old girl couldn't leave you alone
Cause sometimes your you-ness
and the smell of your cologne
Causes me to wonder what I'm thankful I can condone

Was afraid of losing you

When you became my lover

But damn "You got me straight tripping boo"

And the way you look tonight

Is causing a sista to stutter

Intriguing me to wonder what will happen

When we meet up under the covers

This ain't Brown Sugar

Besides my name ain't Sid

But what we share is unique

And to define it would be an injustice

Cause you are a perfect lyric over a tight beat

Like a warm summer day, you're like a shirt with no sleeves

So, I'm ending this poem saying Happy Birthday Boo

I hope you understand how this love is serious

Cause I need for you

To understand

What a beautiful man

You are to me

I need you to see

How much you've touched my inner energy

You have invaded my heart

Invaded my home

Invaded my thoughts

Hell, invaded this poem

Entered my life

Ignited my life

Excited my life

Blessed my life

Damn

It's Like that

Soul's Emancipation

Damn

It's Like that

My soul's proclamation

Soul looked at Anthony as he made his way to the stage and pulled her into his arms. "What are you trying to do to me?" Anthony whispered into Soul's ear as the crowd wolf whistled and clapped.

"Love you man. Just love you," Soul replied kissing him.

"I don't know how you can top the way you just made me feel right now."

"I do baby, I got one more gift for you. And even though you have had it before, the way Ima give it to you tonight, this will definitely be the gift that keeps giving.

Chapter 24

♥

S oul lay in her bed and snuggled under the covers. She smiled thinking about how beautiful the past month had been. Since Anthony's birthday they were inseparable. When they finally made it home from True Visions on Anthony's birthday, they made love all night long, and the next day, only getting out of bed so she could cook him a mid day breakfast. They finally turned their phones on around 7 so they could return all the calls from their friends and family. Soul sighed as she thought of the numerous calls from Key that awaited her on her voice messages, and she noticed that with each call he got angrier and angrier. In his final call he said that he was leaving town to handle some business and would get back with her when he returned. Soul prayed that Key was gone on another of his long stints and so far, it seemed her prayers had been answered. She hadn't received any calls from Key, and although something inside of Soul told her she still needed to tell Anthony about Key, she hadn't been able to broach the subject yet.

Soul honestly didn't understand it. She and Anthony talked about everything. She knew of all his past relationship fiascos, and he knew hers including details of her relationship with Key, but for some reason Soul couldn't bring herself to tell Anthony that Key, the subject of said relationship was back in town. In her mind, Soul had convinced herself it was no big deal, but in her heart, Soul knew that if the shoe were on the other foot, she would be pissed. And now with Anthony gone out of town on business, Soul figured it would just have to wait. Closing her eyes, Soul vowed to tell Anthony the truth when he returned which fortunately and unfortunately for her was today. Soul glanced at the clock. She had several hours before Anthony's flight was scheduled to come in. She picked up the phone and dialed Danielle's number. When she didn't answer, Soul dialed Simone's number. Simone didn't answer either, which was strange for her since she made it a practice to stay at home as often as possible on her off days. Soul was glad things were back to normal with she and Simone. It was crazy how they could fight like cats and dogs, and then be back friends in the next instance. Soul figured it would be like that for the rest of their lives since the same process had been going on since the beginning of time. Laying back in the bed, Soul continued thinking about Anthony. Things were going great between them. They couldn't be any closer than they were, and when she was away from him, her heart literally ached with the pain of not being near him, even if it was just for a short moment of time. When he knocked on her door, her heart would beat a mile a minute with the anticipation of seeing him, and she still got butterflies in her stomach at the sound of his voice. Soul had never felt a love like this, and she thanked God for him every chance she got.

***

Soul woke up to the sound of her ringing phone. Looking at the clock, Soul adjusted her eyes to see who was calling. Anthony. Soul quickly grabbed the phone as a smile spread across her face. "Hey."

"Hey yourself sleepy head." Anthony said referring to Soul's groggy voice. "I didn't mean to wake you."

"Oh baby, that's okay. I was just lying in the bed, and I must have dosed off. How was the conference?"

"It was good, but I miss you. I haven't been able to stop thinking about you, and you know I couldn't sleep right not having you in my arms."

"I miss you too. Is your flight still leaving at one?"

"Yeah, and it is scheduled to arrive at four thirty. Hey, I promised the guys we would come hang with them for a few hours. I hope that's okay. They have booked this cruise liner on the lake, and they invited us to take a ride. There's going to be drinks, food, you name it."

"Well, honestly baby, I was looking forward to spending some alone time with you."

"I know babe, and I promise you we will. But you know how our friends are when they think we've been neglecting them."

"I guess," Soul sighed. But after that, we are coming straight to this house."

"I plan on it, trust me."

"What should I wear?"

"Thaddeus said it was a relaxed affair, so I am sure you will be fine with whatever you put on. I'm going to get dressed here, so we can drive straight to the boat."

"I was hoping to get a quickie before we left."

"You don't do quickies, remember," Anthony laughed.

"I can make an exception. It has been three whole days since I saw my man."

"I promise you babe, I'll make up for it. Besides, the boat leaves dock at seven, and it will probably take us thirty to forty-five minutes to make the drive from the airport."

"Once again you are right," Soul sighed. Well, I guess I will begin my regular Saturday affair, cleaning up, and then I'll start getting dressed. Can you at least tell me what you're wearing?

"I'm just going to throw on some slacks and a dress shirt."

"Oh. Now see I'm glad I asked. I don't want you to be the only one dressed up and I'm in these streets looking like a bum. I guess I can dig through this closet and find a dress or something."

"Whatever you wear will be fine and you never look like a bum. No other lady can compete with you anyway."

"Flattery will get you everywhere mister. I love you, and I'll see you soon," Soul said before hanging up. Climbing out of the bed, she walked downstairs and turned the radio on, pumping the volume up as she began to clean her apartment. An hour later, Soul sat in a chair in her closet trying to figure out what to wear. She wanted to keep it causal and cool since she really wasn't sure what the dress code was. She finally settled on a simple wrap dress and a pair of open toed sandals. Soul decided on a bath instead of her normal shower so the steam wouldn't damage her freshly done silk press. Her stylist complained the entire time, warning her about the damage that microbraids could do to her hair. Soul listed quietly as she waited patiently for him to finish. She was used to his fits since they went through them every time she put braids in her hair.

"I don't know why you put those braids in your hair anyway. It is gorgeous just like this," he remarked as he flat ironed her brown and blond streaked hair.

"I told you; wigs and weave are easier for me to deal with because of my schedule," Soul sighed.

"Well, why are you here today? You know you're just going to put some weave in later."

"Maybe but my baby likes my hair, and since he's coming back in town, I thought I would do something special for him."

Soul was glad that she had asked her stylist to wrap her hair back up when he finished despite his protests because now all she had to do was put her shower cap over it, then unwrap it later when it was time to leave. Soul thanked the hair God's that today wasn't the normal humid Texas day that would normally cause her hair to swell back into its natural state. Soul looked in her mirror. The coral dress went well with her streaked hair, and she knew once Anthony saw her, he would not want to stay at the party long.

***

By the time Soul arrived at the airport and found a parking spot it was four fifteen. Soul found the arrival gate for Anthony's flight and entered the waiting area. She couldn't wait to see Anthony. Although he had only been away for three days at a young entrepreneur's conference, Soul felt like it had been an eternity. Her stomach felt like it was in knots, as she paced back and forth trying to release some of the nervous energy. Soul couldn't understand why she felt so anxious, but she knew she couldn't wait until her man stepped off that plan.

***

Anthony's heart was beating so loud he was sure everyone on the plane could hear it. The two women sitting across from him smiled at him in an appreciative manner, and the older black gentleman sitting next to him patted him on the leg to calm his tapping foot.

"Don't worry sonny, I remember how it is to be in your shoes," the elderly man said with a smile.

Anthony could only smile as he imagined the look on Soul's face when he stepped off the plane. God, how he loved this woman. Even though they had technically been together less than six months Anthony felt like he had waited a lifetime to meet Soul. She completed his puzzle like no other piece ever could. His hand shook out of sheer nervousness and no matter how hard he tried he couldn't calm his emotions. The elderly gentleman once again looked at Anthony's shaking hands and chuckled.

"Okay, our flight will be landing in the next five minutes. Please buckle up and thank you again for flying American Airlines," the voice announced over the intercom.

"This is it," Anthony thought to himself. "Now or never. Thanks again he said nervously turning to the eleven people sitting around him. My mama told me I could always count on the kindness of a stranger, and I see she was right. Do any of you need to see the picture again?"

"You've showed it to us five times," one of the women sitting across from him remarked. "Don't worry, she will love this."

Anthony said a quick prayer to God and thanked him for bringing Soul into his life just as the intercom announced their arrival. He took a deep breathe and prayed his legs would hold him up. He waited until all the other passengers departed the plane, including the eleven strangers who were critical to his plan. He took a deep breathe and begin to walk slowly down the flight tunnel.

***

Soul couldn't contain her excitement as Anthony's flight finally arrived. She, along with the other waiting guests, walked over to the entryway where their friends and loved ones would soon enter. Slowly each passenger straggled from around the corner. They all seemed to be in a great mood for such a long flight, and many of them seemed to stare at her as if they knew her. "Damn," she thought to herself, "I really must be looking good." It was just like Anthony to be one of the last few passengers. Soul hoped Anthony didn't miss his flight. Just when it seemed there were no more passengers, several men and women came around the corner each bearing a red rose. "Ah," Soul thought, "maybe Anthony got me one too."

"Excuse me," the first gentleman said walking over to her, "I believe this is for you."

"I'm sorry, there must be some mistake," Soul stammered.

"Are you Soul Jackson?"

"Yes," Soul replied shocked that he knew her name.

"Then there's no mistake."

Each of the other people who walked off the flight carrying a rose walked over to her and handed her each of their beautiful red roses until Soul had eleven of the most beautiful roses she had ever laid her eyes on. It seemed as if all eyes were on her. No one was rushing to collect their baggage; everyone was simply standing around watching her every move. Suddenly out of the corner of her eye, Soul spied Anthony walking towards her carrying one single rose. A huge smile spread across her face, and she ran over to hug him.

"Here baby," he said handing her his rose. I hope I will always complete you just as you have completed me.

Anthony gently pushed her away from him and looked at her with so much love that Soul thought she would burst.

"Soul," Anthony said dropping to one knee.

Oh God, he can't be. Yes! Yes! Yes! "Anthony baby," Soul said covering her mouth to hold the sob that threatened to escape.

"Shh," he said, "let me talk. I know it seems like it was just yesterday that you stepped into my life, but to me it seems like an eternity that I have waited on someone like you to enter it. You fulfill my every need, and I want to spend the rest of my life trying to fulfill yours. When a man knows, he knows, and there is no time limit on what he knows. You have become my weakness, now let me become your strength. Soul," Anthony said reaching into his pocket and pulling out a velvet box, "will you marry me?"

"Yes baby of course," Soul said crying as tears flowed from her eyes.

Anthony slipped the most beautiful diamond Soul had ever laid her eyes on, on her finger. He grabbed her and pulled her into a kiss as the airport patrons clapped loudly. Soul couldn't believe what had just happened, but she knew she was the happiest woman on the planet. Many people walked over to congratulate them as they finally began to make their way to the baggage claims area. It was as if the entire airport had heard about Anthony's proposal as several people continued to stop them even as they attempted to make their way to Soul's car.

"I thought we would never make it out of there," Anthony replied with a huge smile as he placed his luggage into the trunk. As he closed the trunk, Soul walked over to him and kissed him like there was no tomorrow.

"I love you so much, and I promise you I am going to be the best wife you could ever imagine."

"I know you are baby," Anthony said kissing her again before he started to laugh.

"What's so funny?" Soul said handing him the keys.

"I was just thinking about how nervous I was walking off that plane. It took all my will power just to make it over to you," he laughed as he opened the passenger door for Soul to get in. "I thought my legs would give out before I even made it to you."

"You? I was nervous, and I didn't even know what was going on. But I thought it was just because I was nervous and anxious to see my man. Oh my God!" she said as if suddenly remembering something.

"What is it baby?" Anthony asked as he expertly maneuvered her truck onto the freeway.

"I've got to call Simone and Danielle, and Granny and your mom and"

"Slow down, baby," he laughed. I promise you can tell Simone and Danielle later, but right now I want you to just focus on us."

"But what about your parents, and your grandmother and my grandmother?" Soul protested.

"Who do you think helped me pick out the ring? And I had to ask your grandparents for your hand in marriage before I left."

"Anthony, you mean to tell me you planned on proposing to me even before you left?"

"Baby, I've wanted to propose to you the moment you stepped on that stage and read me that poem for my birthday."

"Ah," Soul said tearing up as she placed her hand on his cheek. "God my makeup is going to be awful by the time we make it to the ship."

"You'll still be the prettiest woman there," Anthony said wiping her tears. "Baby, I promise that I will be there to wipe every tear that falls from your eye from this point forward. I will never let anything, or anyone come between us. You are my partner, and soul mate, and I will do everything in my power to make you happy."

Soul could not stop the tears that flowed from her eyes. She was glad she had brought her make-up, because it was going to need some retouching.

***

Soul adjusted her make-up as best as she could as Anthony pulled into a parking space near the front of the ship's deck.

"I can't believe we got lucky enough to find a space this close," she commented as she reapplied her lipstick.

"Me either. Come on, we better hurry before the ship pulls out."

Soul took one final glance in the car mirror before stepping out of the truck. Anthony led her up the ship's deck where the host waited to greet them. "You must be Anthony and Soul? We've been waiting on you. You're our final guest," the host said with a smile.

"I guess we're right on time," Soul said smiling. "We'd better hurry up before the ship pulls off."

"Don't worry ma'am. I promise we won't set off without you. Please follow me."

"I don't see anyone, where are all the guests?" Soul asked turning to Anthony.

"Oh, most of the guests are below deck and some are at the back near the jazz band," the host replied. "Please follow me," he said leading Soul and Anthony below deck.

Soul noticed the glimmer from her ring as the reflection of the setting sun hit it. She couldn't wait to call Danielle and Simone and share her happy news. Maybe later she could sneak away and give them a quick call. They were going to be so shocked.

"Here we are," the hostess said opening the door to elegant banquet room below deck.

"Congratulations!"

Soul was greeted to the shouts of the people waiting as she and Anthony entered the room. Slowly she spanned the room as tears quickly filled her eyes. All of she and Anthony's friends and family greeted them with hugs and smiles. Soul was so shocked, she couldn't move.

"How?" she stammered turning to Anthony.

"Didn't I tell you I was going to make it my business to make you happy for the rest of your life?"

"I love you so much," Soul cried as she kissed Anthony.

"Hey, get a room, you freaks!"

Soul turned to see Danielle and Simone standing beside them with huge smiles on their faces.

"Guess what!" Soul said twinkling her fingers at them.

"Girl you are late. Who do you think helped your baby here plan this here shindig?" Simone added.

"You two hookers knew about this and didn't say anything?"

"Hey, a girl, got to do, what a girls got to do," Danielle said hugging her tightly.

"Congrats cuz," Simone said joining in the hug. "After all you have been through, you deserve someone like Anthony who loves you like you deserve to be loved," Simone said seeing the tears brimming in Soul's eyes. The three friends stood in a three-way hug crying until Anthony stepped in.

"Alright ghetto girls. Ya'll truly look GHETTO standing in the middle of the room crying. "Come here," he said taking Simone and wiping her tears then giving her a kiss on the cheek. "Now you," he said pulling Danielle to him, and wiping her tears, then giving her a kiss on the cheek.

"Hey, what about me?"

"Baby, I saved the best for last. Remember every tear," he said. "Every single tear."

"I love you Anthony," Soul said giving him another kiss.

"I love you too," he whispered in her ear before he was swamped by congratulatory hugs and handshakes from all his friends.

Chapter 25

"**B**aby, are you going to do this every morning?" Anthony asked yawning.

"Do what," Soul said innocently.

"You know," Anthony playfully tickled Soul's side.

Every morning for the past month, Anthony had spent the night at Soul's place, and she knew he was referring to the fact that as soon as she woke up, she would reach over to her nightstand where she kept a silk cloth and jewelry cleaner. Every morning when Anthony woke up, he would find her sitting up in bed cleaning her engagement ring.

"Do what," Soul asked again sitting the jewelry cleaner and cloth back on the nightstand before sliding back under the covers and snuggling into Anthony's chest. "Give me a kiss man."

"No woman! You've got morning breath," Anthony said snarling up his nose.

"As do you. Now give me a kiss."

"Uh, Uh," Anthony said shaking his head and tucking his lips in.

"Okay. Fine," Soul turned her back to Anthony, pretending to go back to sleep.

"Come here babe. I was just playing."

Soul turned over and pretended to snore loudly.

"Since you're sleep, I guess I can have my way with you," Anthony said kissing Soul on her back and neck.

Soul immediately melted with the desire to make love with Anthony as she pressed against him in a spoon position. There was something about his touch that felt so comforting, so safe, so loving.

Anthony slid his hand under Soul's T-shirt and began to caress her nipples, tugging and pulling on them causing Soul to moan.

"Come here," Anthony whispered in Soul's ear causing the hairs on her neck to stand as Anthony turned her towards him, before sliding his tongue in her mouth. Reaching inside the nightstand to get a condom to put on, Anthony rolled on top of Soul, sliding inside of her as she wrapped her legs around him to feel the full impact of his lovemaking.

"Who's is this?"

"Yo Yo Yours baby."

"Whose?" Anthony asked going even deeper inside Soul pulling her legs around his neck.

"Yours baby. Damn this feels good."

Anthony bit his lip while he looked at Soul while he continued to thrust roughly inside of her.

"Anthony!" Soul moaned as her legs begin to shake.

"Come for daddy."

"Anthonyyyyy, oh shit baby I'm about to come," Soul breathed heavily.

Anthony continued to pump even harder, knowing he and Soul were both near their desired goal.

"Oh Shit," Anthony moaned as he came before collapsing onto Soul's chest trying to catch his breath.

Soul rubbed his back. "You okay." She asked as Anthony lifted to give her a kiss.

"Yes indeed." Anthony gently pulled himself out of Soul, before he carefully rolled the condom off. "Damn, this shit is good," he said reaching for the silk cloth she used to polish her ring.

"Wait!" Soul jumped up and ran to the bathroom, quickly returning with a warm towel to find an amused Anthony smirking at her.

"You are too much."

"I know, Soul said bending down to give him another kiss. She sat down and began to clean the product of their morning love off him.

"I love you," Anthony said leaning back and closing his eyes.

"I love you more."

"You know if you ever give my stuff away, I'm a have to kill you."

"Yeah, and you know that if you give my stuff away, it *will* be a double homicide," Soul joked sticking her tongue out at Anthony.

"I'm serious," Anthony opened one eye to look at Soul.

"Me too," Soul said winking at him.

***

Anthony and Soul walked into the clothing store. They were just supposed to be going to the mall to exchange the shirt that she had purchased for him while he was at his conference. But of course, she had dragged him into two shoe stores and now into one of her favorite stores.

"Baby, I promise you this will only take about 15 minutes."

"Yeah right."

"No, I promise. I promise. I just want to see if they have this dress on sale that I've been eyeing. Please!"

"Soul, you have fifteen minutes, and then I am going next door to Champs."

"Okay, I promise," Soul smiled giving Anthony a quick kiss on the cheek.

She dragged Anthony into the store and quickly began browsing the sales rack where she spotted the dress she had been eyeing and continued to browse through the racks where she found two pair of jeans and three shirts.

"Thirteen minutes," Anthony warned.

"Okay, Okay, I'm going to go try these on, but just so you know, I'm just trying to look good for you."

"Umph."

Soul walked into the dressing room as Anthony walked to the front of the store. She slipped into the blue jean spaghetti strapped dress that had a baby doll cut. "This is so cute. It is going to be perfect with my brown wedge sandals," she thought.

"How does this look baby?" Soul said coming out of the dressing room and spinning around.

"It looks good than a muthafucka," the sound of Key's voice stopped her in mid spin.

"Key."

"Oh, so you remember me now. The way you've been dodging my calls, I thought you forgot who the fuck I was. Maybe you forgot my name cause of that nigga I saw you walk in with."

"Anthony," Soul said covering her mouth. She quickly scanned the store for Anthony. He was standing outside of the store talking to a short stocky bald man wearing a T-shirt with Anthony's fraternity letters emblazed across the front.

"Or maybe this is why," Key said taking her hand to examine her engagement ring.

"Key, I,"

"You what Soul? You forgot to tell me you were engaged? You forgot to tell me you didn't want to be with me anymore? I told you time doesn't mean anything with me. You"

"Hey baby, what's taking so long," Anthony said as he approached. He noticed Key holding Soul's hand and stopped dead in his tracks.

"Hey baby," Soul said walking over to stand by Anthony before she grabbed his hand. Please God, don't let Key make a scene. Please, Soul silently prayed.

Anthony slid his arm around her waist never taking his eyes off Key.

Key didn't break his stare.

"I came out to show you this dress and you were gone. Key was standing here. Then he started admiring my engagement ring." The words rushed out so fast, Soul could hardly breathe.

"Oh yeah. What's up man? I'm Anthony, Soul's fiancé," Anthony stated, his eyes never leaving Keys.

"Fiancé huh?"

"So, you live around here?" Anthony tightened the hold onto Soul's waist.

"Nah, I'm a man of the streets. I just came back in town to check on some unfinished business, but it seems like it's already been taken care of," Key replied as he looked Anthony up and down in that way black men do when they feel they have something to prove.

"Yeah, well when you gone too long things have a way of taking care of themselves," Anthony said giving Soul a kiss on the cheek, his eyes still never leaving Key.

It seemed like time just stopped. Key and Anthony locked eyes until Key's phone began to ring. MO3's voice broke the silence reminding them all that everybody aint your friend.

Key glanced at the caller ID display and clicked a button. "Say man, I told you I needed to see you and your boy ASAP. Both of ya'll better have yo young ass in this mall right now." Key turned his attention back to Anthony and Soul. "I got some business to take care of, so I'm a holla at you Soul. You know it's always good to see you," he said taking Soul's free hand and kissing it. "My man, take care of her, cause if you don't, I'm sure there's always a nigga willing to do it for you." Key put his phone to his ear and walked off.

"What the fuck was that about?" Anthony hissed into her ear.

Soul sighed as she turned to Anthony to explain what she should have said the first time she knew Key was back in town. Soul recalled she and Key's chance encounter on Anthony's birthday and explained that she just needed to explain things to Key so he would understand things were over between them.

"Do you still have feelings for him?"

"I'll always care about Key, but that's it. I care about his well being. You're the man I'm in love with, not Key. As you know, Key and I went through a lot of things, and for twelve years he was something comfortable. I know that sounds strange, but he was kind of like my fallback man. When I worried that maybe I was destined to be alone, there was always our old reliable, yet unreliable relationship," Soul said putting her hands in mock quotes when she said relationship, "that I had with Key. Even though I knew he wasn't the best God could offer me, I didn't want to be alone. So, I would let him run in and out of my life in between all my other boyfriends. In fact, it had been over two years since I had even seen Key, more less talked to him, and then he just shows up again. But then I met you, and I never gave Key a second thought. I knew God had sent me the best he had to offer. I'm so sorry baby, I know I should have told you he was back in town, and I really should have explained to you the dynamics between he and I, but never found the appropriate time. I promise you babe, you are the love of my life, and Key nor any other man can take me from you," Soul said standing on her tip toes to give him a kiss.

Anthony hugged her, "Well, you better make sure he knows it, cause If I see him looking at you like that again, one of us might end up six feet under, and that's my word.

Chapter 26

"Ms. Jackson, you have a special delivery," the school secretary said entering Soul's class with a beautiful bouquet of flowers.

"Are those for me?" Soul asked as a huge smile covered her face.

"Yes ma'am. Somebody really loves you!"

"He better, if he plans on marrying me," Soul joked taking the flowers and placing them on her desk. "Thank you, Johnita."

"Oh no problem, I figured they would help you make it through the day," the school secretary said closing the door behind her.

"Go Ms. J. Go Ms. J.," Alicia, one of Soul's favorite students poked fun at her.

Soul slid open the envelope and read the card which simply stated, *Soul, forever my lady.* Soul began laughing as the thought of the hit song by the R&B group Jodeci crossed her mind. Anthony was too much. How did she ever get so lucky?

"Ah look at the smile on her face," Alejandro joked. "I guess that means no homework right Miss?"

"Actually, I wasn't planning on giving you homework, but since you insist on being such a smart mouth, maybe I should give you enough homework to keep you busy for the next couple of days," Soul replied with the most serious expression she could muster as she tried to conceal her giggles from the horrified expressions on her student's faces.

"Ah, Ms. J, he was just playing," Alicia interjected.

"And I was too! Gotcha! Now make sure you stay out of grown folk's business," Soul teased as the lunch bell rang. "All right, you guys can go. Your homework assignment is to simply think of what you plan on doing your research paper on. Make sure it is some type of current event, and that it's a hot topic. No need to write anything down, just think. That's all. See you all Monday and have a good weekend and stay out of trouble."

As soon as the students left the room, Soul clicked on her cell phone and dialed Anthony's cell number. His voice mail picked up, and Soul decided not to leave him a message, but try him back later. He was probably in a meeting as usual. Since he had decided to go ahead and venture into his own real estate business, he had been incredibly busy especially since he still had to service his current clients.

Soul gathered her lunch and purse preparing to go meet her lunch crew for her daily dose of laughter.

"Hey," Key's gravely voice caused her to drop her purse. "Dang girl, when did you become so clumsy?" he laughed easily.

"Key, I, what are you doing here?"

"Are you going to stare at me or pick your stuff off of the floor?" Key asked bending down to collect Soul's belongings from the floor.

Soul quickly bent down to collect the remainder of her belongings from the floor as Key handed her the things he had in his hand. "I see you still carrying all that lipstick?" Key said laughing.

"Key, you didn't answer my question. What are you doing here?"

"I had some business to take care of and I was in the neighborhood, so I thought I would check in and see if you got the flowers I sent, but I can see you did," Key gestured towards the flowers that sat on Soul's desk.

"You sent those?"

"Forever my lady," Key said pulling her close to him.

"Stop it Key." Soul angrily pulled away from him. "I'm engaged, and you know it."

"Well, why can't you look me in the eyes and say it?"

"Key, this is ridiculous!"

"Okay, then look me in my eyes, and tell me you don't love me?"

"Key,"

"You can't."

"Key, I love Anthony,"

"Say it, Soul. Tell me you don't love me," Key said pulling her towards him as his lips gently brushed hers.

"Ms. Jackson, I forgot my notebook," Alejandro said yanking the door open as he and Shakeem entered the room. They stopped short when they saw Key standing there. "Uh, my bad Miss, we didn't know you had company," Alejandro glanced at Shakeem with a confused expression on his face.

"No, it's not a problem," Soul said walking quickly over to the boys. "Come on in."

"Key, this is Alejandro and Shakeem, two of my best students. Boys, this is my old friend Key,"

"What's up ya'll? Best students huh? Well, it's nice to meet you," Key said extending his hand to Alejandro, who shook it nervously as he looked down not making eye contact with Key.

"Boy, didn't you learn to always look a man in the face when you shake his hand? Makes him know you can hold your own?"

"Key, leave them alone. Here you go Alejandro," Soul said walking over to pick up the notebook Alejandro had left on his desk. "You boys have a good weekend. What's your homework assignment?" Soul asked placing her hands on Shakeem's shoulder.

"We know Ms. Jackson, research paper, research paper," Shakeem sighed.

"Ah, I'm sure they'll get their assignment done. Wouldn't want to disappoint Ms. Jackson now, would we?" Key said looking the boys up and down.

"Nah," Alejandro said looking Key in the eyes.

"Good."

Alejandro and Shakeem looked at Key before leaving the room.

"Look Soul," I need to get out of here," Key said suddenly, "But I need to talk to you tonight," he said writing something on the back of the flower card Soul had left on her desk.

"Key, there isn't anything left for us to say."

"Soul, you owe me this. I promise this one last request, and then I will leave you alone to live ya little happy life with pretty boy."

"Why can't we talk now? I mean you're here already which to be honest, I'm not even sure how you got in the building and more less knew exactly where my classroom was."

"I got some business to take care of."

"That's what I'm talking about. It is always business with you. No Key, I'm not meeting you tonight or any other night for that matter," Soul said angrily.

"What?" Key said stepping toward her. "You will meet me tonight, and any other night unless you want me to make life a living hell for you and that punk ass fiancé of yours," he said grabbing her and kissing her roughly as Soul tried to free herself from his grasp.

"Stop it," Soul huffed finally freeing herself from his rough hold.

"Yeah whatever, but you know me. I mean what I say," Key said releasing her arm and walking out of the door.

"And you say what you mean," Soul said as tears formed in the corner of her eyes.

<h1 style="text-align:center">Chapter 27</h1>

"**E**xcuse me sir," the receptionist said waving her hand in front of Ajax and his date.

"Oh, I'm sorry Miss Lady. I just thought I saw someone I knew," Ajax said bringing his attention back to the hotel clerk.

"Me too," his date added.

"Oh, that's no problem. OK," the receptionist said typing and looking at the screen. "Ah, here's your reservation right here. You're going to be in room 614. It has a view of the city just as you requested. If you could sign here sir," the receptionist said smiling sweetly at Ajax. "Is that all I can do for you sir?"

"Yes, that is all you can do for us," Ajax's date said stressing the word 'us', as she glared at the clerk.

Ajax smirked as he led his date to the elevators. "I love it when you get jealous," he said whispering in her ear. "You know that's sexy as hell."

"Me sexy? Yes. Me jealous? That would be a no. I have never,"

Ajax shut his date up with a long passionate kiss that warned to lead up to something a little freakier if the elevator doors hadn't clanked open and an elderly couple stepped on.

Ajax continued to kiss his date seductively on the back of her neck. "I missed you," he said whispering into her ear as he noticed the elderly lady stealing glances towards he and his date.

"I missed you too," she said absentmindedly.

"What's the matter baby?" Ajax said noticing her distracted look. He had to admit this one was fine as hell. He couldn't believe he had been kicking it with her so much these past few months. He hadn't even thought of getting none from anyone else lately. His boys would never believe this. It wasn't like he was sprung or anything, but baby sure had it going on.

"Nothing bae," his date smiled before wrapping her arms tighter around him. "I'm just worried about a friend of mine. She has a way of getting herself into trouble without realizing it. I just don't want her to mess up a good thing."

"Yeah, I know what you mean. Sometimes we don't know a good thing when it's staring us in the face."

"Isn't that the truth," the elderly lady interrupted, as she looked at her husband. "Young love is such a beautiful thing. Are you newlyweds?" she asked.

"No ma'am, not yet," Ajax winked at the elderly couple.

This brother thinks he got some game, his date thought to herself.

"Well, you sure are a cute couple. I remember when Ernie and I used to be the same way," she said giving her husband a disgusted look.

"Yeah well, I remember when you used to have a girly shape like this young lady too, but you don't hear me complaining, do you Margaret Ann?"

"Shut up!" the elderly woman pouted whacking her husband on the head with her purse.

"Don't you tell me to shut up. You shut up, and don't hit me with that old handbag again. It wouldn't be nice if I clobbered you with this here old cane."

Ajax and his date did their best to hold their laughter.

"Well, your old battleax of a mother didn't raise a fool because I see that cane is still on the floor," the lady said just as the elevator door opened. The couple hobbled off the elevator as they continued to argue.

Ajax's date finally let free all the laughter she had been holding in. "I hope I don't get like that when I get that old."

"Oh, don't worry baby, you're like that now," Ajax said playfully swatting her on the butt as they stepped off the elevator and found their way to their hotel room.

"Oh, If I'm that way, let's just call this a night, and go our separate ways."

"Girl quit playing. Come here cutie," Ajax said pulling her towards him as he began to kiss his date. He fumbled to open the door to their room and immediately pulled her inside.

***

"Damn girl" Ajax lay breathlessly on top of his date. You been keeping big daddy's stuff nice and tight?"

"There is no need to pump up my head. I already know I got some good stuff."

"I just bet you do. I guess I wasn't too bad either. Everybody in the hotel heard you screaming my name Ma." Ajax kissed the top of his date's forehead before rolling off her and gently pulling himself out as he carefully held on to the tip of the condom to ensure no future problems.

"Hey baby, can you hand me the phone on your way into the bathroom."

"Why? You need to call your man to tell him how good I am?"

"Whatever," she said smacking her lips together. "I'm calling my girl to check on her."

"Oh yeah, let me grab my celly, I need to call my boy really quick too."

"I just bet you do."

"Yeah, I need to tell him how good that pussy is," Ajax said reaching over to grab his cell before walking in the bathroom.

Yeah right, his date thought. Boy my ass. Just when I think this negro is okay, the true player comes out of hiding. Oh well, it's just sex, she tried to convince herself before dialing the number to her own girl.

Chapter 28

Key's coal black body was smooth to the touch. Soul knew there were plenty of women who would have died to be in her place, and there used to be a time when she felt like the luckiest woman in the world to be in this place, but tonight there was one problem, he wasn't Anthony.

Key put his arms around her and held her tight. "Damn girl I missed you." he said as he began to kiss her neck.

Back in the day, this would have been exactly what Soul wanted, but now, it put a vile taste in her mouth. Despite her better judgement, Soul had only agreed to meet Key to make her amends, apologize for not telling him about Anthony from the jump, and wish him well with his life, so she and Anthony could move on with theirs. She knew a part of her would always care about Key's well-being, but it was nothing compared to how she felt about Anthony.

Key continued to suck on her neck, as he made a slow descent towards her chest, "I know you want to tell me to taste it, don't you?" Tell me to taste it," Key repeated when she didn't respond. Key didn't wait for an answer, as he found his way down to Soul's waist. He dropped to his knees yanking her underwear down from under the dress she had thrown on, before sliding his head under her dress, and attempting to taste Soul despite her efforts to push his head away. as tears began flowing down Soul's face.

"What are you doing? Key stop it. You promised we would just talk, and I could go on my way." Soul said as Key forcefully pushed her legs apart before sinking his tongue deep inside of her.

"Key," she began.

"Uhm," Key groaned. "This pussy tastes good," he said moving his head deeper into her.

"Key."

He lifted her dress up, so she could watch him perform his tongue tricks.

"Key," she moaned. "I," she opened her mouth. "I"

"I know baby. I miss you too. I want us to be together. I love you baby. That nigga can't do this, can he?" Key said dipping his tongue inside of Soul again.

Key's touch used to send chills down her spine, but now it was only sending waves of disgust. "Key stop," Soul whimpered attempting to move his head.

"Uh Uh," Key said mistaking her words of resistance for those of pleasure.

"No Key, I'm serious," Soul said grabbing his head with force. He looked into her eyes with a smile on his face. "Did you hear what I said? Stop. I can't do this. I'm leaving." Soul attempted to remove his hands from his waist.

"What the fuck you mean stop?" Key growled, the smile from before now replaced with a frown. Key pulled her towards him as they fell on the bed. "Quit playing Soul."

"Key I'm not playing. Now let me up."

"Humph, you betta quit playing girl," Key laughed. He grabbed Soul's face attempting to kiss her again.

Soul turned her head, and Key began to suck on her neck. She felt a nauseated feeling begin to rise in her stomach. Oh God what have I gotten myself into, Soul thought to herself. "Key please let me up,"

Key attempted to slide into her.

"Key!" Soul cried. He grabbed her face towards his roughly and covered her mouth with his as he slid his tongue into her mouth. Soul began to cry. "Key don't," she whimpered. "Key, stop dammit!"

"What the fuck you mean stop. I just told you I still love you, and you gone say some stupid shit like don't!" Key said angrily as he pushed himself off her.

"This is wrong, I only came here to talk so you could understand there is nothing more between us," Soul cried as the tears now flowed freely.

Key looked at her with so much fire in his eyes, that if she didn't know better, she would have sworn that he would have just taken what he wanted or knocked the hell out of her. But she did know better, and she knew that in her many years of knowing and loving Key, he had never laid a hand on her and never would. In his own way, he respected her too much for that. And even though Key was one of the most street brothers, she was his one weak spot. She had heard stories of Key's wrath on others, and as mad as he used to get at her, he never touched her. He used to tell Soul she was his Achilles, and she knew he meant that. Soul used to think that Key was her destiny, and that she had to watch over him to make sure he didn't end up in an early grave, but now she knew better. The comfort of being with Key, didn't replace the conflict that came with him. The only people that could keep Key out of jail or a grave, were him and God, and for reasons beyond Soul's own understanding that hurt her to her core. She just didn't want to be another person to give up on him, but she knew it was time she let go of the tie that bound them together.

She watched the fire in Key's eyes turn into hurt as he looked at her questioningly.

"It's that nigga aint it?" Key sighed sitting up.

"I love him Key," Soul whispered as she sat on the bed beside him.

"Then why are you here with me?"

"Key, I care about you, but I'm in love with Anthony, and I will do anything to make sure that you don't come between mine and his relationship. Today when you said,"

"When I said I would make your life a living hell? Humph! I meant it,"

"Why, Key? Why don't you want me to be happy?"

"Because it ain't with me?" Key was quiet for a long time, before Soul felt him turn his body towards her. "Does he make you happy?"

"Yes," she whispered. "He's everything I have ever wanted in a man."

"Everything I'm not you mean," Key's phone started to ring as he glanced at the caller ID. "What nigga? Man, I'm busy. I can't keep bailing you out of ya stupid ass situations. What! You the one fucked up with that broad that was taking care of you. Nigga whateva. Yeah, you handle yo business, and I'm a handle mine." Key said slamming the phone closed. "My damn big brother gets on my muthafuckin nerves." Key returned his attention to Soul.

"See Key that's what I'm talking about. I've never even met your brother. There are things that I should know about you that I have no clue. With Anthony it's different."

"Be quiet Soul, I need to think" Key said placing his fingers to his temples. Soul watched him closely as he sat and seemed to contemplate everything life held. For some reason, Soul knew she had to make Key understand, or she was sure he really would do everything in his power to make her life with Anthony a living hell. He walked over to the in-room mini bar and poured himself a drink before walking back over and sitting on the bed, lighting a blunt that was lying on the nightstand. He took a long drag before turning towards Soul and placing his hand under her chin to wipe the tears from her eyes. "Damn girl, this is messed up. From the first day you let me hit it, I was in love. I will never respect another woman like I respect you. You made an ordinary brother like me feel special when I was with you. Man, I used to brag to all my boys about how I had a college girl, and about how smart you was and shit. You believed in me when I didn't believe in myself. You a good ass woman. You educated, sexy, and got some damn good stuff," Key joked. "I just can't let you go. Ain't no other nigga supposed to be banging this but me.

"Key," Soul began.

"Shh! Now that's your problem.   You don't know how to listen. When I was in jail, my counselor talked about listening versus actively listening. Right now, you listening, which is what she said is when people listen, but not really listen, cause they trying to think ahead to what they gone say next. I need you to actively listen," Key said seemingly pleased with himself for remembering what he had learned. "Now what was I saying? Oh yeah, no other nigga can love you like I do, in my opinion, but if this nigga makes you happy, then I guess I got to accept that shit. I won't try to see you again or call you or anything. I'll just accept it and be gone. Are you sure this is what you want?"

Gone. Forever. The thought of never seeing Key again scared Soul. No matter how long she and Key would go on hiatus, they would always eventually find their way to one another. He was uncomfortable comfort. Soul knew that no matter who she was dating, if things didn't go well, she could always just wait for Key to find her again. But she also knew that with Key she was settling and if she and Anthony were going to be one, she had to free herself from Key, and the bondage that he held over her. Letting Key go would be the first step in showing that she had faith in what she and Anthony were creating. Soul thought about how much she really loved Anthony, and realized Key was simply a comfortable addiction, and since she knew addictions were simply games that your mind played with your body, Soul knew that if she wanted to be with Anthony, it was time to put the games away.

Chapter 29

The closer Anthony got to the Winterland Suites, the harder his heartbeat pounded. There had to be a mistake. Ajax was his boy, but his love for ass and his latest honey must have been playing tricks on his eyes.

"Man, this is crazy. I need to turn around and go home," Anthony murmured out loud to no one in particular, since he was the only one in the truck. There was no way in hell Soul would be at the hotel with anyone but him. If the seriousness in Ajax's tone didn't force him to drive over, the nagging feeling of sickness would have. Anthony thought about Ajax phone's call not even fifteen minutes ago.

"What up A?" "What up?"

"What you doin?"

"Chilin' watching a Kevin Hart comedy special. You know same old same old."

"Say dog is Soul there with you?"

"Nah. Why you ask me that?"

"I'm just asking."

"Come on Ajax, you mean to tell me you called me late at night to ask if Soul was here. Boy, as much lying as you do to them females, you would think you could do a little better with ya boy."

"Ah man, it ain't like that. I was just wondering if you knew where she was."

"She said something about hanging out with Simone or something like that, but you still ain't told me why you so interested in the whereabouts of wifey to be."

"You sure she said Simone and not Danielle."

"Yeah man. I know what she said. Besides, Danielle just called my phone looking for Soul to see if she knew where Simone was."

"Say dog, I think we need to talk."

Now as Anthony stood in front of the hotel entrance, he prayed Ajax was wrong. Soul wasn't like most women. Why would she want to cheat on him? She knew he loved her. He gave Soul whatever she wanted before she even asked. Anthony couldn't count the times he had gotten up in the middle of the night out of their warm bed to go put gas in her car, so she wouldn't have to worry about it the next day. And shit, sex, well, Anthony made sure to give her as much as she could take. But even though Anthony's pride told him one thing, his heart pulled his attention in another direction.

The weight of the hotel door seemed to be almost too overbearing to open. To Anthony, it felt as if he were walking in slow motion as he made his way to the receptionist.

"Good evening, Sir. How can I help you?" the receptionist flashed him her best flirtatious smile.

"How are you doing ma'am? Could you ring Soul Jackson's room?"

"Sure. Do you know the room number?"

"Nah, I sure don't."

"Unfortunately, sir, I'm not allowed to give out guest information. Would you like to use the courtesy phone and maybe try calling your sister," she said hopefully.

"Fiancé"

"Excuse me?"

"Fiancé. I'm trying to find my fiancés' room."

"Oh, I'm sorry. I must have misunderstood."

"No problem."

"Why does every sexy black man that comes in here tonight have to be taken?" the receptionist grumbled.

"I'm sorry, were you saying something."

"Oh no sir," the receptionist blurted realizing she had spoken her thoughts aloud, "I was just asking if you were sure you didn't want to use the courtesy phone."

"Nah, I don't think so. Let me just try her again from my cell and double check"

Anthony let out a sigh of relief as he pulled his cell phone out. "Damn battery," he said noticing his phone had died and was going into recharge mode. "Excuse me, where did you say that courtesy phone was located?"

"Oh yes sir, there's one right around the corner in the business center," the receptionist was noticeably less friendly now that she knew Anthony was a taken man.

"Thanks." Anthony made his way around the corner but decided against calling Soul since she was standing just short of him with her arms around a short dark brother.

Chapter 30

A nthony could feel his heart beating out of his chest. He couldn't believe what he was seeing as he watched Soul, his girl, his fiancé, his everything wrap her arms tightly around the man's neck. The glare from her engagement ring blinded Anthony as he blinked back the tears that had formed in the corners of his eyes. The man whispered something in her ear as she giggled and playfully pushed him away.

Anthony felt like he was watching a movie rather than the real-life horror scene right in front of his eyes as he watched Soul lovingly pick something off the man's face, before reaching over to give him a kiss on the cheek. To Anthony, it all seemed so comfortable, too comfortable for a one-night stand.

Anthony stood opening and closing his fist hoping to release the volcano of anger that was building inside of him threatening to erupt.

The man reached over and held Soul's hand. She began to play with her engagement ring as if remembering that she belonged to someone else.

"Oh, so now you remember that you're engaged," Anthony growled storming over to Soul. The look of pure shock on Soul's face told Anthony everything he needed to know.

"Anthony what are you doing here?"

"What the fuck you mean? What am I doing here? Here's a question. What the fuck you doing here, all wrapped up with some nigga?"

"Say hold up homeboy. You need to watch the way you talking to a muthafuckin lady," Key interrupted angrily.

"Say punk ass nigga, you need to get the fuck out of my face," Anthony said turning his attention for the first time to Soul's friend. A look of familiarity crossed Anthony's face as he realized this wasn't his first time seeing the man. "Ain't this a bitch. So, you cheating on me with some wanna be thug ass nigga. Nigga, who you supposed to be?

Pac? 50? I shoulda kicked yo ass that day in the store when I thought you was pushing up on my girl then," Anthony said moving closer to Key.

"Shit, you bad. No time like the present," Key said walking up even closer on Anthony.

"Anthony baby," Soul said stepping in between the two men, one ready to fight for her love, the other ready to fight to prove he was worthy of her love.

"Bitch, don't baby me, get your muthafuckin hands off me! How long you been fucking him? I thought what you had with him was over," Anthony said through clenched teeth before sarcastically chuckling. "I guess it wasn't so over after all or you wouldn't be here in some hotel with him acting like you aren't my soon to be wife. Well, what used to be my soon to be wife."

"Baby, it's not what you think. I promise," Soul pleaded tears forming in her eyes. "Please let's go somewhere and talk. I promise I can explain everything."

Anthony wanted to believe her. Everything in his heart told him to believe her. But his pride and the pain told him different.

"Key. Go. Please," Soul said never turning away from Anthony.

"I ain't going nowhere till I know you a'ight."

"Bitch, you ain't got to worry about her. This my muthafuckin girl!"

"Say nigga, I ain't gone be your bitch no more."

"You'll be my bitch for as long as I say you my bitch. If I tell you to bend over or drop to your knees, you better do it too. You hear me bitch!"

Key pushed Soul out of the way and swung at Anthony.

Just at that moment Ajax and his date ran up. Ajax grabbed Anthony just as the hotel security grabbed Key.

"Let it go dog!" Ajax yelled at Anthony.

"Fuck that! This nigga fuckin my girl! I'm a kill his hoe ass!"

"How you gone kill me from your grave, cause when I get loose, you bout to catch a bullet!"

"Let's go Sir," security said dragging Key away.

"Let me go!" Anthony said angrily as he attempted to shake Ajax's hands off him.

"Not until you calm down."

"I'm cool dog. Let me go!"

Anthony, are you okay?" Soul said regaining her composure.

"Stay the fuck away from me. This shit is over," Anthony said snatching away from both Soul and Ajax.

"Baby wait!" Soul pleaded with Anthony as she attempted to grab his shirt.

The cold hard look in Anthony's eyes stopped Soul dead in her tracks as he looked her up and down like she was a stranger on the streets rather than the woman he was preparing to spend his entire life with just this morning.

Anthony straightened his shirt and walked out of the hotel.

"Hold up dog. Shit, I knew he would be headed here. I'm a check on him, you better stay with her," Ajax said glancing back at his date before jogging off in the direction Anthony had headed.

"Okay baby," his date replied with a disappointed look on her face. She walked over and put her arm around Soul, who stood in the middle of the lobby with tears streaming down her face. "Are you okay?"

Soul turned her attention for the first time on Ajax's date wondering why some strange woman was hugging her like they were old friends.

Chapter 31

♥

"Simone, I've got to stop Anthony. I've got to explain! It's not what he thinks!"

"Calm down Soul. You need to get yourself together before you attempt to explain anything."

"No, you don't understand. I need him to know," Soul whimpered tears streaming down her face as she attempted to run out the door.

"Soul, not now," Simone said grabbing Soul's arm firmly. "Give him some time to calm down. Anthony's not thinking clearly, and I don't think it would be a good idea to deal with him right now. Come on, let's go upstairs so you can pull yourself together." Simone led Soul to the elevator just as the doors opened.

Soul felt drained, weak, and nauseous. Even the short elevator ride itself made her feel like throwing up.

Simone leaned into the wall never saying a word. She just stared ahead at the elevator numbers beeping as it passed each floor until it finally reached their destination.

Leading Soul to a room, Simone pulled out the door card to swipe it. "What were you thinking girl?" Simone asked opening the door and holding it open for Soul to enter the room. Simone propped the dead bolt in the door so that it wouldn't lock Ajax out of the room.

"I don't know," Soul sighed. "I just wanted to explain things to Key. Tell him about the engagement, you know. He had flowers delivered to the school, then he just showed up, and there were too many loose ends to tie up," Soul said purposely neglecting to tell Simone about Key's threatening words.

"Please help me understand why you feel the need to explain things to Key. First the store, now this," Simone said kicking off her shoes. "Did Key ever feel the need to explain things to you when he was no where to be found? Hell to the no!"

"Simone, I don't need you to be my judge, I need you to be my friend."

"No, you want me to be your supporter, but since I am your friend, I'm going to tell you what you need to hear, not what you *want* to hear. There are thousands of women who would die to be with a man like Anthony. Fine, successful, caring, and loves the hell out of you. But for reasons that I can't understand, you fucked it up because you felt compelled to explain some shit to Key of all people? What the hell were you thinking? Then the two of you are all wrapped up in the lobby. What the hell was Anthony supposed to think? I'm surprised he didn't beat both your asses. Not only were you disrespecting your relationship with Anthony, but you would have also made a fool of yourself if I hadn't stopped you."

"Oh yeah, like you never mess up! Wait, wait!" Soul said as if suddenly remembering something. "Hold the damn press, flag on the field, false start on the track. What are you doing here anyway? I know you aren't fucking Ajax?" Soul said looking around the room for the first time. "You fucking Ajax dog? The king hoe of hoes! Oh, so I guess now you want to be part of his hoe-asis too. Ain't this a bitch! You sitting here trying to tell me how I'm messing up, but what do you call this?" Soul said waving her hand across the room.

"That's cool Soul, you want to take your anger out on me. Cool. I'm a let you have this tonight," Simone got up to fix herself a drink from the mini bar.

"I can't believe you. This is unbelievable!" Soul screamed. "You're settling for Ajax of all people? I mean don't get me wrong. He's cool and all, but this little whatever," Soul said once again waving her hand as if dismissing the entire situation, "is crazy!"

Simone continued to sip on her drink. She walked to the hotel balcony and lit a black and mild, closing her eyes.

Soul stomped out on the balcony following Simone, "Oh I guess you don't have anything to say now huh? You had tons of advice for me, but when it comes to your own f-up's, the cat got your tongue."

Simone slanted her mouth to the side and blew out her smoke. "Okay Soul. Again, I'm going to let you have this one, being as that you probably just lost the best thing that ever happened to you. But you will not sit here and talk to me like I'm a child, and you will not pass judgment on me and Ajax's relationship without knowing the facts."

Simone downed her drink before waking back into the room to the mini bar to refill her drink. She walked to the window and looked into the night sky. Damn a relationship. Simone couldn't believe the word had actually left her mouth. Did she really want a relationship with Ajax of all people? Her thoughts drifted back to the night she first hooked up with him. It was at one of Soul's and Anthony's regular little Friday card games. She remembered thinking once again how arrogant Ajax seemed to be every time she had been around him, how he talked about women like all of them were bitches and hoes, and how he always seemed to be constantly bragging about his latest conquest. It was then as she listened to him joking and bragging about how he had two twin sisters fighting over him, that he became her personal challenge. She knew he wanted to get with her because he flirted to no end, so she decided to give him a taste of his own medicine. She figured not too many women had ever turned Ajax down, with those drop-dead gorgeous dimples, and smooth butter complexion, and besides, it had been a while for her, and her body could use a little attention. She remembered how she was in the kitchen, and he came in brushing against her as she searched through the shelves for some tequila salt. He rubbed against her butt and whispered in her ear wanting to know when she was going to give him some. She could smell the vodka on his breath, and she remembered how he grew hard right there in the kitchen. She turned around and slipped her tongue inside his mouth. Something she rarely did, as she really wasn't one for kissing. She slipped her hand inside his pants and massaged his growing erection. Just as she knew he was giving in to her tongue dance, she pushed him away, slipped her hand out of his pants, and told him to meet her at her place. She gave him the address and told him to be there that very night if he ever wanted a chance to have sex with her, and that he better be worth her time or else. Then she poured some tequila salt into her palm, dipped her finger it, and rubbed it across his lips. She licked it off and walked out of the kitchen and went back to join the rest of the party. Ajax returned to the party a few minutes later. He later explained to her that he had to get his erection back down before he could walk back into the room. He said goodnight to everyone, got his coat, and left. No one noticed that she too left about twenty minutes after he did. When she got to her apartment, he was there waiting. She laughed at the thought. They could barely make it into the house before their clothes were off. She took charge of every sexual position they found, and he ended up not leaving until Monday morning.

It was in that weekend that she saw a different side of him as they lay in bed talking and cuddling. He even cooked her breakfast in bed. She laughed as she remembered how during one of their many sex acts that weekend, he looked her in the eyes and seriously asked "Damn girl, you trying to make a brother fall in love?" She laughed and kept riding him like a cowgirl at a rodeo since she knew good coochie could make the strongest man talk. Funny how the joked turned out. And even though the one night turned into a weekend, Simone did follow her original plan. Ajax called everyday for at least a week, and she never answered until he finally stopped calling.

It wasn't until she saw him again at Anthony's mom house that she realized the tough act was just that, an act. She called him and apologized. He came over and they had the second-best sex she had ever had in her life, only second to that first weekend together.

And the rest was history. They had been kicking it secretly since then. He wanted to let their friends know, but she begged him not to, saying she didn't want their friends all in their business yet. Despite Simone reminding him they were keeping things light; she and Ajax were practically together almost every night. Simone knew she had fallen for him a long time ago, but she didn't want to admit it to anyone, especially herself because that would be too much like making it true. She just wasn't sure she was ready to be in love. Look where it had gotten Soul, who was sitting on the bed with her back to her. Simone couldn't ignore Soul's sobs, and she could feel Soul's heart breaking as if it were her very own. The sight of Soul reminded Simone of why she couldn't love Ajax. She walked over and sat beside Soul putting her arm around her, as Soul's sobs grew louder.

"I'm sorry cuz," Soul said between tears. "I really am happy for you. It's just that this thing between Anthony and I, and Key and I, has my whole head screwed up. And then when I realized that you were here with Ajax, it just kind of took me by surprise."

"Hey, you don't have to explain. We all say things we don't mean. I really shouldn't have been so hard on you. I know you were only doing what you thought was right, and I know you really love Anthony. If you say nothing happened between you and Key, I believe you. And I'm sure," Simone continued, "that once you let Anthony cool down, and you explain things to him, he'll forgive you. It may be some time, but we will be back to planning a wedding in no time."

"I hope so girl. I love Anthony. There is no me without him," Soul wiped her tears and tried to smile. "Hey Simone, can I ask you a question?"

"Sure."

"This thing between you and Ajax, is this the first time you two, you know?"

"Yeah, I know, and no it isn't."

"Is it serious?"

"I thought you said one question."

"Come on girl. Inquiring minds want to know," Soul said attempting to smile.

Simone thought for a while before finally answering, "Yes nosy, I think it is starting to get serious."

"Are you falling in love?"

"Dang, for a teacher, you sure can't count."

"Hey, I don't teach math. Now answer the question."

Simone thought again for a minute. What the hell, she already knew the answer. "Yeah, she finally admitted. "I think I am."

"Wow."

"Humph," Simone laughed. "Wow doesn't even begin to cover it."

Soul reached over and squeezed Simone's hand remembering her own old fears of falling in love with Anthony, and trying to push back her new fears of losing him.

Ajax stood back from the door. He couldn't move. He didn't mean to listen to their conversation, but he couldn't help it. Now he needed a moment to get himself back together. A moment to breathe, a moment to think, a moment to control the fear that was growing. Fear that Soul and Simone would know that he had heard their conversation and could read what was written on his face. He had fallen in love with Simone too.

Chapter 32

As soon as Soul walked into the school building, she knew it was going to be one of those days. Just as she clocked in, an irate parent showed up in the main office ranting about a referral Soul had written on her son the previous day. Soul sighed shaking her head, knowing this was going to be a long day. Maybe she had been a little hasty, but she was sick of the woman's son and his constant rude comments. Normally Soul didn't let the boy's stupid comment's bother her, but yesterday was different. Soul was in an extremely bad mood since Anthony still wouldn't answer any of her calls, and to make matters worse, she had run out of gas two blocks from the school, which really made her miss Anthony since he usually kept her car filled with gas.

So, when Jack Franklin made a smart aleck comment to her when Soul had asked him to tuck in his shirt, she had screamed at him telling him that there wasn't a salary for smart asses, put him out of the class, and wrote a referral sending him to the principal's office.

Soul waited on the rest of her team to show up for their usual parent conferences, as Jack Franklin's mom sat tapping her feet impatiently.

"Ms. Franklin, if you like, we can go ahead and discuss the problems with Jack and I," Soul said turning in the direction of the impatient woman.

"No, what I would like is for you to refrain from referring to my son as a smart ass," Jack's mother spat with anger.

Soul sighed knowing she had overstepped her boundaries, but Jack was constantly giving all his teachers some type of grief, and his mom was constantly at the school bailing him out. Nothing was ever Jack's fault, and his mom made sure to let everyone know it. Soul was thankful when the rest of the team members walked in the door. Thirty minutes later, Soul and her team finally walked out of the school conference room with just enough time for her to grab her morning coffee from the teacher workroom. By the time, her conference period rolled around, she was just glad to have made it through the day without crying. Every time she called Anthony, or sent him a text message, and he wouldn't answer, Soul wanted to scream. She was trying to give him time to think things over, but each day without Anthony was like slow torture to Soul. Key, however, had been a man of his word. He hadn't shown up anymore, or even tried to call her, which was fine with Soul.

Soul arranged the papers in a stack and prepared the long process of grading another set of essays.

"Hey Ms. Jackson, you got a minute?"

Soul turned at the sound of the light tapping on the door to find Shakeem's grandmother standing in her doorway.

"Hey Mrs. White, come on in," Soul said walking over to embrace the older lady. "I had just written your name on a call list. I noticed Shakeem hasn't been here all week. Is everything okay?"

"Actually, that's what I'm here for," the older lady said sitting down in a seat. Her shoulder slumped and Soul could tell the old lady was tired. That was the problem with so many of these kids, too many grandparents having to raise their kid's kids. It seemed Soul was seeing more and more older people who should be out enjoying their golden years at school attending parent conferences and hearings.

"Well Ms. Jackson, I don't know what to do about Shakeem anymore. That boy is getting more hard-headed each day, and his granddaddy and I don't know what to do with him anymore. You know he's in jail, don't you?"

"Jail? Are you serious?"

"Yes ma'am, he went last weekend for drugs. Police said he threw the rest out of the car, so they only found a bag on him."

"That's not good, but not a cause for him to be there an entire week. When are they going to release him?"

"He has a court date in a month, and I just wanted to see what you thought being that you have been working with him and trying to keep him on track. I know he has a great deal of respect for you and all, and like I said I'm at my wit's end with that boy. Besides the fact that sometimes I don't understand all that lawyer mambo jumbo, and them lawyers can sure make you feel stupid sometimes. His granddaddy said we should send him to stay with his mama, but she's in and out of jail and smoking that stuff. And his daddy ain't even an option. I just don't know where we went wrong," Shakeem's grandmother sniffled as tears rolled down her face.

Soul walked over and placed her arm around the old woman. "It's okay, Mrs. White, I'll go to court with you that day and see what's going on." Soul could hear her friends now. They always warned Soul that she got entirely too involved with her students, but Soul was always taught that it takes a village to raise a child, and that's just what she believed. She knew that even when she became an administrator it would be hard for her to not take things so personally. "Here you go," Soul said handing the old woman some Kleenex.

"Thank you so much Ms. Jackson. I can see why Shakeem has taken such a liking to you."

"Well, I like him too, and once we get him out of this, I am going to kill him myself if he gets in anymore trouble."

"And you have my permission to do so," Shakeem's grandmother smiled. "Here you go," she said handing Soul Shakeem's court date and information. "Do you need a ride to the court baby? I can have my husband stop by and pick you up from the school."

"No Ma'am," Soul laughed.

"Are you sure you don't mind? I mean it is after work and I know you already put in so much time with these kids during regular work hours. Besides, I'm sure that there's some handsome young man who can't wait for you to get home every day," the old lady smiled sweetly.

"It's okay. Really. I don't mind," Soul patted her on the hand and tried not to think of the handsome young man who used to wait on her every day, even occasionally popping in on her at school to check on her or have lunch with her.

Soul somehow managed to get through the rest of the day. As soon as the bell rang for dismissal Soul grabbed her things and checked her phone. Not surprisingly, there were no messages from Anthony. Soul fought back the tears as she started her car, Mary J's smooth voice telling of all her pain and trials.

***

Soul entered the court and asked for directions to the juvenile court area. When she found the area, Shakeems' grandparents waited on a bench looking as tired as ever.

"Oh Ms. Jackson, you came!" Shakeem's grandmother said as she noticed Soul approaching.

"I told you I would, have you heard anything?"

"No, we were just waiting for them to call his name and case. Here, have a seat," Shakeem's grandmother said as she slid over to make room for Soul on the bench.

Soul's mind drifted to Anthony. It had been a month, and he still was not taking her calls despite her calling multiple times every day. She wondered what he would say about her being at the courthouse. Knowing Anthony, he would fuss about her getting too involved with her student's personal lives, all the while driving her to the courthouse himself just to sit and wait with her. Soul chuckled to herself knowing Anthony probably would also end the day trying to become a mentor or big brother to Shakeem before it was all said and done.

"Shakeeem White, anybody here for a Shakeem White?" the tired looking bailiff asked without enthusiasm. Soul helped Shakeem's grandparents up and led them into the courtroom. Tears streamed down Shakeem's grandmother's face as soon as she saw her grandson standing there in his county uniform. Shakeem seemed to fight his own tears knowing that jail and court were no place to show signs of weakness. Soul on the other hand, was pissed beyond reason that Shakeem would even put his grandparents through such an ordeal. She couldn't imagine having her mother go through something so traumatic, much less her grandparents. When he saw the disappointed and angry look on her face, Shakeem put his head down in embarrassment.

Soul listened as the court appointed lawyer discussed the logistics of Shakeem's case. The lawyer pointed out that Shakeem was a good kid and that this being his first offense, he should receive probation. The judge didn't seem very impressed. Soul figured he was tired of seeing teenage criminals and probably just wanted to go home to his family. For him, Shakeem was probably just another hood on the street.

"Where are the parents?" the judge asked looking over his wire framed glasses.

"Right here your honor," Soul said pulling Mr. and Mrs. White up.

"And you are?"

"I'm his teacher, these are his grandparents."

"Mom and Dad?"

"His grandparents are his guardians," the lawyer interjected.

"Uh," the judge added.

"Will the young man in question be placed back in the home with the grandparents?"

"Yes, your honor," the lawyer stated.

"And how am I to assume, that a few months from now, this same young man won't be standing in front of me again."

"You honor, if I may," Soul spoke up. The judge signaled for her to go ahead with a gesture of his hand.

"My name is Soul Jackson, and as I stated earlier, I am the teacher of this young man. I understand that you really don't have a reason to release Shakeem. Believe me, teachers of all people, know that when dealing with kids everything is a gamble. However, it is my belief that Shakeem White is really a good kid. He has a good heart, and I know he has a promising future ahead of him. You may think the streets would be a better place with one less thug locked up, but when I look at this young man, I don't see a thug. I see hope and a future leader. Some of our greatest leaders and entertainers had to find their way in life because they were forced too. I honestly think that Shakeem will be one of those kinds of people. He has two loving adults in his life, and a teacher who believes in him."

"That's all good and dandy, but how can I be sure that this young man is going to make a change?"

"You can't your honor. There is nothing that is a sure guarantee. Everything in life is a gamble, but sometimes you must be willing to take a chance. If no one ever took a chance on Alexander Graham Bell, we may have never had a telephone. If Dr. King wasn't willing to take a chance, we wouldn't even have the opportunity to stand in this court today. Please your honor, I believe in Shakeem, and all I'm asking is that you take a chance on him."

The judge looked closely at Shakeem, and then over towards Soul and Shakeem's grandparents. He sighed, "I'm going to take a chance on you, young man," he said turning his attention back towards Shakeem. "I hope this serves as a lesson for you. You are lucky to have grandparents who care about you and a teacher who thinks so highly of you. Most kids who enter this court don't have anyone who cares enough about them to come to court on their behalf, but you have three. I pray that you don't disappoint these people who have so much invested in you. You will have six months probation and will be assigned a probation officer to ensure you are staying out of trouble with routine checkins. For now young man you will be released into the hands of your guardian," the judge said pounding his gavel on the desk. Shakeem walked over to his grandparents and Soul. His grandfather released a weary sigh, and his grandmother grabbed him into her arms. As soon as she released him, Soul popped him upside of his head before pulling him into her own hug.

"Don't you ever have your grandparents or me worried like this again! Do you understand?"

"Yes ma'am," Shakeem said unable to hold the tears back any longer. "That's my word."

"Oh, I know that's your word, and I am going to see to it that you keep it," Soul said with a sigh knowing that it was easier said than done.

Chapter 33

As Anthony got closer to Soul's school his heart began to beat faster. He used to love coming to this area for his meetings with the city housing authority since he would often drop in at Soul's school and have lunch with her, or just drop in to say hi. But now since the night at the hotel, Anthony couldn't even stomach going remotely close to anything that reminded him of her. Despite feelings of betrayal, Anthony found himself driving even slower as he got closer to Soul's school and despite the urge to speed up, he strained to catch a glimpse of her coming out of the school. Her car wasn't parked in its usual spot. He glanced at the clock on his dashboard, it was only four p.m. Soul was usually one of the last people to leave, even on Fridays, so Anthony couldn't understand why her car wouldn't be in its usual spot. Maybe she left early to go be with her new man, or maybe he dropped her off at school. Anthony knew he would only drive himself crazy trying to analyze the what ifs about Soul, but he couldn't help it. The past month had been torture. Even after everything, Anthony still loved Soul as strongly as he had the day he proposed to her, and he couldn't get her off his mind. Last night he dreamed about their wedding, and when he woke up smiling to tell her about it, he was faced with the reality that she wasn't laying beside him. Yes, she had been calling him nonstop, but he couldn't bring himself to talk to her. Anthony knew he would have to eventually face her, but his heart wasn't strong enough to do it right now, and he didn't want to hear any of his friends and family trying to reason with him, which is why it took him so long to face any of them. The only reason he was out of the house now was because he couldn't afford to miss this meeting with the city's housing authority if he wanted to get the grant money he desperately needed to get his community development corporation up and running by teaming up with the city.

Anthony sighed. It was Soul who he had shared his dreams with, and she who had worked so hard to get everything going as if his future were her very own. She put just as much effort in getting his business to the next level as he had. She believed in him. Anthony just couldn't understand why she didn't believe in them.

Even now she was propelling him towards success through their recent breakup since all he was willing to do was work. In fact, the only thing he really came out of the house to do was work. Anthony worked all day at his real estate business with his fraternity brothers, then he worked all night at meetings like the one he had today with the housing authority. He had even gone out of town to another entrepreneur's convention. Anything to manage his time and take his mind off Soul.

Anthony drove through the rough neighborhood. Drug dealers hung out on the corners, as kids walked home from school. He used to hate that Soul worked in such a rough area, but she would remind him that she took care of herself in the area long before he came into her life, and she wouldn't leave kids who deserved good educators more than any group. Though he wasn't a stranger to the hood, he still hated the thought of her working in such a bad neighborhood with all her late-night meetings. She would even go to the apartments and drop kids off or to talk to parents when she or they had a concern. In fact, it was Soul's passion for her school community that led Anthony to choose the area for his own business venture. He knew that if she believed she could help this community, he had to support her, and like the old saying went, Anthony knew he couldn't beat her, so he joined her.

Anthony parked his car in the parking lot of the southern division of the city's housing authority building. More than anything, Anthony wanted to call Soul to just hear her voice. Soul had always been Anthony's peace in moments like this because she had a way of calming any doubts and fears he had without even voicing them to her, but today, he would have to do this for himself, by himself.

Anthony gathered his paperwork and prepared for his meeting with the people who held his future in his hands. He checked his reflection in the rearview mirror and straightened his tie before jumping out of the truck and heading into the building.

***

It was nearly 6:30 when Anthony finally emerged out of the housing authority building. Anthony looked at his phone and noticed he had two missed calls from Thaddeus. Anthony sighed. "I'll deal with that later," he thought to himself.

His meeting had gone extremely well, and with the support of the city, Anthony was one step closer to getting his business off and running. Now that his proposal had been accepted, and all paperwork had been submitted to the city, everything was going great. With the addition of the grant money that the officials said he was eligible for, Anthony knew it would only be a matter of time before he would start making a difference in the community that Soul believed in so much. He sighed as he thought of her. God how he wished he could share his good news with her. No matter how he tried, Anthony couldn't get her out of his mind. Anthony even thought he saw her as he glanced across the street. He shook his head and climbed into the truck. Anthony didn't know how, but he had to get her out of his mind. Never in a million years did Anthony think a woman could affect his life like Soul had.

Antony pumped up the rap track and tried to take his mind off her as he glanced again at the woman hugging the older couple and teenager across the street in front of the courthouse.

Chapter 34

"Simone, I really don't feel like going out," Soul whined for what had to be the hundredth time in an hour.

"Oh yeah, you're going out!" Simone demanded as she reapplied lip gloss to her already shiny lips. It has been a month. You are not going to sit here another Saturday night crying over some trifling negro.

"Simone, Anthony is not trifling, I'm the one who messed up."

"Oh, I know. I just wanted to make you feel better," Simone said blowing a kiss to her reflection in the mirror. "Do these jeans make my butt look big?" Simone asked as she turned around to examine her butt.

"Yep."

"Good! Simone said walking out of the bathroom. "So, what are you going to wear?"

"What do you mean, I'm wearing this," Soul said referring to the Nike sweatsuit she had on.

"The hell you are! Not with me you ain't sis. You know our motto: Diva one, Diva all."

"I thought we were just going out to eat."

"Yes, we are, but you know how Cajun Catch gets on a Saturday. It's the club of restaurants."

"Yeah, and it's the restaurant that doesn't want you negros standing around drinking one drink all night, running away paying customers like me," Soul joked.

Simone threw a pillow at Soul and walked into the closet. "Okay, let's see what we have going on in here."

"Heyyyyy! You guys better be ready to go." Danielle shouted from downstairs.

"Danielle, how in the hell did you get in my house?" Soul shouted from where she lay across her bed.

"I used the emergency key," Danielle said walking into the room. "Oooohhh, and by the way you're looking, it is an emergency. You know the motto, Diva one"

"Diva all. Yeah, I know, I know. Listen since I'm not as divafied as the two of you, why don't you guys just let me go back to bed and the two of you can go out and enjoy yourself.

"Soul, you will not lie in bed, and cry again tonight," Simone warned.

Which is exactly what Soul was doing when Simone showed up unannounced at her door an hour earlier. The only reason Soul answered the door was because she prayed it was Anthony, though she should have known better. He had done a damn good job of dodging every attempt she had made to contact him. She even showed up at his job, and he refused to see her.

"He needs time baby," his mother had said when Soul called her.

"Life isn't worth living without Anthony."

"Soul Jackson, I don't want to hear you say that again. As much as I love my son you are a strong woman whose existence is not defined by a man. Any man can enhance your happiness, but he never defines it. Now my son loves you more than he knows himself, and you were wrong for not being completely honest with him, cause once you bring lies into a relationship, it's hard to get them out. But Anthony's biggest fault is that he doesn't want to listen. Once he has calmed down, explain everything like you did to me, and he will realize it was one big mistake."

"Maybe you're right," Soul said sighing.

"I know, I'm right. I carried his big head for nine months, and I know 'Ant' like I know the back of my hand. He's just stubborn as his daddy, and his biggest crime is not wanting to love, but loving too strongly. He's suffering too. Trust me. I had to almost beat his door down just to get him to talk to me. Just give him time and if you need to talk again, you just call me."

"Yes ma'am."

"Now quit crying and get yourself together. You two will work this out before you know it."

Soul thought about the call she had made to Anthony's mom several weeks ago. Everyday Soul kept hoping that Anthony would reach out and at least give her a chance to explain but after a week of dodging her calls, Soul knew she had no other choice but to call the woman he loved even more than he loved Soul, his mama. Soul knew she had to explain her side, knowing that if his mother was in her corner, everything would be okay. But even though she knew Anthony's mother loved her dearly and probably pleaded her case just as hard as Soul would have if Anthony would give her the chance, he still hadn't returned any of Soul's calls, come by, or even come to get his things. It was as if he wanted to erase everything about their relationship.

"Oh yes! This is more like it," Simone snapped her fingers, interrupting Soul's thoughts. She emerged from the closet with a blue jean mini skirt, a cream turtleneck, and a cream leather blazer with matching cream boots.

Soul sighed again and covered her face with the blanket.

"Honey moping is not going to bring Anthony back. He just needs some time," Danielle said sitting beside her on the bed.

"It's been a month," Soul could feel the tears form in the corners of her eyes.

Danielle glanced at Simone and began playing with a string hanging from her shirt. Danielle was giving true diva in a stonewashed pair of jeans with matching jacket, lime green blouse and matching lime green pumps. Her golden locks were pinned in a bun.

"Hey, do you have some scissors?" Danielle asked suddenly.

Danielle went into the bathroom and came back with a small pair of purple scissors. She was just about to cut the strand on her shirt when she suddenly stopped as if remembering something. "Hey are these your coochie scissors?" Danielle stopped in mid stride as a look of disgust crossed her face.

"What?"

"Now Soul, don't play dumb. Every woman I know has a pair of coochie scissors somewhere under their shelf to give herself a little porn star trim. You know when the forest is growing a little too wild."

"Girl, ain't that the truth," Simone piped in. "I keep mine by my bed. Sometimes I get fancy and get a mirror to see way down," she said jumping on Soul's bed and demonstrating her legs spread open as she pretended to give herself a trim.

"Simone, you're sick. Get off my bed," Soul couldn't help the laugh that escaped her. "Besides, you heffas need to move into modern times and dump the scissors and get you an actual trimmer."

"Ok Ms. Fancy coochie, so you can still smile. Well good. Go get dressed, so I can tell you about the time I accidentally cut myself," Simone winced.

"Okay, okay." Soul dragged herself out the bed and picked up the clothes Simone had lain out.

"Diva one," Danielle and Simone said at the same time.

"Yeah, yeah, yeah. Diva all."

Cajun Catch was packed. After waiting nearly an hour they were finally seated. Soul, Simone, and Danielle laughed at all the young girls in the short skirts sharing every piece of business they owned. They laughed even harder at the brothers who were trying to holler at them. Simone was right. Cajun Catch was like an unofficial club. Soul temporarily forgot her troubles and laughed it up with her girls like the old days. They ate and sipped on drinks as they tried to ignore the admiring glances of a group of ugly brothers who kept looking their way. Soul excused herself to go to the restroom.

This was a great idea Simone, Soul seems to be enjoying herself," Danielle said as she bit into her dessert.

"Yeah, it may not be the cure but at least it helped a little."

"I think everything will be okay."

"I hope so. It would be a shame for Soul to have gotten Anthony ripe for somebody else's picking."

"Damn straight."

Soul was on her way back from the restroom. She had really enjoyed hanging out with her girls and she would have to be sure to thank them. She had even managed to forget about Anthony and their problems for a while. "What a blessing it is to have good friends," Soul thought. Soul was so caught up in her thoughts that she wasn't paying attention as she ran right into Thaddeus, Anthony's frat.

"Soul," he said with a surprised look on his face.

"Hey! How have you been?" Soul reached over to hug Thaddeus to the obvious displeasure of the young lady standing beside him. "Oh, I'm sorry, Thaddeus," Soul said noticing the jealous look on his dates face.

"Angie, this is Soul. Soul, Angie."

"Hello," Soul said turning to smile at her. "Damn insecure bitches get on my nerves," Soul thought, inwardly rolling her eyes.

"So, how do you two know each other?"

"I'm An," she paused, "I'm engaged to one of Thaddeus's friends."

"Really! Who?"

"Hey Angie, I think our table is ready," Thaddeus interrupted. "Soul, it was great seeing you. You take care."

"Hey, can I talk to you for a sec?"

"I don't think now is a good time. You know they'll give away our table in a heartbeat. I'll call you."

"Damn baby, why you in such a rush. We've got to wait on Cookie nem. They should be finished parking the car unless they're trying to get a little freaky. Oh, never mind, here they go. Cookie! Anthony! Over here," Angie said waving.

At the sound of Anthony's name, Soul's heart dropped. She turned to see Anthony entering the restaurant with a cute light skinned sister.

Soul's heart was beating so fast, she couldn't breathe. As bad as she wanted to leave, her feet were planted to the ground. As soon as Anthony saw her, he stopped dead in his tracks. "Cookie" didn't seem to notice as she pulled him their way. Anthony threw a questioning glance at Thaddeus, who just shrugged his shoulders and mouthed "sorry".

Cookie was a tall yellow sister with long wavy black hair that hung to her butt. Soul couldn't tell if her hazel eyes were gifts from God or EyeMasters. Her perfect white teeth gleamed like the million dollars she paid for them. Soul couldn't help but admit the sister was gorgeous, and obviously the reason why Anthony wasn't returning any of Soul's call and hadn't tried to talk to her. And to think, she had been lying in bed weeping and moaning about him while Anthony was out banging some video vixen beauty look alike. The sudden thought of Anthony having sex with someone else suddenly made Soul sick, and the combination of the seafood and alcohol Soul had consumed earlier threatened to surface. Before Anthony could say anything, she ran to the bathroom.

"Soul, wait," Anthony said running after Soul as she ran into the bathroom and flew into the stall pissing off the girl who was about to go in there.

"What the fu!"

"Sorry," Soul squeezed out just as she began to throw up what her heart and stomach couldn't hold in. Soul was not sure what came out more, tears or food.

"Damn girl, you all right?" the girl asked now feeling sorry for her.

Soul's answer was another round of sickness.

"Hey, you the girl with the cute boots on. I remember seeing you when you walked in. You better be glad I'm a shoe person or I wouldn't have noticed. I think you were with two girls, one had on some cute lime green pumps. Do you know where she got those? I have some purple and pink ones, but those lime green ones were too cute.

"Uh excuse me, uh would you mind getting her?"

"Damn my bad, no problem. I'm tripping. I'll be right back," the girl said as the door swung open.

Soul flushed the toilet and leaned against the wall. How could she go back out there? How could she face Anthony? The awful taste of vomit in her mouth forced her to come out of the stall. Thank God no one else was in the bathroom. She walked to the sink and rinsed her mouth out, then splashed a little cold water over her face. Just as she reached for a paper towel, the door swung open, and Simone and Danielle rushed in, followed by Anthony and the girl who was in the bathroom earlier.

"Hey, you okay? You were throwing up?" Danielle asked.

"She sure was. Came busting up in here, cutting in front of me and everything."

"Hey thanks for letting us know, but can you give us a sec?" Danielle asked sweetly.

"I guess," she hesitated, "but ya'll need to hurry up, cause I gots to use it and the other stall is out of order.

"Sure. No problem, we'll be out in a jiffy." Danielle replied.

"Anthony, what are you doing in here? This is a ladies room, and don't you have your own lady to tend to?" Soul asked angrily.

"I was standing outside waiting on you when that girl came out, talking about how some girl with cute boots was in here throwing up."

"Well, I 'm fine now. So, you can go back to your little date."

Anthony's face looked defeated, but he didn't move.

"Come on Anthony. I'm going to go pay for our meal. Let's give her a moment," Simone said.

Anthony hesitated then finally agreed to leave with Simone.

"Simone man, it wasn't like that," Anthony said as soon as the door closed behind them. "No matter what happened, I can't help but loving ya girl still. Man, I been closed up in my house so much, even my boys starting to worry. I never should have let Thaddeus talk me into coming here and going on this date with some dumb video vixen wannabe just so he could get with her girl."

"Anthony," Simone interrupted "you don't have to explain anything to me, besides Ajax told me you were moping around too," Simone gently smiled at Anthony touching his arm.

"Damn, he must really like you to be telling his boy's business and all."

"Whatever," Simone said smiling.

"Whatever my ass. You care about him just as much as he cares about you. You know I love you girl, but if I have to hear your name one more time, I'm going to start calling my boy PW."

"Huh?" Simone said with a smile.

"Quit frontin, you know. Pussy whipped," Anthony chuckled.

"You crazy!" Simone said trying to play off how happy Anthony's comments had made her.

"Crazy, I may be, whipped, you and Ajax are."

"What!"

"Yeah, but don't feel bad, your girl had me whipped too," Anthony sighed glancing back towards the bathroom.

"Anthony listen, she loves you. She may have f'd up, but she loves you. Can't nobody take your place. Talk to her. Try to work things out. You two have given me hope that true love still exists, and there is no way that a connection that strong could be broken this quickly."

"Thanks Simone, you're a great woman."

"I hope your boy knows that."

"Trust me, he knows, and we won't hear the end of it."

Simone and Anthony exchanged hugs.

"I guess I should get back to Thaddeus and our guest before they send a search party for me. I bet Thaddeus and Angie won't try to fix me up ever again. I'm sure old girl is not too thrilled with me, which is good, I'll take natural beauty over bought beauty any day."

Simone and Anthony walked to the front of the restaurant seconds before Danielle and Soul emerged from the bathroom.

"Are you sure you're okay.

"I'm fine Dani, really. I'll be okay.

"Yeah but I'm sure this has to be a tough pill to swallow.

"Danielle, I really don't want to talk about it anymore. Anthony's moved on. Period. End of story. If he could get over what we had in one month, well that's fine. No explanation required. No explanation needed."

"Are you sure?"

"Positive. Let's go."

"Are you feeling better?" the girl from earlier inquired as she passed them on her way back to the bathroom.

"Yeah, hey thanks."

"No problem. I'm sure that fine man who was so worried about you helped."

"I'm sure he did, Soul mumbled. I'm quite sure he did."

Chapter 35

♥

nthony glanced at the glowing lights on the alarm clock. 1:57. He had been staring at the ceiling for the past two hours. Every time he closed his eyes, Anthony kept picturing the look on Soul's face when he and Cookie walked into the restaurant. He never should have let Thaddeus talk him into going on a date anyway. He was perfectly fine wallowing in his own misery. As soon as Anthony saw Cookie, he began to miss Soul even more. Everything about her said attention seeker and fake. Yeah, she was cute, but she was video vixen cute. Cookie explained that she was getting herself prepared to be an actress by investing in her career, in other words, her body. Everything about her was fake, from the overdone long weave to the fake eyes, to the fake breast. Yeah, his baby wore weaves too, but everything about her was subtle and classy. She was what LL Cool J would call a *round the way girl*. It's like Halle Berry and Sanaa Lathan. Halle is gorgeous, but Hollywood gorgeous. Sanaa is gorgeous, but more like the neighborhood cutie. That was how he felt about Cookie. Some men may have gotten caught up in her beauty, but from the time they were introduced all Anthony found himself doing was comparing her to Soul. Damn, Anthony didn't even know how they got here.

Anthony was prepared to have given Soul the world. Never had he felt a love like the one he felt when he was around Soul, and even after things went down, he still wanted her back in his life, as his wife. He was so tempted to call her that Anthony erased her number but immediately went back and reprogrammed it in his phone. Anthony had settled for simply turning his phone completely off to ignore the temptation of answering Soul's persistent calls or breaking down and calling her himself. In fact, the only thing keeping Anthony from literally driving over to Soul's house was his pride, and his mama wouldn't let him forget it either.

Like the other day, after trying to reach him all day, and not being successful, his moms got in her car and drove over to his place. She banged on the door like she was working for Dallas's finest, and then finally started screaming at the top of her lungs, "Boy, if you don't open this damn door!" Anthony knew he was in for it when he opened the door, and she whacked him upside the head with her purse.

"Boy, don't you ever have me worried about you like that again. Why in the hell haven't you been answering your phone? Huh? Anthony Timothy Robinson, you better answer me!"

"Mama, I"

"Shut up! Have you been eating? You look like you lost fifteen pounds. Boy you better answer me! I said," Anthony's mom raised her voice another octave or two, "Have you been eating?"

"Mama, I"

"Shut up, when I'm talking to you. Now I know you think you grown, and you are, but I brought life into you, and I raised you, and I know when you hurt. I'm not going to tell you not to hurt, cause it's okay to hurt. Soul was wrong, and even though I'm not taking sides, I know sitting here shutting the world out is not going to solve anything. If you think being in a relationship is hard work, you in a heap of trouble when you get married. You can't run at the first sign of trouble, or your daddy and I would have been over and done with a long time ago. Baby, you're a strong man, but your stubborn pride is going to be the death of you. You better face your problems and realize your solutions. You need to talk to Soul, but first you need to talk to God. Sometimes God got to knock you down to make you look up. And believe me when I say, God knows who he can trust his troubles to, that's why they say only the strong survive. Everything about you and Soul's relationship was picture perfect, but how many Sundays did you go to church? How many mornings did ya'll wake up and pray together, or thank God for him helping you to find your way to each other? You know I love you," Marvella Robinson said, touching Anthony's check. "You are my son, and you done made me proud, but don't be a fool. Don't let pride keep you from being happy. If you want that woman, go get her. If you don't, let her go, get yourself together, and move on, and if you're not sure, pray about it. Oh, and clean this mess up," his mom said peeking around Anthony and into his place. "Here," she added handing him a sack with plastic containers filled with food. Get yourself together and answer your phone the next time you see your mother calling. I'm not driving all the way back over here no more. You hear me?"

"Yes ma'am."

Anthony's mom kissed him on the cheek and walked off.

"Hey mama."

"Yeah?"

"I love you."

"Love you too baby," Anthony's mom said with a wink.

So, Anthony did just what his mama said. He ate, shaved, showered, and cleaned his place. Then he finally turned his phone back on. He had multiple combined text and voice messages, most of them from Soul. Listening to his voicemails, the sound of her voice almost drove Anthony back to bed, but he remembered what his mama said, and instead said a quick prayer asking God to help him through this and guide him towards the answers he sought.

Then he finally called his boys who insisted he meet them for drinks. He should have known better. He got sloppy drunk, and then proceeded to embarrass himself by babbling and crying about Soul. His boys finally got him home where they all crashed because Thaddeus was worried that Anthony would die from alcohol poisoning or something. Man, he was glad that they were like brothers, or he may have been too embarrassed to talk to them. The funny thing about men is that even though Anthony knew he made a fool of himself, they never mentioned it again, it was like a code or something. Everybody was allowed at least one crying moment, no questions asked, no dwelling on it the next day. The funny thing that surprised Anthony was the advice that each of his boys gave him when they were alone at the bar. Ajax, who caught his chance when Thaddeus left to go to the bathroom surprisingly advised Anthony to try to work things out and apologized for even calling Anthony in the first place.

"Nah dude, you did what you thought was right. And if the shoe were on the other foot, I would have done the same thing."

"Yeah dog, but maybe I should have done some better investigations, or hell even confronted her myself. At least that way if things weren't what they seemed I wouldn't have gotten you involved."

"Man, I was involved the day I asked her to marry me. Besides, what if I had found out later that something was jumping down and that you knew or suspected something at one time or another, I would have been pissed off."

"Yeah, I guess you're right, but at least I would have known for sure. I mean, dang you still don't know what, if anything, was going on, because you won't talk to her. But for what it's worth, I don't think anything happened. I mean I saw how tore up she was when you left. Shit dog, Simone almost had to tie her up to keep her from coming after you.

"Speaking of Simone, what's up with that? You just hitting it or what?"

Ajax took a long swig of beer. "I don't know man. I think I got myself involved deeper than I bargained."

"Well, I tell you what. Simone is good peeps, and I don't want to see her hurt. You know you my boy and all, but you know how you get when it comes to women."

"I know dog. I know. The problem is, Simone ain't your average woman, Ajax said taking another long sip of his drink. "Say, I'll be right back, let me step outside and make a quick call," he said, giving Anthony a pound before sliding off the barstool.

"Where's he going?" Thaddeus asked walking up.

"He went to make a phone call."

"To who?"

"Probably Simone."

"That's wild huh?"

"Yeah. That's wild for real."

"Shit I don't know why either one of us is surprised. Simone fine as hell, and the way they argued, there had to be some sexual tension."

"True that," Anthony said sipping on his drink.

"So, what's up dog. You aw'ight or what?"

"Humph! Or what."

"Damn, I never would have pegged Soul for the cheating type. She seemed to be all into you and everything. And then to catch her with another nigga. Damn."

Anthony sighed. He felt his stomach tighten up, "So you think she cheated on me?"

"Nah dog, that ain't what I'm saying. I mean I ain't really saying she did cheat or she didn't cheat. All I'm saying is that I never thought ya'll would be in this kind of situation. Hell, to be honest, I envied what the two of you had. Made me want to get that kind of love for myself, which is why I have been on the dating scene so much lately truth be told. I guess looking for my Soul."

"Yeah well, don't look too hard. Shit ain't all it's cracked up to be."

"I hear you. Say, this chick, I've been dating has a friend that's fly as hell."

"Nah dog, I think I'll pass."

"Man, I'm telling you. This chick is bad with a capital B. Say bartender let me get another round," Thaddeus added gesturing to the bartender who promptly refilled all three shot glasses. "I mean 'A' what you gone do? Sit around and cry all day. No offense dog, but you are my boy. I don't want to see you like this, besides you know you were there for me, when Susan left, and we all thought I'd never get over her. Hell, it was you, who told me to move on."

Anthony swallowed the drink sitting in front of him, before gesturing to the bartender for another.

"You sure sir? You look like you have had enough."

"It's cool dog," Thaddeus interjected. We got him, he ain't driving."

"Okay man, it's on you." The bartender poured Anthony another tequila shot. As soon as he sat the drink in front of him, Anthony downed it quickly.

"So, what's up man, you want to go out with Cookie or what? Well, her real name is Marisa, but everybody calls her Cookie."

Anthony thought for a minute. "Yeah man. Why not?" he finally answered. "Bartender, another shot. I think I'm gonna need it." There were two things Anthony knew. One, never accept a blind date, and two, never accept a blind date when you were drunk. But he had and look where it had gotten him. All he had really wanted to do was relax and work on his proposal, but Daniel insisted that one date couldn't hurt anything. Somehow, Anthony had known that he was wrong, he just didn't know how wrong until he walked in that restaurant and saw Soul.

Chapter 36

"Who in the hell is calling me at this hour?" Soul's ringing phone jarred her from her sleep.

Soul squinted to look at the time as the phone stopped ringing only to start ringing again a few seconds later. 2:47 A.M. Soul had only been asleep about twenty minutes, but it felt like it had been hours. Not able to get the image of Anthony and his date out of her mind, Soul had tossed and turned since the moment she got in the bed. Confusion was the only way Soul could describe what she was feeling. Why did Anthony even come to check on her, like he cared or something? If he cared, he would have returned her calls, not went on some damn date.

"Hello," Soul answered not even bothering to look at the caller ID. "Hello," she repeated raising her voice. "Look I don't have time for you to play on my muthafu..."

"Soul."

Soul's heart stopped. The sound of Anthony's voice shocked her so much she almost dropped the phone. He was the last person she expected to be calling.

"You're the last person I expected to call. I thought you would be with your video vixen."

Anthony chuckled. Damn they were so connected, they even thought alike. "Soul, I need to talk to you."

"Really," Soul responded dryly.

"Yeah, really."

"And what makes the fact that you want to talk to me now so important that you had to wake me up at three fucking o' clock in the morning. Why didn't you want to talk when I was calling you back-to-back, not able to eat or sleep?"

"I needed time to think."

"Think! You know what Anthony. I 'think' I am hanging up now!" Soul disconnected the call, and slammed the phone on the nightstand as the tears immediately began to flow down her face. The banging on the door and the simultaneous ringing of her phone scared her to death.

She looked at her Caller ID. Anthony. She got up and peeped out her window. Anthony's SUV was parked out front. Shit! Soul quickly glanced at her reflection in the mirror before storming down the stairs. She snatched the door open and prepared to give Anthony the cursing of his life, but the man standing in front of her caused her to pause just to try to catch her breath. Wearing basketball shorts and a cut up red muscle shirt that she had bought him a week after they became engaged, the words "Mr. Right" scrolled across his chest seemed to fit him perfectly. Soul quickly regained her composure, "Who in the hell do you think you are coming over here at this hour of the night. You got a lot of nerves."

"Soul, I really need to talk to you. Can I come in," Anthony said stuffing his hands inside his pockets, the only thing he could do at that moment to resist the temptation of grabbing Soul and making love to her right there in the doorway. Her tight hot pink boy shorts clung to every curve of her hips. Her hair pulled back into a ponytail and the sleep lines pressed into one side of her face, gave her that round the way look he had come to love so much.

"You know what Anthony, this is ridiculous. You made yourself very clear tonight when you walked in with your little date." Soul felt the tears begin to run down her face. She quickly turned her back to Anthony and went and sat on the sofa. He walked in behind her and closed the door. He looked around noticing that her normally tidy place looked as dirty as his own place before his mother told him to get it together. He could hear an old Shirley Murdock song playing upstairs. Anthony went and sat beside Soul on the couch. She sat with her hands holding the sides of her head. Her entire body expression had defeat all over it. He noticed she was still wearing her engagement ring. It sparkled like she had just shined it again that very morning.

"Come here," Anthony said taking her into his arms.

"Don't," Soul couldn't help herself as she began crying harder.

"Baby, I don't want anybody but you. I just need time. I never should have let Thaddeus talk me into going on that date. I was just so tired of thinking about you and not being able to hold you in my arms. And then I kept seeing you in that nigga's arms and I would lose it all over again."

Soul sighed. She looked into Anthony's eyes and could see the hurt he felt. She began to cry again. "I'm sorry baby. I never meant to hurt you. It's just that Key and I had so much history, and I felt like I needed to explain things to him so he would know the only man for me is and will always be, the man sitting here with me right now. I would do anything to protect what we have, but in this situation, I should have listened to Simone and Danielle."

"You should have trusted me. Talked to me," Anthony said wiping the tears from Soul's eyes. "What was I supposed to think when the woman I'm about to marry is in a hotel with another man?" This time the tears formed in the corners of Anthony's eyes, but unlike Soul, he didn't bother turning away to hide them.

"I'm sorry baby. I'm so sorry," Soul moaned kissing his tears. "I never meant to hurt you," she whispered in his ear suddenly overwhelmed by heat and passion. "I'm sorry. I'm so sorry," Soul whispered over and over as she continued to kiss Anthony as she climbed on top of him and straddled his legs, slowly pulling the shirt over his head.

"Baby, don't," Anthony said weakly. "This isn't going to solve."

"Shh. I'm sorry, I'm sorry," Soul cried as her tears mixed with those that ran down Anthony's face. Soul kissed Anthony like her life depended on it, nibbling his ear and neck, as he grew harder beneath her. Standing, Soul pulled her shorts off, her eyes never leaving Anthony's. Not able to fight the passion inside of him any longer, Anthony pulled Soul's pussy into his face sniffing the aroma he had missed so much. He could feel the steam radiating from her as she begged him with her eyes to taste her. And he did, plunging his tongue deep inside of her, tears mixing with Soul's wet juices. Soul snatched the t-shirt off her as she felt her legs weaken as she stood over Anthony watching his head and tongue disappearing inside of her. Soul grabbed the back of the sofa to stop herself from crumbling to the floor as her orgasm quickly overtook her trembling body as Anthony wrapped his arms tightly around her waist. Her chest rose and fell as she tried to catch her breath. Soul lifted Anthony's chin and looked into Anthony's eyes.

"I love you Anthony," Soul couldn't stop the tears from flowing down her face as she watched Anthony's own tears fall down his face. Soul began to kiss Anthony tasting the juices of her very own passion. Reaching her hands inside Anthony's shorts, she pulled his hard erection out before dropping to her knees and swallowing him into her mouth as he began to curse and moan her name. She tasted him with such force that he finally grabbed her face pulling him to her and kissing her. Straddling him, Soul slid onto him, slowly moving up and down. The meeting of his skin and hers the only noise outside of their tears. Anthony grabbed onto her back as Soul began to ride him faster. He began to shake and kiss her more intensely as they both exploded into each other. His juices mixing with hers, hers mingling with his. She screamed loud enough to let the world know she had missed her man as he grunted the same, holding onto her, pumping the last of his juices inside of her. She collapsed onto his chest, the sound of her whimpering the only thing that now disturbed the night.

Anthony laid his head back against the sofa. He closed his eyes, and the tears continued to stream down his own face. He couldn't deny the love he had of Soul, but the image of her doing this to someone else still forced its way back into his mind. He knew what Soul insisted, and most of him believed her, but there was still that small part that wondered why she even felt the need to go and explain something to someone she said no longer meant anything to her.

"I love you Anthony," Soul whispered in his ear. "Please don't leave me. I'm so sorry. I love you so much."

"Shh!"

Soul laid her head on Anthony's chest and listened to his heartbeat. Shirley Murdock's voice floated down the stairs. "Never again, will I let you let go. Now that your home, I missed you so," Shirley sang.

"Raise up baby."

"Hmm?" Soul realized she had fallen into a light sleep.

"Can you get me a towel or something," Anthony said kissing Soul's forehead.

"Sure baby." Soul slowly slid off Anthony. She blew him a kiss before dashing into the guest bath.

He could hear her opening cabinets and turning on the water. What was he thinking? This wasn't supposed to happen like this. Or was it? He knew that showing up at this hour could only lead to one thing, knowing he could never resist the woman he had fallen in love with almost the first day he laid eyes on her. While driving to Soul's, Anthony had told himself they were going to just talk things through, but as soon as Soul opened the door, he knew that was a lie. In fact, more than anything at that very moment, Anthony wanted to just say f it and pretend the last month had never happened so they could just pick up from the last good time he and his lady had shared, with the events that happened in between a mere memory, but it could never be that easy.

Soul looked in the mirror as she began to clean herself with the warm towel. She frowned despite the warm glowing feeling that illuminated from her skin. How did this happen? She was no dumb ass. She knew you never had sex with someone right after breaking up, especially someone you loved. It always confused things. Do you go on and try to act like everything is okay, never really discussing what brought you to the place of breaking up in the first place, or do you just go back to your separate places. This was by no means just a booty call. With Anthony nothing was just anything. Soul threw the towel in the hamper. She grabbed the robe hanging on the door and pulled it on before snatching a clean towel for Anthony. She wet it with warm, soapy water and sighed. She knew this moment of passion would surely come back to haunt her.

Anthony had his head leaned against the sofa with his eyes closed. His chest rose and fell.

"Hey," Soul said nudging him. Looks like sleep is catching up with somebody."

"Yeah," he chuckled. I guess so. Thanks," he said taking the towel from her outstretched hand. She sat down beside him avoiding his eyes.

Anthony cleaned himself and began searching for his shirt.

"I think your looking for this," Soul said reaching down to get the shirt she didn't even remember pulling off him.

As she handed him his shorts, their hands touched and their eyes locked.

"Soul. Anthony," they said simultaneously. They laughed a nervous laugh.

"You first," Anthony said taking the shirt and pulling it on quickly. Soul's eyes watched his every move.

"No go ahead," Soul smiled. "It's not like I know what I'm about to say anyway."

Anthony chuckled and moved a stray hair out of her face. "Me either. Why do you think I let you go first?"

They smiled.

"Maybe this," Soul began.

"Wasn't the right thing to do," Anthony interjected.

"Yeah," Soul finished.

"I'm not sure if I can handle this now. My feelings aren't in check. Sex confuses my heart and clouds my judgment. Makes me want to forget everything and start over." There, Anthony had said it.

"But we can't. We haven't solved anything. Haven't really figured out how to make sure we get back to that place, our place, again," Soul sighed.

"Do you love me?" Anthony blurted out.

"More than life itself."

Anthony breathe out a sigh of relief.

"Anthony, do you think what we had is worth working to save?"

"More than life itself," Anthony repeated imitating her earlier words. "We just need time to work things out and get things together. To grow. You know the old saying. If you love something, let it go. If it comes back to you, it's yours. If it doesn't,"

"It never was," Soul said finishing Anthony's thought. "Anthony, I'm coming back."

"I'm counting on it." Anthony grabbed Soul and held her in his arms. "I should go," Anthony said finally pulling away.

"Don't. Stay."

"But we just,"

"No, that's not what I mean. Just until morning. Let me fall asleep. Here. In your arms. Then just leave. Don't wake me, just go. I need this."

"He looked into her eyes, "You sure?"

"More than life itself."

"How can I resist?" Anthony grabbed a blanket off the sofa and made a pallet for them. Soul grabbed pillows from off the sofa and lay them beside Anthony's feet. Anthony climbed on the floor, and she snuggled into his waiting arms. He pulled the cover over them and kissed her on the cheek. "I'm coming back," he whispered into her ear.

"I'm counting on it," she said before closing her eyes. "Dear God," Soul prayed silently, "please let morning take her sweet time getting here."

Chapter 37

S oul looked at the clock. Five more minutes and she could finally start her weekend.

"Ms. Jackson."

"Yes Shakeem?"

"What if we don't finish our test?"

"I guess we will have to finish it Monday. How many people are still working on their test?" Several students raised their hands. Soul sighed, "Fine. Alicia, please collect the test and sit them on my desk. We'll finish Monday. Maybe some of you should take this extra time to do some refreshing of chapter eight," Soul hinted. "Okay, let's get ourselves together. Everyone, please check your areas and make sure you have nothing on the floor. Make sure you have your reading assignments written in your homework planners." The students groaned but immediately opened their planners and jotted the assignment down. They knew Soul's expectations were high of each of them. Either you're sinking or thinking Soul often reminded her students if they got off track or fell below her expectations.

The bell rang and the students waited impatiently for her to release them. Soul glanced around the room to make sure everything was back in order. "Okay, have a good week"

The students shot past her as usual before she could even get the last words out. Soul walked back to her desk and began to gather her things.

"Hey Ms. Jackson," Albert said wheeling his cart inside her room. "You getting out kind of early today huh?" he chuckled dumping a trash can into the larger one on his cart. "You got class tonight?"

"Nah, I plan on going home and getting straight in bed with a bowl of vanilla ice cream and Captain Crunch cereal."

He chuckled, "That's a new one on me."

"Really, we used to eat it all the time when I was little, and I have been craving some lately."

"Well, the big day is almost here huh? You ready?

"Please God don't let him ask me about the wedding. "What big day?"

"Graduation."

Soul let out a sigh of relief. "Yeah, it is," she said brightening up. "You would think as much money as I have spent going to school that graduation would be embedded in my mind."

"Ha, well with everything you're always working on, I can see how it may have slipped your mind, but don't let it slip too far away. I'm still banking on being head maintenance soon as you get your own school."

"Hey, I'm still counting on it too," Soul smiled at the older man as she grabbed her purse and bag. Have a good weekend," she said with a sneeze.

"You still sick."

"Yeah, I guess this bug is getting the best of me. Oh yeah, I left that box of pizza for you. I ordered pizza for my Honor Roll students, and we had some left over."

"Thank you, Ms. J., You get on out of here and try to get some rest this weekend, so you can feel better by Monday."

"Okay. See you later. Oh shoot. I'm forgetting my book," Soul said turning back to her desk to grab her book *The Purpose Driven Life* by Rick Warren.

"Hey, is that a good book? I've heard a lot about it, and the wife and her book church group are reading it and she keeps harassing me to read it."

"I've had it for years, but never gotten around to reading it until now, but It's worth it. You're supposed to read a chapter a day but sometimes I read more and sometimes I don't read it at all, so I guess it balances out. Plus, I have the journal, so it also helps me keep track of important points. I have gotten a lot out of the book, and I think it's really helping me deal wit a lot of my issues."

"Issues! You're too young to have issues. What kind of issues do you have?"

"Mr. Albert, more than you could ever imagine," Soul smiled weakly. "See you later."

Soul lay in bed reading The Purpose Driven Life. She stopped every few minutes to reflect and write in her journal. The thought of Anthony popped in her head. She tried desperately to push his image out of her head. It had been almost six weeks since she last saw him. Most days she did a good job going about her daily activities and pretending like he didn't exist, but then there were those days that something would remind her of him. A car, a song, a person. Anything, and she would burst into tears. Too bad she hadn't started reading this book before she met Anthony, maybe she would have been prepared for the gift that God had sent her.

Soul closed her eyes and lay back on the pillow. "If you love something let it go. If it comes back to you, it's yours. If it wasn't it never was," she repeated over and over. Soul smiled thinking about the words she and Anthony had spoken the night he had shown up to her place and made love before falling asleep on the floor only to wake up again and make love again before he finally left.

The ringing phone jarred her from her sleep. Soul looked at the clock. She must have dosed off. It was nine thirty. She looked at the caller ID.

"John- Cooks Hospital," Soul grabbed the phone. "Hello."

"Soul?"

"Yeah?"

"This is Ajax. I'm at St. Cooks. Can you come down here?"

"Oh my God. Is it Anthony? Is he okay? What happened?"

"Soul. It's not Anthony. It's Simone. She's been in a car accident."

<h1 style="text-align:center">Chapter 38</h1>

♥

Danielle looked forward to her nightly calls from Devon. Though he had flown back to visit her quite a few times, they decided to take things slow, which was fine with Danielle since she didn't want to find herself in another bad situation. Danielle would never admit it to anyone, but the first time she had returned home from visiting Devon, she came home to find Jackson on her doorstep. Her first instinct was to take off running in the opposite direction, but he assured her that he wasn't there to hurt her. He made promises that things would get better and begged her to take him back. And for a moment she had even considered it. She and Jackson had even hooked up a couple of nights, but something had changed in Danielle's heart. Yes, she still loved Jackson, but it was not until Devon came to visit her, that she realized she was no longer in love with Jackson, and quite frankly wondered if she had actually ever loved Jackson. Danielle laughed as she thought of all the times her friends tried to warn her about Jackson's wayward behavior, but as Simone loved to remind her "bought sense is better than told sense any day." One day as she laid in the bed thinking about all the bad times she and Jackson had gone through, she cashed in on some of her sense. When Jackson showed up for one of his regular booty calls, she told him it was over for good. Of course, he didn't believe her, and Danielle wasn't surprised. He had heard her say it was over many times before and each time she took him back.

"Come on Danielle, you know you still love me," Jackson said with a short laugh.

"I never said I didn't love you anymore, but it's time I started loving myself too."

"Whatever. You'll change your mind tomorrow."

"Not this time Jackson."

He had just laughed and walked off, but she was determined to stick to her guns. When he called, she wouldn't answer. At first it was hard, but with each passing day she found herself growing stronger. Danielle chuckled to herself thinking how just last week, she had seen him in the mall walking with the same nurse from when she was in the hospital, and all she found herself doing was laughing, not crying, not creating a scene, just laughing. In fact, she didn't feel the need to even let him know she had busted him. Yes, she thought breathing a sigh of relief; she could finally say it was over and mean it. Danielle fixed herself a glass of wine and allowed the smooth sounds of jazz to cover her. When the phone rang, she didn't have to wonder who was on the other end, she knew. She and Devon called each other every night at the same time. It was becoming second nature.

"Hey you," Danielle said answering the phone as a huge smile covered her face.

"Hey baby, it's Jackson."

All Danielle could do was laugh. After all Soul had been through with Key and Anthony, she should have known better than to ever answer the phone without first looking to see who was calling. "Expect the Unexpected," she said laughing.

"What is that supposed to mean?"

"Nothing. What do you want Jackson? I told you it was over."

"Yeah, you did, and how many times have I heard that?" Danielle could tell he had been drinking from the slur in his voice.

"You're right. You have heard it many times before. The only difference now is that this time I mean it."

"I need to see you. Danielle, open the door. I'm outside."

Danielle got up and walked over to the window. Sure enough, Jackson's truck was parked out front.

"Go home Jackson."

"I am home."

"Not anymore."

"Please baby, open the door," he pleaded. "Besides I've been drinking, and I shouldn't be driving. Remember you used to tell me that all the time."

"Yes, and you never listened. As you loved to remind me you are a grown man who has never had a wreck, so I don't see why tonight will be any different."

"Come on baby. I really have had a lot to drink, and I just want to see you. Let's talk. We can work this out."

"It's over Jackson," Danielle said meaning every word. "I'm hanging up now."

Danielle hung the phone up and expected Jackson to immediately call her back. Instead, she was surprised to hear the ignition to his truck start as he slowly pulled away.

"Good. Maybe now he will leave me alone and bother someone else."

***

"Who does she think she is?" Jackson said aloud. "She's nothing without me. When she comes around begging me to come back to her, I won't be anywhere around. I've got plenty of women who want to be with me. Hell, her own friends probably want me. That's probably why they used to hate on me so much," Jackson said laughing at his own humor. Whoa!" he said grabbing the wheel, as he swerved back into his own lane.

"It's over," Danielle's words rang through his head. Jackson didn't want to admit it, but he knew this time was different. Danielle had never been so firm and persistent as she seemed to be lately. It was like he didn't even know her. Last week, he saw her in the mall, and she seemed so carefree and full of life, like she was happy just being by herself. He even thought he saw her glance in his direction, and almost panicked since he was walking arm in arm with the nurse from the hospital. But if she did notice him, she didn't even blink in their direction. She just kept shopping and smiling, even laughing to herself. Jackson reached for the bottle lying in the seat beside him and took a long swig of the alcohol.

"Damn!" he said taking another drink as his cell phone began to ring. Jackson smiled to himself. "I knew it wasn't over," he said searching for his phone. He finally found it only to see that it was the nurse not Danielle. Jackson declined the call before reaching for his bottle of liquor. He tried to open the bottle and simultaneously scroll to his contacts to call Danielle as he pressed the gas faster and faster without even realizing it. He was so busy with the task at hand, that he didn't realize he had once again driven into the oncoming lane until the lights and blaring horn forced him to look up.

***

Danielle glanced at the ringing phone, praying it wasn't Jackson again. John- Cooks Hospital flashed across the screen. "Hello."

"Danielle this is Ajax. I'm at St. Cooks. Simone and I were in a bad accident.

You need to get her now. We're in ICU."

"I'm on my way," Danielle said grabbing her keys and rushing out of the house.

Chapter 39

S oul whipped her car into an empty parking space, barely bringing it to a full stop before grabbing her purse and making a mad dash into the hospital. She rushed to the front desk and began pounding on the window.

"Excuse me, I'm looking for someone. Her name is Simone Alexander.

"I'm sorry, what was the name?"

"Simone Alexander."

"Do you know what she was brought in for?"

"A car accident, I think."

"Soul, over here," Danielle said rushing up. "Come on. She's in ICU."

"Oh God! What happened?"

"I don't know." Danielle grabbed Soul's hand and rushed towards the elevators.

"I mean what did Ajax say?" Soul said impatiently pressing the elevator button over and over.

"Just what I told you." The doors opened and Danielle and Soul rushed in quickly.

"When Ajax called, all he told me was to get here because he and Simone had been in an accident, and she was in ICU."

The doors clanged open, and Danielle and Soul rushed out.

Ajax was standing in front of a large set of double doors pacing back and forth. His shirt was torn, and blood was dripping down the side of his face.

"Oh my God! Ajax!" Danielle screamed rushing up to him. "What happened?"

Ajax turned around just as Danielle and Soul rushed up to him.

"Are you okay? Is she okay? What happened?" the words came spilling out of Soul's mouth quicker than her brain could process.

"We were driving, and Simone had just taken her seat belt off to get her cell phone that had dropped under her seat. Then the next thing I knew this SUV comes barreling around the corner in our lane, and slams into us. Simone flew threw the windshield. I couldn't do anything to help her. I tried to grab onto her, but the impact of the wreck made my airbag deploy and I couldn't catch her.

"Oh God," Danielle whimpered. "Why didn't her airbag activate?"

"I don't know. It was all so fast.

"Is she?"

"She's in surgery. I didn't know what to do."

Danielle leaned into Ajax's chest and began to cry.

At that moment a doctor came out of the double doors. "Are you the family of Simone Alexander?"

"Yes," everyone answered in unison.

"Are you her husband sir?"

"I'm her boyfriend. Is she going to be okay?""Well sir, your girlfriend suffered a great deal of trauma. There was a lot of internal bleeding from her injures and several broken bones. Right now, we need consent to go back in and operate.

"Operate? I don't understand." Danielle piped in.

"Unfortunately, there is swelling around her brain."

"The brain. Doc, look, I'm not understanding, what does all this mean? Can you just give it to me straight?"

"Well, once we receive consent, we will prepare Ms. Alexander for emergency surgery. Then we will go in the brain and try to stop the bleeding. However, it is imperative that we get her prepared for surgery immediately. I'm going to be honest Sir without the surgery she could die.

Die. Did Soul hear him correctly? This had to be a dream. Soul leaned against the wall. The room started to spin. She tried grabbing a nearby chair for support, but it seemed so far away.

"Soul are you okay?" Soul could hear Ajax talking but his voice seemed so far away.

Soul tried answering but couldn't find the words. She felt herself go weak before everything went pitch black.

✳✳✳

"Is she going to be okay?" Danielle asked from where she stood in the doorway.

"She'll be fine," the nurse replied as she checked Soul's blood pressure.

"Hey," Ajax said walking into the room. "How is she?"

"She'll be fine once she wakes up. How's Simone?"

"I don't know. She's still in surgery. We just have to wait and see at this point. Her mom should be arriving soon, but they let me go ahead and get all the paperwork started since her mom gave her consent."

"Do you mind sitting here with Soul? I'd like to go to the chapel for a while."

"Sure, no problem. Hey Dani, are you sure you're okay? I can't have all three of you in the hospital.

"Nah, I'm fine," Danielle said smiling weakly. "Two is enough. Some people will do anything for attention, and those two are so competitive," Danielle joked attempting to make Ajax smile. "Do you want anything back?"

"I'm cool, can you call Simone's mom and see what time her flight gets here."

"Sure," Danielle started out the room.

"Hey Ajax."

"Yeah?

"This is good."

"What?"

"You and Simone. I'm glad she has you. Who would have ever thought," Danielle said with a slight smile before leaving the room."

"Okay, looks like we're all finished," the nurse said checking the last of Soul's vitals. "She must have given you a real scare," the nurse said as she tucked the covers around Soul. "She'll be fine once she wakes up. Probably stress."

"I guess," Ajax murmured absentmindedly. He knew he was being selfish, but he wished Danielle would hurry back. He didn't want to be away from Simone too long.

"Yeah, most expectant mothers are quite stressed in the early parts of their pregnancy. She was quite dehydrated and needs to go to her doctor ASAP to get her prenatal vitamins started."

"She's pregnant?" Ajax asked incredulously.

"You didn't know."

"I'm not her boyfriend."

"I'm sorry, I just thought. Shit. Now I'm going to get another write up," the nurse said as a worried look crossed her face.

"Oh no, it's cool. We're friends. My girlfriend is her cousin. It's just that I didn't know she was pregnant. How far along is she?"

"I guess about six weeks?"

"Damn!"

"Is that a good damn or a bad damn?"

"Depends on who you ask," Ajax said picking up the phone as the nurse left the room."

"Ant. What up dog? Hey you here yet? I'm coming down to meet you. I know I promised myself I would mind my own business, but we got to talk."

***

"Soul," Anthony said moving closer to the bed.

"Hey," she said weakly struggling to open her eyes. She tried to sit up, but the overwhelming nauseated feeling caused her to lie back down.

"Uh, I feel awful. What happened?"

"You fainted baby. You okay?"

"Yeah, I think so." Soul laid back and closed her eyes. "How's Simone?" she asked suddenly remembering why she came to the hospital in the first place.

"She's still in surgery."

"Is she going to be okay?"

"We just have to wait babe," Anthony said with caution so as not too upset Soul.

"How could this be happening? Anthony, I can't lose Simone. She's not just anybody, she's my BGC, that's best girl cousin, as she named it. You know how far we go back. We've always been a team, from high school debate to college roommates. Simone has gotten me through so much, and I just feel so helpless." Soul began crying.

"It's okay," Anthony walked over to the bed and sat down, pulling Soul into his arms and holding her. He loved her so much that her pain felt like his own. If he could take everything that was hurting her away, he'd do just that. He rocked her and waited for her to be okay.

After a long time, her tears subsided, and her shoulders relaxed a little. Soul pulled away from Anthony looking into his eyes.

"Thank you."

"For what?"

"For being here. For letting me cry. For even loving me," Soul said pausing hoping she hadn't stepped on a line they weren't ready to cross yet.

"Soul, can I ask you something?"

"Of course."

"Do you still love me?"

"Of course."

"Do you want to be with anyone else?"

"Not even Idris Elba," Soul said smiling.

"Humph. When was the last time you had sex?"

"With another person, or by myself?"

"Come on Soul, I'm serious," Anthony said searching Soul's eyes.

"Okay. The last person I had sex with was you. That night, well technically that morning. In the living room. Truth only."

Anthony released a sigh of relief, "No more secrets, right?"

"Of course, baby. I promise. Why are you asking me all these questions?"

"Soul, is there something you want to tell me?"

"Uh, I love you," Soul said hesitantly.

"I know baby, and I love you too. But is there something else you want to tell me?" Anthony said placing his hands on her belly.

"Anthony what are you talking about?" Soul asked looking questioningly into his eyes.

"The baby Soul. Were you planning on telling me about the baby?"

"What baby? I'm not pregnant. I mean I know I'm getting a little fat, but not that fat!"

"Baby, it's cool. I mean we can work this out. You know I'm not the type of brother that doesn't take care of my responsibilities."

"I know baby, but I'm not pregnant."

"Are you sure?"

"Yes!"

Anthony let go of her hand and turned to the side. Ajax was sure the nurse told him Soul was pregnant.

"Baby why would you think I was pregnant?"

"Ajax."

"Ajax?"

"Yeah, the nurse told Ajax you were pregnant."

"What the hell! She must have gotten me mixed up with someone else. Where is this damn nurse? Who in the hell does she think she is? First and foremost,"

"Soul calm down. Pregnant or not, you did just faint, so chill out."

"What up man," Ajax said entering the room with Danielle. "Everything cool in here. You guys need some privacy?"

"Nah dog, we cool," Anthony said looking at Soul."

"Ajax who is this damn nurse who told you I was pregnant?"

"Pregnant?" Danielle screamed walking in behind Ajax.

"Dog, are you sure you heard her right," Anthony said turning to Ajax.

"Man, I'm positive. She said something about stress and expectant mothers. Hell, I even asked her how far along you were, and she said as far as she could tell six weeks.

"Pregnant," Danielle said doing a little shimmy. "I'm going to be an aunt!"

"Hello. I'm not pregnant. Is anyone listening here?" Soul said waving her hand.

"Hey! There she goes right there. Nurse, can you come here?" Ajax said.

"Yes sir," the nurse said stepping into the room full of puzzled faces.

"Ma'am, earlier you told my friend," Anthony began.

"Where do you get off telling him I'm pregnant?" Soul interrupted.

"Ma'am, I am so sorry I didn't mean to blurt anything out. Hold on," the nurse said closing the door. "I'm really sorry ma'am. I just thought that he was your boyfriend or husband, and he already knew. I really didn't mean any harm. Please don't tell my supervisor. I'm new and could probably get written up."

"Okay look," Soul said softening up. "Just tell me why you would think I was pregnant?"

"Uhm, do you want everyone to step out?" The nurse asked nervously. "I really don't want to get in any trouble."

"No, at this point it's cool," Soul said. "It's not like everyone isn't invested in understanding why you would even think such a thing. So, they may as well hear too."

Well, it's right here on your chart," she said walking over to pick up Soul's chart. See it says, dehydration, stress, approximate six-week-old fetus in good condition." She said running her finger over the chart.

Everyone turned to look at Soul who was clearly as shocked as they were.

"This, this is a mistake. I mean I'm not pregnant."

"You have been sick lately," Danielle added.

"Yeah, but it's just a bug, probably something I picked up from one of my students."

"Have you been nauseated, throwing up, tired?" the nurse asked.

"Yeah, but that could just be a virus." Soul said although she remembered that she hadn't been able to eat anything the past week or so without it coming right back up.

"Do you mind me asking but when was your last period?" the nurse asked.

"Last month, or wait, was it the month before? Where's my purse?"

"Here baby," Anthony said giving her the purse from near the sink. He knew Soul kept track of her period through her app.

Soul began searching in her purse for her phone. She opened her apps and scrolled to her women's health app, quickly opening it and scrolling to the tab that monitored her period. Her eyes frantically scanned the page as she looked at the icons on the monthly calendar. How did she miss this?

"Oh God!" Soul said covering her mouth.

"What is it baby?" Anthony said gently reaching for her hand.

"I missed my period last month," Soul said closing her eyes and laying back on the pillow.

Chapter 40

♥

"Excuse me" the policeman said entering the room that was full of shocked faces. "I need to speak with the gentleman who was brought in with the young lady in the car accident on Frandella Road."

"That's me," Ajax said moving towards the door.

"I need to ask you a few questions. Do you want to step outside?"

"It's okay. Everybody here is family."

"Fine," the officer said flipping open his notepad. "Could you tell me what happened?"

"I mean, everything happened pretty quickly. Simone and I were coming around the corner where Frandella interchanges with Agnew. Simone dropped her cell phone under the seat. She had just unsnapped her seat belt so she could reach further under the seat. Suddenly, this SUV comes swerving around the corner, and it's all in our lane. I started flashing my lights and blowing on the horn, but it just kept coming at us. The next thing I know it rams right into us, and Simone is flying through the windshield."

"Is that it?"

"That's the last thing I remember because I blacked out for a short period of time."

"Thank you sir. I just needed to make sure that I had all facts straight before filing a report. When we catch this person, I want to make sure we have everything straight so we can throw the book at em'. Besides if that young lady dies, they're going down for vehicular manslaughter."

"What do you mean if you catch this driver? You mean to tell me you don't have this clown in custody!"

"Unfortunately, not sir, he fled the scene," the officer shut his notebook. "I'm sure the person who hit you was a drunk driver. In most case when the driver flees the scene, there is alcohol involved."

"A drunk driver hit us?" Ajax pounded his fist on the cabinet angrily.

"I can't say that for sure, but I'm willing to bet money on it. No matter how hard we try, we can't get 'em to stay off the streets. People think they're okay to drive, because they've only had a few drinks, and they don't give a damn about getting behind the wheel and hurting innocent people."

"Do you at least have any leads?"

"Right now, it's too early to tell, but based on the paint left on your Mustang, we know it was a red or maroon colored vehicle. Are you sure there isn't anything else you can tell us?"

"I'm sorry sir, I wish I could be of more help, but like I said it all happened pretty quickly."

"Well, we have your information. If anything comes up, we'll be in contact. Here's the info where your car was towed," the officer handed Ajax a card before leaving the room. Ajax crumbled the card in his hand.

"Damn, this shit pisses me off. I can't believe some drunk driver ran us off the road. That muthafucker had to know they were too drunk to get on the road. Should have had their ass somewhere at home."

Anthony walked over to Ajax and put his hand on his shoulder. "She's going to be okay, dog. I know we don't understand it now, but everything happens for a reason," Anthony said looking more at Soul than Ajax.

"Yeah, and I may have never known that I'm pregnant," Soul sighed.

"Oh, at some point you would have known," Danielle said coming over to rub her friend's belly.

"Excuse me," the nurse said walking back into the room.

"Is it Simone?" Ajax asked anxiously.

"No, I didn't mean to worry you. The doctor just wants me to do a few more routine checks on your friend here, and I think we'll be ready to release her."

"Oh, okay. Do I have to leave?" Anthony asked.

"Go Anthony. I'm fine," Soul assured him.

"Are you sure?"

"I'm positive. Now go. All of you. Go check on Simone. I promise I'll be fine."

Ajax led Danielle out the door, as Anthony slowly followed. Soul lay back in the bed as the nurse began to check her vitals. She closed her eyes and prayed that she would really be alright.

***

Jackson looked behind him to make sure that no one was following him. He kept expecting to see sirens and police car lights flashing behind him at any second. The building he pulled behind would seem deserted to someone driving by, but Jackson knew better. He was just glad this place was only a few blocks away. He tried to steady his shaking hands, but the pounding of his heart only made things worse. Surprised that he made it this far, he turned the ignition off as smoke continued to come from under the crushed hood. He got out to examine the damage. The hood was crushed, paint was all over the passenger side, and the front windshield was smashed in. He cursed as he noticed that one of his rims was bent in, and the tire axel seemed to barely hold the tire onto the truck.

"What the fuck you want?" a rough voice said, pushing a gun into the side of his temple.

"Man, this J. Get that fucking gun out of my head and open the damn garage."

"Dog, you better start announcing yourself. You know your brother don't play when it come to business."

"Yeah, well, you better recognize who the fuck I am," Jackson glared at the teenager standing in front of him. He would never understand why his brother allowed dumb ass teenagers to handle his business. One day they were going to fuck up and get his brother in plenty of shit. "Where's my brother?" Jackson lifted the door to the garage before tossing the keys to the teenager. "Pull her in."

"I don't work for you dog," the teenager said with glazed eyes.

"Nigga, you better do what the fuck I said before I have my brother get on that ass. And be careful."

"For what? You done already fucked it up," the teenager said laughing.

He wanted to slap the taste out of the boy, but he knew he had more problems to deal with right now. He headed to the back where he knew his brother would be. He really didn't want to hear his shit, but he knew he was the only one who could get him out of the mess that he was in. If his girl would have just let him in, he could be getting some, instead of hiding out in a damn garage full on stolen cars.

As soon as he walked into the office, his brother glared at him with disgust. "Look man, before you even get started, I really need your help."

"Nigga, you always need my help."

Weed smoke surrounded him. The combination of weed and the alcohol was suddenly making Jackson sick to his stomach, not to mention the pounding in his head. He probably had a concussion, but he couldn't afford going to a hospital, at least not now anyway.   Damn, why couldn't he get his shit together. His brother was sitting there looking at him like he was one of the teenage punks he employed.

"What is it now J?"

"Look man, I need to keep my truck here, and I need some wheels to roll."

"What the fuck I look like? You got ya own damn ride."

"Damn, can you just help me for once without questioning me?"

"Help you? Nigga, that's all I do is help yo stupid ass. What you done fucked up now? Bro you my brother, but it seems like every time I look up J, you always doing stupid shit that require me to step in and fix it. Shit, I'm the youngest, and you act like you can't even handle yo damn business like a man. Hell, we both had it hard growing up, but I didn't let it stop me. I'm a hustler, and I do what I have to do to make it work. Nigga you got to get some hustle in you too. Shit I sacrificed everything I wanted, love, family, the woman who should have been my wife. Every fucking thing! Whatever it took to come up. I was tired of watching every brother come up but me, so I did what it took to survive. But you J, you act like you can't handle shit for yourself. First Mama had to take care of you, now every bitch on the street got to take care of you, and when they got sick of yo ass cause slanging dick don't pay bills, here you come running to have me clean up your messes.

Jackson hung his head. "Look man, I'm in some serious shit. I had an accident, and my truck is messed up."

"We'll I guess you better file on your insurance, cause I don't do freebies."

"Nah man, you don't understand. I left the scene."

"You what?"

"I had to. I had been drinking. I tried to see if everybody was okay, but I heard the sirens, so I freaked out, and left."

"Nigga, how you know the police didn't follow you here?"

"Do you think I'm that stupid?"

"Yeah."

"Well, I'm not. Look all I'm asking is for you to help me out this one last time."

"Nigga, I'm so sick of you and yo weak ass shit." Jackson's brother glared at him knowing no matter how he felt about his brother, family was family. He thought about how he used to admire his big brother. Watched him beat their daddy's ass every time he came home drunk and tried beat the hell out of their mama. Knowing that this wouldn't be the last time he would have to bail his brother out, he walked over and threw a pair of keys in his direction. "Tell the boys I said to handle the shit for you and get the fuck out of my face. And you better pray you didn't lead any type of five-o to my business, cause if you did, I'm beat the shit out of you."

"Thanks, little bro. I promise I'm going to get my shit together. I promise."

Jackson's brother didn't even bother to answer as he walked over to his desk and took a long drag of the weed as he closed his eyes.

Jackson watched as his brother blew weed smoke into the air with his eyes closed dismissing him completely. He knew he could count on him. People would think they couldn't stand each other, but he knew better. There was love between the two. It was just that life on the streets had changed the way they cared, a job where the required skills were ruthlessness and respect. Tonight, had been a wake-up call for him. Jackson prayed the people he hit were okay, and he wanted to stay with them to make sure they were ok, but he had to save himself first. His brother was right, Jackson knew he had to get his life together before it was too late.

Chapter 41

"Soul, are you sure you don't want to go home and rest," Anthony pleaded for what seemed like the hundredth time.

The doctor had just released Soul, and she was being her usual stubborn self.

"Yeah, we'll call you as soon as we know something," Danielle added.

"Are you going home?" Soul asked turning to her Danielle.

"Well no. I was going to wait here until Ajax got back from the airport with Ms. Dee," Danielle said referring to Simone's mother.

"Then I ain't going nowhere either. She's my cousin and I'm waiting right here until I know she's fine," Soul walked over to a couch in the waiting room and sat down. Simone had been in surgery for nearly five hours, and Soul planned on being right there with everyone else when the surgery was complete.

Danielle and Anthony looked at each other knowingly. They both knew that once Soul had her mind set on something, she was determined to do it, pregnant or not. Soul knew she was being stubborn, but she didn't care. Like earlier, even though she knew her period was late and saw the results on her chart, once everyone left out of the room, Soul still made the nurse take a urine sample and bring the actual test to the room for her to see. Then, she still wasn't convinced, and probably would have tried to take another one if the nurse hadn't finally convinced Soul that another test was useless and would only result in a higher medical bill.

"Okay baby, well at least let me get you something to eat," Anthony said in a frustrated tone.

"Fine, get me a honey bun and a Twix out of the machine."

Anthony was about to say something about junk food being bad for the baby, but the look on Soul's face made him change his mind.

"Dani, you want anything?"

"Yeah, can you bring me some water or something?"

"Sure, I'll be right back."

As soon as Anthony left the room, Danielle plopped down in the chair nearest Soul. It was nearly five in the morning, and the waiting room was empty except for them.

"Are you okay? Soul asked with concern.

"All things considered I should be asking you. I mean you did just find out you were pregnant and in front of a room full of people. Are you ok?"

"Not really, I just need some time to process everything that has happened." Soul closed her eyes, leaning her head back on the wall.

"You and me both. I keep trying to tell myself that everything will be ok, but it's hard. What if Simone"

"Simone will be fine. She's too stubborn not to be."

"You're right Soul. This is the time where we must trust in what God allows. Speaking of what God allows, I can't believe I'm going to be an aunt," Danielle said attempting to change the subject back to Soul's newfound news.

"I can't believe I'm going to be a mother."

"Soul, you really had no idea?"

"Hell nah! Do you think I really would have kept something like this from you and Simone?"

"It just seems so unbelievable."

"Yeah, well believe it. I guess with school and everything going on between me and Anthony I didn't pay any attention to a missed period."

"It's fate."

"It's bullshit. How in the hell am I going to have a baby at this point of my life?"

"But you love Anthony. What's the problem? Oh, and you know all that cursing is not good for my niece or nephew. I assume you will be stopping soon, as in today."

"Danielle don't start with me about what is right and wrong for this baby. One thing at a time. Of course I love Anthony, but I don't want him to think he has to be with me because of a baby. You know that's not fair to him."

"Girl stop!" Danielle said turning to Soul, "Anthony loves you. He's going to take great care of you and this baby."

"Yeah, that's if I have it."

"What the hell do you mean if?"

"Here you go ladies," Anthony walked in with the snacks, handing each of the ladies their requested items. "Is everything ok in here?"

Danielle glared at Soul but kept her mouth closed for the time being. She thought about continuing the discussion, but she knew it would only get her friend riled up and push her closer to the wrong decision. No, she would just wait until they were alone and slap some sense into her.

"Where's my Twix? Soul asked.

"Uh they didn't have any, but I bought your honey bun and a granola bar instead."

"I just bet you did. Well give them here. Beggars can't be choosy."

"As soon as the cafeteria opens, I'll go downstairs and get you some breakfast."

"Uh don't mention breakfast. Let's take this one meal at a time. I'm not trying to get fat nor kill myself with morning sickness."

Anthony laughed and settled in the seat beside her. "You okay?"

"I'm good baby."

"You sure."

"I'm positive," Soul said biting into the honey bun.

"What's wrong babe?" Anthony said noticing she had paused after the first bite. "You want something else?"

"Nah this is cool. I'm just waiting to see if it's coming back up." After a few more minutes of waiting, Soul seemed satisfied that the food agreed with her stomach. She finished the honey bun, took a sip of the juice Anthony had brought her, and tossed the granola bar into her purse. "I'll save it for later," she said noticing Anthony's glance. "Scoot down."

"Huh?"

"I want to lie down."

"Soul, are you sure you wouldn't rather go home? You have got to be exhausted. I don't know why you didn't just stay in the hospital room for the night"

Soul answered by gently nudging Anthony to the other end of the sofa. "Because they said it was ok for me to leave. Now scoot."

"Okay, okay."

Why don't you go ask one of the nurses for a blanket," Danielle suggested to Anthony.

"Good idea." Anthony began gently moving Soul so he could go retrieve a blanket.

"No!" Soul interrupted.

"No?"

"I want you to stay. I'll just use your jacket." Soul smirked at Danielle knowing Dani was just trying to get her alone to argue about Soul's last comment.

"Are you sure?"

"Yes, Anthony, I'm positive."

Anthony slid down to the far end of the couch. Soul laid her head in his lap and propped her foot on the sofa's railing. She closed her eyes and in moments was snoring loudly.

Danielle too had closed her eyes and was sitting sideways in the chair with her jacket thrown across her. She tried to go to sleep but couldn't. Something was wrong, and it wasn't just the whole Simone situation. There was something else that was bothering her, but she couldn't put her finger on it.

Anthony closed his eyes, but the only thing he could think about was the fact that he was going to be a father.

He loved Soul so much, and now she was having his baby. He couldn't be happier. "Thank you God," he whispered, "for helping me to come back to what's mine."

***

"Baby, wake up. The doctor's here," Anthony said gently nudging Soul.

"Huh what? Oh," Soul yawned slowly sitting up. She looked at the clock. 7:45. Soul didn't realize she had been sleeping so hard. She didn't even hear Ajax and Ms. Dee come in. Damn this baby was already starting to wear her down.

"Doctor," Ajax said walking over to him. He grabbed Ms. Dee's hand and pulled her next to him. "How is she?"

"Well, the surgery seems to have been a success. Right now, she's in a light coma, but she can still hear you."

"Coma," Simone's mother gasped.

"Yes, but this is quite common after a patient goes through a procedure of this magnitude. It's like the brain needs to rest for awhile."

"Is she going to be okay? Is there any damage?" Danielle asked.

"Well right now as far as we can tell, everything is working, but of course we'll know more when she comes out of the coma."

"And how long will that be?" Soul asked as Anthony grabbed her hand.

"To be honest, we don't know. It could be a day, or it could be days. It could be a month, or it could be months. As I said right now it's pretty much a waiting game."

"Can we see her?"

"For a minute, but let's keep it short and to a minimum of two visitors for now."

"Thanks Doctor," Ajax said grabbing his hand.

"Sure."

"Well, I know I'm going in," Simone's mother said. "Who's the number two?"

Ajax looked around the room. Soul could tell he really wanted to go in but was trying to be considerate of Simone's two life-long friends.

"Ajax I think you should go in," Soul said.

"Me too," Danielle added.

"Thanks," Ajax said with a grateful look. He and Ms. Dee immediately rushed to follow the doctor.

Anthony, Soul and Danielle sat silently in the waiting room until Ajax returned. His eyes were red, and he looked more tired than ever.

"You two can go in," he said weakly trying to contain his emotions. Ms. Dee is still in there, but you can step in for a sec."

"Thanks," Danielle said.

"Dog you okay," Anthony said walking up to his friend.

Ajax didn't reply. He only shook his head and looked down at the floor as the tears began to fall.

"Come on Soul," Danielle said walking over to help her friend up. "Let's give them some privacy."

Soul could already feel the tears falling down her own face. She was already emotional, and she was sure it would only get worse in the coming months.

"It's not fair man," she heard Ajax mumble as they walked out. "Why her? Why now?"

Soul and Danielle were not prepared for what they saw when they entered the room.

"Oh God!" Danielle said as she burst into tears.

Soul too burst into tears as Ms. Dee came over and pulled both girls into her arms.

"It's okay girls. She's going to be okay. We just got to pray. My daughter's a fighter and you two know that better than anyone here."

Soul tried to stop the tears, but they only flowed harder as she once again looked at Simone.

Her face was swollen and bruised. Tubes were coming from everywhere, and a huge bandage covered her head from the operation. She had bandages on her arms and legs and Soul could only imagine the pain her cousin was going through. Soul began to cry even harder as thoughts of her own mother's death flooded through her mind. She hated hospitals, and seeing Simone laying in such a terrible condition only made her hate even stronger.

"Okay, I'm going to have to ask one of you to leave. She really needs her rest," the nurse said walking in.

"Okay, we're going," Danielle said trying to wipe the tears that wouldn't stop.

"Girls, go home and get some rest," Ms. Dee piped in.

"But"

"No buts. I mean it. She's going to need your strength. Ajax and I will be here. You can come back later. Besides, there's no need in us all sitting in that waiting room."

"But what if," Danielle began.

"I will call you if anything happens," Ms. Dee said firmly. "Now go."

"Yes Ma'am," Soul and Danielle agreed in unison.

"She'll be alright. She has to be alright," Danielle said as she pulled Soul into her chest, and they began to cry again. Soul walked over and touched Simone's free arm. "We'll be back sweetie, we promise."

"Go, Go," Ms. Dee said trying to hold back her own tears.

"Yes ma'am," Soul and Danielle said hugging Ms. Dee before leaving the room.

The two friends made it as far as the hallway before they grabbed each other and started crying again.

Chapter 42

It had been nearly two weeks and Simone was still in a coma. The doctors said it was hard to tell if she was improving but her body did seem to be healing.

Ajax had been wonderful. He had proven himself to be a great man plus much more. He was at the hospital all day, every day, sitting beside Simone trying to raise everyone's spirit, and plain and simple, proving that he had fallen in love with her. Wrinkled jeans and t-shirts had replaced his usually well-maintained look. He needed to shave and needed a hair cut but he refused to leave Simone's side too long. Ms. Dee had to make him go home a couple of times to sleep and shower, but he returned after a few hours usually with notes and questions that he had found on the internet regarding Simone's condition. Anytime the doctor would start Simone on new meds, Ajax would come back the next day full of questions about the medicine.

He was wonderful and if anyone had any doubts about he and Simone's relationship, they were long gone.

Anthony was equally as attentive. He had been at Soul's beck and call. He insisted on staying with her and although they hadn't made love, Anthony slept in the bed with Soul every night where he usually fell asleep rubbing on Soul's stomach. It was Anthony who would hold her at night when she woke up crying with worry about Simone. Soul didn't want to admit it, but she was beginning to hope again. She knew Anthony loved her and would be a great father, but she had to make sure he wanted her back because of love, not obligation, and that he had forgiven her so they could truly move on with the past being just that, the past. Soul knew it was easier to forgive than to forget, and she wanted to be sure the baby didn't just make Anthony forgive her now and later regret the decision when he couldn't forget.

When Soul had mentioned to Anthony that she might not keep the baby, he blew up. The last time she saw him that upset was the night he found her with Key. And although they hadn't discussed it anymore, she knew Anthony was praying Soul would keep the baby.

Damn it Soul, I can't believe you would even consider punishing an innocent child because of our mistakes. Shit, you're a teacher, and you're the one who's always talking about how much you love kids. You give that crazy Shakeem and Alejandro all the chances in the world, and they seem to constantly be one shot away from murder or prison. But now you're here telling me you may not even let our baby have a chance at life. That's bullshit and you know it," Anthony had yelled.

The only thing Soul could do was sigh. She knew Anthony was right, but she was so confused. Soul knew she would never forgive herself if she destroyed something she and Anthony had created, but she wanted to be sure this was what Anthony really wanted. Deep down, Soul knew there was nothing more she wanted than to have Anthony's baby and start their family, but they hadn't even talked about resuming their wedding more less a wedding and a baby.

"Give it to God," Danielle had told her, "And this time don't take it back."

"What do you mean?"

"I mean when you give this situation to God, don't keep trying to fix it yourself. Give it to him and wait for an answer and really listen to it. That's what I keep reminding myself with this entire situation with Simone."

"Yeah, but how do you know when it's God's voice versus your own voice telling you something you just want to hear?"

"Pray girl, and I promise you'll know."

And that's exactly what Soul had been doing. Every chance she got. Praying. Praying for Simone, and praying for answers about the baby and Anthony, but as of today neither situation had been fixed. Simone was still in a coma, and she still didn't know what to do about Anthony and the baby. Soul knew what her heart was telling her, but she had listened to her heart before. This time she was trying to wait and listen to God.

"Good morning babe," Anthony said noticing Soul was awake.

"Good morning, Soul turned towards Anthony giving him a brief kiss. God how she still loved this man.

"You feeling okay. Need anything?"

Soul smiled and touched Anthony's cheek, rubbing the hairs on his chin like she so often loved to do. "I'm fine baby but I got an idea. Why don't we go to church today before we go to the hospital?"

"You must have read my mind. I wanted to go last Sunday but I knew you wanted to be at the hospital in case Simone woke up, but last night I was praying, and I realized how much I would like us to start going to church together, especially if we are going to grow as a family."

Soul sighed, "Anthony."

"Wait," Anthony interrupted, "let's just agree to go to church together," he begged looking into her eyes.

"You're right baby, let's just take it one day at a time, and this day will start with church."

"Thank you baby."

"No, thank you for being so patient and understanding."

***

St. Lukes was packed as usual. Soul and Anthony made their way to the center pew just as the services began.

The praise dancers performed a beautiful dance to an upbeat number, and then the choir began to sing.

Soul cried the entire time as they sang *The Battle is Not Yours* by Yolanda Adams, and *Great is Your Mercy* by John P. Kee. Anthony kept stealing worried glances in her direction. As soon as the choir started singing *Impossible* Soul felt overwhelmed by the spirit and began to cry out, "Thank you Jesus."

Granny Lewis who had noticed Soul and Anthony when they first came in finally came and sat by her granddaughter and wrapped her in her arms. As soon as she felt her grandmother's loving arms around her, Soul burst into tears even more.

"It's okay baby. Everything's going to be okay. God has it all in his hands. He didn't bring you to it, not to bring you through it," Soul's grandmother rocked her back and forth as the ushers fanned her to calm her down.

As the choir sang how God could do the impossible, Soul felt her spirit uplifted.

"You okay baby?" Anthony whispered as Soul's tears subsided.

She shook her head yes, as she continued to allow her grandmother to comfort her.

"She'll be okay honey," Granny Lewis said attempting to reassure Anthony. "Sometimes the spirit just overwhelms your soul. I must admit I almost shouted myself when the two of you walked in here together. Praise God!"

Soul sat up and wiped her eyes with a tissue the usher handed her before walking off once she was sure Soul was okay.

"You sure you okay baby?"

"I'm fine," Soul said smiling weakly at Anthony. She took his hand in one hand and her grandmother's hand in the other, "I love both of you so much," she whispered kissing each of them on their cheek before excusing herself to go to the restroom. When she returned, the preacher was already up preaching. Granny Lewis had returned to her seat at the front beside Mrs. Luella.

"God is such a merciful God. He can do some extraordinary things with ordinary people including you. Just quit fighting his will. Some of you waiting for answers that God done already gave. In fact, he left you a voice mail and sent you a text message and e-mail, but you haven't listened to them or checked them, so they keep bouncing back reading mail undeliverable and user account over quota."

"Amen," a few members shouted.

"But I'm here to tell you quit doubting God's plans. He don't make no mistakes and he don't need your help. God wants you to surrender your life to him, and I promise that blessing you been waiting on is going to come. I know ya'll ready for me to hurry to my seat and I promise you I'm not going to hold you much longer, but God told me there's somebody here who needs this message."

"Take your time," someone shouted.

"Thank you brother, I believe I will. Let me explain something," the preacher said wiping his brow. "You have got to surrender everything, that's everythang," he said stressing *thang*, "to God. In fact, I was reading a book the other day, and it said, "If you don't surrender to God, you surrender to chaos, and some of you got a chaos blanket wrapped around you, just all snuggled up," he said pretending to wrap a blanket around him which invoked a lot of laughter from the congregation.

"But I'm here to tell you, don't surrender to the problems. Don't surrender to the trials. Don't surrender to the chaos. Quit trying to be God and fix everything. Ain't nobody perfect but God, and if there is somebody in here who thinks they're perfect, you need to leave right now cause ain't nothing I can do for you. I need some people here who want to surrender. If you know you need to surrender your life to God, stand on your feet and give God some praise. Praise him!" he shouted, "Praise him! Ah yeah! Tell him Lord, I surrender it all. That problem that's keeping me from sleeping at night, tell him I surrender it to you."

"I surrender Lord," Anthony whispered. Soul squeezed his hand as she saw tears brimming in his eyes.

"That person on your job that been hating on you, trying to block your blessing, go to work tomorrow and tell him you can't stop me, cause I surrendered it to God," the preacher sang jumping up and down.

"That child you been worried about or that man or woman, boyfriend or girlfriend, husband or wife, tell him Lord, oh Lord, I surrender. That loved one laying in the hospital that the doctors can't give you a prognosis about, surrender it to God," he sang. "Surrender," he sang "Surrender it to God. Snatch it from chaos, "he said pretending to yank something, "and tell it Chaos," he sang "Oh Chaos. I don't need you to handle this here problem no more. I thank you mightily for holding on to it for me, but now I'm a give it to God, cause he said he got this one, and I'm sorry," he sang, "but he don't need no help. So chaos, you can go on about your business, cause I surrendered it to God. Turn to your neighbor and tell him God got this one!"

"God got this," Soul and Anthony said turning to each other.

"Ah yeah!" the preacher shouted walking back and forth, "Somebody shout surrender!"

"Surrender!" the congregation shouted.

"Surrender!" he shouted.

"Surrender!"

"Surrender it all to God," the preacher said walking back to the mic. "Surrender it all. Amen? Amen."

"Amen, the congregation repeated as Soul, and Anthony stood to their feet clapping. Several people were crying, including them.

"Baby," Soul said turning to Anthony with tears in her eyes. "You sure you ready to be a daddy?"

"Yes baby," Anthony said catching his breathe as tears dropped down his face.

"Good, cause I surrender," Soul said as she grabbed him into her embrace.

Chapter 43

Anthony and Soul had just returned from eating with Granny Lewis and Anthony's grandmother Mrs. Luella after church. They had gone to the same soul food restaurant they went to so many Sundays ago when their grandmothers first decided to fix them up.

"Who knew that Sunday, that you and I would be at this point?" Soul said digging into her macaroni?"

"We did," Luella said. "We always knew that we had great matchmaking skills."

"Yes, you did ladies. A toast to you," Anthony said raising his glass of tea.

"Granny, Anthony and I need to tell you something," Soul said putting down her fork."

"Ya'll getting married again. Praise God!" Her grandmother said interrupting Soul.

"Granny, can I finish?" Soul hesitated before going on. I know you have always wanted me to get married and have a house full of kids running around the house so you could spoil them to death. Unfortunately, that is not going to happen."

"What do you mean? You two are here together. You seem happy."

"We are happy," Anthony added.

"Good, then what's the problem," Mrs. Luella asked.

"The problem is that things don't always happen in the order we expect them to happen," Soul said. "What I am trying to say is that I'm pregnant," Soul said looking down.

"What!" their grandmothers shouted as several customers glanced their way.

"Oh baby," her grandmother said, "that's no reason to put your head down. You're a grown woman, with a man that loves you. It is Anthony's ain't it?"

"Yes ma'am. It's Anthony's," Soul laughed.

"Then there's nothing for you to be ashamed of. People get pregnant everyday. Especially when they do that hokey pokey thing you two young people probably like to do," Granny Lewis smirked. "You just make sure you thank God you got a man who loves you and will take care of his family. You understand?"

"Yes ma'am. Thank you Granny," Soul said with tears in her eyes.

"Oh! My baby is having a baby,"

"I can't believe your mama didn't tell me," Luella said with a puzzled look on her face.

"Well, Nana, she doesn't exactly know yet," Anthony said.

"Oh Lord! That woman is going to flip out. She been praying for the two of you to work things out since you first broke up. Why did ya'll break up?"

"Luella, get out of them kid's business. What matters is that they back together, and that we gone be some great grandmothers," Granny Lewis said smiling.

"I look too young to be a great grandmother," Luella said.

"Child me too, but I guess we better get used to it. So, when is the wedding?"

Anthony and Soul looked at each other. "We hadn't really thought about that yet. Things have happened so quickly," Soul said.

"Well, we better start thinking, because you're going to be a little busy real soon," Granny Lewis said with a smile.

"I guess your right," Soul said rubbing her stomach. She looked at Anthony and smiled.

"Okay ladies. Now that all the excitement is over, I guess we should be going. Soul and I need to get to the hospital," Anthony said signaling for the check.

"Simone is going to be okay baby," Soul's grandmother said noticing the sadness surface in Soul's face. "God is still in the miracle business."

"Amen," Luella added.

Anthony paid for the check, before going to get the SUV. They drove to the church and dropped Granny Lewis and Mrs. Luella off right after Anthony made his grandmother promise not to say anything to his mother about Soul's pregnancy until they had a chance to talk to her themselves.

She promised, although Anthony was not sure how long the promise would hold. "You know that old lady likes to gossip," he told Soul as they drove off.

Arriving at Soul's they went upstairs to change clothes before going to the hospital. Just as Anthony and Soul were getting ready to walk out the door, both Anthony's and

Soul's cell phone started ringing at the same time. "It's Danielle," Soul said looking at the caller ID.

"Ajax," Anthony said looking at his own phone.

Soul felt her stomach drop and sat in the nearest chair. Anthony grabbed Soul's phone and answered both his and hers at the same time.

"Hello, he said into both phones at the same time. "Ajax. Danielle. Both of you were calling at the same time. Is Simone okay? Wait. Danielle, hold on. I can't understand you. Ajax is talking too. What?" He paused, "We're on our way right over." He ended both calls turning to Soul.

"Baby, what is?" Soul asked nervously.

"It's Simone. She woke up."

Chapter 44

By the time Soul and Anthony arrived at the hospital, it seemed like Simone's entire family was there. There were so many people in the waiting room, it felt like a family reunion.

"Hey baby," Ms. Dee said grabbing Soul and hugging her. "I told you my baby was a fighter."

"Yes ma'am, you did. Can I see her?" Soul asked with a huge grin on her face.

"Well, the doctors are in there with her and Ajax. You know they had to nearly drag me out of there once my baby woke up. I was just sitting there praying with my head down, and Ajax was in the corner, then all the sudden I heard a weak voice ask, 'Mama what are you doing here?' I looked up and praise God, my baby was awake. Girl I could have run up and down the hospital corridor I was so thankful."

"Where's Danielle?"

"She went to the chapel."

"I'm going to run down there and find her. I'll be right back baby," Soul said turning to Anthony.

"No problem, I'm going to see if I can go find Ajax."

Soul kissed Ms. Dee on the cheek and rushed to the elevators. She pushed the second button to go to the chapel, where she found Danielle sitting there praying.

"Hey girl," Soul said walking up to her and gently touching her on the shoulder.

Danielle looked up and grabbed Soul. They both started crying tears of joy.

"It's a miracle."

"Girl, it ain't no miracle. It's God."

"You know you right. I was just sitting here giving him his glory," Danielle said.

"Well, let me get some of that, because we sure got a lot of thanking to do today, auntie."

"You mean."

"I'm going to be a mommy."

"Two prayers answered in one day," Danielle smiled grabbing Soul's hand as they begin to pray.

When they got back upstairs, Ajax was standing in the hallway with Anthony. He had a huge grin on his face. He grabbed Soul and Danielle in a bear hug. I hear we got a lot to celebrate today," he said.

"Yes, Simone is back, and you and I are going to be an aunt and uncle," Danielle laughed.

"You might be an aunt, but I'm going to be a Godfather," Ajax said.

"What? Well, I'm going to be a Godmother then."

Ajax laughed, "Hey don't try to leave my baby out of this. She would beat all of us down.

"Now you know I can't have just one Godmother," Soul said with joy as she walked over to hug Anthony.

"Baby, you can have whatever you want," Anthony whispered in her ear, kissing Soul on the neck.

The doctor came out and spoke to Ajax and Ms. Dee about Simone's condition. She was still in a lot of pain, but with therapy and time, she would be back to her old self soon.

"Can we go see her?" Soul asked with excitement.

"Sure," the doctor said, "but let's keep the visits short. She is still tired, and we don't want to wear her down."

"You two go," Ajax said looking at Ms. Dee, "I mean if that's okay with you."

"Of course, I've already been in and"

Before she could finish the words, Soul had grabbed Danielle and pulled her in the direction of Simone's room.

Simone was lying with her eyes closed, as they knocked gently on the door. "Hey you," Soul said.

"I was wondering where you two were," Simone said weakly.

"Girl, we had to give some shout outs to God," Danielle added jokingly.

"You alright?" Soul asked.

"Well, other than looking a complete fool, having half my head shaved, and being in a coma, I'm fine," Simone laughed as she begin coughing.

"Hey, take it easy," Soul said walking over to sit down.

"Ajax," Simone began.

"Has been great," Danielle interrupted. "Girl you would not believe how he has been these past few weeks. He would hardly leave you alone. Ms. Dee is completely in love with him. Girl that man got a love jones for you."

Simone smiled.

"Girl, go ahead and smile. You deserve to. And don't you ever scare us like that again."

"Yeah," Danielle added. "Besides it's not good for Soul's baby."

"Dang Danielle, you couldn't wait to open your big mouth," Soul said turning to glare at Danielle.

"Baby," Simone whispered hoarsely.

"Child, yeah. You not going to believe what you've been missing."

Soul laughed. It felt good to have her circle complete again. "It's amazing what happens when you surrender", Soul whispered to herself.

Chapter 45

Anthony looked at Soul. For nine months pregnant, she was the most beautiful woman he had ever laid his eyes on. She looked positively radiant in her gown that clung to her curves despite her huge belly. Anthony thought back to the day he and Soul met in the club, he knew there was something special about her. She was so sassy, and tough, but he could tell she had a heart of gold. A tear fell from his eye as he thought about how far they had come. If someone had told him they would be at this point in their lives a few months ago, he wouldn't have believed it.

Soul looked at all the smiling faces as she walked down the aisle. It was a beautiful afternoon, the perfect day for a wedding. Anthony looked ravishing in his tuxedo. His love was like an energy pulling her towards him as she walked down the aisle, and Soul knew she was the luckiest woman in the world.

The bridal music began to play, and all eyes turned to the door to examine the bride who was positively glowing. She reached the front of the church finally, and there wasn't a dry eye in the house. After all they had been through, this was truly a blessing.

Anthony looked at Ajax, who even had tears in his eyes. He reached in his pocket and handed him the ring.

"Who gives this bride away?" the minister asked.

"I do," her father said turning to give his daughter a kiss on the cheek, before placing her hand inside her future husband's hand.

"Dearly beloved, we are gathered together here in the sight of God, and in the face of this congregation, to join together this man and this woman in holy matrimony," the minister began.

Anthony looked across to Soul. "I love you," he mouthed as she beamed.

"Jonathan Dewayne Thompson, do you take Simone Denise Alexander to be your wedded wife to live together in marriage? Do you promise to love, comfort, honor and keep her for better or worse, for richer or poorer, in sickness and in health? And forsaking all others, be faithful only to her so long as you both shall live?"

"I do," Ajax said smiling at Simone.

"Simone Denise Alexander, do you take Jonathan Dewayne Thompson as your husband, to live together in marriage? Do you promise to love, comfort, honor and keep him for better or worse, for richer or poorer, in sickness and in health. And forsaking all others, be faithful only to him so long as you both shall live?"

"I do," Simone repeated. The minister looked at Simone and Ajax and shook his head for them to begin their personal commitment vow.

"Simone Denise Alexander, I take you to be my lawfully wedded wife," Ajax began.

"Jonathan Dewayne Thompson, I take you to be my lawfully wedded husband," Simone repeated.

"Before these witnesses, I vow to love you and care for you as long as we both shall live. I take you, with all your faults and strengths, as I offer myself to you with my faults and strengths. I will help you when you need help and will turn to you when I need help. I choose you as the person with whom I will spend my life," they said in unison.

Soul wiped a tear from her eye as she smiled thinking of her own wedding months ago. Once Simone woke up, Anthony decided that he didn't want to waste another moment of their life together. Soul was elated but argued that she wouldn't have enough time to plan the proper wedding.

"Baby, I don't care about a wedding, I just want you to be my wife. We can plan a big wedding after the baby is born," Anthony had said.

"But what about Simone, I can't get married without my girl," Soul argued.

"Well, we'll do it here in the hospital."

"But"

"But nothing woman. I've waited too long for this, and I'm not taking no for an answer."

And that was it. Anthony pulled some strings, and two weeks later they were married with promises to their parents and grandparents of a big wedding to come. As soon as they had exchanged vows, and were pronounced man and wife, Ajax toasted to their new love, and then made a proposal of his own.

"Simone," he began, as he dropped to one knee. "I never thought I could love a woman the way I love you. You are my world. When I thought I had lost you, my world ceased to exist anymore. I knew that I didn't want to spend another day without you as my better half. Simone Alexander, will you be my wife," he said popping open a huge engagement box.

Simone looked around at the room full of faces that were now all looking at her.

"Girl, you better say yes, before I do," Danielle whispered to her.

"Hey, you better save that yes for me," Devon had spoken up from the corner. He had flown down to check on Danielle with all the Simone drama and was now smiling at her from where he sat in the audience. He had shortly requested a job transfer soon after and was now visiting every weekend until he got his permanent transfer.

"Baby, will you?" Ajax prompted.

Simone looked at him with tears in her eyes. "Till death do us part."

So as soon as she and Anthony were married, Soul spent the rest of her free time planning Simone's wedding with Danielle and Ms. Dee. Simone said her one stipulation was that Ajax had to wait until her face was better, and she could at least limp down the aisle. He agreed and made her promise to speed up her recovery process, arguing that he couldn't wait another day to make her his wife.

The minister smiled, "Then by the power vested in me, I now pronounce you husband and wife. You may now kiss your bride."

Ajax lifted the veil to his wife's face and gave her a kiss so long the minister had to clear his throat.

"I present to you Mr. and Mrs. Jonathan Dewayne Thompson."

Ajax and Simone turned to face all their family and friends as they jumped the broom that had been laid before them before walking down the aisle as husband and wife.

Danielle blew a kiss as she passed Devon in the audience who mouthed "I love you."

Anthony grabbed Soul's hand as they walked back down the aisle. "How are my wife and son?" he asked with a smile.

"Blessed," Soul said smiling, "Truly blessed.

Chapter 46

Soul sat at the computer typing lesson plans for the upcoming six weeks. She wanted to make sure that her students wouldn't fall behind while she was out on maternity leave. Soul had only been off school for a few days, but she was already bored out of her mind, although she knew that would change any day now. Life couldn't be any more wonderful. Soul and Anthony were doing terrific. Anthony's business was booming with the city partnership, not to mention that he still maintained his real estate ventures with his fraternity brothers. Simone and Ajax had just returned from their honeymoon and were so in love it was sickening, and Danielle was just as bad especially since Devon's transfer had finally been approved and he had moved to the city permanently. For once in Soul's life, she and all her friends were in good relationships at the same time!

Soul saved the lesson plans she had been working on and wobbled around the house cleaning and tidying things though there really wasn't anything to clean. Her co-worker Maxine used to kid her about the fact that every time she called to chat, Soul was always in the process of cleaning house. Today was no different. Soul's energy level was off the charts today, so she decided to clean the entire house and cook Anthony dinner. She glanced through the cupboard and refrigerator to make sure she had all the ingredients to make her famous homemade lasagna before picking up the phone to call her grandmother.

"Hello."

"Hey baby,"

"Anthony?"

"Yeah babe."

"I picked up the phone to call granny and you were on the other line. The phone didn't even ring," Soul said sitting on a nearby stool.

"Oh. We'll I was just calling to see how my two babies were doing?"

"We're fine, just like we were an hour ago when you last called," Soul said smiling.

"Don't sass me woman," Anthony joked. "You feeling okay?"

"I'm fine sweetie. In fact, I'm fixing your favorite dinner tonight."

"You served on a platter?"

"You are so nasty! Get off this phone."

"Okay, but I want my dinner waiting on me when I get home."

"Goodbye Mr. Robinson."

"Goodbye Mrs. Robinson."

Soul hung up the phone and walked back into the study to log into the student database. She planned on calling Shakeem's grandmother to check on his progress as soon as she called her own grandmother. By the time, she made it back into the kitchen, she was so out of breath, she had to sit down. The baby was kicking and moving something fierce, and Soul had to take several deep breathes before she was able to relax enough to dial her grandmother's number. "Calm down AJ," Soul said rubbing her hands across her belly. Anthony and Soul had decided to name their son Anthony Jr. and today he was being as stubborn as his daddy.

"Hello," Soul's grandmother said answering the phone and coughing.

"Hey granny. You still feeling under the weather?"

"Yeah baby, I couldn't even go to work today."

"Don't start granny," Soul laughed. "You ain't got no job."

"I do have a job. You know I sit with old people," Soul's grandmother said referring to her job of home health care. Soul loved messing with her grandmother and joking about the fact that she didn't have a real job, but the truth was her grandmother had more money than anyone in the family. Whenever someone would ask her to borrow money, she loved to rub it in their face that for a no job having woman she had more money than any of them! Soul figured her grandmother's job was just something to keep her busy and occupy her days while Soul's grandfather was at work. Soul's friends were all astounded that her grandparents were both still working in their senior years. Most people of their age were somewhere enjoying their golden years, but not her grandparents. They had to keep themselves busy or they just didn't feel right. It wasn't like they had to work. They had built their own house when they were newlyweds and they didn't believe in owing people, so just about everything they owned was paid for.

"Anyway," her grandmother continued. "How are you feeling today?"

"I'm fine. Bored, but fine. I've cleaned so much today I don't have anything else to do."

"You had a lot of energy today?" her grandmother asked.

"Yes, too much."

"You got your bags packed for the hospital?"

"Yes, why do you ask me that?"

"Cause that baby is on his way."

"I wish, but the most I've had are a few pains, and they weren't nearly strong enough to be labor pains."

"I'm telling you baby, you are going into labor today. Tell Anthony to make sure to call me, I'll have your Uncle Lenny bring me to the hospital."

"Okay, so you're psychic now?" Soul laughed.

"You don't have to be psychic to know that baby is coming today. Now I'm going to get some rest and call your Uncle Lenny, so he'll be on standby. I'll see you later," her grandmother said before hanging up the phone.

Soul laughed at her grandmother's antics as she searched for Shakeem's name in the database so she could retrieve his grandparent's number. Soul dialed the number slowly as she continued to rub her swollen belly.

"Hello, may I speak to Mrs. White?" Soul asked when the phone was picked up.

"Who's calling?" the old woman asked from the other end of the phone.

"This is Mrs. Robinson."

"Who?"

"I'm sorry, this is Ms. Jackson, Shakeem's teacher."

"Oh hey Ms. Jackson, I thought you was a bill collector or something."

"I'm sorry, I keep forgetting that my student's parents don't all know me by my married name."

"That's right suga. I forgot Shakeem told me you done went and got married and pregnant!"

"Yes ma'am. I'm on maternity leave now, but I wanted to check on Shakeem. Ow!" Soul stopped midsentence grabbing her side.

"You okay baby?"

"Yes ma'am, probably just Braxton Hicks," Soul said referring to the sharp pain in her side.

"You sure,"

"I'm positive, now tell me how's Shakeem," Soul asked again trying not to focus on the increasing pain.

"He's okay, but he's started coming home later and later, and some shady looking character came around here looking for him the other day. I'm worried that he's going to get himself back into trouble," Shakeem's grandmother admitted.

Soul sighed. She really didn't know how to keep Shakeem on track. For some reason he had become her little project this year, and she was going to make sure that he made it through high school and graduated even if it killed her. "Mrs. White, would you have Shakeem give me a call when he comes in?"

"Sure, let me grab a pen."

Soul waited as the old woman went to retrieve pen and paper to write her number down. Another sharp pain shot through her body. Soul grabbed the table and held onto the edge until the pain subsided.

"Okay, I'm back," Shakeem's grandmother said returning to the phone.

Soul gave Shakeem's grandmother her home and cell number just as Anthony's picture flashed across her screen indicating the incoming call.

"Well Mrs. White, it was good talking to you, but my husband is on the other line."

"Oh, that's no problem honey. I'll be sure to have Shakeem give you a call."

"Thank you," Soul replied before switching over to answer Anthony's incoming call. "Yes dear?"

"Hey, I'm coming home for lunch. Do you want me to bring you anything?"

"Whatever, it doesn't matter."

"Well, I'm around the corner. Is Whataburger okay?"

"That's fine baby," Soul said as another sharp pain caused her to grab the table again.

"Baby, are you okay?" Anthony asked noticing that she was breathing hard.

"I'm fine, I've just been having some sharp pains."

"Oh shit! I'm on my way,"

"Calm down baby. They're probably just Braxton Hicks again. You know if we go back to the hospital again with false labor the doctor is going to kill us."

"Yeah but,"

"But nothing. If it was the real deal I would know."

"Are you sure? You didn't know the last time," he joked.

"Well, I will know this time. Uh oh," Soul said looking down.

"What is it?"

"Remember when I said I would know for sure this time?"

"Yeah, what is it baby?" Anthony asked urgently.

"I know."

"How do you know?"

"Because my water just broke," Soul said wincing.

"I'm on my way."

***

Anthony glanced down at his glowing wife and son and knew life couldn't get any better. They had barely made it to the hospital on time, as he broke every law in the book to get Soul to the emergency room before she delivered their son right there in his SUV.

"He's beautiful," Anthony said taking his son into his arms as tears ran down his face. "Hey little man. I'm your daddy," Anthony beamed with pride as he smiled down at the small figure in his arms. "I love you so much."

"Hey what about me?"

"I love both of you," Anthony said turning to his wife before bending down to give her a kiss.

"Hey, that's what got you in this predicament in the first place," Ajax said as he, Simone, Danielle, Devon and Thaddeus walked into the room

"Oh my God, let me see my Godson," Danielle exclaimed.

"You mean my Godson," Simone interjected.

"Okay you two, don't start," Soul laughed. "And just so you all know, I'm fine."

"Some people always need attention. Excuse you, there's a new baby here. You may as well give up the thought of needing attention. From this point on, nobody cares about you," Danielle joked.

"Hey!"

"I care about you," Anthony said kissing Soul again.

"Thank you hubby" Soul said smiling. "And just for that, don't even let them hold AJ."

"Girl don't make me fight you and Anthony. Give me that baby," Danielle said walking over and taking the baby from Anthony as Simone, Thaddeus, Devon, and Ajax all gathered around her.

"You done good dog," Ajax said giving Anthony a pat on the back.

"Why do men always say that? Must I remind you who did all the work?" Simone said walking over to put her arms around Ajax.

"Yes wifey, you remind me every other time you think I'm wrong, no need to change today."

"Whatever," Simone replied, kissing Ajax on the cheek.

"Where's my baby?" Soul's grandmother said bursting into the room followed by her grandfather and Uncle Lenny.

"Hi Granny," Soul said smiling.

"I told you that baby was coming today, didn't I?"

"Yes, old woman, you were right," Soul said laughing.

"Let me see my great grandson," Granny Lewis said sitting in a chair near the bed. Danielle walked over and placed the baby into her arms. "He's beautiful, isn't he?" Soul's grandmother said turning to Soul's grandfather to show him the new baby.

"Fine looking fellow," Soul's grandfather beamed with pride.

"Okay, I'm going to have to ask some of you to leave," the nurse said entering the room.

"Okay, we're going to step outside," Danielle said motioning for the rest of the crew to step outside. "We'll be back a little later. You get some rest. Simone and I are going to drag these men to do some shopping for our new Godson."

"I'm not shopping," Thaddeus interjected.

"Me either," Devon added.

"And don't even think about dragging me into all those baby stores," Ajax agreed.

"We'll fine, then we will drop you off, and we'll go shopping. That way we can spend as much money as we want," Simone smiled.

"When you put it like that, I think we will go shopping," Ajax said as they walked out of the door followed by Soul's uncle Lenny.

Soul, Anthony and her grandparents all burst into laughter at their friend's craziness as the nurse checked Soul and baby AJ to make sure they were both okay.

"Well, we're going to get going too. You need some rest," Soul's grandmother said standing up. She walked over and kissed her granddaughter on the forehead. "Anthony, take care of my two babies. We'll see you tomorrow."

Anthony walked over and kissed Soul's grandmother on the cheek before walking over to shake her grandfather's hand.

"Bye baby," Soul's grandfather said walking over to kiss her on the cheek. "Get some rest."

"I will," she said closing her eyes.

As soon as Soul's grandparents were gone, Anthony walked over to the bassinet. AJ slept peacefully and just as Anthony started to place the baby in the basinet, he stopped and begin cradling the baby's face against his own. "My little man," he whispered. He turned to say something to Soul, but she had fallen into a deep sleep. Anthony smiled at his new family as he sat in the nearby chair and placed AJ across his chest. Yes, life was good. He really had been blessed with his heart's desires.

Chapter 47

♥

Anthony walked back into the kitchen and wrapped his arms around Soul as he began to nibble on her neck.

"Alright Mr. Robinson, you know we have to wait two more weeks."

"I know, but I don't think I can wait any longer," Anthony said pressing his body into Soul's. Soul giggled and continued to wash the dishes. They had just had dinner, and Anthony had laid AJ down for a nap. These past four weeks had seemed to fly by, and Soul was dreading going back to work. She didn't know how she would stand being away from AJ, though she knew he would be in capable hands since he had a spot waiting for him at Auntie Danielle's daycare. Between their family and friends, AJ was going to be spoiled rotten. If Danielle and Simone weren't showing up with new clothes, Ajax was showing up with baby Nikes. And Anthony's parents, grandmother, and her grandparents regularly fought over whose time it was to baby sit, even though they knew Anthony and Soul weren't going to let AJ out of their sight for too long.

"Hey, let me finish up. You go take a bath, and let's snuggle up and watch some movies before AJ's next feeding. You know that boy is just like his daddy, he has to eat when he's ready."

"This is true, I don't know how I'm going to keep both of you full."

"Well, if you let me, I've got an idea how you can feed me now," he said squeezing Soul's butt and running his tongue along her neckline.

"Would you quit trying to tempt me. We have two more weeks, so get used to it," Soul said kissing him on the cheek. "I'm going to fix a few more bottles before I go bathe," Soul reached into the cupboard to retrieve AJ's bottles. "I forgot to pick up some more milk when I was at the store," Soul said groaning. "Maybe we have enough to make it through the night."

"Don't worry, I'll finish up in here and run to the store. Anyways, I need to run by the office and get a file."

"Hey what about our movie?"

"I promise to be back before the previews even start rolling."

"Can't it wait until Monday?"

"It could, but I need these papers so I can fax them over to a client in the morning."

"Baby, it's late, and you know I hate for you to go into that building this late at night by yourself. You know that's a bad neighborhood. Anything could happen."

"This, from the woman who works in that neighborhood too. If I recall, it wasn't but a few months ago that I wanted you to quit leaving so late from school, and if I recall, you were the one who told me not to worry, and that the neighborhood was fine. It was your belief in those kids and that neighborhood that caused me to choose it for the housing project, so don't get wishy washy on me now," Anthony said smirking.

"Fine Anthony. You just better be back here by the time I get out of the tub."

"Yes dear," Anthony said putting the last of the dishes into the dishwasher. He grabbed Soul and pulled her into his arms planting another long kiss on her lips."

"What was that for?"

"For being the best and sexiest wife and mother in this world. I love you."

"I love you too," Soul said giving him a quick kiss, "but you still aren't getting any."

Anthony swatted Soul on her butt again, as he grabbed his keys from the key holder. He ran upstairs to check on AJ who was still sleeping soundly in his bassinet. Anthony bent down and kissed the boy who was his spitting image. "Love you little guy. Daddy will be right back." Anthony blew a kiss towards Soul as she walked into their bedroom with a towel in her arm. He set the alarm before walking into the garage to get into his SUV. Mary J Blige's soulful voice filled the truck. Anthony smiled not at all surprised that his wife had been listening to the Mary J satellite station. He planned on surprising Soul with concert tickets as soon as Mary went on tour. Anthony made the short trip to the grocery store to get little AJ's milk, before he went by the office to retrieve the files he needed to fax to his client. Making sure to set the alarm before locking up, Anthony looked around to make sure no one was around, before jogging back to his truck. He hummed along to the sounds of Mary J as he thought about his wife and baby. Anthony wondered how one man could get so lucky.

"Not lucky, just blessed," Anthony laughed aloud to himself as he approached the red light. He was so busy staring at the picture of his wife and son that he kept on the dashboard, that he didn't notice the two teenagers who pulled up behind him and were now approaching his truck until it was too late.

Chapter 48

Soul was awakened to AJ's cries coming from the baby monitor that lay on the floor near the sofa where she slept. She looked at the clock; it was nearly 11:45. She must have fallen asleep waiting on Anthony to return. Soul grabbed a bottle from the refrigerator and placed it in the bottle warmer before grabbing the phone. She dialed Anthony's cell phone number as she climbed the stairs to get AJ from the nursery.

"Where is that man?" Soul wondered aloud as she walked into the nursery. "Hey little guy," Soul bent down to pick a crying AJ up from his bassinet. She dialed Anthony's number again, as she walked back downstairs. "What's the matter with mama's baby? Are you hungry?" Soul walked back into the kitchen and retrieved the bottle she had placed in the bottle warmer. She grabbed a nearby receiving blanket and went to sit on the sofa. As she fed AJ, she dialed Anthony's office number. When there was no answer, Soul began to get worried. "He's fine," she assured herself. "He probably just stopped over to Simone and Ajax's. Soul tried calling both Ajax and Simone's cell phone but neither picked up. "I'm sure he just got caught up. Nothing to worry about," Soul tried convincing herself, but Soul couldn't shake the anxious feeling that was pulling its way from the pit of her stomach to the forefront of her mind.

Soul looked at her baby boy who was dozing back off to sleep now that his stomach was full. She smiled looking at the little boy who was his daddy's twin. "Let's go lay you down, then I'll try daddy again."

***

Ajax rolled off his wife as they both tried to catch their breathe.

"Woman, I don't think I will ever get tired of being inside of you."

"You better not" Simone said smiling at her husband as she reached for her phone to see who was calling her so late at night. A frown crossed her face, as she unlocked her phone and saw a missed call from Soul. "Soul called. That's not like her to call this late. Let me call her back and make sure everything is ok." Simone said as she dialed her cousin.

"Yeah, looks like she called me too," Ajax said picking up his phone.

"Hey, everything ok? Ajax and I saw we both had missed calls. No, he's not here," Simone said into the phone. "She's looking for Anthony," Simone whispered to her husband. "Well what time did he leave? I'm sure everything is fine. You know how hardworking that man is. He probably just got caught up with work stuff as usual. Ok. Yeah, we will let you know if we hear from him. Night cuz." Simone ended the call. "That's not like Anthony. Soul is worried out of her mind," Simone said looking at Ajax.

"How long ago did he leave?" Ajax asked as opened his contact list to try calling Anthony himself.

"Soul said he left around 8:00. He was going to go grab AJ some more milk and grab a file from his office."

Ajax dialed Anthony's number, but it went to voicemail. A few seconds later his phone started ringing as an unknown number displayed on the caller ID screen.

"Is that him?" Simone asked.

Ajax shushed Simone as he connected the call. "Hello. Yes, I did, who is this?" Wait, what!" Ajax said immediately jumping up out of the bed and grabbing a pair of sweatpants on the floor. "When? "Where did this happen?" Fuck! Yeah, Ok!" Ajax shouted into the phone as he dashed around the room grabbing a wrinkled t-shirt out of the hamper and a pair of shoes. "We need to go!" he shouted as he ran around the room frantically trying to put on the shirt and shoes on simultaneously.

"Ajax you're scaring me. What's going on!" Simone said jumping out of the bed.

"Just do what I said Simone!" Ajax felt his heart pounding out of his chest.

Scrambling into the nearest clothing she could locate to throw on, Simone ran into the living room where she found her husband trying to catch his breath as tears streamed down his face. "Where the fuck are my keys!"

"Baby, what is it? You're scaring me!" Simone grabbed his arm forcing him to look at her.

"It's Anthony baby. Some teenagers tried carjacking him and he was shot."

"Oh my God! What!"

"We got to go." Ajax yelled as he tried to steady his shaking hands.

Simone took one look at her husband and grabbed the keys. "Let's go, I'm driving."

***

Soul tried Anthony's cell and work number again. "Where in the world could that man be," Soul said aloud. She jumped at the sound of the knocking sound on the front door. Finally! "Anthony, I am going to kill you!" Soul shouted as she went to open the door. "Where have you been?" she asked just as she heard AJ start crying once again probably awakened this time from the banging on the door. "And why didn't you come through the garage, now your little dude is up just in time for daddy to put him back to sleep," Soul said as she opened the door surprised to find Ajax and Simone at her door and not her husband.

"Ajax. Simone. What are you two doing here at this hour. I didn't mean to wake you earlier and have you both worried".

"Soul, it's Anthony."

Soul felt queasy as the uneasy feeling from earlier returned. "What do you mean it's Anthony."

"We need you to go with us," Ajax said tears once again forming in his eyes just as baby AJ's cries became louder.

"Here, I'll get him," Simone said pushing past Soul and making her way into the house to retrieve baby AJ.

"Ajax, what do you mean, it's Anthony."

"Soul, Anthony," Ajax hesitated as he tried to find the words, "Anthony was shot."

Soul laughed as the tears streamed down her face. "This is a joke, right? My husband is standing outside pulling some type of prank on me." Soul pushed past Ajax and peered outside. "Anthony, this isn't funny," she yelled.

"Soul, sweetie we would never play a joke like that on you," Simone said coming around the corner with a now quiet baby AJ, tears running down her face.

"Noooo," Soul screamed as she crumbled to the floor. Simone handed Ajax the baby and wrapped her cousin in her arms. "I'm so sorry cousin. We need to go sweetie, come on let me help you throw on some clothes.

Chapter 49

Soul, Ajax, and Simone arrived at the hospital. Soul felt like her legs were made of bricks as she struggled to make her way to the main entrance of the hospital where Thaddeus, Danielle and Devon greeted them.

"Anthony's parents are already here," Danielle said walking over to hug Soul. "Do you want me to take the baby," she asked noticing Soul seemed to be moving slow.

"No, I just want my husband."

"Come on, they're this way," Thaddeus interjected leading the group in the direction of the ICU waiting area. The group made their way to the waiting area where they found Anthony's parents. Marvela Robinson looked like her entire world had been crushed and Anthony' normally calm and unbothered father sat solemnly, tears streaming down his face. The older man stood to greet them all, and Ajax immediately pulled him into an embrace. Marvela hugged Soul as the two ladies cried.

"Here give me my grandson," Marvela said attempting to compose herself as she took AJ and sat down in the chair next to her husband.

"Has there been any update?" Ajax asked.

"Not yet," a nurse just came up and asked us some questions about Anthony's medical history before rushing back into the back, but that was a while ago and no one has come,"

"Are you the family of Anthony Robinson," an older balding white man asked, interrupting Anthony's father.

"Yes," Soul spoke up. "I'm his wife and these are his parents and friends. And you are?"

"Detective Jones and Davis," the younger detective said flashing his badge.

"Do you know what happened to my boy?" Anthony's father asked.

"Well, as far as we can tell Mr. Robinson was the apparent victim of a carjacking."

"Did you catch the bastard that did this?" Ajax said anger all over his face.

"Yes Sir. We've taken them downtown for questioning. Two young teenagers from the generation of the unsaved," the older detective attempted to joke. When he noticed he was the only one smiling, he cleared his throat and continued. "They seem to be a part of a carjacking ring. They're going down for a long time, plus we found drugs on them. Ma'am, I need to ask you some questions," the detective said turning to Soul. "We want to get these boys booked tonight. We think they may work for one of the city's heavy hitters, and hopefully we can take him down too."

"If it will help you get them off the street, by all means ask away," Soul sighed.

"Were you with your husband today?"

"Yes, we were home all day with our newborn and had just settled down for the night and we were planning to watch a movie."

"And what time did your husband leave home?"

"Around 8:00," Soul said wiping away the tears that had once again began."

"Where was your husband headed when he left?"

"He was headed to get our son some milk, and to his office to pick up a file that he needed so he could fax some information to a client."

"And what does your husband do?"

"He has his own company, a partnership with the city to provide housing to low income and single mothers. He also has another real estate venture."

"Is there anyone who would want your husband dead? Any enemies?"

"No of course not. I thought you said it was a carjacking by some teenagers?"

"Yes, but we have to rule out all possibilities."

"Where is your husband's office located?"

"The southern sector, on Parrott, near my school. I'm a teacher," Soul added.

"Are you sure there was no one that wanted your husband dead. You said you're a teacher. These boys were teenagers. Do you have any students who wanted to hurt you or your husband? Any students who may have it out for you?"

"No! Sir, neither me nor my husband have any enemies to my knowledge. My students love me, and their parents do too. Besides I've been on maternity leave for the past four weeks."

"Okay ma'am, we just have to make sure we've covered all our bases."

"Do you know the names of the teenagers," Soul asked suddenly. "You said it was by my school, and I have been in that area for years. Maybe I know them."

"I'm sorry ma'am, I can't give out that information especially since this is still an ongoing investigation."

"But how can you rule out everything if you don't know whether I know these kids as you say," Soul asked angrily.

The two detectives looked at each other before shrugging, just as the younger detective's phone started ringing.

"Detective Jones, "he said walking away from the group. "They did! Good! That was fast. We're on our way. Looks like we will be closing this case quicker than we thought," the detective announced as he walked back over to the group.

"Who are they," Soul asked again, as a sinking feeling began to flow through her.

"Well since we're about to close the case," the older detective shrugged in the direction of his younger counterpart.

"The younger detective shrugged, "Two boys. A Hispanic and Black teenager. An Alejandro Torres and a Shakeem White. It seems as if the Shakeem White was our trigger man, and he swears it was an accident. But I'm told they just gave us the name of their boss who is a much bigger fish."

Soul covered her mouth as the room begin to spin.

"You're kidding," Detective Davis, the older detective, spoke excitedly.

"No man, I'm not. They gave us his name, and this one is going to get the PD some good press, the boys are headed to pick him up now. The streets are going to be a lot safer now that Keyshon Franklin is off of the streets" the detective said more to his partner than anyone else in the room.

"Who did you say," Simone said suddenly looking at Soul, who immediately stood up but was seemingly frozen in the spot she stood.

"Keyshon Franklin. Down at the precinct he is known as one of the biggest drug dealers and notorious criminals in the city, but on the street, people call him Key. He is in and out of the city so much, it's been hard to pin anything on him."

Just at that moment, a doctor came from the back. "Family of Anthony Robinson? Is there anyone here for Anthony Robinson?"

Soul attempted to open her mouth, but the only thing she could get out was a gasp before the room went black and she passed out.

Epilogue

Key looked at his brother sitting across from him with a smug expression on his face. He was dressed from head to toe, creased jeans and polo shirt. Key would never figure out what women saw in his brother besides good looks. They were just dumb bitches who wanted a man so badly they were willing to settle for anything. Not like Soul.

Soul. He wanted to talk to her so bad that it hurt, but he loved her enough to let her live her life, even if it was with somebody else. He promised her he wouldn't interfere with her new life, and he had tried to keep his promise. But if this shit went to court, he may have to ask her to be a character witness.

Out of all the runs he had sent Shakeem and Alejandro on, this was the first time they had fucked up. He couldn't believe they got caught. They knew the rules. The gun was just for show, unless necessary. Get the car and be out. He couldn't believe those stupid ass teenagers gave the cops his name. It was a shame he was going to have to end their lives so early. Soul would be sad since they were her students and shit, but they chose to live the life of a street hustler.

He wished he had told his brother to sneak some weed in, because he needed something to calm his nerves now more than ever. He was so sick of police interrogating him. He knew he was hated at the precinct, and the beating he took proved it. His face was still swollen, and his arm hurt like hell. He thought of how the officers laughed as they told the captain how Key hurt himself trying to escape. When he got out of this mess, he was going to sue the whole damn city. They thought he gave them trouble before, but it was about to be some hell to pay. The police were pulling all stops to make something stick against him. Talking about how he could be charged as an accessory to attempted homicide. Then they were all in his face talking about how he was the reason a husband

and a father lay in a hospital fighting for his life. Shit, that didn't have nothing to do with him. Truth be told, he wanted to be a husband and a father one day too.

"It took you a whole week to come check on me. As much shit as I done bailed you out of. I guess you got another bitch taking care of your shit, so fuck me."

"Nah little brother, it ain't nothing like that. They wouldn't let me see you. They kept saying that the only person who could see you was your lawyer."

Key didn't know whether to believe his brother or not. But he figured it didn't matter. He was all he had right now.

"Man look, don't worry, we gone get you out of this. You done always took care of me, and now it's my turn. Tell me what you want me to do."

Key took a deep breathe. "I need you to put pressure on my lawyer. Make him understand how it's in his best interest to get me out of this shit. Then I need you to make some family stops if you know what I mean. Express to some people how important family is, especially grandparents and parents. These teenagers seem to take that for granted."

"No doubt, I'm a let shit cool for a minute, then I'm all on it. Wouldn't want nobody to think I'm threatening them."

Key nodded his head in agreement. "But when you do visit them, remind them death is everywhere."

"Everywhere." Key's brother nodded his head knowingly. "You know I got your back."

"I know dog. I know."

"Well, let me get out of here. I need to go get something to calm my nerves. I promised my new girl, I would watch her kids for her, and Lisa's son Teddy Jr is bad as hell."

"A'ight. And J,"

"Yeah Key"

"Thanks man."

"I always got ya back little brother, no matter what," Jackson said as he walked out of the room.